FORT VE
State Histo
Officer's Row Tour Guide

As you walk down Officer's Row, you return to the Fort Verde of Territorial Arizona. The officers' quarters overlook the parade ground and the nautically inspired flagpole. The flagpole was so constructed because of the difficulty in transporting a 60 foot pine log from the high country by mule team. The officers' quarters are open for inspection and are furnished to acquaint you with the military life-style of the 1880s

OFFICERS QUARTERS 1871-81

In 1881 fire destroyed the Married Officers housing — an imposing 2-story structure identical to the Commanding Officers Quarters. Several families often occupied apartments in a house this size. The building was not rebuilt after the fire because of Army budget cuts and the thrust of the Indian campaigns had shifted to Southeast Arizona and Mexico.

COMMANDING OFFICERS HOUSE

COMMANDING OFFICERS HOUSE — Chalipun, Tonto Apache Chief, with 300 of his followers in attendance, officially surrendered to General George Crook in 1873 on the front porch of this building.

Fort Verde's Commanding Officer was typically the senior company Captain having served in the Army for nearly two decades. His salary of 166.00 dollars per month — hardly enough to live lavishly — was enough for his wife to have gradually assembled the respectable household furnishings necessary for them to assume their role in the center of military society. The master bedroom to the right of the vestibule was cloaked in privacy to strict Victorian standards, though the parlor and dining room to the left were elegantly furnished for the entertaining that befell the commander. The KOW (military acronym for Commanding Officer's Wife, the K substituted as a military courtesy) employed an enlisted man called a striker to help with cooking and household chores. His quarters were up the stairs from the kitchen and adjoined the children's room. Very few of the strikers were of temperment to serve as nursemaids, although some became quite fond of the children thus finding a homelife not available in the barracks. In addition to the home-like atmosphere, the striker earned an extra $5.00 dollars bringing his monthly pay to $18.00.

BACHELOR OFFICERS QUARTERS

Bachelor Officers lived a somewhat spartan life-style, not altogether unexpected considering the low pay, slow promotion, frequent moves, and the amount of time spent in the field. Although these quarters were designed to have three bedrooms, doubling up was common so that almost constantly needed repairs could be made.

The building's outer walls were of pice construction. Pice is a technique of casting massive adobe units in a temporary wooden form. This was simpler and faster than making adobe bricks, and the resulting pice was less susceptible to water damage.

The communal kitchen in the rear of the building also served as quarters for the officers' striker. The parlor, officially assigned to the senior officer in residence, was used by all occupants of the Bachelor Officers Quarters when it was not needed for an extra bedroom. Army regulations authorized a Lieutenant one room and a kitchen, a Captain two rooms and a kitchen and so on up the ranks. These standards were largely ignored by the frontier Army.

MARRIED OFFICERS HOUSING 1871-1891

Foundation of another two story building destroyed sometime after the fort was abandoned.

DOCTOR'S QUARTERS

The Post Surgeon was allowed these rather spaceous accommodations because patients were treated and surgery performed in the Doctor's residence. The

Post Hospital, located at the Northwest corner of the parade ground, was operated by the Hospital Matron and used strictly for quarantine and convalescence. Each permanent military command was required to have a physician. The low pay and primitive conditions attracted few doctors, so most military doctors were civilian physicians on contract. The contract was usually for two years and earned him considerable service in the field. These surgeons were attracted to the Army for a variety of reasons. Some were incompetent and unsuccessful in their civilian practice, others had hopes of finding wealth by establishing western mines or homesteads. By far the most prominent were the Natural History scientists who looked at frontier service as a free specimen collecting trip.

DOCTOR'S QUARTERS — Many physicians serving at Fort Verde achieved fame as natural scientists Drs. Mearns, Coues and Palmer were but a few Fort Verde surgeons that made outstanding contributions to Ornithology, Archaeology and Botany during their frontier service.

HEROES, MAVERICKS
AND BOUNDERS

Also by Hugh David

The Fitzrovians

HEROES, MAVERICKS AND BOUNDERS

The English Gentleman
from Lord Curzon to James Bond

HUGH DAVID

Michael Joseph   London

MICHAEL JOSEPH LTD
Published by the Penguin Group
27 Wrights Lane, London W8 5TZ, England
Viking Penguin Inc, 375 Hudson Street, New York, New York 10014, USA
Penguin Books Australia Ltd, Ringwood, Victoria, Australia
Penguin Books Canada Ltd, 10 Alcorn Avenue, Suite 300, Toronto, Ontario, Canada M4V 3B2
Penguin Books (NZ) Ltd, 182–190 Wairau Road, Auckland 10, New Zealand

Penguin Books Ltd, Registered Offices: Harmondsworth, Middlesex, England

First published in Great Britain 1991

Made and printed in England by Clays Ltd, St Ives plc
Filmset in Monophoto 11 on 13 pt Garamond
Diagrams drawn by K. Smith

A CIP catalogue record for this book is available from the British Library
ISBN 0 7181 3264 5

The moral right of the author has been asserted

Contents

List of Illustrations

Copyright holders are in italics.

Introduction

O, when degree is shaked,
Which is the ladder of all high designs,
The enterprise is sick. How could communities,
Degree, in schools, and brotherhoods in cities,
Peaceful commerce from dividable shores,
The primogenity and due of birth,
Prerogative of age, crowns, sceptres, laurels,
But by degree, stand in authentic place?
Take but degree away, untune that string,
And hark what dischord follows.
– William Shakespeare, *Troilus and Cressida*, I.iii.101–110

Today one is far more likely to spot a gentleman in the late-night film or a television drama series than to rub shoulders with him, even in Jermyn Street or Piccadilly. Like the Cavalier, the swell, the toff, the masher – or, for that matter, the rake and the spiv – in the real world his hour, it seems, has passed.

Charles Ryder and Sebastian Flyte – as played by Jeremy Irons and Anthony Andrews in Granada Television's adaptation of *Brideshead Revisited* – were both recognizable English gentlemen. For all his bumbling, the Bertie Wooster of the more recent Granada series *Jeeves and Wooster* was another. Every one of the male members of the Bellamy household in the London Weekend Television series *Upstairs, Downstairs* and (virtually) every man in the BBC's epoch-making *Forsyte Saga* (and the equally-ambitious radio adaptation of John Galsworthy's novel sequence *The Forsyte Chronicles*) was a gentleman too. In the cinema David Niven, Rex Harrison and Noël Coward were never less than gentlemen, whatever part they played. Nor was Dirk Bogarde. Nor was James Stewart. Then, of course, there was Leslie Howard . . .

Off the screen, however, like the debutantes he used to escort around town, the country estates from which he derived his wealth and even his own 'gentleman's club', the traditional gentleman has become virtually extinct in postwar Britain. Economic factors – the introduction of death duties and inheritance tax as much as 'the servant problem' – are largely responsible for this, but changing social circumstances have also played their part: *Gad, sir, these days peers are not so much born as made!* Degree has been so fundamentally 'shaked' during the course of this century, and the social pyramid so irrevocably eroded, that plain Jack is now generally indistinguishable from the *déclassé* man he would once have readily acknowledged as his master. Caps are no longer doffed, forelocks are no longer tugged; and the real McCoy passes unnoticed in a crowd of ersatz gentlemen, his Jermyn Street suit ironically slightly more crumpled than their snappy Next or M&S double-breasted two-pieces.

Purely as an index of the extent of this change, it is only necessary to point out that Balliol College, Oxford now undertakes to accept 'a percentage' of undergraduates with comprehensive school backgrounds. The green-liveried flunkies at Harrods are also happy to open the door for customers who arrive wearing shorts, T-shirts and all the paraphernalia of the peripatetic tourist. Even more poignant is the fact that the Prime Minister of Great Britain is the son of an itinerant circus performer, while Her Majesty the Queen is appealing to British industry to find salaried niches for younger members of the Royal family, at least two of the immediate members of which are already earning a living in what once would have been peremptorily dismissed as 'trade'.

None of these situations would have been imaginable 100 or even seventy-five years ago when the 'prerogative of age, crowns, sceptres, laurels' still stood in 'authentic place'.

Thus it is only in comparatively recent years that the traditional, Eton-and-Balliol gentleman has been both marginalized and minimalized. It is certainly true that there are very few individuals alive today who can *afford* to be gentlemen, at least in the manner in which Bertie Wooster and all the other members of the Drones' Club – to say nothing of that dutiful Victorian George Nathaniel Curzon or even the Cold War spy Guy Burgess – would have understood the term. And even among the few *soi-disant* gents of today who do have the money, very very few finally pass muster; for as novels such as Anthony Trollope's *The Way of Live Now* and George Gissing's *Born in Exile* had already demonstrated by the end of the nineteenth century, there was always more to being a gentleman than the mere possession of wealth. Such intangible qualities as style (as opposed to 'fashion' – would any real gentleman ever wear an earring?), honour, manners and the possession of that famous stiff upper lip are also among his attributes. And it has to be admitted that all are seemingly in equally short supply in today's aggressively 'go-getting', nominally egalitarian, meritocratic, post-monetarist society.

In consequence, perhaps, the very words 'gentleman' and 'gentlemen' have virtually disappeared from common usage (apart from on the doors of public conveniences. America might have the 'men's room', but in Britain the little male stick-figure is always below the word 'GENTLEMEN' or 'GENTS'.) When the words are heard at all the context is almost invariably joshing or heavily ironic, and they are surrounded by an almost audible set of inverted commas: *You're an officer and a gentleman . . . a gentleman and a scholar . . . a gentleman of leisure . . . a gentleman-farmer . . . a gentleman of this parish . . . a real gent . . . My Lords, ladies and gentlemen . . . Gentlemen gentlemen . . . Time, gentlemen, please! . . .*

Other, synonymous phrases have fallen into a similar linguistic limbo: it is perhaps only London taxi-drivers who can now infallibly distinguish between a 'squire' and a 'mate'. But the dogged persistence of so many gentlemen-phrases in the colloquial vocabulary is in itself significant. So too is the fact that they still have an altogether different connotative value from such ostensibly similar examples of bar-room banter as *a real man, take it like a man, a man's work* and *sort out the men from the boys.* Taken together, the existence of the two suggests that, despite his own virtual disappearance, the *ideal* of 'the English gentleman' still remains a potent force in society. Somehow it has remained separate from the more neutral concept of 'a man'. Nowadays a gentleman might not have much in common with Geoffrey Chaucer's 'verray parfit gentil knight' – but equally, it seems, he still doesn't need to work, to 'take it' or to be 'sorted out' from the common herd.

So who then is – or was – he?

In the following pages I shall argue that the English gentleman as we currently perceive him had his origins in the final third of the nineteenth century, and that he was not so much born as made. Other books and other writers have followed his earlier incarnations and evolution from the feudal squire.[1] Here I am concerned only with the honourable, starched-collared but still recognizably modern individual whom Eton, Harrow, Marlborough, Rugby (where Dr Arnold had to all intents and purposes started it all) and 200 other public schools groomed for a precise role in the Imperial hierarchy of the 1880s and 1890s – and with the problem confronting his sons and grandsons as they attempted to live up to that role in an altered and still altering world.

For the sake of convenience I have intentionally counted as gentlemen many aristocrats whom – as specialists in 'degree' – both William Shakespeare and the editors of today's *Burke's Peerage* and *Debrett* would place several steps higher up the social ladder. Actions speak louder than words; and many a Lord This and Hon. John That was to prove himself a member of the same breed as plain Mr Other. (On the other hand, just like the mere possession of money, merely belonging to an aristocratic family has never in itself been a guarantee of gentility, and titled 'cads' and 'bounders' have always existed. Lord Byron was one such and, closer to our own times, the Lords Alfred Douglas and Lucan two more, albeit in very different ways.)

Similarly, I have also counted as gentlemen many individuals whom sticklers for form would very likely have regarded as mere 'men'; ill-bred upstarts who entered the form-book through the tradesmen's entrance rather than the front door. W. G. Grace and C. B. Fry fall into this category; so too does Stanley Matthews – although ironically the nominally working-class Sir Stanley (as he now is) did more to further such gentlemanly notions as sportsmanship and fair play in the 1940s than anyone else.

But then merely being in the right place at the right time could always make one more of a 'gentleman' than 'primogenity and due of birth' and the strict application of rule-of-thumb criteria. Neither Matthews's nor Fry's – nor, come to that, Lord Curzon's – grandfather earned in excess of £1,000 a year for example; and yet that was the standard by which Bertrand Russell assessed whether or not any man was a true gentleman.

In the light of all this, I have not made any attempt to define the term 'gentleman'. To have done so would have been unnecessarily reductive; besides, anyone who has ever tried to sort out the 'gentlemen' from the 'players' or used any of the terms quoted above will know exactly what and whom I mean.

However, none of the out-and-out, copper-bottomed gentlemen

who figure in what follows would have cavilled if the spirit of Sapper's description of Roger Vane, the hero of one of his early (pre-Bulldog Drummond) novels, had been applied to him. Written in 1919, Sapper's words in fact prompted this book. It is fitting, then, that they should stand as its epigraph, providing as they do the definitive *terminus a quo* for any investigation of the character of the modern English gentleman:

> . . . he had been in the eleven at Eton, and was a scratch golfer. He had a fine seat on a horse and rode straight; he could play a passable game of polo, and was a good shot. Possessing as he did sufficient money to prevent the necessity of working, he had not taken the something he was supposed to be doing in the City very seriously. He had put in a periodical appearance at a desk and drawn pictures on the blotting paper; for the remainder of the time he amused himself. He belonged, in fact, to the Breed; the Breed that has always existed in England, and will always exist to the world's end. You may meet its members in London and Fiji; in the lands that lie beyond the mountains and at Henley; in the swamps where the stagnant vegetation rots and stinks; in the great deserts where the night air strikes cold. They are always the same, and they are branded with the stamp of the Breed. They shake your hand as a man shakes it; they meet your eye as a man meets it. Just now a generation of them lie around Ypres and La Bassée, Neuve Chapelle and Bapaume. The graves are overgrown and the crosses are marked with indelible pencil. Dead, yes; but not the Breed. The Breed never dies.[2]

A large number of gentlemen have demonstrated that the courtesy of their breed lives on – and an appreciable number of ladies have proved that it never was a wholly masculine attribute – through their kindness to me during the writing of this book. For their unstinting help I must especially thank my agent Bill Hamilton; and Simon Blow, Antonia Byatt, George Carey-Foster, Lady Rose Cholmondeley, Michael Church and *The Independent on Sunday*, Hugh Corbett-Palmer, Jack Hewit, Anthony Howard, Philippa Ingram, Lady Jackling, Adam Johnson, the staff of T. M. Lewin & Sons Ltd, Gordon Marsden and *History Today*, Lord Mayhew, Nicholas Mosley, the Hon. Lady Mosley, Philip Mould, Jeremy Paxman, Barrie Penrose, Roland Philipps, the Rt. Hon. Enoch Powell MP, Richard Pyatt, Ivor Spencer, Sir Stephen and Lady Spender, Ken Thomson, the Revd Kenneth Wolfe and Lord Young of Dartington.

I am particularly grateful to Susan Watt and Alexander Stilwell at Michael Joseph Ltd for their support; and for the initial enthusiasm of Peter Robinson, my *quondam* editor, whose idea this book originally was. Between them, my father and Ray Dicks saved me from being caught in the slips by their tactful, patient explanation of bodyline bowling.

As always, the staff of the London Library have gone well beyond the call of duty in finding and showing me books which might otherwise have escaped my attention. I also have been helped by efficient (but anonymous) personnel in the libraries of the House of Lords and the London Boroughs of Bromley and Lambeth.

Raffles had his Bunny, Bertie Wooster his Jeeves; during a particularly fraught period of research and writing Edmund Hall was similarly indispensable to me. Peter Ellis later took over the role of amanuensis, volunteering to read a sprawling, untidy manuscript, pointing out many an error and solecism, cooking even more meals and ensuring that coffee and Scotch were always available. I am deeply grateful to them both.

HUGH DAVID
London, February 1991

CHAPTER ONE

The Old School Tie

I do not doubt but if he could have been, he
would have been an Etonian.
                    – Lord Rosebery on Lord Aberdeen

The Hon. Arthur Fitz-Gerald Kinnaird chose to celebrate the victory of his Old Etonians' XI in the final of the 1882 Football Association Challenge Cup by standing on his head in the middle of the pitch. It was a grand, glorious gesture and, according to a modern historian of the FA Cup, it received 'the equivalent of a standing ovation by his fellow Etonians'.[1]

Hurrah! Well might they have cheered. Well might they have thrown their hats in the air, those Old Etonians who packed the pavilion and filled the hard wooden seats at Surrey County Cricket Club's ground, the Kennington Oval, where the Cup Final was played between 1872 and 1892. *Hurrah!* Kinnaird's men had done it again, beating Blackburn Rovers just as convincingly as they had thrashed the local Clapham Rovers team in the Cup Final only three years previously. *Hurrah!* The Battle of Waterloo had been won on the playing fields of Eton. Now on a south London cricket pitch the school had snatched an equally famous victory, one which only confirmed its unshakeable belief in itself and the inherent superiority of its sort of gentlemen over even professional players.

Not that, in the 1880s at least, such a belief needed very much bolstering. Kinnaird's scratch team had been FA Cup finalists in three of the previous four years. They were the unchallenged *victores ludorum* and, more crucially, their triumphs came at exactly the same time as an Etonian pre-eminence began to be noticed in fields far wider than the Kennington Oval. For the early 1880s saw the beginning of a third of a century during which the College came to enjoy an almost feudal domination over every aspect of public life in Britain and its then numerous overseas colonies.

Among the 101 Cabinet ministers who were to hold office between 1886 and 1916, no fewer than thirty-five were Old Etonians. (Of the remainder, thirty-four had been educated at the other 200-odd public schools then recognized by the Headmasters' Conference, while just thirty-two came from Britain's vastly greater number of grammar, elementary and secondary schools.)[2] During the same period, other Old Etonians enjoyed an even greater hegemony in what were then called 'the Professions'. They ruled supreme in the higher reaches of the Bar. They dominated the Foreign and Diplomatic service, and they virtually ran both the Home and Colonial civil services. They were equally well represented in the army. Eton supplied well over twice as many of the infantry officers who served in the Boer War (1899–1902) as any other public school – no less than 610 of them when, by contrast, Harrow provided just 281 and Marlborough and Charterhouse could each muster only 191.[3]

In addition, Old Etonians held sway over what would later become known as the Establishment, in exactly the same way that their successors would effectively control British arts and letters in the mid twentieth century.[4] Throughout the eighties and nineties they edited *The Times*, filled many of the senior positions in the Church of England and adorned the boards of many public bodies. The Hon. Arthur Fitz-Gerald Kinnaird himself (who became the eleventh Lord Kinnaird on the death of his father in 1887) was at various times President of the YMCA, a director of Barclays Bank Limited, a Fellow of the Royal Geographical Society and, for three years in succession, Lord High Commissioner to the Church of Scotland. Fittingly – and seemingly eternally – he also presided over the Football Association from 1890 until his death in 1923.

He was hardly unique. In the City of London and in Whitehall, in the gentlemen's clubs of St James's and in English cathedral closes, there were many others with a similar record of public service. And in regimental messes and at any number of the Old Etonian dinners

2

which enlivened the daily round in British embassies and colonial out-stations throughout the world, there were still more for whom Eton was a *modus vivendi* as much as a *raison d'être*. Over 'tiffin' or tea, their talk was of the old days, of past headmasters, provosts and fellows. After dinner, their toasts were to the continuing success of their famous contemporaries. And still later in the evening, their clubby, port-fuelled reminiscences were full of stories of 'Pop' and 'Speeches', scholars, oppidans and houses.

To any visiting outsider, it would all have seemed intimidatingly incomprehensible. Such was the prestige of Eton in the last years of the nineteenth century, however, that there were not that many true outsiders. The previous fifty years had seen the publication of an astonishing number of fond memoirs and dull (and often privately-printed) autobiographies, all of which sought to give their readers at least an insight into the College's ethos and traditions. Predating *Tom Brown's Schooldays* by nearly a decade, a shyly pseudonymous volume entitled *The Confessions of an Etonian* and ascribed to one 'I.E.M.' had appeared in 1846. Eight years later, a separate – and rather longer – *Confessions of an Etonian* was published. Other volumes advertised at this time included Sir Edward Creasey's *Memories of Eminent Etonians* and H. S. Cookesley's *Brief Memoirs of an Eton Boy*. By 1898 there were enough of these Eton books around – and, we must conclude, a sufficiently large pool of potential readers – to justify the publication of *An Eton Bibliography*.

There was, therefore, plenty to celebrate when more than two hundred Old Etonians arrived at the Monico restaurant in Piccadilly Circus on 28 October 1898 for one of their regular dinners. By then the College really had spread its light blue mantle over every aspect of late Victorian life. It really did seem as though the nation itself – and certainly the Empire – would crumble without the devoted service of a legion of Old Etonians. Indeed, the ostensible excuse for that dinner at the Monico was to toast the appointment of the most illustrious Old Etonian of the day, the recently-ennobled George Nathaniel Curzon, as Viceroy of India. But, Eton being Eton, after the five-course meal Curzon and his fellow-guests also raised their glasses to the almost simultaneous promotions of two more of their number. Lord Minto had just been given the Governor Generalship of Canada, and the Revd J. E. C. Welldon was about to be enthroned as Bishop of Calcutta.

The former Liberal prime minister and race-horse owner, the Earl of Rosebery presided at the feast. Devoted as he was to the College – more than thirty years later he was to ask to hear the 'Eton Boating Song' as he lay on his deathbed – he was a natural choice. And quite naturally too, his speech continued the self-congratulatory mood of the evening. 'In all my life I have met only one Old Etonian who did not like Eton,' he observed – adding that 'he speedily went to the Devil!'

The moral of the story was not lost on any of his listeners. The boisterous manner in which they cheered and drummed the tables with their fists bore out their own, similarly deep devotion to Eton. To the majority of them, indeed, the words of the 'Eton Boating Song' which they had been singing ever since William Johnson Cory composed it in 1863 expressed the essential spirit of the place: it really was 'the best of schools'. But among the Cabinet ministers, bishops, aristocrats, young bloods and rather older roués who made up Lord Rosebery's audience, there would undoubtedly have been one or two with heads clear enough and memories sufficiently long to recall that that had not always been the case.

Less than one hundred years previously, virtually all the public schools in Britain had still been in what one modern writer has described as their 'brutal and permissive age'.[5] And at that period, far from being 'the best of schools', Eton rated among the worst. At exactly the time when the elderly King George III was often to be seen wandering through its courts and cloisters, stopping to greet any boys or masters he happened to encounter and knowing most of them by name, the College was at its lowest ebb. Academic standards were at a discount, and discipline and morality almost non-existent. The College even supported a brothel, solely for the use of its sixth-form boys, although it is highly unlikely that the King ever knew about that.

Originally established in 1440 to provide a free education for seventy local 'Scholars', by 1800 the 'College Rioiall of oure Ladie of Eton beside Windesor' had changed out of all recognition. It had grown substantially, with those Scholars heavily outnumbered by hundreds of fee-paying oppidans or townsmen, their Latin name reflecting the fact that they originally lived out of the College proper. And inevitably, the charitable objectives of its founder, King Henry VI, had been largely overtaken by the needs of these newcomers.

Predominantly aristocratic – between 1753 and 1790 only thirty-five boys out of a total entry of some three thousand were the sons of those whom the College registers summarily categorized as 'tradesmen' – they were cosseted, fawned on and pampered by the College authorities. Until comparatively recently the courtesy-titles of Lord Thomas This, the Hon. Richard That or plain Sir Harry The Other were still pricked out in red ink on the Eton year-rolls. They not-infrequently arrived with their own tutors and servants, and wanted as little contact with the Scholars as possible. Whatever their demands, Eton was happy to oblige. And as a direct result, until it was finally closed down in the 1840s, generation after generation of Scholars were left virtually to their own devices in the College's notorious and unsupervised Long Chamber.

Some 170 feet (forty-two metres) from end to end, fifteen feet (nearly five metres) in height and entirely unheated until 1784, the Long Chamber had no glass in its windows, so that in winter rain and snow soaked the Scholars' beds. There were no washing or toilet facilities, and absolutely no privacy. By all accounts it was filthy, insanitary and infested by rats. As late as 1834 an official report noted grimly that 'the inmates of a workhouse or a gaol are better fed and lodged than the scholars of Eton'[6] – a fact which was confirmed in 1858 when the Long Chamber was finally rebuilt and two cartloads of rats' bones were removed from beneath the floorboards.

It is reasonable to infer that, on his stumbling strolls, the kindly but confused George III would have been kept as far from the Long Chamber as he was from the brothel. However, it is more difficult to believe that such a frequent visitor to the College could have been unaware of the brutality and violence which characterized every aspect of its life, for the tyrannical suzerainty of its prefects, or 'praepositors', who at their mildest just turned a blind eye to the vicious bullying which was such a feature of life in the Long Chamber, was merely an adolescent parody of the equally barbarous regime imposed by a succession of uninterested and frequently undistinguished headmasters. We can only conclude that, like the privations endured by the enlisted men in his Navy, George accepted these excesses as necessary and inevitable. Indeed, the comparison is not so far-fetched; during the last years of his reign Eton was run by a man who has subsequently been depicted as the scholastic equivalent of HMS *Bounty*'s Captain Bligh.

Histories of the College still refer to Dr John Keate as its longest-serving Headmaster. Rightly so, since he held the position for virtually a quarter of a century, from 1809 until 1834. They also mention that he numbered among his pupils no less than two future prime ministers: Lord Derby and William Ewart Gladstone. Only the most up-to-date and objective, however, record the details of his long career. For the grotesque Dr Keate achieved an ambivalent sort of fame in his own lifetime solely through his fondness for corporal punishment.

Scarcely five feet in height and prone to foam at the mouth in moments of anger or excitement, he possessed what Alexander Kinglake, the author of *Eothen*, later described as 'the pluck of ten battalions'. And with the total recall which in itself suggests something of Keate's shattering impact on the youngsters in his charge, Kinglake went on:

> You could not put him out of humour, that is out of the ill-humour which he thought to be fitting for a Head Master. His red, shaggy eyebrows were so prominent that he habitually used them as arms and hands for the purpose of pointing out any object towards which he wished to direct attention. He wore a fancy dress, partly resembling the costume of Napoleon, partly that of a widow woman.

In surviving caricatures by some of his pupils Keate does indeed resemble a pocket Napoleon. His actions, however, were more akin to those of a school-house Stalin. He thought nothing of ordering the birching of an entire year, and more than once actually performed the task himself. In the summer of 1810 he personally gave six lashes to every member of his lower fifth, one hundred or so boys, who had taken to coming in late for chapel. If nothing else, this was a formidable physical achievement: one of his predecessors at Eton was confined to bed for a week with torn ligaments after administering ten strokes of the birch to each of the seventy boys in one particular year.

Even by the standards of his time, however, Keate was excessive. But neither the repressive authoritarianism for which the birch came to stand nor the frighteningly violent ethos engendered by its use in ritualized floggings before an assembled house or year-group was entirely confined to Eton. Both were facts of life in the vast majority of English public schools at this period. For, although conditions in their dormitories might not have been quite as bad as those in Eton's

Long Chamber and their 'beaks' and 'dons' were not necessarily as sadistic as Dr Keate, virtually all the schools manifested at least some symptoms of the decadence and depravity which marked that brutal and permissive age. In many this amounted to little more than a general neglect of pupils' moral and physical welfare, as the diary of a young Wykehamist of the period makes very clear:

> *Thurs. May 25th, 1820*: Sat up all night with 3 other fellows swigging wine and playing cards. We had 3 bottles and a fine ham. Shirked chapel next morning. We had about 2 hours' sleep and I was told I looked very unwell next morning, I felt very sleepy. Meredith was much worse than I . . .[7]

But there was of course another side to this neglect. In the claustrophobic anarchy of many dormitories bullying of the grossest kind, bare-knuckle fights, indecent behaviour and downright immorality were endemic and ubiquitous. Boys as young as twelve or thirteen had little or no protection from the attentions – violent, romantic or otherwise – of the be-whiskered and fully adult men who lingered in many sixth-forms until the age of nineteen or even twenty.

In his novel *Tom Brown's Schooldays*, first published in 1857, Thomas Hughes could not bring himself to describe the depths to which Rugby had sunk by the early nineteenth century. Primarily writing to prepare his own eight-year-old son for life there and respecting the juvenile susceptibilities of his earliest readers, he merely noted that in 1828 Dr Thomas Arnold had inherited a 'school, and school-house, in a state of monstrous licence and misrule'. The 'great man' apparently worked wonders and was popularly supposed to have turned Rugby into something of a model school within a decade. But even this latter term is relative. In later chapters of what he called his 'true history', Hughes – who had himself been a pupil at Rugby in the late 1830s – still gave graphic descriptions of how Tom Brown was tossed in a blanket and set to roast before an open fire. The 'licence and misrule' might have gone but, he hinted, the place remained indisputably 'rough and hard'. Arnold had not been able to wholly eradicate practices like bullying. That still went on, although by the 1830s it was apparently confined to 'nooks and corners'.[8]

Looking back to his own days as a pupil at Westminster School in the 1750s, the poet William Cowper also caught something of this atmosphere of violence and degradation in a vituperative attack on the public school system in general. His target, however, was more specific, and in tones of boiling irony, he went on to describe the coarse philistinism which every school instilled in the name of education:

> Would you have your son should be a sot or dunce,
> Lascivious, headstrong, or all these at once [. . .]
> Train him in public with a mob of boys,
> Childish in mischief only and in noise,
> Else of mannish growth, and five in ten
> In infidelity and lewdness, men.
> There shall he learn, ere sixteen winters old,
> That authors are most useful pawned or sold;
> That pedantry is all that schools impart,
> But taverns teach the knowledge of the heart . . .

There was more than an element of truth in this. Even at Eton educational standards were minimal. This was not so much because no one gave any thought to their improvement; it was simply because there was no real reason for them to have been otherwise. Until around the middle of the nineteenth century, the fathers of even the College's most nobly-born pupils would have entirely concurred with the thoughts of Thomas Hughes's Squire Brown on the eve of Tom's departure for Rugby in the late 1830s.[9] 'What is he sent to school for?' the squire asks himself. The answer comes almost immediately. Tom is not going to school to be educated: he is going so that he will 'turn out a brave, helpful, truth-telling Englishman, and a gentleman, and a Christian.'[10]

And that, of course, is exactly how he does turn out. By the end of Hughes's novel the diffident young scrap which the Tally-ho coach to Leicester had deposited into the care of Dr Arnold has become a sturdy, upright, Bible-reading member of Rugby's School House. He has never seriously been in the running for its Balliol scholarship; rather more importantly, however, he has become captain of the cricket team and an all-round 'good fellow' who can be relied upon to play a straight bat in any situation.

Precisely because of this complacent, rentier attitude of generation after generation of real-life Squire Browns – in itself a reflection of a scarcely-changing social climate – Tom was hardly unique. Like him, hundreds if not thousands of upper- and upper-middle-class boys left English public schools in the late eighteenth and early nineteenth centuries to spend the rest of their lives doing little more than administering the family estates on which they had themselves grown up, something which in those days 'a sot or dunce, / Lascivious, headstrong, or all these at once' could do every bit as well as a highly-educated man. Nor, it has to be said, were the subsequent academic hurdles which faced those younger sons who left public school to embark on virtually predetermined careers in the Church, the army and the law particularly high.

There was no real incentive for change. And consequently the lessons taught in the classrooms of Eton, Westminster, Rugby and just about every other school remained as ineluctably medieval as the conditions in their dormitories until about the time that Queen Victoria came to the throne in 1837. They consisted of little more than the endless construing (translating) of passages from Homer and Virgil, together with what Thomas Hughes described as

> the time-honoured institution of the Vulgus (commonly supposed to have been established by William of Wykeham at Winchester, and imported to Rugby by Arnold, more for the sake of the lines which were learnt by heart with it, than for its own intrinsic value, as I've always understood), [which] is a short exercise, in Greek or Latin verse, on a given subject, the minimum number of lines being fixed for each form.[11]

William of Wykeham, the founder of both Winchester College and New College, Oxford, was born in around 1323 and died in 1404 – only four years after Geoffrey Chaucer. His classically-based curriculum, however, remained virtually unchanged for almost a quadri-centennium, and the consequences were inevitable. At about the same time that Jane Austen was beginning to write novels at her kitchen table in Hampshire, William Cowper noted that scarcely one in fifty of the ex public school boys of his day could either speak or write English correctly.

But within half a century of Cowper's death in 1800 everything was looking rather different. By 1850 Jane Austen's relatively sophisticated Mr Bennett had long since replaced Mr Pinchwife, the awful, ignorant, blustering husband in William Wycherley's Restoration comedy *The Country Wife* (1674), as the epitome of the English gentleman.

By then, too, radical newspapers and periodicals like the *Edinburgh Review* were lampooning the public schools' academic inadequacies and attacking the birching and violence by which they maintained an anachronistic status quo. They were even savaging the schools' most cherished customs. Fagging, the *Edinburgh Review* declared as early as 1816, was 'the only regular institution of slave labour enforced by brute violence which now exists on these islands'.

In this, however, they were only reflecting a general attitude. For, beyond the public schools' dormitories and cloisters, the times themselves were changing. In the wider world, a rising tide of Whig reform was beginning to reshape the face of Britain. The Reform Bill was passed in 1832; but almost twenty years previously the House of Commons had appointed the Brougham Committee to begin an equally radical reform of what were even then perceived as the short-comings of the public school system. Its report, when it eventually appeared (in 1818, five years after Jane Austen's *Pride and Prejudice*), was severely critical. And in this respect it can be seen as paving the way for the great clean-up which Arnold was to instigate at Rugby only ten years later.

Far-reaching though that was, however, Arnold too was only react-ing to the mood of the times. He did undoubtedly inculcate in his young charges what Thomas Hughes summarized as a concern 'for whatsoever is true, and manly, and lovely, and of good report', and thus sketch the blueprint on which the character of the ideal public schoolboy of the late nineteenth century would be based. But it would still be overstating the case to conclude that it was purely Arnold's influence which persuaded Eton and virtually every other school to abandon Wykehamist tradition and pursue the same ends within a matter of fifty years. What we would now call market forces were also closely involved.

On the one hand, the schools – nearly all of which even then existed as charitable foundations – were simply failing to so much as break even. In Eton's case the damage wreaked by Dr Keate was so severe that, as late as 1841, it was still unable to recruit its full complement of scholars. Seen in a wider, national context, however, the financial problems faced by individual headmasters and governors paled into insignificance. More worrying for those whose re-sponsibilities were rather broader was the inescapable fact that the public schools were also failing dismally in their primary role as the educators of a ruling élite. By the middle of the nineteenth century it was apparent that their medieval curricula were just not up to the task of training the young men who were being called upon to dispense justice, run the railways and generally ensure that things got done in some of the farthest-flung territories of an Empire upon which the sun never set. Nor, for that matter, was the Vulgus really preparing their cousins and brothers for the new rigours of life at the Bar, in the army or even the Home civil service.

The demands for radical change were thus irresistible, and the public schools had little choice but to confront the modern world. Accordingly, they regularized their uniforms, updated their charters – Eton adopted an entirely new constitution in 1871 – revised their curricula, and began singing their own praises from a whole hymnal of newly-composed songs. As we have already seen, the 'Eton Boating Song' dates from precisely this period, and Harrovians began singing 'Forty Years On' only a few years later. Throughout the 1850s and 1860s too, individual schools disinterred (or sometimes invented) traditions that would give them a new distinction. At Eton, the wild excesses of its historic 'Montem' celebrations were curtailed in 1847 – and replaced by a cricket match.

Nor was that all. School after school also set about what amounted to a wholesale re-evaluation of its role in society. As a result, new laboratories were built, dormitories were swept and ancient libraries extended. School cadet forces, 'volunteer' companies and officer training corps were established, armed and drilled; and a now-familiar regime of 'character-building' games, parades, communal showers and compulsory chapel instituted on campuses in every part of the kingdom. In the name of 'moral and religious training', full-time school chaplains and matrons were appointed. New swimming pools were dug, new gymnasia carved out of echoing panelled halls and new sports pitches levelled and sown and mown. In 1860 Rugby had just one fives court; after two decades of frantic activity another eight had been added, together with a number of cricket pitches, another gymnasium and a swimming pool.

'Play up! Play up! and play the game!' The stirring refrain of Sir Henry Newbolt's poem 'Vitae Lampada', first published in 1879, perfectly expressed the sentiments of a legion of the newly-appointed housemasters who patrolled the boundaries and touchlines of this new world of 'manliness' and 'order'.

*

The shake-up proved immensely successful. Purely by their own efforts, the public schools managed to restore their prestige within a generation. More importantly, they established a new tradition which was to survive virtually unaltered for the century and more which separates two of the most characteristic public school novels to have appeared in the wake of *Tom Brown's Schooldays*, Frederick W. Farrar's *Eric, or Little By Little*, first published in 1858, and Michael Campbell's more recent *Lord Dismiss Us* (1968).

Indeed, the very continuance of that essentially Victorian tradition into the second half of the twentieth century was the subject of Lindsay Anderson's apocalyptic film *If . . .* (another, even more symbolic expression of the mood of 1968). In it, three disaffected sixth-formers are only able to break free of the wing-collared starchiness of a College House where first-year 'scums' still warm the lavatory seats for cane-carrying, sadistic 'whips'; where boaters have still to be raised to 'masters, their wives and the friends of College'; where a 'homosexual flirtatiousness' still pervades the dormitories; where the local grammar school boys are still called 'smudges' and every one else is a 'bloody oik', by machine-gunning their headmaster, teachers and parents.

In 1968, it is fair to say, they did have a point; change was long overdue. Thomas Arnold had had his day. Immensely influential in the mid nineteenth century, his ideas lacked the flexibility demanded by liberal and progressive teachers – 'Trust me!' implores the headmaster in *If . . .* only seconds before he is shot – by the industrialists who were pressing for a second great reformation of the public schools, and not least by the girls who were starting to gain admission to a few of their sixth-forms.

But a century earlier, what amounted to a grafting of the square-jawed, straight-batting ideals of the Victorian world on to three or more centuries of archaic complacency had also had unforeseen consequences. For the renaissance of the public schools served more than immediate, Imperial ends. It undoubtedly helped make the railways of India and West Africa run more efficiently, but it also produced a new breed of men.

In the early 1860s, at precisely the time when the young Arthur Fitz-Gerald Kinnaird was beginning to make his name at Eton, the College was visited by the members of another parliamentary commission. Their 1,800-page report was published in 1864, and explicitly noted that it was schools like Eton which 'had perhaps the largest share in moulding the character of an English gentleman'.

CHAPTER TWO

Anglo-Saxon Attitudes

But in spite of all temptations
To belong to other nations,
He remains an Englishman!
– W. S. Gilbert, *HMS Pinafore*, 1878

Today it is easy to pillory, and very much more difficult to understand, the young, public school-educated English gentleman of the early years of the twentieth century. Notions of Blimpishness and jingoism colour our thoughts, while images drawn from the novels and stories of P. G. Wodehouse, John Buchan and (rather more accurately) Joseph Conrad and Rudyard Kipling crowd our minds.

Unreconstructed by the social volcano that was the First World War, on first sight characters as different as the young Rupert Brooke and the diplomat and traveller Aubrey Herbert seem arrogant and even vaguely repellent figures. Everything about them and their contemporaries, from their incessant cigar smoking to their inbred chauvinism and blind, innate conservatism makes them seem little more than early caricatures of what Edward Heath once called 'the unacceptable face of capitalism'. More fundamentally, however, in a markedly more egalitarian society it is difficult to comprehend their blithe acceptance of wealth and the privileges which it could buy.

And they, or at least their families, did have wealth. For the most part it came from land, as indeed it always had. In the late nineteenth century Lord Portsmouth owned 46,984 acres – and in 1883 alone

drew from them an income of no less than £36,271. In the same year
Lord Scarscale's more modest holding, just 9,929 acres, still brought
in £17,859.[1] Increasingly, however, wealth was coming to mean 'new
money', for throughout the nineteenth century a parvenu mercantile
class had been emerging. It has recently been calculated that, while at
the time of the Battle of Waterloo (1815) there were fewer than 500
'businessmen' in England with incomes of more than £5,000, by 1875
that number had increased eight-fold.[2]

Thus insulated from the pressures of life, the gentleman of the
period could quite literally afford the insouciance which P. G. Wodehouse in particular was later to capture so well. Money gave Bertie
Wooster and all the other members of the Drones' Club a certain
position, and they did their best to live up to it. In London for the
two or three months of the Season, they gave themselves up entirely
to pleasure, as the diary entries of one young man in the summer
of 1914 make very clear:

> *July 7th* To dine with Ld & Lady Londesborough [. . .] After dinner a
> lot more people arrived & there was a dance. I stuck it out to the
> bitter end & got back at 2 a.m. [. . .] I enjoyed it immensely; my
> 1st ball in London!
>
> *July 8th* To the Duke of Portland's house [. . .] my dancing is
> improving. I got in at 4.
>
> *July 9th* I was up again at 6 & walked to Barracks [. . .] on to Lady
> Salisbury's ball [. . .] I have now become fond of dancing & love
> going out!!
>
> *July 10th* I've had no more than 8 hrs sleep in the last 72 hrs.[3]

In this context it is not particularly relevant that the author of those
words was no mere drone but the Prince of Wales, later King
Edward VIII and subsequently the Duke of Windsor. Many lesser
men were familiar with the same world and happy to share what
Lady Cynthia Asquith was later to describe as the 'almost mythical'
affluence of it all:

> striped awnings, linkmen with flaring torches; powdered liveried
> footmen; soaring marble staircases; tiaras, smiling hostesses; azaleas in
> gilt baskets; white waistcoats, violins, elbows sawing the air, names on
> pasteboard cards, quails in aspic, macedoine, strawberries and cream,
> tired faces of cloakroom attendants, washed streets in blue dawns . . .[4]

And it is their stuffed self-importance, their very ostentatiousness – the silken affluence and extravagant posing which are so well caught in portraits by the American-born society painter John Singer Sargent – which we notice today. But with the benefit of hindsight we can also see how the 'gadding about' in white ties and tails of these gentlemen had a dual purpose.

On one level it served to establish their credentials within what Benjamin Disraeli had earlier described as 'the upper ten thousand'. Like belonging to the right clubs, it was simply expected of them. On quite another it also proclaimed their social superiority. It effectively cowed the army of footmen, servants and cloakroom attendants who made it all possible; and, more curiously perhaps, it also delighted the lower-middle classes who, until about 1939, were enthusiastic voyeurs of the antics of their 'betters'. Today only pop-stars and royalty get the treatment, but in the years before 1914 and throughout most of the twenties and thirties the arrival of any white-tied guest at a major reception or society wedding (such as that of Oswald Mosley in 1920) was greeted by the respectful cheers of a crowd of onlookers on the other side of the road.

As much as the card-carrying aristos and invitees, they also 'knew their place'. Writing as late as 1935, the novelist Patrick Hamilton, a neurasthenically-sensitive observer of social mores, pin-pointed exactly where that place was when he delineated the worm's-eye view of Bob, a London barman-cum-waiter of the period:

> On going up to any table he held his tray lightly in the fingers of both hands, and balancing it perpendicularly upon the table, said either 'Yessir' or 'Goodeveningsir' according to the case. In resting the tray thus upon the table *he was able to achieve a minute bow. Without the tray he could not have bowed*, would not have known what to do with his hands, and could only have stood there looking limp and inadequate. Similarly, in the indecisive conversation which invariably followed amongst those he served, the tray was a barrier, a counter, a thing behind which *he could resolutely stand and wait, deferent and official*.[5]

There was too an arrogance behind the starched shirt-fronts – and it was arrogance of the very worst kind. In London, it manifested itself in sheer extravagance, but during the succession of country-house weekends which filled the autumn and winter months it could be seen in its true colours as little more than callousness. In his autobiography, the Duke of Windsor recalled that his father, King George V had once, and only semi-flippantly, opined that servants slept in trees.[6] Out on the grouse moors, with only a momentary twinge of conscience, he would also personally bring down over 1,000 birds during the course of a single six-hour shoot.[7]

There was nothing particularly special about either attitude. In his memoirs, Edward Lyttelton recalled how, as an Eton schoolboy, he would throw soft fives balls at dogs – and stones at cart drivers.[8] In his rather tellingly-titled memoirs *Men, Women & Things*, the Duke of Portland noted that, between 1867 and 1900, Lord de Grey 'personally killed no fewer than 370,728 head of game, including 142,343 pheasants, 97,759 partridges, 56,460 grouse, 29,858 rabbits and 27,686 hares'.[9]

Life was simpler then; the blacks blacker and the whites whiter. Today no one has much time or sympathy for such boors, for the type of men whom Ford Madox Ford was to describe only a decade later. They 'administered the world', he wrote – but

> If they saw policemen misbehave, railway porters lack civility, an insufficiency of street lamps, defects in public services or in foreign countries, they saw it, either with nonchalant Balliol voices or with letters to *The Times*, asking in regretful indignation: 'Has the British This or That come to *this*?' Or they wrote, in the serious reviews of which so many still survived, articles taking under their care, manners, the Arts, diplomacy, inter-Imperial trade, or the personal reputations of deceased statesmen and men of letters.[10]

Perspectives have changed, with the result that, quite as much as the square-jawed heroes of books by John Buchan, Sapper and Dornford Yates, even such 'regular' empire-administrators as George Nathaniel Curzon and King George V's father, King Edward VII are now as remote from us as, say, Cardinal Wolsey and King Henry VIII. Already they have become historical figures whose realities are concealed behind the dates and retrospective analyses of the history books. 'The past is another country', as L. P. Hartley wrote; and it seems that they really did do things differently there.

And yet, until comparatively recently, the rather earnest attitudes and what must now be considered the equally dubious attributes of the early twentieth-century English gentleman were shared, or at least aspired to, by the majority of his compatriots. In the early 1920s,

Sapper's first readers found the hearty, monied, muscle-bound Bulldog Drummond as congenial a hero as, forty years later, their grandchildren did James Bond or, for that matter, Kingsley Amis's Jim Dixon.

What amounted to this virtual deification had its roots in the second half of the nineteenth century. It was then that the gentleman, and more specifically the whole public school ethos from which he sprang, became inextricably associated with notions of 'Englishness'; then that the gentleman became both a role-model and, to a lesser but increasing extent, an Aunt Sally.

Indeed, it is hardly overstating the case to say that by the 1860s both that posturing, patrician gentleman and the public schools from which he sprang had been given official, government approval. It is certainly difficult to put any other gloss on the conclusions of the 1,800-page report of the Clarendon Commission which was presented to Parliament in 1864.

Set up three years previously to 'inquire into the revenues and management of certain colleges and schools, and the studies pursued and instruction given therein', the Commission had looked at length at every aspect of life in nine sample schools.[11] And – unsurprisingly perhaps, since with one exception it was composed of men who had themselves attended one or other of those self-same schools – it expressed itself well pleased with what it saw.

In this respect it was almost irrelevant that its members (they included the Earl of Devon, Lord Lyttelton, Sir Stafford Northcote and The Revd W. H. Thomson) were hardly more than well-intentioned amateurs. Clarendon himself complained that one was 'idle' and another 'weak'. In private letters he also described a third as 'quirky', and wrote off a fourth as downright 'mad'. Nor was it really noticed that, like the members of more than one parliamentary commission before and since, the majority were also only barely competent as part-time committee-men, and showed scant interest in the subject of their research. For, incredible as it seems today, during the whole of their three-year investigation they managed to spend just one day at Eton, one at Westminster and one at Charterhouse. Only the post-Arnold Rugby significantly detained them. But while the examination of an ordinary comprehensive can now take a trained team of Her Majesty's Inspectors two weeks or longer, even there Clarendon and his colleagues were finished in no more than seventy-two hours.

No one minded very much. Seemingly, it was enough that the commissioners were all gentlemen. Certainly, given their own backgrounds, it was virtually inevitable that their report should have fulsomely acknowledged 'the obligations which England owes' to the public school system. It was almost over-egging the pudding, however, when they went on to paint a glowing picture of the schools' role in national life:

> It is not easy to estimate the degree in which the English people are indebted to these schools for the qualities on which they pique themselves most – for their capacity to govern others and control themselves, their aptitude for combining freedom with order, their public spirit, their vigour and manliness of character, their strong but not slavish respect for public opinion, their love of healthy sports and exercise. These schools have been the chief nurseries of our statesmen; in them, and in schools modelled after them, men of all the various classes that make up English society, destined for every profession and career, have been brought up on a footing of social equality, and have contracted the most enduring friendships, and some of the ruling habits, of their lives.[12]

But, complacently as Clarendon's conclusions read today – although they found all their nine schools to some extent 'too indulgent to idleness', he and his fellow commissioners fought shy of suggesting any radical curricular reforms – at the time of their publication the report's recommendations were widely welcomed. Quite simply, they said exactly what Parliament and large sections of the country wished to hear. Both really did pique themselves on their notions of fair play, decency, manliness and no-nonsense justice.

Thus it was to its public schools that the England of the eighteen-sixties, seventies and eighties increasingly looked for an image of itself – and, inevitably, to their own schooldays that its rulers and leaders turned for notions of Englishness.

It should, therefore, come as no real surprise to discover that Lord Curzon, Viceroy of India and sometime His Imperial Majesty's Principal Secretary of State for Foreign Affairs, nursed a lifelong affection for the Eton he first encountered in 1872. No matter that friends and enemies alike called him resolutely unsentimental, dully dutiful or just plain 'cold' – it was Stanley Baldwin who remembered receiving from him 'the sort of greeting a corpse would give an undertaker' – until the very end of his life Curzon preserved at Kedleston Hall, his family seat in Derbyshire, the very desk he had occupied while an Eton Colleger in the mid 1870s.

What is perhaps more surprising is the durability of what we might conveniently call this Eton-England axis. It survived the First World War virtually unscathed. Even more remarkably, it was hardly dented by the Second. William Johnson Cory's 'Eton Boating Song' had referred to 'the chain which is round us now', and that chain proved unexpectedly strong. Not only did it bind young Etonians together – as late as the 1940s the young Nicholas Mosley realized that 'to other Etonians, being a member of the school was more important than one's father being in gaol'[13] – it was no less strong in later life. At Eton and elsewhere, its emotional shackles continued to ensnare generation after generation as hopelessly as they had done Curzon.

And in the twentieth century, it held no one so fast as it did Guy Burgess. The future spy had been sent to Eton in 1924, slightly more than half a century after Curzon, and in one part of his mind at least he too never really left. As his friend and biographer Tom Driberg was to note,[14] even during the enforced exile in Moscow which followed his defection with Donald Maclean in 1951, Burgess continued to sport an Old Etonian bow-tie. In much the same way as the Gilbert and Sullivan tunes he also liked to sing, that proud relic of his schooldays became, in T. S. Eliot's phrase, a precise objective correlative of the old country the traitor so perversely continued to love.

Burgess may have been a one-off, a fallen pillar of the Establishment who broke as many rules as he kept – and, on his own terms at least, he did not break that many – but it is still impossible to overstate the importance of what was to become a symbiotic relationship between the nation and its public schools in the last thirty years of the nineteenth century and the early years of this. Socially and architecturally, well before Dr Arnold even arrived at Rugby, a handful of these schools at least really could claim to be part of the fabric of the nation. Even today, one has only to stroll through the quadrangles, cloisters and chapels at Eton, Westminster or Winchester to appreciate how closely they were modelled on the monastic establishments attached to roughly contemporaneous cathedrals and abbeys. The briefest dip into the vast pool of public school literature will also reveal that, as late as the nineteenth century, the facilities available in even a senior boy's study differed only marginally from the medieval starkness of a monk's cell. None of this was accidental. Nor was the parallel entirely confined to the older schools. The shortest of walks down the wood-panelled corridors of Rugby or Oundle immediately suggests a connection with a later generation of Restoration halls, Georgian country houses and spacious, portrait-filled eighteenth-century rectories. Indeed, it is hardly over-stressing the point to suggest that, up until relatively recently, public schools were only ever offering a 'home-from-home' to their pupils. It is even possible to argue that, at least until about the middle of the nineteenth century, attending any one of them amounted to – and was intended as no more than – a brief sojourn in broadly familiar surroundings. That, fundamentally, is what is described in books like *Tom Brown's School-days*: an adolescent interlude separating a childhood spent at home from an adult return there or, more rarely, a career in the panelled exchanges and boardrooms of commerce or the lofty, gilded corridors of government.[15]

And despite (or quite probably because of) the shake-ups which followed visits by the Clarendon commissioners and other 'outsiders', the schools were reluctant to rock this particular boat. As late as the beginning of the twentieth century many were still doing everything possible to consolidate their own position at the heart of a fast-fading aristocratic, squirarchical system. And the lengths to which they were prepared to go are vividly demonstrated by the history of Christ's Hospital School.

Familiarly known as 'the Bluecoat School' because of the long Elizabethan cassocks still worn by its pupils, Christ's Hospital had been established as a charitable foundation in the City of London in 1552. It was a unique institution which Desmond Graham has rather brutally described as 'a public school – but one for those without money'.[16] It sat well in the City, but 350 years after its foundation it became necessary for the whole school to move, and in 1902 it decamped to newly-built premises near Horsham in Sussex.

Most of its pupils still came from London elementary schools and paid no fees, but the new Christ's Hospital (which had taken five years to build) was nothing like the intimidatingly solid London County Council 'three-deckers' in which they had sat their scholarships. Instead, it was seen as more appropriate for all 700 of the school's 'Blues' – its élite 'Grecians', its more ordinary 'Housey boys' and junior 'swabs' (fags) – to move into a gargantuan Edwardian pastiche of an English country house.

Image was all. For just as the below-stairs realities of life in even the grandest of country houses could be mean and brutish, the private domestic arrangements at the new school differed little from those at any other, despite its first headmaster's comment that 'the new buildings are splendid; entirely adequate; refreshingly up to date'.[17] Rough plank beds still filled the house dormitories; and as the poet Keith Douglas (a Grecian in the late 1930s) was to discover, a study was still monkish in its facilities. His own, as he described in a letter, was 'a dirty little room' in which

> The wooden and plaster walls are green (dark) up to about waist high and then yellow plaster, or window. These walls are covered with initials and burnt lettering of various kinds (particularly the lower part of the door, which is brown). Indelible finger-marks of past owners are profusely distributed. I have a little table, a lot of books, an armchair, a deckchair and a settle.[18]

In direct contrast, the more public face of the new Christ's Hospital easily outdid the modest, homely quads at Eton and Westminster. In sheer scale the new building dwarfed every nearby village. Set in its own estate of some 300 acres, and approached from the Horsham road via a broad, tree-lined avenue, the main school was built of good red brick in a mock-Tudor style with an elaborate Perpendicular gateway, wide cloisters and long, mullioned windows looking out over a broad central quadrangle. Ranged around it and only slightly less grand were the boarding houses, each one the size of a modest country mansion and bearing the name of a distinguished Old Blue – Pepys, Coleridge, Lamb and Leigh Hunt among them. Opening directly on to the parade ground-sized quad, the new dining hall boasted one of the largest unsupported roofs in Europe, while the adjoining chapel, whose walls were later covered with vast murals by Sir Frank Brangwyn, resembled nothing so much as the great hall at Hampton Court Palace.

Empty today except during the school's daily service, that chapel can now be seen as the apotheosis of Victorian aspiration. Even more than the rest of the school, it is a massive, echoing monument to the grandiloquence of spirit of which Eton, Rugby and Westminster were the finest flowers, and the new Christ's Hospital unknowingly the last expression.

There is, seemingly, no record of the hymns which the Christ's

Hospital Blues sang as they settled down at their new school in the early years of this century. But it is tempting to imagine their raising the beamed roof of the cavernous, mock-Tudor chapel with lusty renditions of the patriotic new 'Children's Song' that Rudyard Kipling included in *Puck of Pook's Hill* (1906).

A novel which is in itself preoccupied with notions of Englishness, *Puck* ranges back through English history and draws unpleasant parallels with happenings in Kipling's own time. It suggests that decadence and a lack of purpose are undermining the national character. At one point it even compares the plight of Roman legionaries guarding Hadrian's wall with the contemporary neglect of the British soldiers who were then patrolling the furthermost frontiers of the British Empire. Ostensibly a children's book, Noël Annan has nevertheless bracketed *Puck of Pook's Hill* with E. M. Forster's *Howard's End* (1910) and Bernard Shaw's rather later play *Heartbreak House*, first produced in 1921. All are to some extent state-of-the-nation works, he argues; with Kipling's at root the attempt of 'a conservative to discern England's destiny'.

And despite its inherent pessimism, *Puck* does discern one. Everything in the past seems to point towards a future in which Kipling's young readers will have crucial roles to play. If they can only preserve a certain purity, the book suggests, England and the Empire will survive. Hence in the 'Children's Song' Kipling exhorts them to dedicate themselves to the highest of ideals. They must make a pact with that destiny and keep faith with the spirit which had previously made England great:

> Land of our Birth, we pledge to thee
> Our love and toil in the years to be,
> When we are grown and take our place
> As men and women with our race.

> Teach us to bear the yoke in youth,
> With steadfastness and careful truth;
> That, in our time, Thy Grace may give
> The Truth whereby the Nations live.

> Teach us to rule ourselves alway,
> Controlled and cleanly night and day,
> That we may bring, if need arise,

No maimed or worthless sacrifice.

Land of our Birth, our faith, our pride,
For whose dear sake our fathers died;
O Motherland, we pledge to thee,
Head, heart and hand through the years to be.

[My italics]

It would of course be a mistake to see Kipling's apostrophizing of the 'Motherland' as anything like as sinister as the Nazis' cynical manipulation of the spirit of *Deutschland, Deutschland, über alles* some thirty years later; but it is equally wrong to assume that he was a right-wing, xenophobic loner. Empire Day, first celebrated in 1902 – coincidentally the same year in which the Christ's Hospital Blues moved into their new school – was only one of several other manifestations of a general feeling that children should be taught that their innate superiority had strings attached.

The brainchild of the otherwise unexceptional Earl of Meath, Empire Day was originally little more than an informal commemoration of Queen Victoria's birthday and the ending of the Boer War. But within fifteen years it had been officially recognized and come to stand for something every bit as atavistic and fundamental as even Kipling could have wished. On 24 May each year, amid much flag-waving, hymn-singing, Bible-reading and general paramilitary brouhaha, the country's schoolchildren were given a day off lessons and specifically encouraged to be aware of their duties and responsibilities as citizens of the greatest empire the world had ever known. Officers' Training Corps paraded, chaplains preached appropriate sermons, and parties of small girls placed chaplets of spring flowers before portraits of the King and (as time progressed) on the steps of the new war memorials which were erected in every town and village.

The movement was at its height in the inter-war years, most particularly in the immediate aftermath of what was then known as the Great War. But ironically – and tellingly, perhaps – the attendant celebrations were to continue for far longer than the Empire. It was not until 1958 that Empire Day was officially renamed Commonwealth Day, the flags were furled and the parades stood down.

It had had its day; but forty years earlier its overt and frankly chauvinistic patriotism reflected the attitudes and aspirations of a wider world as much as it did the bell-clanging ritual which governed everyday life in boarding schools. The Empire itself was still expanding – between the death of Queen Victoria in 1901 and the outbreak of the Great War it acquired new territories with a greater area than the whole of the United States – and no one seriously questioned its right to do so. Still less did anyone challenge Britain's right to rule them as she wished. Imbued from their schooldays with a deep love of country, a generation of Old Boys made sure of that.

Indeed, it was their particular, rather sentimental, common-room patriotism which went on to shape the national response during the Great War. It was implicit in Lord Kitchener's recruiting slogan 'Your Country Needs You!', and made perfectly explicit in Rupert Brooke's best-known poem 'The Soldier', a somewhat mawkish lyric composed by the Old Rugbeian at the very end of 1914:

> If I should die, think only this of me:
>   That there's some corner of a foreign field
> That is forever England. There shall be
>   In that rich earth a richer dust concealed;
>   A dust whom England bore, shaped, made aware . . .

In succeeding lines, Brooke rather labours his point with complex metaphors suggesting that his remains would bring to that foreign field something of the 'sights and sounds . . . and gentleness' of England. It is sentimental and all rather too redolent of colonialism and the proselytizing, muscular zeal which drove missionaries to bring other aspects of English life to even farther flung fields.

More modest in their scope, but still perhaps the most perfect expression of the patrician sentiments of the time, are the opening lines of the stirring hymn which Sir Cecil Spring-Rice, the British Ambassador to the United States composed in 1916:

> I vow to thee, my country – all earthly things above –
> Entire and whole and perfect the service of my love . . .

By 1916 the impact of the Great War had rather clouded the issue. By then a deeper, more natural patriotism had long-since filled the national consciousness. All the same, the hymn acquires an extra resonance – and something, indeed, of its original force – when we learn that in his youth Spring-Rice too had been an Eton scholar, an exact contemporary, and later a lifelong friend, of Lord Curzon's.

There are many more literary testaments to the enduring power of the later nineteenth-century Eton-England axis. However, in his poem 'Clifton College' (first published in 1908 in a collection significantly entitled *Clifton College and Other School Poems*), Sir Henry Newbolt spelt out the connection better than anyone. Addressing himself to a young boy – 'my son' – shortly to go up to Clifton, the author of 'Drake's Drum' and that other quintessentially public school poem 'Vitae Lampada' concluded with the lines:

> Today and here the fight's begun,
> Of the great fellowship you're free;
> *Henceforth the School and you are one,*
> *And what you are, the race shall be.*
>
> [My italics]

Nor was this Edwardian celebration of 'Motherland' and 'race' wholly confined to literature. It can be seen in the broad avenues and massive Imperial architecture which Sir Edwin Lutyens and Sir Herbert Baker deemed appropriate for New Delhi when the capital of British India was moved from Calcutta to the banks of the river Jumna in 1912. It is even reflected in the construction of the doomed White Star liner, the s.s. *Titanic*. Built at Harland and Wolff's Belfast yard, she was no less than 882 feet (269 metres) long and a generous 92 feet (28 metres) wide. With a gross displacement of 46,328 tons, for the four days and seventeen hours that she floated before hitting an iceberg on her maiden voyage in April 1912, she was quite simply the largest passenger vessel ever to put to sea.

She was far, far bigger than the four-funnelled German liners with names like the *Kaiser Wilhelm der Grosse*, the *Kronprinz Wilhelm*, the *Fürst Bismarck* and the *Kronprinzessin Cecile* which had dominated the Atlantic run in the early years of the century. Most importantly of all, she was also British, a gargantuan steel symbol of national self-confidence in which the nation's élite could make themselves at home. And exactly who comprised that élite and precisely what they could expect was spelt out in a contemporary account of the appearance of the *Titanic*. For while it scarcely mentioned the spartan conditions endured by her steerage passengers – largely foreign emigrants en route to the

New World – this waxed lyrical about the 'prodigal spirit' and 'magnificence' of the first-class accommodation:

> The dining rooms, state rooms, and common rooms were furnished in various periods and styles, copied faithfully from old models, so that English gentlemen might sit in rooms panelled and adorned like those of Haddon Hall, and fair women might have their beauty reflected in oval mirrors hanging upon walls like those of Versailles when Marie Antoinette played with her ladies.[19]

But perhaps it was music which best expressed the full range of the proud but complex Edwardian notion of 'Englishness'. For before the Great War a generation of talented (and still largely underrated) English composers was celebrating the virtues of its native land every bit as effectively as its poets and engineers. Well before 1914, figures like Sir Charles Villiers Stanford, Sir John Stainer, the bucolic sportsman-baronet Sir Hubert Parry (who composed the familiar setting of William Blake's 'Jerusalem') and others of the grandiloquently 'public' Victorian school had handed on the baton to younger men.

Although he spent most of his life in France and fits more closely into a northern European or Scandinavian tradition – he was both a pupil and friend of Edvard Grieg – the Yorkshire-born Frederick Delius continued to find inspiration for much of his work in the English countryside he had known as a boy. This was particularly true in the period 1900–14, from which date his second opera *A Village Romeo and Juliet* (1901) and several of his best-known tone-poems and orchestral pieces. 'Brigg Fair' was written in 1907, 'On Hearing the First Cuckoo in Spring' in 1912, and 'North Country Sketches' in 1913.

Even closer to the 'richer dust' of England, the Eton-educated George Butterworth was born in 1885, and completed relatively little before he was killed during the Battle of the Somme in 1916. An almost exact contemporary of Rupert Brooke, he shared something of the poet's sentimental attachment to the soil, even going so far as to join Cecil Sharpe and Ralph Vaughan Williams in their research into English folk song. Consequently, even more than Delius's, the music Butterworth composed in the years immediately before the outbreak of the Great War is ineffably English. Its very titles say it all. There is his song-cycle 'A Shropshire Lad' (1912), based on the poems of A. E. Housman, and a set of 'Eleven Folksongs from Sussex' which dates from the same year. There is his orchestral suite 'The Banks of Green Willow', and above all there are his two 'English Idylls'. In different ways, every piece reveals what one modern critic has called 'a personality sensitively responsive to the peace, contrasts and contours of the English countryside'.

Nearly thirty years older than George Butterworth, and far more closely allied to Stanford and Parry, Edward Elgar (who was knighted in 1904 and became Master of the King's Music in 1924) could also be responsive to the moods and character of the English countryside. Worcestershire born, he had composed his autobiographical suite of 'Enigma Variations' in 1899, while the second movement of his earlier 'Serenade for Strings' was apparently inspired by memories of the River Severn. But it was his later and more characteristically swaggering music – the Symphony No. 1, 'Sea Pictures' and his five 'Pomp and Circumstance Marches' – that gave the swelling imperial theme its most eloquent expression.

The first two of the 'Pomp and Circumstance Marches' date from 1901, the third was written in 1904 and the fourth in 1907. (The fifth was not completed until 1930, and the interval shows. Where the others are confident, it sounds hedged around by doubts and duplicity.) But it was of course the first which caught the public imagination – even without the words which are now inseparable from its trio section. They were added later by A. C. Benson – inevitably another Etonian – and encapsulate better than any other single lyric the aspirations of their generation:

> Land of Hope and Glory, Mother of the Free,
> How shall we extoll thee, who are born of thee?
> Wider still and wider shall thy bounds be set;
> God who made thee mighty, make thee mightier yet.

This then was the intellectual background against which the English gentleman grew up in the early years of the century. It would be foolish to assume that, as a matter of course, he read the poetry of Rupert Brooke, or even A. E. Housman – as simplistic, indeed, as imagining that he was always at the Queen's Hall or prepared to make the trip to the Three Choirs Festival to hear premières of the latest works by Elgar, Delius and Butterworth. But he inhabited the same world and, as we have already seen, was quite likely to have shared classrooms and dormitories with the likes of the above.

Typically, he was less eloquent than they. His Englishness was cruder and more strident than theirs; his pronouncements about it – when he made them at all – less polished. But, for all that, he too expressed the mood of the times, and deserves an equal hearing. Here, for instance, is the young and ineluctably English George Curzon, reluctantly crossing the Atlantic on the German liner *Fürst Bismarck* in 1892:

> Of the hundreds of first class passengers crowding the great vessel, barely one has the appearance of a gentleman or lady. The majority are commercial Germans – with the unredeemed Teutonic type of face, figure, manner and dress. God! What a people! How coarse! How hideous! How utterly wanting in the least element of distinction![20]

Nor was Curzon's antipathy to foreigners confined to Germans. During that same Atlantic crossing he went on to note that 'middle-class Americans [are] the least attractive species of the human genus'.[21] In the following eight years he was also to write off Frenchmen – *all* Frenchmen – because they have 'no manhood about them. Every one of them like a hair cutter. All curl of the lip and smirk in address, but no real bonhomie or frankness'.[22] Later, the 'life of mingled splendour and frippery, and of taste, half cultured and half debased, of the Persian monarch and, it may be said, of the Persian aristocracy in general'[23] was also to incur his displeasure.

But more significant, perhaps, was his attitude to Indians. In a letter he wrote to Alfred Lyttelton, two years after his appointment as Viceroy, Curzon explained that:

> We cannot take the Natives up into the administration. They are crooked-minded and corrupt. We have got therefore to go on ruling them and we can only do it with success by being both kindly and virtuous. I daresay I am talking rather like a schoolmaster; but after all the millions I have to manage are less than school children.[24]

Patronizing and awful as such sentiments sound today, they were not entirely confined to Curzon. Nor was Curzon himself, in the early part of his life at least, anything like their truest mouthpiece. At that time he even enjoyed a reputation for comparative free-thinking. Although in the early 1880s he had not been able to bring himself to join the Liberal party (then led by his friend William Ewart Gladstone), by the decade's end he had made one of the very first constructive plans for the reform of the House of Lords.

For all that, Curzon remained little more than a product of his time and social position, a willing victim of the jingoistic Englishness that was explicitly inculcated in members of his class. But although it was their public schools which made them into 'little Englanders', in many cases it was the universities to which they matriculated that finally buffed and polished those bruised and Bible-battered public school young men into 'acceptable' members of society.

Even there, however, hierarchies existed. George Nathaniel Curzon would no more have thought of going up to a Cambridge college than he would of squandering his talents by following his father into the obscurity of Holy Orders. Instead, for him and more than a generation of serious-minded Etonians the road led inexorably to Oxford, and specifically to the gates of Balliol.

Founded nearly two centuries before Eton, in 1263, Balliol College, Oxford had a long history of intellectual rigour. But a decade or so before Curzon arrived in 1878 it had also become recognized as the temple of patrician orthodoxy. Indeed, its rather gloomy, neo-Gothic architecture – the stern brick face it turned on the Broad and the cold, weird charmlessness of its chapel and quad, so much at odds with the honeyed seventeenth- or eighteenth-century charm of neighbouring colleges – only seemed to reflect its reputation for relentless high-mindedness.

There were few 'hearties' at Balliol; it was just not that sort of place. Curzon's junior by two decades, Raymond Asquith noted that among his fellow candidates for a scholarship were 'a very large number of diseased and hideous people. My vis-à-vis is an intellectual looking man with a black beard and flaxen undergrowth over the rest of his face'.[25] Passing out top of the list, in 1897 Asquith (son of the Liberal politician H. H. Asquith) was nevertheless happy to go up to a Balliol that was still 'for the most part composed of niggers and Scotchmen'[26] – and still heavily under the influence of the man who had become its Master in 1870.

Dr Benjamin Jowett's connection with Balliol began when he was elected a Fellow in 1838. He was ordained in 1842, and appointed Oxford's Regius Professor of Greek in 1855. But his real career spanned the twenty-three years between 1870 and his death in 1893 during which he held that mastership. Under his regime of cold baths and scholarship, the College became the recognized finishing school for any public schoolboy with pretensions to high office or public service. So much was this the case, in fact, that shortly before his death Jowett was able to issue an invitation to a Balliol reception at which guests would meet 'members of the two Houses of Parliament, and other members of the College'.

His pride in what he had achieved was perhaps forgivable, although a streak of arrogance did figure strongly in Jowett's make-up. He certainly did not suffer fools gladly – or indeed at all. An intimate of Robert Browning, Algernon Swinburne and Matthew Arnold (the son of Rugby's 'good doctor') he was one of the great scholars of his time, and published definitive translations of Thucydides, Aristotle and the *Dialogues* of Plato. Within and even beyond the university his reputation was such that there was more than mere undergraduate irreverence in the lines about Jowett in 'The Masque of B-ll--1', a collection of doggerel describing forty members of the College community which first appeared in 1881:

> First come I. My name is J-W-TT.
> There's no knowledge but I know it.
> I am Master of this College,
> What I don't know isn't knowledge.

He had an almost Olympian distinction. In part this was due to his high collars, white ties, black tailcoats and curiously squeaky voice, but at a deeper level it probably had more to do with his conviction that being up at Balliol was a privilege – and privileges, as all good Victorians knew, had to be earned.

Jowett was a quintessentially good Victorian, and once summed up his aims in a single sentence: 'I should like to make all my old pupils properly ambitious, if I could, of living like men and doing silently a real work'. In this he provided us with a vital clue. For he suggests that the xenophobia, chauvinism, anti-semitism, racism and snobbery of Curzon and generation after generation of his students, their contemporaries and to some extent of Jowett himself was only one side of the coin. We might call it the public manifestation of their Englishness, an explicit demonstration of their implicit notions of national superiority.

Underlying it was something far deeper, ultimately of greater importance, but very much more difficult to characterize or even caricature. For both Jowett and his students were imbued with a sense of

Duty and the importance of doing 'real work'. This is apparent even in Curzon's first recorded public utterance. In 1867, at the age of eight, he had laid the foundation stone of a new school at Kedleston and made a short speech. The words were written for him by his father, but they are nevertheless worth quoting:

> I am very much pleased at being desired by my Father to lay the first stone of this school, which I hope will be an ornament to the village and a blessing to the parish; and I trust that many children here may learn those truths which may fit them to fulfil their duty towards their God, their parents and their neighbours as long as they live.[27]

It is no accident that in the manuscript record of this admittedly rather priggish effusion the initial letters of the words 'Father' and 'God' are capitalized. For it is impossible to understand the attitudes of the English gentleman at the turn of the century without acknowledging his acceptance of the 'duty' he was under and all that that entailed. For good or ill (and, as we shall see, the cons frequently outweighed the pros) it informed his every action. Not unnaturally, it also coloured his view of the world. Here, for instance, is the Duke of Windsor again, meditating in his autobiography about the character of his father, King George V:

> through everything cut the sharp concept of duty summed up for him in that precept that, copied in his round hand, he kept on his writing desk: 'I shall pass through this world but once. Any good thing, therefore, that I can do or any kindness that I can show any human being, let me do it now. Let me not defer or neglect it, for I shall not pass this way again.' These lines are attributed to an American Quaker of the early nineteenth century, Stephen Grellet. I was made while very young to memorize them, and they were often to influence my actions in later life. If through my family's position my childhood was spared the mundane struggle that is the common lot, I nevertheless had my full share of discipline. For *the concept of duty was drilled into me, and I never had the sense that the days belonged to me alone.*[28]

Born in 1894, a generation later than Curzon, not even the party-going Prince was above this concern for others. And although in later life his commitment to this country might be said to have deserted him, Curzon's did not. Despite his contempt for the Indians over whom he was given suzerainty, his respect for Britain and the British Empire never wavered. The remarks he made to an audience in Derby in 1904 held good for the rest of his life:

> To me the Empire is so sacred and so noble a thing that I cannot understand people quarrelling about it, or even holding opposite opinions about it.[29]

To fully understand both Curzon's character and the attitudes of the English patrician class from which he sprang and of which he was such an exemplar, however, it is necessary to see this statement in context. For later in his life Curzon was also quite capable of remarking that:

> Our so called working classes are rotting at the core; and it is the upper classes and the older generation of working men who alone set the tone.[30]

Bulldog Drummond would have agreed with that. So too would Rupert Brooke and – cocking an eyebrow at the faithful Jeeves – even Bertie Wooster. For all of them too recognized their duty to set that tone. Not to have done so just wouldn't have been cricket.

CHAPTER THREE

Playing Hard

*The man who is good at cricket is good at
anything.*
  – *Daily News*, 12 November 1920

'Queen's weather' they called it in the 1880s and 1890s when, whatever
the season, bright clear sunshine marked virtually every one of Queen
Victoria's public appearances.

The old Queen had died at the beginning of 1901 at the age of
eighty-one, but out of affection for her memory perhaps, the phrase
stuck – and so, seemingly, did the weather. Even now, in the popular
mind at least, there is a notion that an unbroken spell of that Queen's
weather continued for the next ten years. For after more than half a
century it is still virtually impossible to conceive of the reign of King
Edward VII as anything other than an endless June afternoon, with a
warm sun shining down from cloudless skies.

To those fortunate enough to have been in its rays – to the descend-
ants of that 'upper ten thousand' which had come to prominence in
the middle of the old century, and the *arrivistes* who had literally
bought their way into what remained of the new King's 'Marlborough
House Set' – it must even have seemed like that at the time. In the
few brief years between 1901 and King Edward's death in 1910 they
at any rate could well have been forgiven for thinking that an English
God was in his Heaven and everything right with the world.

In London the first years of the new century were enlivened by a succession of Coronation balls, at which the Royal presence added extra glitter and fizz to Lady Cynthia Asquith's 'almost mythical' world of striped awnings, soaring marble staircases and azaleas in gilt baskets. According to the 1908 edition of *Baedecker's Guide to London*, the capital was 'not only the largest but one of the finest cities in the world'. The West End in particular was fast acquiring the reputation for breathless modernity and sophistication of which it would boast in the 1920s, and never quite lose. After darkness fell, electric lamps illuminated its major thoroughfares, while beneath them a rapidly-expanding underground railway network already linked Piccadilly Circus – 'the hub of the Empire' – with distant suburbs in the north and west.

The pace of life had quickened, and as if to symbolize the new vivacity the first few years of the new century witnessed a rash of theatre-building as hectic as that which had overtaken London in the late 1880s. As early as 1902 the Victorian interior of the Criterion restaurant and theatre complex in Piccadilly Circus was stripped out and replaced by an effulgent riot of 'rococo' plasterwork and Art Nouveau tiling deemed more in keeping with the spirit of the new age. And appropriately enough the theatre reopened, on the evening of 10 February 1903, with a play entitled *A Clean Slate*.

The following year saw the opening of the 4,000-seat London Coliseum, specifically built to stage anything from Sarah Bernhardt's lavish production of Racine's *Phèdre* to full horse races. It coped with both, as well as appearances by the likes of George Robey and Vesta Tilley (but only the nearby Hippodrome [1900] could have housed the 1909 epic *The North Pole* which featured the appearance of seventy polar bears). Front-of-house facilities at the Coliseum were as spec-tacularly elaborate as its stage machinery. Telegrams could be sent and stamps bought; and although it never worked, there was even an electric light railway linking the specially-constructed royal entrance in St Martin's Lane to a royal box at the back of the stalls. According to a contemporary programme the whole vast edifice combined 'the social advantages of the refined and elegant surroundings of a Club; the comfort and attractiveness of a Café, besides being the THEATRE DE LUXE OF LONDON and the pleasantest family resort imaginable'.

Even more in keeping with the mood of the times was the new Gaiety Theatre in the Strand (1903) where the impresario George Edwardes presented revue and what would become known as 'revuedeville'. The sets were more lavish and the famous 'Gaiety Girls' even more gorgeous than those who had appeared at the old Gaiety Theatre in Leicester Square. Max Beerbohm was not alone in apostrophizing their fashionable hour-glass beauty, their 'splendid nonchalance' and the way they all seemed 'to wonder why they were born, and born to be so beautiful'. Bouquets in hand, a legion of 'Stage-Door Johnnies' continued to court the attentions of Phyllis le Grand, Gertie Millar (off-stage the wife of Lionel Monckton, composer of *The Arcadians* and *The Orchid*, the show with which the Gaiety opened) and all the other satin-clad 'queens'.

Just as the Gaiety Girls had always been, they were photographed and feted; pampered, paraded and not infrequently propositioned. At the end of the old century the Maharajah of Cooch Behar had approached Edna May, 'his hands full of gems', while Rosie Boote actually left the company to marry the Marquess of Headfort. But then there had been something slightly shameful, if not scandalous, about it all; it was simply not done for a gentleman to consort with a showgirl. By 1903 all that had changed. King Edward himself wrote to Edwardes shortly before the opening of his new theatre: 'I've loved the Gaiety, I love you, and I love the Girls. I am bringing Queen Alexandra to the first night.' He did; and they arrived late.

In other ways too London was coming to terms with the new dispensation. By 1905 an almost Napoleonically straight avenue that was tellingly called Kingsway and the curving, white stone arrogance of the Aldwych had replaced a huddle of smaller, meaner streets at the southern end of Drury Lane. And fashionable London was soon flocking to two more new theatres, the Strand (originally known as the Waldorf) and its twin, the 'Georgian' Aldwych, which had been central to the development. Separating them was the opulent Waldorf Hotel, one of several five-star establishments which also opened at this time, along with the very first 'nightclubs'. Among the former, King Edward and the surviving members of the raffish and unashamedly philistine Marlborough House Set favoured the fashionable Cavendish Hotel in Jermyn Street, run by the redoubtable Rosa Lewis. But by 1910 the discerning and the merely wealthy would have found little to choose between its palm court, dining room and private suites and those at the Waldorf, the Ritz (which had opened in 1903) and the nearby Piccadilly.

Wordsworth had stood on Westminster Bridge exactly a hundred years too early.

> Earth has not anything to show more fair:
> Dull would he be of soul who could pass by
> A sight so touching in its majesty,

he had written in 1802. Now, a century later, a different, far more cosmopolitan generation of Londoners was looking on a very different city with very different eyes. For although they might well have echoed the poet's words, it was for very different reasons.

Out of town too, it seemed as if a sixty-year accretion of Victorian dust, decorum and dead leaves had suddenly been swept away. And then as now it was the doings of the King and the so-called 'fast set' which attracted most attention. The tedious months of Court mourning were hardly over before they were once again seen at the annual Eton and Harrow match, at the Cowes regatta and especially at the Epsom, Newmarket, Doncaster and Ascot races; the ladies parading beneath lacy white parasols, the men uncomfortable in full morning dress.

Since his days as the 'playboy' Prince of Wales, the new King had taken a keen interest in horse racing and the turf. (With eight victories in English classic races over a period of less than fifteen years, he still ranks among the twenty most successful race horse owners of all time.) Now, comfortably seated in the elegant, white-painted, neo-Gothic grandstands, or strolling more visibly about Ascot's Royal Enclosure, his hedonistic, monied set was also suddenly horse-mad and cheering on the royal runners every bit as loudly as they did those of the Liberal statesman, the Earl of Rosebery. Nor were they alone. It was a matter of national rejoicing when the King's horse Minoru was first past the post in the 2,000 Guineas in 1907 and then went on to win the Derby as well, just as his first champion, Persimmon, had done in 1896.

But, for all its royal and aristocratic connections, even racing is nowhere near as redolent of the long June afternoon of Edwardian England as is cricket. For however much flat-racing deserved its description as 'the sport of kings', at the beginning of this century it was cricket which became the sport of gentlemen, and specifically of the new breed of gentlemen which was then coming to prominence. By 1900 the modest game which had been played at village green level since the end of the eighteenth century had acquired an almost totemic significance in English life. At village, county and first-class level, it was enjoying a popularity unimaginable before or since. New leagues had been formed, not just in the southern shire counties but in the industrial heartlands of Durham, Yorkshire and North-umberland as well. Eighty thousand people turned out to watch Surrey play Yorkshire at the Oval in 1906, while the annual Gentleman and Players match had rapidly become one of the key dates in the social calendar – and was to remain so until the series was discontinued in 1962.

Not without cause then, the twenty years before the outbreak of the First World War are still frequently referred to as the game's 'golden age', when it remained largely the province of the amateur and a matter of 'striped blazers, champagne, parasols and languid grace'. As a modern history of the game puts it, right up until about 1914, 'the front-foot drive was the hallmark of the amateur batsman – the straight knee yards down the wicket, the ball despatched through the off-side with lordly disdain'.[1]

The exotic K. S. Ranjitsinjhi was perhaps the most perfect embodi-ment of all this. A real Indian prince who travelled to England to play for Sussex, he had become a mainstay of the national team by the beginning of the century. He scored a career best of 285 runs for Sussex in 1901, took six wickets for fifty-three for a London County XI in the same season and throughout his career played with an easy elegance which pleased the crowds and delighted the Press. It was the *Daily News* which noted that 'he handles the bat like a walking-stick and dispenses runs like a millionaire disgorges sovereigns'. Off the field too, he was a star. Despite the fact that newspapers habitually described him as 'dusky', the nation took him to its heart. Shrewd entrepreneurs cashed in on his popularity and flooded the market with 'Ranjiana'. There were Ranji matches and even bottles of a patent Ranji hair-restorer – from the sales of which the unassuming player apparently earned not one penny.

On a rather different level, C. Aubrey Smith was a home-bred player who came to exemplify cricket's unique and ineffable 'English-ness'. Somehow he found the time to play for Sussex and serve as England's skipper on a South African tour while still acting on the West End stage with the likes of Mrs Patrick Campbell and Ellen Terry.

There are close and fascinating connections between the evolution of gentlemen like Smith and the development of the modern game. Both can even be said to have started in the same year, since modern historians claim that cricket as we know it today dates from 1864, the very year in which the Clarendon Commission published its report on the public schools. Certainly it was in 1864 that overarm bowling was finally allowed in first-class matches and an England XI first visited Australia (albeit as an unofficial, last-minute replacement for a cancelled lecture tour by the ailing Charles Dickens). It was in 1864 too that John Wisden's *Cricketers' Almanac* was first published and one William Gilbert Grace made his debut in county cricket.

In retrospect it was probably the arrival of Grace which had the greatest impact. Right from the start he was a formidable player. Not quite sixteen when he took to the field for that game in 1864, he still made a first innings score of 170, playing for South Wales in a match against the Gentlemen of Sussex and Brighton. He was to continue in much the same vein for the next forty years. As a batsman he hit a career best of 344 runs in 1876. As a bowler he was equally effective until well into middle age. In 1886, when he was nearly forty but still playing for the MCC, he took ten wickets for only forty-nine runs in a match against an Oxford University XI.

But there was more to Grace than that, for he represented an entirely new type of player – one who was, in essence, a Player rather than a Gentleman. And, inevitably perhaps, by the time he retired from the first-class game in 1908 these new brooms for whom cricket was more than a socially-acceptable pastime were in the ascendant. In the strict sense of the word they were still amateurs and continued to wear striped blazers; but however much they enjoyed the champagne, there was a new seriousness in the way they took up their positions at the crease. Quite simply, they were dedicated sportsmen – and they were playing to win. R. E. Foster, for instance (one of seven brothers who all played for Worcestershire) remains the only man ever to have skippered England in both soccer and cricket. A. E. Stoddart achieved a similar distinction as captain of both his country's rugby and cricket teams, and also went on to play golf and hockey at international level.

More because of his background than any outstanding prowess, however, B. J. T. Bosanquet is probably the best example of this new type of player. A well-connected Old Etonian, the caption to one of *Vanity Fair* magazine's 'Spy' cartoons suggests that he was little more than a Drone, a life-member of the country house set: 'His friends make persistent efforts to see more of him . . . but the short interval between close of play and the beginning of dances gives them little opportunity.' But the record books tell a different story. Far from being a 'languid' social cricketer, Bosanquet was the inventor of the notorious 'googly' – a ball delivered with an orthodox leg-break action which, because of a twist of the wrist at the moment of release, arrives from an unexpected angle – and thus in many eyes guilty of injecting an ungentlemanly urgency into the game.

Despite all this, in the last quarter of the nineteenth century it was 'W.G.', thick-set and magnificently bearded, who bestrode the wicket like a colossus. He too always publicly maintained his amateur status, while at the same time displaying a markedly more modern attitude that Ranji's, Smith's or even Bosanquet's. Put at its most basic, Grace had a shrewd – and as it turned out, very accurate – appreciation of his own worth. And through a no-nonsense – and, it has to be said, occasionally downright crooked – attitude to money, he came to benefit substantially from the game he so personified. Three separate testimonial matches in the 1895 season alone earned him some £9,000. But even that was little more than small change. It has been estimated that other fees, honoraria and the very generous touring expenses he received during his forty-three years in first-class cricket amounted to more than one million pounds.

Despite – or possibly because of – this, by the turn of the century the country doctor with an unfortunately high-pitched voice had been promoted into a position left vacant by the death of W. E. Gladstone in 1898: without question, he was the most famous Englishman in the world. He was a 'star' long before that term was coined. There are stories that county cricket grounds used to put out boards reading; 'Admission threepence – if W. G. Grace plays, admission sixpence'. They are very probably true, as is the entirely characteristic one told about Grace's behaviour at the wicket. Given out in one match, he immediately rounded on the umpire: 'They've come to see me bat, not you umpire. Play on!', he declared – and remained at the crease.

As unsporting as some of his financial deals though that outburst was, in one sense Grace was right. He had quickly recognized that he was the right man in the right place at the right time. He did not have a title; he was not part of the traditional, upper-class Eton-and-Oxford-educated élite. He was not even a professional. He could simply play cricket better than anyone else. Yet – for all the world like the wealthy businessmen who had bought their way into King Edward VII's Marlborough House circle – his very palpable success de-monstrated that proficiency in 'the game' could in itself be a passport to acceptability and even material comfort in a markedly more mobile society. Literally and metaphorically, the first googlies were being bowled at the twentieth-century Eton-and-England gentleman, almost before he had come of age.

With all this going on, it is perhaps not surprising that in the years immediately before 1914 cricket and the cricketing metaphor came to feature largely in popular literature. The game is described and used for various purposes by Sir James Barrie, A. A. Milne, Rupert Brooke and Siegfried Sassoon, among many others. A keen amateur player, Sir Arthur Conan Doyle went so far as to write a (rather undist-inguished) poem commemorating the glorious day when he took Grace's wicket in an amateur match.

A generation younger, at the turn of the century the young Pelham Grenville Wodehouse was also establishing a reputation as a promising bowler for the Dulwich College First XI. And although he did not go on to play at any higher level, cricket remained one of the abiding interests of his life. It is not, for instance, totally irrelevant that he was to name Bertie Wooster's faithful butler Jeeves after the Warwick-shire cricketer Percy Jeeves, who was killed on active service during the First World War.

Even Wodehouse, however, wrote about cricket as a social diversion. The odd village or county game was no more than a 'lark' to the likes of Bertie Wooster and Psmith. But to many writers it was more important than that. As much as half a century earlier, Thomas Hughes had used success on the pitch as a symbol of Tom Brown's wider triumph at Rugby; as we have already seen, Tom ended up as captain of the First XI. Now, even as Wodehouse was beginning his career, the game was being used as a metaphor of excellence by quite another author.

Something of a cricketer himself, Ernest William Hornung did not bother unduly with *Wisden* and the small print of the score-book when, in a story entitled 'A Bad Night', he came to describe how one A. J. Raffles played for England in a Test Match against the Aus-tralians. There was no reason why he should have done. By 1905, when that story was first published, Raffles was far too established a character to need such dogged documentary back up.

He had first appeared in 1899, in a volume of stories entitled *The Amateur Cracksman*. But within less than a decade there had been two further collections. *The Black Mask* was published in 1901, and *A Thief in the Night* followed some four years later. Both of these show signs of having been written for the market; inevitably so perhaps, for by 1905 Sir Gerald du Maurier was already impersonating Hornung's suave gentleman-crook on the West End stage – John Barrymore, Ronald Coleman and David Niven would all reinterpret him for succeeding generations – and Raffles's popularity was at its height.

The principal reason for this (and still today the subject of some critical debate) seems to have been 'A. J.'s' similarity to the even more popular Sherlock Holmes. For although Raffles is nominally a villain and, in public at least, Holmes remained the very soul of probity, the connections between the two are close and tangled.

Holmes was the earlier creation. Sir Arthur Conan Doyle had introduced the great detective and the dogged, dependable Dr Watson, his chronicler and assistant, in *A Study in Scarlet* which was published in 1887, twelve years before *The Amateur Cracksman*. And it is almost incontrovertible that Hornung had Conan Doyle's work and the Holmes-Watson model in mind when he came to delineate the relationship between A. J. Raffles and Bunny Manders, *his* chronicler and assistant. Critics have even suggested that Hornung stole Raffles's name from the title of a lesser Conan Doyle story, 'The Doings of Raffles Haw'.

None of this should unduly surprise us, for Hornung was the friend, and later the brother-in-law, of Conan Doyle. Indeed, he went some way towards atoning for his plagiarism (if such it can be called) by dedicating *The Amateur Cracksman*, 'To A.C.D. This Form of Flattery'. For his own part, Conan Doyle was seemingly happy enough to accept the tribute. He noted in his autobiography *Memories and Adventures* that 'Raffles was a kind of inversion of Sherlock Holmes, Bunny playing Watson'.

The similarities between Raffles and Holmes, however, cannot be pushed too far. Indeed, the differences between them are rather more illuminating. Discussing Hornung's stories in *Memories and Adventures*, Conan Doyle himself pointed out the most obvious:

> I think there are few finer examples of short-story writing in our language than these, though I confess they are rather dangerous in

their suggestion. I told [Hornung] so before he put pen to paper, and
the result has, I fear, borne me out. You must not make the criminal a
hero.[2]

In classical, Aristotelian terms Conan Doyle is undoubtedly right,
even if a more recent interest in a generation of flawed 'anti-heroes'
has weakened his imperative. Yet it was facile – and indeed wrong –
of him to have seen Raffles as merely a criminal. Certainly he did
commit crimes, but his moral code was very much in tune with his
times; far more so, indeed, than Sherlock Holmes's. For whereas the
great detective was a lonely brooding outsider, observing society with
a clinical, forensic detachment, at least at the outset the amateur
cracksman was a fully paid-up member of that society and the very
epitome of the turn-of-the-century English gentleman.

Hornung did not trouble to reveal that his hero's Christian name
was Arthur until mid-way through the third story in *The Black Mask*;[3]
and by then that was one of the very few things a devoted reader did
not know about Raffles. His character and past life had after all been
lovingly chronicled in the opening pages of *The Amateur Cracksman*.
They established The Legend: how – inevitably – Raffles had been
educated at (an unnamed) public school and then progressed to
Oxford; how, in his early thirties and attired in 'one of his innumerable
blazers', he was now very much the man about town; how he had
rooms in the Albany; and how, to Bunny at least, he was a full-blown
Hero.

Bunny, it should be added, had not made much of his life since
leaving school. Although he had fagged for Raffles, been a 'literary
little cuss' and even edited the school magazine, there is no suggestion
that he accompanied his mentor to Oxford. Rather, there is every
indication that he had gone on to lead a rather dissolute life. He had
come into some family money, but spent so much of it within a mere
three years that when we first meet him he is only hours away from
ruin and disgrace. Grossly overdrawn at his bank, he has nevertheless
done what in Edwardian times was still unthinkable and written
cheques to cover gambling losses of some £200 and, in a state of near
hysteria, throws himself upon Raffles's mercy.

'You've plunged enough', Raffles tells him and, intoxicated by the
realization that Raffles at least is on his side, that 'A. J. Raffles would
be my friend!', at the beginning of *The Amateur Cracksman* Bunny sees

only what he wants to see in Raffles – or rather, Hornung allows him to describe only the Raffles that he (Hornung) wants us to know. Bunny does both proud and catalogues his former fag-master's virtues as devotedly as any Boswell. He reports that Raffles is 'beyond comparison the most masterful man whom I have ever known'. He describes his 'indolent, athletic figure; his pale, sharp, clean-shaven features; his curly black hair; his strong unscrupulous mouth [and] the clear beam of his wonderful eye, cold and luminous as a star'. Later, he hymns Raffles the cricketer, the England and Gentlemens' XI all-rounder, specifically applauding 'his perfect command of pitch and break, his beautifully easy action, which never varied with the varying pace, his great ball on the leg-stump'. And almost as afterthought, he goes on to mention Raffles's 'consummate daring and extraordinary nerve' as well as 'the fine streak of aestheticism in his complex composition'.[4]

These are attributes which still have an appeal today – no wonder that both Ronald Coleman and David Niven were cast in the part! – but they are only one side of Raffles's nature. For just as Conan Doyle was oversimplifying things when he declared that 'You must not make a criminal a hero', in those first few pages Bunny too was actually doing Raffles a disservice. For, intentionally or unintentionally, the more he wrote, the more Hornung said about the mores of his day. Through the character of A. J. Raffles he was exploring the doubts and preoccupations of a whole social class. Crucially, for instance, he early on explained that 'A.J.' was not rich. In a vital exchange at the very outset of *The Amateur Cracksman* he had him say to Bunny: 'Do you think that because a fellow has rooms in this place [the Albany], and belongs to a club or two, and plays a little cricket, he must necessarily have a balance at the bank? I tell you, my dear man, that at this moment I'm as hard up as ever you were'.

With a certain number of his first readers those two sentences must have touched a raw nerve, for as we have seen, the final years of the nineteenth century saw the end of the automatic link between power and money. Raffles's need to maintain appearances, to belong to the right clubs and be seen in the right places was thoroughly Curzonian, and affected just about every facet of his character. Indeed, his perpetual need for money seemingly overrode morality and every other consideration:

'Cricket' said Raffles, 'like everything else, is good enough sport until you discover a better. As a source of excitement it isn't in it with other things you wot of, Bunny, and the involuntary comparison becomes a bore. What's the satisfaction of taking a man's wicket when you want his spoons? Still, if you can bowl a bit your low cunning won't get rusty, and always looking for the weak spot's just the kind of mental exercise one wants. Yes, perhaps there's some affinity between the two things after all. But I'd chuck up cricket tomorrow, Bunny, if it wasn't for the glorious protection it affords a person of my proclivities.'[5]

Significantly, however, Raffles never does 'chuck up' cricket; not quite. In 'A Bad Night', for instance, he abandons his plans to go off without Bunny and do 'a one-man-job' when he is unexpectly selected to play in the Second Test Match. Nevertheless, story after story in all three volumes contains lines in which Raffles *appears* to put money before everything else. 'My dear fellow, I would rob St Paul's Cathedral if I could', he tells Bunny in 'A Costume Piece'. Occasionally, he even attempts to justify himself – most notably in that opening story of *The Amateur Cracksman*, 'The Ides of March':

'Why should I work when I could steal? Why settle down to some humdrum uncongenial billet, when excitement, romance, danger, and a decent living were all going begging together. Of course, it's very wrong, but we can't all be moralists, and the distribution of wealth is very wrong to begin with.[6]

Crucially, however, in virtually every case Raffles's professed amorality and dare-devil words amount to nothing. Time and again, moral scruples overcome his baser instincts – as indeed they might in a man who can quote Swinburne by heart, who has a reproduction of 'The Blessed Damozel' hanging on his sitting-room wall and, apparently, 'the best of sisters married to a country parson in the eastern counties'.

Frequently, however, it is a close-run thing. The early story, 'A Jubilee Present' is quintessential Raffles, full of doubts and moral quandaries. In barely a dozen pages Hornung gives us the full flavour of the man. Visiting the Room of Gold in the British Museum, his connoisseur's eye appreciates the beauty of what his criminal eye still simultaneously sees as a 'good, portable piece'. 'Why, it's as thin as paper', he says, 'and enamelled like a middle-aged lady of quality! But, by Jove, it's one of the most beautiful things I ever saw in my life, Bunny. I should like to have it for its own sake, by all my gods!'

And have it of course he does. For a few vital seconds Raffles the criminal gains ascendancy over Raffles the connoisseur. He clubs the warder who is guarding it, snatches the cup from its showcase and, with Bunny in breathless pursuit, succeeds in making his escape from the British Museum.

It is a shocking, atypical moment. But, such was Hornung's craftsmanship, it was one that was both carefully prepared for and no less carefully defused. Right at the beginning of the story Bunny had told us that 'a number of the immorally rich' had clubbed together to present the £8,000 cup to the nation. However, Raffles already knew that 'two of the richly immoral' were planning 'to snaffle it for themselves'. *His* theft of the cup, therefore, can be seen as an altruistic – and implicitly moral – gesture.

But the story does not end there. Adding uncertainty to uncertainty, Hornung goes on to describe how the cup stood for days on Raffles's chimney-piece, and how Raffles adored in ('It is the joy of my heart, the light of my life, and the delight of mine eye') but was still capable of realizing that 'taking it was an offence against the laws of the land'. Even the devoted Bunny is uneasy at this ungentlemanly conduct. But only in the final few paragraphs of the story is everything resolved:

> 'Bunny,' he cried, flinging his newspaper across the room, 'I've got an idea after your own heart. I know where I can place it after all!'
> 'Do you mean the cup?'
> 'I do.'
> 'Then I congratulate you.'
> 'Thanks.'
> 'Upon the recovery of your senses.'[7]

The cup disappears and, in the very best Holmes-Watson tradition, Raffles is left centre-stage, patiently explaining to Bunny that he has posted it to Queen Victoria as a Diamond Jubilee present:

> 'My dear Bunny, we have been reigned over for sixty years by infinitely the finest monarch the world has ever seen. The world is taking the present opportunity of signifying the fact for all it is worth. Every nation is laying of its best at her royal feet; every class in the community

45

is doing its little level – except ours. All I have done is to remove one reproach from our fraternity.'[8]

The sententious rhetoric is good enough for Bunny – in his mind it re-establishes Raffles as 'the sportsman he always was' – and is just about sufficient to renew the faith of the reader. But Hornung has still lifted a corner of the curtain. Raffles *did* steal the cup – and injure the British Museum warder in the process. He *did* actively enjoy possessing it . . .

Mindful perhaps of the wages of sin, Hornung allowed his hero to live for just another three years. At the end of *The Black Mask* he described how Raffles was killed by a sniper's bullet in the Boer War, sometime after Lord Roberts's capture of Bloemfontein in 1900. It was, of course, a hero's death.

Strictly speaking then, Raffles was a Victorian. However, two-thirds of the Raffles canon was written and published in the Edwardian era; and as we have seen, the man himself perfectly embodied the ambivalence of the new age. Despite his protestations of loyalty to 'the finest monarch the world has ever seen', he never really belonged in the old century. He was far more at home at country house weekends during which the Marchioness of Melrose's diamond-and-saphire necklace could virtually be taken from round her neck (as in the story 'Gentlemen and Players'), and at that type of London dinner party which offered the perfect cover for his attempt to steal the Kenworthy diamonds. His was a world in which the well-cut sleeve of a dinner jacket could conceal a life-preserver – and for that matter a world in which, for the first time, an illegitimate swindler could stand for – and be elected to – Parliament.

By nature Horatio Bottomley was an Edwardian too. He was born in 1860 (in the East End of London) and had already acquired a certain notoriety before Queen Victoria's death in 1901. On the one hand there was his claim that his mother's husband was not his father at all; that he was in actual fact the son of the nineteenth-century Secularist demagogue Charles Bradlaugh. (In adult life he did closely resemble him; Bottomley's 'enormous upper lip' immediately reminded Frank Harris of Bradlaugh.) On quite another there was his involvement in what has become known as the 'Hansard Bubble'.

Back in the mid-1880s Bottomley had abandoned his early career as

a law court shorthand writer and founded two London local newspapers. Two quickly became three and then four as their proprietor's
business interests expanded to include printing companies and national
journals. Then, in 1886, Bottomley was able to announce that his
newly-formed company, the Hansard Publishing and Printing Union,
had won the contract to publish parliamentary debates and was going
public. For a couple of years all went well, and the Union paid
handsome dividends to its shareholders. But in 1891 the bubble burst.
Shareholders were informed that the company was to be liquidated
since it 'is in possession of no assets other than a trifling balance (if
any) at the bank . . . has no property whatsoever, and its whole capital
appears to be lost.'[9]

Quite where it all went was never discovered – although it was
noted that Bottomley had paid himself more than £100,000 – but
something of the complex financial irregularity which underlay the
Union was revealed when, after prolonged investigations, Bottomley
and others were tried for conspiracy in 1893. The twenty-four-day
trial excited considerable Press and public interest, not least because
Bottomley elected to conduct his own defence. By all accounts he was
an electrifying advocate, a trifle flashy, perhaps – Harris noticed that
grammar occasionally deserted him and he was incapable of sounding
the letter 'h' – but he was certainly the master of his brief. Judge, jury
and public gallery were on his side from the start, in spite of the
weight of evidence against him. Indeed, the jury took less than thirty
minutes to find him not guilty. 'That makes thirteen of us', muttered
the judge, while a barrister-friend of Frank Harris summed up what
must have been the Establishment's more private reaction when he
called Bottomley 'a damned clever *outsider*!'[10]

Bottomley himself would probably have approved of that. He *was*
an outsider; he never tired of pointing out that he had been raised in
an orphanage and educated at 'the University of Life'. All the same,
within ten years of the Hansard Union trial he had rebuilt his life,
amassed a fortune and, in a manner strongly reminiscent of W. G.
Grace, cashed in on society's new openness. His most recent biographer, Alan Hyman has ably summarized how, in the early years of the
new century, his whole career and lifestyle mimicked the new Marlborough House morality:

he was managing director of over twenty Westralian mining companies;

47

he became the proprietor of an evening newspaper, the *Sun*; he frequently went to see his racehorses in training and always watched them run; he backed theatrical shows and took a personal interest in them; and he supervised the alterations and improvements being carried out at enormous expense at [his country home] The Dicker.[11]

There was no stopping him. In 1906 he finally realized a long-held dream and entered the House of Commons as the Liberal Member for the constituency we can only assume he called South 'Ackney, having obtained (as he did not fail to mention in his maiden speech) 'the largest majority secured by a metropolitan member sitting on this side'. Seeking an even wider constituency, that year he also founded and began editing a weekly magazine, a down-market penny-dreadful which he called *John Bull*. 'POLITICS WITHOUT PARTY – CRITICISM WITHOUT CANT', cried its masthead, while regular features included a column entitled 'The World, the Flesh and the Devil' (written by Bottomley himself and underpinning his hopes that *John Bull*'s writers would be 'no respecters of persons, of place, or of power') and an Open Letter addressed to a celebrity of the moment.

In the light of all that he had achieved, there was a certain inevitability in the fact that the very first of these Letters (also penned by Bottomley) was addressed to King Edward VII. It ended:

> With Your Majesty on the throne, Parliament is almost a redundancy. You are more of a democrat than most of its members.
>
> GOD SAVE THE KING
> Your faithful liege,
> *John Bull*

Although it appears that they never met, and were certainly never on any terms of intimacy, there were great similarities between the new King and his 'faithful liege'. For with a speed which bewildered as much as it dismayed the courtiers he inherited from his mother, Edward VII's accession to the throne in 1901 brought to an end a whole era. In very literal terms it propelled society into the twentieth century. The new King was not prepared to compromise or 'trim', and saw no reason why merely becoming King should in any way affect the rather rakish lifestyle he had enjoyed for the previous thirty years. In particular, he refused to drop his circle of friends – an act of defiance which, as we shall see, was to be repeated by his grandson thirty-five years later, but with immeasurably greater consequences.

Universally regarded as at best 'fast' and at worst downright unsuit-
able companions for a future sovereign, almost without exception
these survivors from Marlborough House days were bluff, baccarat-
playing, brandy-drinking *arrivistes*; Graces and Bottomleys to a man,
but with a little added *gravitas* and 'bottom'. Unlike any previous
courtiers, they had got where they were not through breeding and background, but through money. Bankers and industrialists, foreign
nationals and (perhaps most scandalously of all, given the climate of
the times) even Jews, they needed no more than cash and a willingness
to spend it lavishly in order to gain the friendship of the bored and
frequently boorish Heir Apparent.

As long as the food was good enough the man they privately called
'Tum-Tum' would dine at their houses, and invite them to dine at his.
It is reliably reported that guests leaving Sandringham after Royal
weekends at this period were weighed on departure to ensure that
they had eaten sufficiently. If their pockets were deep enough 'Teddy'
would also join his chums for cards at their Mayfair clubs; and if the
company was right he would graciously consent to spend weekends at
the newly-built sham-Gothic country houses which (like Bottomley's
Dicker) perfectly expressed their new pretensions. More seriously, he
was also willing to be more than acquiescent about their licentious amorality.

He had married Princess Alexandra, the daughter of King Christian IX
of Denmark, in 1863; but within ten years it was common knowledge that
the Prince of Wales was not entirely faithful to his wife. (Always to some
extent cut off from her husband, family and adopted country because of
her limited command of its language, by the time she became Queen-
Consort in 1901 Alexandra was also partially deaf due to the effects of
hereditary otosclerosis and crippled by rheumatism.) Rumours about the
Prince's affairs first with Lillie Langtry and then with Daisy, Countess of
Warwick leaked out over the following two decades and, together with
Press reports of various scandals and divorces among the Marlborough
House Set, began to influence behaviour at virtually every level of
society. In the latter half of the 1870s, for instance, there were no more
than 460 divorces in England; but within thirty years that number had
virtually doubled. In the period between 1906 and 1910 there were 809.
The figure are small (principally for legal reasons: at the beginning of this
century only one in 500 marriages ended in formal divorce) but the
increase is significant.

So too is the public reaction to Edward's behaviour after he became King in 1901. For it quickly became apparent that, just as he was unwilling to 'cut' his surviving friends from Marlborough House days, he was also not going to allow the throne to come between him and the last and greatest of his mistresses, Mrs Alice Keppel, with whom he had become infatuated in 1898. Lively, intelligent and witty; a good conversationalist and, according to one contemporary account, 'the most perfect mistress in the history of royal infidelity', Mrs Keppel gave Edward everything which his elegant but ailing wife could not. He was fascinated by her, going so far as to name one of his racehorses Ecila, her Christian name spelt backwards. Always accompanied by her husband ('the most agreeable cuckold in the history of royal infidelity'[12]), Mrs Keppel was invited everywhere the King went and – except at Arundel Castle, Hatfield and Welbeck, respectively the homes of the Duke of Norfolk, Lord Salisbury and the Duke of Portland – treated as his second wife. And to judge from a letter written by the young Hugh Walpole in 1905, their relationship was not only common knowledge but accepted with a sang-froid which would have been quite unthinkable only half a century earlier. Then a Cambridge undergraduate, Walpole had been invited to spend his summer vacation tutoring Mrs Keppel's nephew. His father (later the Bishop of Edinburgh) wrote to express his strong opposition – to which Walpole replied:

My dear Father,
I am, I must confess, extremely astonished by your letter. I thought both you and Mother knew exactly what Mrs Keppel's reputation was. As it is known to the whole of England, I must say I hardly expected you to be so surprised. I gathered that you both knew exactly what she was, i.e. the King's mistress . . .[13]

In 1905 the twenty-one-year-old Hugh Walpole was hardly at the centre of things. (Only after another quarter of a century – and some assiduous jostling – could the newly-knighted Sir Hugh genuinely claim to be *in medias res*.) But his relative obscurity as well as his social and geographical distance from the salons and fashionable dining-rooms of Edwardian London make his letter even more revealing. Things were changing far beyond the purlieus of Mayfair and St James's. Men from King Edward VII down were bowling googlies at established convention, playing hard and playing to win. No longer could they automatically be assumed to embody the virtues of Chaucer's 'verray parfit gentil knight'. Changing social circumstances meant that they were every bit as likely to mature into a Harry Flashman as a Tom Brown. By the time Raffles and Bunny lit their Sullivans and Raffles proposed a toast to 'The Queen, God bless her!' in the closing lines of 'A Jubilee Present' there was even a difference in the way the whisky glasses clinked.

CHAPTER FOUR

'Lovely Lads'

The fighting man shall from the sun
Take warmth, and life from the glowing earth;
Speed with the light-foot winds to run,
And with the trees to newer birth;
And find, when fighting shall be done,
Great rest, and fullness after dearth.
– Julian Grenfell, 'Into Battle'.

❖

It wasn't all cynicism; quite the reverse. The new worldliness of the likes of Raffles, Bottomley and the Marlborough House Set was actually little more than a metropolitan phenomenon, and away from the bright lights what was arguably a far more 'English' way of life was also coming to fruition during and in the immediate aftermath of the Edwardian era.

With the dawn of the new century the fashion for country house weekends had become more popular than ever – inevitably so perhaps since, as Kenneth Rose has demonstrated[1] it too virtually owed its existence to King Edward. Right up until the second half of the 1890s Parliament and the Law Courts were still sitting, and the Cabinet still meeting, on Saturday mornings. The very word 'weekend' did not appear in *The Times* until 1892. But ten years later everything had changed. Other than at the height of the Season – when such dereliction of duty would have been simply unthinkable – by 1902 it had become quite 'the thing' for the privileged rich to desert London for 'Saturday-to-Mondays' at country houses in every part of the home counties. But whereas those thrown by the Marlborough House Set tended to be rigorously traditional, with hearty breakfasts of kedgeree and devilled kidneys preceding whole days of huntin', shootin' or fishin' and long nights of cards and brandy, elsewhere things were taking a different turn.

Surprising and atypical though it seems to us today, in its own way the young Virginia Woolf's decision to join Rupert Brooke for a nude bathe during a 'Neo-Pagan' weekend at Granchester in 1909 was just as 'Edwardian' as the more robust and open philandering of the King's set. For throughout the first decade of this century a range of groups and individuals were already experimenting with what we would now call alternative lifestyles.

In 1907 Bernard and Charlotte Shaw, enthusiastically assisted by Sidney and Beatrice Webb, organized the first Fabian summer school at Llanbedr in north Wales. There, a group of 'elementary teachers and minor civil servants' had endured (or perhaps enjoyed) a regime of 'Swedish drill', vegetarian food, discussion and uplifting dialectic. Brooke himself, though he attended the 1908 school, was probably more inclined to the views of the sexual free-thinker Edward Carpenter who had his own community at Millthorpe in Derbyshire than to such earnestness. Certainly his description of a 1909 holiday on Dartmoor owes more to Carpenter's concept of the 'Simple Life' than anything he could have picked up at public school (Rugby) or from the Fabians:

> I am leading the healthy life. I rise early, twist myself about on a kind of pulley that is supposed to make my chest immense (but doesn't), eat no meat, wear very little, do not part my hair, take frequent cold baths, work ten hours a day and rush madly about the mountains in flannels and rainstorms for hours.[2]

Even in 1909, however, in polite 'adult' circles at least it was generally felt that Brooke, the 'young Apollo' who 'goldenhaired/Stands dreaming on the verge of strife/Magnificently unprepared/For the long littleness of life',[3] had gone too far. He and his like were welcome to their naturism, vegetarianism and mountain walks, of course; but along with Carpenter, Fabianism and the Webbs, they were still considered 'cranky'. It was the more 'spiritual' world inhabited by members of the clannish and almost incestuously close social and intellectual élite that had grown up around the young George Curzon in the late 1880s which was then seen as offering the most viable alternative to the venality and showy materialism of the Marlborough House Set.

It is wrong, however, to imagine a watertight division between this group, known for the previous twenty years as the Souls, and the King's men. Coming from very much the same backgrounds and perforce moving in very much the same social circles, they were inevitably acquainted. Indeed a figure such as Thomas Lister, the 4th Baron Ribblesdale (1854–1925) who married Carzon's lifelong friend Charlotte 'Charty' Tennant and was thus brought into the very centre of 'Soul culture', succeeded in maintaining a foot in both camps. He was perhaps the best example of the English country gentleman of his day, and is depicted as such in a magnificent full-length portrait completed by John Singer Sargent in 1902 (and now in the National Gallery). But if there is still something of the Souls in his lean, sardonic face – and Edward VII nicknamed him 'the Ancestor' because of it – his aestheticism is tempered by the riding whip he holds and the spurs attached to his boots. Ribblesdale was devoted to hunting in all its forms, and was at various times also an army officer and courtier. His ubiquity is further demonstrated by the fact that, after his wife's premature death in 1911, he became a permanent resident at that one-time Marlborough House stronghold, the Cavendish Hotel.

Despite such overlaps, it is still difficult to imagine George Nathaniel Curzon of all people having much in common with, say, Sir Charles Mordaunt, a prominent member of the early Marlborough House Set. For it was Mordaunt who, in bringing a suit for divorce against his wife in 1870, also brought about the appearance of the Prince of Wales in a court of law, the first time this had happened since the fourteenth century.

Such behaviour would also have been frowned upon at Taplow Court, Lord and Lady Desborough's 3,000-acre estate near Windsor; at Stanway, the home of Lord and Lady Elcho and at the many other houses like Panshanger, Gosford and Whittingehame at which the Souls held court – but so too would Brooke's nude bathing and disinclination to part his hair. On the other hand, the conversation would have been as unlaced as even Brooke could have wished, embracing everything from academic philosophy and literature to music and the politics of the day, since the Souls on the whole rightly saw themselves as the guardians of that high-minded liberalism which had been an essential, if fragile, part of English life for far longer than 'Tum-Tum'. They were the epitome of what we today regard as 'gentility'. They were the sons and grandsons (and daughters and granddaughters) of gentlemen. In 1910 they were a power in the land;

and, were it not for the Great War, the enduring Whig sensibilities of families such as the Tennants, the Wyndhams, the Grenfells (Willie Grenfell was created Lord Desborough in 1905), the Elchos, the Lytteltons and to a lesser extent the Asquiths would have had a greater and more lasting effect on society than the amoral legacy of Marlborough House.

It was not, of course, to be. Nevertheless, at the time of King Edward VII's death in 1910 the pattern of what could have been was clear enough. By then the original Souls were getting old – Curzon himself was only fifty-one, but his friend A. J. Balfour ('King Arthur' to his fellow-Souls) was already over sixty – and what we might call the Curzonian baton had been handed over to their children, an even more closely-knit group which called itself the Coterie (*see table*). And albeit in different ways, like Rupert Brooke and Virginia Woolf this new generation was already well-advanced in adapting the rather self-consciously intellectual, High Victorian principles of its parents to the demands of the new century.

Crucially, however, as a group they were as uninterested in wholesale revisionism as they were in naturism. For as we shall see, they – and particularly the men – were the products of precisely the same background as their parents. In all but a very few instances they had attended the same schools and gone up to the same university colleges as their fathers. Their 'revolt' was thus nothing like as fundamental as that of the predominantly middle-class generation born in the immediate aftermath of the Second World War which reached maturity in the common-rooms of a score or more or the 'glass-and-concrete' universities and polytechnics that sprang up during the middle and late 1960s. And yet, had they only been allowed to reach maturity, the Coterie would undoubtedly have brought the traditional English gentleman into the twentieth century. To understand the extent of the promise, however, a brief digression is necessary.

To all intents and purposes, the Souls had come into being during a dinner party at the Bachelors' Club in London which George Curzon gave for a group of his closest friends on 10 July 1889. There were some forty people present; if this was not enough to suggest that the far-from-wealthy Curzon intended the meal to be more than a casual social evening, the 'doggerel appalling' he penned to mark the occasion left neither posterity nor his guests in any doubt:

THE SOULS AND THE COTERIE

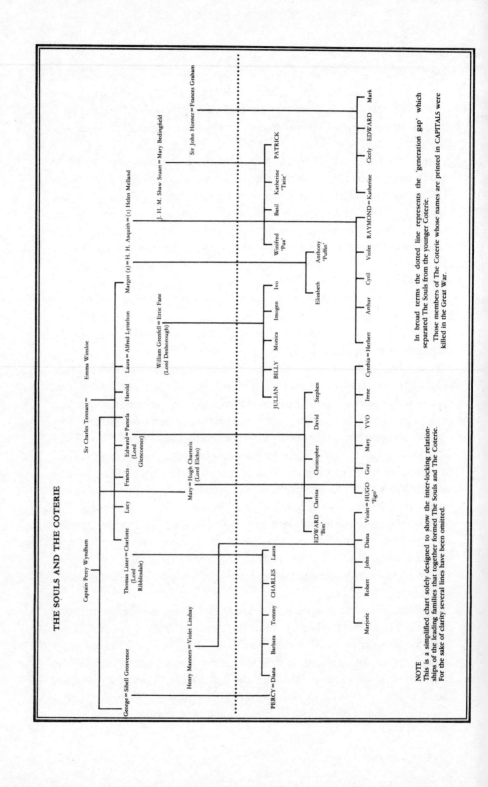

NOTE

This is a simplified chart solely designed to show the inter-locking relationships of the leading families that together formed The Souls and The Coterie. For the sake of clarity several lines have been omitted.

In broad terms the dotted line represents the 'generation gap' which separated The Souls from the younger Coterie.

Those members of The Coterie whose names are printed in CAPITALS were killed in the Great War.

Was there e'er such a sight?
Souls sparkled and spirits expanded;
For of them critics sang,
That tho' christened the Gang,
By a spiritual link they were banded.

Curzon's questionable abilities as a poet need not detain us. What was important about the gathering was his seemingly conscious decision to weld his friends into a semi-formal 'gang' – and in this connection it is not entirely fanciful to see the 'spiritual link [by which] they were banded' as little more than the chain that bound Curzon and his fellow Old Etonians. For possession of the appropriate old school tie was one of the fundamental passports into the inevitably patrician world of the Souls.

Among Curzon's original forty were several men who were to become key members of the group. Among them, A. J. Balfour, Harry Cust, John Horner, Alfred Lyttelton, Edward Tennant (later Lord Glenconner) and the Charteris brothers, Evan and Hugo (later Lord Elcho) had all been their host's rough contemporaries at Eton. Horner and William Grenfell (one of the very few Old Harrovian Souls) had just preceded him at Balliol, while H. H. Asquith was to arrive there a few years later. Harry Cust, Alfred Lyttelton and Edward Tennant had been fellow-students at Trinity College, Cambridge. From their earliest days then, there was a common bond linking many of the Souls. And though in later life their paths diverged (ironically Curzon was one of the earliest to peel off) their differing careers exemplified a now-familiar devotion to duty and public service. Curzon's is well-enough known; but those of some of his colleagues, each of them at the very centre of the Souls, illustrate the level of the group's influence.

By 1910, for instance, Asquith was Prime Minister. Balfour had already preceded him in that office and remained leader of the Conservative party. At a less exalted level Harry Cust, William Grenfell, Edward Tennant and Alfred Lyttelton had all also been Members of Parliament. Dates, seats and parties are all recorded in contemporary volumes of *Who's Who* and, more dolefully, in the appropriate volumes of *Who Was Who* (1897–1916; 1916–28; 1929–40 and 1941–50). From their tightly-printed columns, too, one can pick up at least a flavour of what it meant to be a Soul – even if Alfred Lyttelton's obituary in

Who Was Who, 1897–1916 is terse to the point of circumspection in its adumbration of the achievements of one of the greatest sportsmen of his day:

> Legal Private Sec. to Sir H. James, Attorney-General, 1882–86; Recorder of Hereford, 1894; Recorder of Oxford, 1895–1903; Chancellor of Diocese of Rochester, 1903; Secretary of State for Colonies, 1903–5; M.P. (L.U.) Leamington, Warwick, 1895–1906. *Recreations*: golf; in early life many other games.

The mesmerically attractive Harry Cust (rumoured to have been the lover of virtually every one of the female Souls, and now generally accepted as the real father of Diana Manners, later Lady Diana Cooper) got even shorter shrift. Coincidentally featuring on the same page in *Who Was Who, 1916–1928* as Lord Curzon's, a life not without its own peculiar distinction is cruelly reduced to a mere fourteen lines. Henry John Cockayne Cust, D.L., J.P. is recorded as having been no more than 'M.P. Stamford, 1890–95; M.P. (C.) Bermondsey, 1900–1906; editor of the Pall Mall Gazette, 1902–6; member of the French Bar'.

In contrast William Grenfell, who lived to the age of eighty-nine, was to be fulsomely celebrated in a later edition of *Who Was Who*. His entry is worth quoting at length for the picture of all-round achievement it paints. Grenfell was hardly the best-known Soul, but his record is in many ways typical:

> **DESBOROUGH**, 1st Baron (*cr.* 1905) of Taplow; **William Henry Grenfell**, K.G., 1928; G.C.V.O., *cr.* 1925; K.C.V.O., *cr.* 1908; J.P., D.L., M.A.; late Chairman of Thames Conservancy Board; President and Chairman of the Bath Club, London, from its foundation in 1894 until 1942; D.C.L. Oxford, 1938; Ex-President, London Chamber of Commerce; Ex-President, British Imperial Council of Commerce [. . .] represented Oxford in three mile race *v.* Cambridge, 1876; rowed *v.* Cambridge, 1877–78; President O.U.A.C. and O.U.B.C.; climbed in the Alps and shot in the Rocky Mountains, India, etc.; swam twice across Niagara; stroked eight across the Channel; special correspondent second Suakim Campaign; M.P. Salisbury, 1880, 1885; M.P. Hereford, 1892 (resigned); Private Secretary to Sir W. Harcourt at Exchequer, 1892; Captain of Yeomen of the Guard, 1925–29; High Sheriff, Bucks, 1890; Mayor of Maidenhead, 1895–97; M.P. (C.) for Wycombe Div. of Bucks, 1900–5; member of Tariff Commission, 1904; Chairman of Pilgrims of Great Britain. 1919–29: President Central Association

of Volunteer Regiments; Chairman of Fresh Water Fish Committee appointed by the Board of Agriculture, and Chairman of the Committee to enquire into the Police of England, Scotland and Wales appointed by the Home Office; won Epée prize Military Tournament, 1904–6; won Punting Championship three years.

Even leaving aside the presidencies, chairmanships and decorations which continued to come Grenfell's way in the years after 1910, this represents a formidable record of Edwardian achievement. But although psychologists might see in the constant busyness of the latter half of Grenfell's life no more than an attempt to compensate for a less-than-perfect marriage, to his elder son Julian such conspicuous success merely presented something of a challenge.

At the time of King Edward's death in the summer of 1910, Julian Crenfell was already twenty-two. The better part of the Coterie had also come of age. Asquith's eldest son Raymond was all of thirty-two. Rather younger, Hugo Charteris was twenty-six. Charles Lister was twenty-three; while Patrick Shaw Stewart and Edward Horner were, like Julian, only a year younger. Among the junior contingent Billy Grenfell was twenty, Yvo Charteris just fourteen, and Edward ('Bim') Tennant a mere thirteen. Already, however, both separately and together they were being held up as the exemplars of all that was 'lovely' about an entire generation.

The adjective is A. E. Housman's. In a poem subsequently included in 'A Shropshire Lad' (and composed, like an avalanche of the lesser prose and poetry of the early 1920s, as a threnody to that so-called 'Lost Generation') he was to write:

> East and west on fields forgotten
>   Bleach the bones of comrades slain,
> Lovely lads and dead and rotten;
>   None that go return again.[4]

Raymond, Hugo, Charles; Patrick, Edward and Julian; Billy, Yvo, Bim and all the others ... they were indeed lovely. And despite changes of fashion, today they stare out of surviving drawings and the miniature studio photographs they left for their weekend hostesses to paste into leather-bound visitors' books with a continuing guilelessness and insouciance that defies time itself. Here is Raymond, straight-faced, unsmiling and strong-jawed; good-looking rather than conventionally handsome. And here Julian; younger, fleshier, coarser, but still ruggedly attractive. Here are Hugo and Bim; both of them leaner, moustachio'd and darkly saturnine. And here, fleetingly and most poignantly of all, is young Yvo; his blond hair plastered down and a wing collar and dinner suit only emphasizing the golden promise that is written in his face.

They were young men, 'golden boys'; definitely, defiantly members of a new generation. (In 1897, within weeks of leaving Winchester, Raymond Asquith had noted in a letter to a school-friend: 'I have just found my governor [father] reading a small volume of poems by Alfred Douglas which has just appeared: of course I took it away immediately; I don't think the poor man can have known what was inside.') But for all the charm and confidence of those images there was something lacking: a sense of purpose, a clear vision of how they might meet the quasi-Oedipal challenge thrown down by their fathers. For just as the nation as a whole saw its life as subjects of the new King, George V, as a *tabula rasa* in 1910, those snapshots too bleed a sepia incomprehension.

If the comparison is not too jarring, it is as if for all their privileges Raymond, Julian, Charles and the rest were feeling exactly the same frustrations which would so beset John Osborne's Jimmy Porter two generations later. 'There aren't any good, brave caused left', he was to rant in 1957. Back in 1910 there didn't seem to be many either; and none at all which offered any real challenge. The realization that this was indeed the case and that they were all to some extent caught in a gilded cage was to affect virtually every member of the Coterie; but it was perhaps only to be expected that Raymond Asquith should have sensed it most acutely.

Not only had his father been Prime Minister since 1908, in the years since he left Winchester and went up to Balliol in 1897 Raymond's own precocious intellect and undoubted academic prowess were the subject of frequent comment. Up at Balliol, then still heavily under the influence of Jowett – his father had been one of the Doctor's favourite pupils – he had found the social and intellectual climate both stimulating and conducive. 'Suffice it to say that those parts of the day which are not taken up with eating, are spent, by the athletic, in drinking, [and] by the more intellectual in smoking or playing poker,' he wrote in his stepmother, Margot, less than a month after his arrival, adopting the rather-too-jaunty air of sophistication characteristic of undergraduate letters home.[5] But although Raymond was later to list his recreations in *Who's Who* as 'shooting, golf, tennis', neither smoking (like many of his contemporaries, he was a lifelong smoker) nor playing poker could truly be said to have occupied his time. Rather, he was the embodiment of Balliol man.

John Buchan, a friend then up at the less rigorous – and markedly less fashionable – Brasenose College, might well have had Raymond in mind when he later described how Balliol students had 'careless good breeding and agreeable worldliness' but remained 'in the things of the mind . . . critical, decorous, chary of enthusiasm.'[6] Whether or not he did, both phrases paint an accurate picture of Raymond at this time. He took expected and inevitable Firsts in Mods, Greats and Law, was President of the Oxford Union, and in 1902 elected a Fellow of All Souls.

Superficially everything seemed pre-ordained and effortless; but crucially, unlike both Curzon (who had also enjoyed an All Souls Fellowship) and his own father, Raymond saw through it all. Like it did to Hamlet, in the early years of the century the earth and even Balliol appeared to him a sterile promontory, and in bad moments too, doubtless 'no other thing but a foul and pestilent congregation of vapours'. Writing to Buchan as early as 1901 he admitted that

> honestly I haven't the ambition of a louse and don't see why I should pretend to it. There are a few things and people at Oxford that I intend to keep close to as long as I decently can, and I don't care a damn about the rest. If one fell in love with a woman or believed in the Newcastle programme or had no dress clothes it might be different. But the world as I see it now is a little barren of motives . . . I suppose I may have what they call a spiritual awakening any day: and then I shall shout and lie and make money with the best of them . . . The law is a lean casuistical business: it fills me with disgust.[7]

Nevertheless, it was the 'damnable professional routine' of the law to which Raymond turned his attention after leaving Balliol. He was called to the Bar in 1904 and despite his distaste for it, evidently displayed something of his father's passionate talent for advocacy. But still the *ennui* remained – to be refined and embroidered upon in a rather later letter to his fiancée Katharine Horner:

I have spent two whole days deciphering the ill-spelt letters and ill-shaped figures of a fraudulent and illiterate bagman and now I have to tell my client that he has no case and consequently no further need for my services. And there were you in your walled garden wasting God's sunlight and your own sweet beauty on a half-witted old woman who cares for nothing but plasmon and manures. I hate this life of guesses and snatches and half-satisfaction and silly hopes and silly regrets. But I am much too tired to do more than hate it.[8]

Less than two years later, in July 1907, Raymond and Katharine were married – the elaborate wedding at St Margaret's, Westminster only emphasizing what was even then outwardly perceived as the glittering success of the bridegroom's life and career. Katharine was attended by two pages and no less than eleven bridesmaids. Afterwards, the cream of London's social and political society attended a reception in the garden of 10 Downing Street.

The following year Helen, their first child was born. Perdita, their second, arrived in 1910 by which time Raymond and Katharine had a London address at 49 Bedford Square (Telephone: MUSEUM 783) as well as the use of the Asquith mansion at 20 Cavendish Square. Raymond was already undertaking lengthy cases on the western circuit and – as only befitted a promising and increasingly successful barrister – was a member of Brooks's and the Athenaeum, the Hampshire County Club and the Prince's Tennis Club.

Deep down however, he was still melancholy and preoccupied, assuaging his doubts with cigarettes and alcohol. In photographs taken at this time his features seem almost invisible beneath a rigid mask of solemnity. It is as if the 'guesses and snatches and half-satisfactions and silly hopes and silly regrets' upon which he had long-since realized that his life was based had somehow intruded between his wide-set eyes and the lens. In a letter to Edward Horner dated 15 June 1910 he wrote: 'The older wines are now all drunk, and I fear that you may be becalmed for a time in the interval between two vintages.' Intended as sage advice to his young brother-in-law on the subject of women, it is tempting to read more into this sentence. For if Edward was becalmed in 1910 so too was Raymond, and on a far, far wider sea.

Julian Grenfell was also biding his time that year, dimly aware that his hour had not yet come but still refusing to compromise with the present. Shortly before leaving Eton in 1906 he had written:

Sound, sound the clarion, fill the fife!
To all the social world say 'Hang it –
I, who for seventeen years of life
Have trod this happy, hustling planet
I won't go woman-hunting yet,
I won't be made a social pet!'

They turned out to be prophetic words, particularly the last line, for Julian was never 'a social pet'. Where Raymond (ten years his senior) was at least outwardly conformist, Julian remained unpredictable, contradictory and frequently as confusing to himself as he was to other people. It was Raymond who was later to remember that his

> notions of how life should be lived were widely different from those which are generally received; but his practice showed a much closer agreement with his theory than commonly obtains between the creed and the conduct of more conventional persons ... Intimate, according to the somewhat exacting standards of the day, I should doubt if he ever was, even with those who knew him best. To me at any rate he seemed to have a spirit essentially solitary and self-contained.[9]

Tommy Lascelles, an Oxford contemporary also recalled that Julian 'always used to boast that he could feel absolutely no interest nor take any pleasure in the society of any living soul but himself'.

In part this combative defensiveness stemmed from the influence of his parents. We have already seen something of the career of his father, who was created the 1st Baron Desborough when Julian was in the midst of adolescence – a fact which in itself may not be without significance. But, as Nicholas Mosley has demonstrated, in all probability Julian's stubborn refusal to be 'a social pet' and conform to the polite mores of the day had its real origins in a determination to escape the fierce possessiveness of his mother. A brilliant hostess and conversationalist, by her own efforts Ettie Grenfell had pushed her way into the very heart of the Souls and was accustomed to getting whatever she wanted. Men flocked to her and, despite the upset it caused her husband and elder sons, she enjoyed a succession of affairs, including one with Julian's friend and exact contemporary Patrick Shaw Stewart.[10]

Set against this background, Julian's eccentric yet still promising career makes a kind of sense. At Eton he had become head of his house and a member of Pop as well as one of the editors of both the *Eton College Chronicle* and its unofficial rival *The Outsider*. His academic achievements later paled in the face of the brilliance of his younger brother Billy, but in general he managed to maintain a position near the top of his classes and was especially gifted at Latin verse composition. However, it was as a sportsman that he really excelled. Slightly over six feet in height and weighing in his final year about eleven and a half stone (160 pounds), he played cricket and fives along with all the usual team games while reserving his principal energies for those in which he could be alone. He boxed and fished and shot, and was Master of the Eton beagle pack.

But although he too had triumphantly progressed to Balliol (he went up in 1906, along with a clutch of other Coterie-Etonians including Patrick Shaw Stewart, Charles Lister and Edward Horner) the defensiveness remained. Raymond and Tommy Lascelles had got the true measure of the man even if, writing encomia after his death in the trenches, they glossed over his true feelings at this time. They neglected to mention for instance how, in company with Lord Ribblesdale's son Charles Lister, Julian was beginning to voice revolutionary and even socialist sentiments. Others, however, did not fail to notice his impatience with

> those who value for its own sake the wealth, the magnificence and the display; those whom conventionality forces to keep servants and whom competition forces to keep an army of servants; those who rate the worth of themselves and others by the amount of these things that they possess and the show that they make of them.[11]

Ultimately, of course, it was all hot air and – like the unpublished collection of bitter philosophical reflections Julian produced during his final year at Oxford[12] – little more than another round in the continuing battle with his mother. That he could espouse such sentiments at all and take the trouble to write seven extended essays on topics such as 'Divided Ideals', 'Selfishness, Service and the Single Aim', 'Darwinism, Theism and Conventionalism' and 'On Calling Names By Their Right Things' (*sic*), each of which tilted at one of the shibboleths of Ettie's world, does, however, demonstrate the depth of his frustration. Far more than Raymond, by 1910 he (and to a lesser extent his brother Billy) was chafing with impatience and eager to take up the challenge, even if he too was still uncertain about what form that challenge would take.

Given this desire to be doing something, it was perhaps inevitable that as soon as he had finished at Oxford that summer, Julian joined the army. By 1911 he had found for himself a niche of sorts as a subaltern in the Royal Dragoons, a heavy cavalry regiment then serving at Muttra in India. The life suited him, principally composed as it was of drill, polo and pig-sticking, a somewhat barbaric pastime which particularly appealed to him: 'if you are lucky he runs on to the spear and if you are unlucky he runs on to you. It is no good prodding at him; you just hold out the spear and say your prayer and the pig does the rest with great gusto.'

But if it satisfied the sporting, active side of Julian's character, even service life could not quell the deeper-seated anger and impatience he felt for the world at large. In letters home from India and then South Africa he sniped at his mother and even friends like Patrick Shaw Stewart who had apparently become 'a really *nasty* character'. Back home on leave during the winter of 1912–13 he teamed up with Billy – but, as Mrs Keppel's daughter Sonia noticed, even at parties both of them seemed 'possessed by the same controlled restlessness as though they were keyed up to the same moment of departure, each with one toe on the line impatient to be off'.

That restlessness remained with him for the next eighteen months. Peacetime soldiering could not wholly contain it. His letters to Ettie and other friends during 1913 and the early part of 1914 suggest that Julian was actively thinking of buying himself out and even standing for Parliament. But before he was able to do anything, matters were taken out of his hands.

The tragi-comic train of events set in motion by the assassination of Archduke Ferdinand of Austria on 28 June 1914 was scarcely noticed in England that summer, and even less so in the more distant parts of the Empire. What had started out as more 'Trouble in the Balkans' had become a 'European question', but still no real concern of ours. Only when the German army invaded Belgium on 4 August did the alarm bells start ringing. Even they, however, could not wholly disrupt England's enjoyment of what came to be seen as the last spell of 'Queen's weather'. In London, the parks were crowded with picnickers during the August Bank Holiday weekend. There was an Anglo-American 'Wild West' exhibition at White City, an evocation of 'Sunny Spain' at Earl's Court and, most popular of all, a new tableau at Madame Tussaud's in which 'lifelike portrait models of

Their Majesties King George and Queen Mary' where grouped with those representing 'H.I.M. The Emperor of Austria, H.M. King Peter of Serbia and other reigning sovereigns of Europe'.

But the ears of the Coterie proved more attuned than most. Julian wrote home that month: 'It must be wonderful to be in England now: I suppose the excitement is beyond all words.' Like many others of his age and class, he realized that suddenly he had been given his cause. The purpose of his life had been made clear. Now suddenly he was able to pick up the gauntlet which had been implicitly thrown down so many years before by his 'governor', by Curzon and the likes of Asquith senior.

Despite the minor differences of attitude which divided them, within a matter of weeks all the senior members of the Coterie had also concluded that this was what they had been waiting for. Dreadful as it was in prospect, they seized on the war, uncannily aware that it would uniquely allow them to prove themselves. Suddenly, they sensed that they had been born, brought up and educated with this end in mind. The war would be their proving-ground, and they were profoundly grateful for it. It was the final, ultimate challenge. Julian had spoken for them all when he apostrophized the warrior-gentleman each now seemed so certain to become in his poem 'Into Battle', composed a few months later:

> The blackbird sings to him, 'Brother, brother,
>   If this be the last song you shall sing,
>   Sing well, for you may not sing another;
>   Brother, sing'.

And in a letter he wrote to his mother Ettie he added: 'Isn't it luck for me to have been born so as to be just the right age and in just the right place?'

Characteristically more guarded, Raymond too was soon 'doing his bit'. Earlier in the year he had been appointed Junior Counsel to the Board of Inland Revenue and – despite a discreet flirtation with atheistic socialism – nominated as the Liberal Parliamentary candidate for Derby. But that did not prevent his speaking at recruiting meetings and actively trying to enlist during the autumn of 1914, even if his private correspondence betrayed a more jaundiced attitude. A letter written to Diana Manners in August 1914 is among the best he ever wrote:

I put my name down for a thing called the London Volunteer Defence Force, organized by Lovat and Desborough, having the following among other advantages (a) it is not yet in existence (b) the War Office may stop it ever coming into existence (c) Patrick [Shaw Stewart] belongs to it (d) no member of it can be called on to perform even the simplest act of duty for several months (e) no member of it can possibly be killed till Goodwood [Races in August] 1915 at earliest. Then I went to a most amusing place called the National Service League Offices, where a vast swarm of well meaning and inefficient patriots are employed for 14 hours a day in first classifying and then rejecting the applications of a still vaster swarm of still more well meaning and inefficient patriots for posts which they are utterly and obviously incapable of filling – deaf mutes who fancy they might be useful as interpreters, baptist ministers who volunteer as *vivandiers* and so forth.[13]

Despite his age – in 1914 army recruitment offices were looking for men below the age of thirty – by the beginning of 1915 Raymond had succeeded in obtaining a commission as a Second Lieutenant in the 3/14th County of London Regiment (he would later transfer to the 3rd Batallion, Grenadier Guards). A couple of months earlier it had become obvious that the war would not be over by Christmas, and virtually all the other male members of the Coterie were also in uniform – and adapting unexpectedly well to a new way of life. In the New Year's Honours List, it was even announced that Julian had been awarded the DSO. The erstwhile foxhunter and beagler had taken only too well to the more earnest business of killing man.

There was, however, already one gap in the ranks. Percy Wyndham who, like Julian, had entered the army as a career had been killed in France on 14 September 1914. He was twenty-seven, and had married Charles Lister's sister Diana only one year previously.

> Brother Bertie went away
> To do his bit the other day
> With a smile on his lips and his
> Lieutenant's pips upon his shoulder bright and gay.
> As the train moved out he said, 'Remember me to all the
>   birds.'
> And he wagg'd his paw and went away to war
> Shouting out these pathetic words:
>
> Goodbye-ee, goodbye-ee,

Wipe the tear, baby dear, from your eye-ee,
Tho' it's hard to part I know, I'll be tickled to death
    to go.
don't cry-ee, don't sigh-ee, there's a silver lining in
    the sky-ee,
Bonsoir, old thing, cheer-i-o, chin, chin,
Nap-poo, toodle-oo, Goodbye-ee

The jauntiness of 'Goodbye-ee' and many another hastily-written music-hall song accurately caught the tone of the day. It was with exactly that attitude, with a lot of bonsoir-ing, cheerio-ing, chin-chin-ing, nappoo-ing and toodle-oo-ing that Raymond, Julian, Percy and the rest prepared to do their bit at the very outbreak of hostilities. But if their willingness to enlist was, as we have seen, to some extent bound up with their attempts to prove themselves men, it was going to take more than a war to stop them remaining gentlemen, for as they were the first to acknowledge, the war had as many obligations as life at home. There are many stories of officers in the trenches endangering their own lives to ensure the safety and comfort of their men. They frequently shared with their platoons the goodies sent to them from home and, as far as discipline allowed, established friendly relations with the 'other ranks' – even if few went as far as Edward Horner who in April 1915 asked his parents to send out a gold tie-pin he wanted to give to his batman.[14]

The spirit of *noblesse oblige* thus remained as strong as ever; nevertheless there were still essential differences between officers and men. (One was quite palpable, for among the more curious statistics of the Great War was the fact that, on average, officers were a full five inches taller than other ranks.) During the Boer War at the very end of the nineteenth century, officers had arrived at the front encumbered by elaborate dressing cases and 'field libraries', specially prepared hampers from Fortnum and Mason, their own made-to-measure shot-guns from Westley-Richards or Purdy and, if they were in a cavalry regiment, even their own thoroughbred hunters. Many were also accompanied by personal valets. Expecting a gentlemanly war, they found instead a most ungentlemanly slaughter. And to a degree almost incomprehensible to us today, in the first months and then years of the Great War very little had changed.

Almost without exception the thousands of public- and grammar-school-educated recruits who enlisted during the opening months of the war and became members of what was known as 'the officer class', both expected and received appropriate treatment from the military authorities as well as the other ranks – as indeed they continue to do today. Officers from the rank of second lieutenant upwards were always referred to as Mr-, for instance; while 'men' were merely addressed by their surnames. And although the risks confronting infantry officers were exactly the same as – if not greater than – those facing their men, except during the few awful hours of actual battle they lived in a different world and fought what sometimes amounted to a war within a war. After Lieutenant Lord Charles Worsley, son of the Earl and Countess of Yarborough, was killed along with many of his platoon of the 7th Cavalry (the Household Brigade) in October 1914 his body was discovered by an equally-nobly-born German officer, Oberleutnant Freiherr von Prankh, who immediately instructed a junior officer to do the decent thing:

> He said that he had found the dead body of an English lord [that officer later recalled] and he decided to have a grave made for this English officer. With several men of my company I fetched the body from the trenches, which were filled with dead enemy soldiers, and had a grave dug in which we buried the body of the dead English officer. His effects, consisting of diaries, various papers and articles of some value (unless I am mistaken a golden engagement ring was among them) were handed to Oberleutnant von Prankh to send to the authorities and to inform the next of kin.[15]

Noblesse oblige indeed; but it went deeper than that. For even in the front line these gentleman-officers saw little reason to alter the habits of a lifetime. In September 1916 a Second Lieutenant reported to his father that dinner consisted of 'Soup, fish (if possible), meat (or fowl when poss.) asparagus, vegetables (always fresh); savoury (always), pudding (always), Whisky, Perrier, Port (every night), Vermouth, Sherry, biscuits, cigarettes and cigars, coffee, tea or cocoa, fruit (if desired)'.[16] Incredibly, at that time he was in the allied trenches at Vimy Ridge.

In other, more subtle ways too the prewar differences in attitude between those who were now officers and the majority who remained among the other ranks were only strengthened by the war. As German snipers soon realized, officers could be picked out – and picked off –

by their uniforms. In contrast to the mass-produced Army-issue tunics worn by privates, officers' tunic jackets were individually tailored (at their own expense) and worn over a shirt and tie. Their jodhpur-trousers were tucked into high leather riding-boots which their batmen kept as highly polished as their 'Sam Browne' service belts. In every respect they were a caste apart. Even their letters home went uncensored, so squeamish were their fellow-officers about violating the time-honoured sanctity of another gentleman's mail. While those of the other ranks had to be left unsealed and were subject to ruthless blue-pencilling, officers' letters were sealed in special envelopes on the outside of which a correspondent had merely to sign his name below a declaration which read: 'I certify on my honour that the contents of this envelope refer to nothing but private and family matters.'

It was all rather redolent of school, of praepositors, prefects, Pop and privilege. As Peter Parker has shown in his book *The Old Lie*, the public school ethos was rekindled in the trenches. It was implicit in the attitudes of many individuals, as we have seen; and it was made quite explicit by the appearance of bodies such as the University and Public Schools Brigade, the very formation of which was specifically intended to demonstrate how much success in the war would depend on 'past members of those schools the names of which appear in the current number of *The Public Schools Year-Book*'.

Originally proposed (naturally enough in a letter to *The Times*) by eight men aged 'between thirty and thirty-five' and thus too old to enlist, it attracted considerable support. Launched at a crowded meeting at Claridge's Hotel (where else?), within a fortnight it had received applications from more than 5,000 men. Most were between the ages of nineteen and thirty-five, but exceptions were made for 'ex-soldiers up to forty-five, and certain ex-non-commissioned officers up to fifty'. All, however, had to be 'Height 5 ft. 3 in. and upwards; Chest 34 in. at least' and medically fit. And it was hoped that they had at least 'attended the Bisley musketry camps and Aldershot training camps with school or university corps', for the intention was ultimately to create a 'Legion of Marksmen'.

Lord Kitchener was delighted at this unexpected fillip to his own finger-pointing recruitment campaign. But although 'the soldierly appearance, splendid marching, and general physique' of the UPS volunteers greatly impressed those who watched them drilling in Hyde Park, the original plans to form a public school legion – or even an

entire regiment – gradually petered out as some 3,000 of the original
volunteers left to take up commissions with other regiments.

'Mud thou art, to mud returnest' . . . the unofficial motto of the
UPS can serve as the epitaph for its endeavours as well as the wider,
gentlemanly ethos which gave it birth. For as the casualties mounted
in the mud of Flanders – 86,000 Englishmen had been killed before
the end of 1914 – it was clear that it was going to take more than the
idealistic decency of the Coterie to win the day.

The 'lovely lads' had been swamped by a reality that was far from
lovely. With the single exception of Julian who in letter after letter
described 'the most *wonderful* fun' he was having ('I *adore* war. It is
like a big picnic without the objectlessness of a picnic. I've never
been so well or so happy'),[17] they were withering spiritually and
emotionally. Again and again Raymond's letters to Katharine describe
a mood of loneliness and detachment:

> It would be a much pleasanter life, if one had one's friends in the
> regiment . . . No, my pretty, don't send me any book by Conrad,
> however good, I couldn't bear it. It gives me a sick headache even to
> write the man's name. And as a matter of fact I never seem to read
> anything except an ode of Horace now and again . . . the monotony of
> the life is already rather appalling and even in this short time the noise
> of the guns has become as idiotic and tediously irritating as the noise
> of motor buses in London. I suppose I am too easily bored to be a
> soldier even in War time.

But seemingly neither Raymond nor any of the other gentlemen who
found themselves at the front in 1915 and 1916 actually resented the
war. The other ranks had an anthology of more or less scatological
songs along the lines of 'I Don't Want to Be a Soldier' (itself a parody
of 'I'll Make a Man of You', the hit number in a London revue called
The Passing Show) that contained the notorious lines, 'I don't want a
bayonet up my arsehole,/I don't want my bollocks shot away' and a
range of official and unofficial trench newspapers in which they could
vent their frustration. But the officers merely sat out 'the duration'
with an almost literally Stoic resignation, for Raymond was by no
means unusual in finding solace in the Classics.

Editions of Homer, Plato, Aristotle, Virgil and Horace (in the
original Greek or Latin, of course) found a place in many an officer's
pack. T. E. Lawrence carried a copy of the *Odyssey* with him across

Mesopotamia. Robert Graves killed time in the trenches by composing his own Latin epigrams, and Harold Macmillan construed Aeschylus while lying out in No Man's Land awaiting rescue after having been wounded during the Battle of Loos in 1915.

Dulce et decorum est pro patria mori . . . In retrospect, Horace seems a peculiarly appropriate poet for Raymond to have chosen – not of course because of Wilfred Owen's description of that line from *Ode III* as 'the old Lie' (his poem 'Dulce et Decorum Est' was written in October 1917 and not published in book form until 1920). But rather because Raymond seems to have responded to the more typically phlegmatic side of the Roman poet. There is surely an echo of the couplet

> *Omnem crede diem tibi diluxisse supremum,*
> *Grata superveniet quae non sperabitur hora.*
> (*Epistles*, I.iv.13–14)

[Tell yourself that every day is your last, then the hour to which you are not looking forward will come as a pleasant surprise.]

in a letter he wrote to Diana Manners at the end of 1915: 'usually one is very equable, looking no further ahead than the next meal and feeling that really life is very much the same everywhere, war or no war . . .'[18]

By the end of 1915 he had very little choice. By then there seemed to be no future hour to which to look forward, and even the present offered only what Cicero (whom fifteen years previously he had written off as 'vain, egotistical, pusillanimous, limited') had called the *consolatio timoris*.

On the afternoon of 12 May Julian had, in his own words, 'stopped a Jack Johnson with my head'. It was more serious than he realized or even the doctors knew; a splinter of metal had penetrated an inch and a half into his brain. Complications set in and, despite an emergency operation, he died a fortnight later, on 26 May. Then, on 30 July, his younger brother Billy was killed leading a charge at Hooge, less than a mile from where Julian had fallen. On 28 August Charles Lister had died of wounds at Gallipoli. The following month the nineteen-year-old Yvo Charteris was killed as he led his men 'over the top' in France.

By then too the notion of a Lost or Tragic Generation was gaining ground at home. Within months of Julian's death Viola Meynell had published a mawkish eulogy in the *Dublin Review*. Beginning 'Julian Grenfell had such shining qualities of youth, such as strength and courage and love, that to others who are young he seems like the perfection of themselves', it ended:

> Charity is a virtue of the earth; its pity, its tolerance and its love, are like white angels dedicated to be the guardians of human failing and grief and sin, and in a sense charity will fade out in heaven like a ghost in daylight. And so even on earth it can stand aside, unneeded, while there go past swift figures, wounded by suffering and loss and death, their faces bright, too bright for resignation and too bright for pity – and to watch such a figure go by is to see the immortal spirit.[19]

Tragically, 1916 and 1917 saw no diminution in that parade of bright-faced swift figures. On 23 April 1916 Yvo Charteris's eldest brother Hugo ('Ego') died in Egypt. Less than six months later, on 22 September, Edward ('Bim') Tennant was killed in the Battle of the Somme. Like Yvo Charteris he was barely nineteen. Edward Horner died on 21 November 1917 at Cambrai; and then on 31 December, Patrick Shaw Stewart 'though hit in the ear by a bullet, carried on, and was finally killed by a shell which burst on the parapet'.

Raymond himself had been hit in the chest by a bullet on 15 September 1916 while leading an attack during the Battle of the Somme. Mortally wounded, he managed to light the inevitable cigarette, but died before he could be taken to a dressing station. He was thirty-seven, and his body was buried close to where he fell. His tombstone bears the inscription:

SMALL TIME, BUT IN THAT SMALL
MOST GREATLY LIVED
THIS STAR OF ENGLAND

By the beginning of 1918 the Coterie no longer existed. In 1910 it had included forty or so young people, men and women, some hardly more than boys and girls. Now, fourteen of its male members were dead. As Viola Meynell and her likes were saying, the heart had been ripped out of a generation; the finest flowering of English manhood had died in the fields of Flanders. But beneath the understandable sentimentality, there was some truth in their desperate protestations that those 'stars' had not died in vain.

Almost a decade before he died, Julian Grenfell had written a letter of condolence to his mother after the death of his childhood nanny. It was long and rambling but contained the central reflection:

> Surely the great maxim is to take everything, and especially death, in the most natural and cheerful way that we possibly can, without letting ourselves be absorbed for one instant in the little petty things or forgetting the great mysterious background that there is to everything. The only way must be what the Greeks insisted upon, and called 'the mean', 'το μετριον'.[20]

That was what the members of the Coterie had been striving for in their various ways throughout the best part of a decade: 'the mean' which would unite the ideals of Dr Arnold and their fathers with the imperatives of the modern world. It was their tragedy – and quite possibly ours who came later – that in ultimately finding it they lost themselves.

Certainly, they proved irreplaceable. For, as we shall see, no one who later attempted to usurp their place as gentlemen could quite match their natural nobleness of spirit. The best, as W. B. Yeats was later to write, would be full of passionate intensity, while the worst simply lacked all conviction.

CHAPTER FIVE

The Hero and the Thug

'Here is the perfect politician who is also the
perfect gentleman,' I said to myself as he
entered the room . . . So much perfection argues
rottenness somewhere.
    – Beatrice Webb on Oswald Mosley

We moved on 11 November – Armistice Day, and we heard the announcement of the Armistice when we were still in the Forest de Mormal on a cheerless, dismal, cold misty day. There was no cheering or demonstration. We were all tired in body and mind, fresh from the tragic fields of battle, and this momentous announcement was too vast in its consequences to be appreciated or accepted with wild excitement. We trekked out of the wood on this dreary day in silence. We read in the papers of the tremendous celebrations in London and Paris, but could not bring ourselves to raise even a cheer.

The experiences of an ordinary gunner,[1] still out near the front line on 11 November 1918 were typical. Despite the artificial razzmatazz in the Place de la Concorde and the rue Royale in Paris and in Piccadilly Circus, Trafalgar Square and the Mall in London, there was a general feeling that an irrevocable corner had been turned. Nothing would ever be the same again. By all accounts the autumn of 1918 had been 'incredibly lovely', the trees had kept their leaves until well into October; but metaphorically at least, on that meteorologically-dull Monday an almost infinitely prolonged spell of Queen's weather had broken. Acutely sensitive to changes of mood and climate, and

75

never one to be swayed by the mob, Virginia Woolf noted in her diary:

Monday, November 11th
Twenty-five minutes ago the guns went off, announcing peace. A siren
hooted on the river. They are hooting still. A few people ran to look
out of windows. The rooks wheeled round and wore for a moment the
look of creatures performing some ceremony, partly of thanksgiving,
partly of valediction over the grave. A very cloudy still day, the smoke
toppling over heavily towards the east; and that too wearing for a
moment a look of something floating, waving, drooping. We looked
out of the window; saw the housepainter give one look at the sky and
go on with his job; the old man toddling along the street . . . closely
followed by his mongrel dog. So far neither bells nor flags, but the
wailing of sirens and intermittent guns.[2]

And it was not just in Bloomsbury that this *lacrimae rerum* note continued
to resound beneath the frenzied, patriotic veneer of victory parades and
national rejoicing. For although Lord Curzon was echoing Shelley
and telling the House of Lords that 'The world's great age begins
anew, The golden years return' (*Hellas*, Chorus II); although 100,000
clapping, cheering people braved the pouring rain and brought
London's West End to a halt on Armistice night, and George Robey's
show at the Alhambra music hall in Leicester Square had to be
abandoned because the audience was 'so uproarious', the underlying
mood was very different from that which had pervaded Queen Victoria's Diamond Jubilee celebrations hardly more than twenty years
previously. Then, and to a lesser extent during the Boer War (1899–
1902), every section of society had remained united in allegiance to
Queen and country. Old-fashioned values still held sway:

> Say not the struggle naught availeth,
> The labour and the wounds are vain,
> The enemy faints not, nor faileth,
>
> And as things are, things remain.

But by the end of 1918 the complacent moral certainties of that Old
Rugbeian and eminently High Victorian Arthur Hugh Clough seemed
rather dated (although, ironically enough, his lines were once more to
help galvanize the nation when Winston Churchill quoted them during
the Second World War). His sturdy forthrightness had been replaced
by the more sceptical musings of a younger generation of poets for
whom the struggle really did seem to have been of naught avail.

Many were already dead, among the 1,089,939 fatalities[3] suffered by Britain and the Empire alone. Rupert Brooke had died in 1915 and the then-unrecognized Isaac Rosenberg in 1918, while Wilfred Owen was killed in action just one week before the Armistice. (Nor were the casualties confined to literature. Little now is made of the fact, but the world of music suffered just as grievously. From the same generation as Brooke, Owen and Rosenberg, and every bit as promising, Brooke's friend, the organist W. Denis Browne was killed in 1915. The composers George Butterworth and Frederick Kelly died in 1916 and Ernest Farrar in 1918. Most tragically of all perhaps, Ivor Gurney, the pre-eminent song composer of his generation, was wounded and gassed in 1917 at the age of twenty-seven, and never fully recovered. He was to die in a mental asylum in 1937.)

The war poetry of Owen, say, or writers such as Siegfried Sassoon, Herbert Read and Edmund Blunden – all of whom survived the war – graphically conveyed a sense of the horror and futility of four years of fighting. But, if anything, the tone of another of the casualties was even bleaker and more pessimistic. Born in 1878, Edward Thomas was older than the writers with whom he is now somewhat randomly bracketed. He differed from them too in that before the outbreak of war he was already a professional writer and journalist, turning out up to three new books a year. He had published everything from critical biographies to nature studies well before 1913, when he was encouraged to try his hand at verse by the American poet Robert Frost.

But it was the war more than Frost which made him a poet; if nothing else the frequent *longueurs* of life in the front line gave him more time than the pressures of Grub Street ever allowed to fashion his frequently highly-elaborate lyrics. Furthermore, the months he spent on the battlefields of France in the months immediately before his death in 1917 seem to have put his previous life into a new perspective. His poem 'Old Men' was composed in December 1914:

> I have mislaid the key. I sniff the spray
> And think of nothing; I see and I hear nothing;
> Yet seem, too, to be listening, lying in wait
> For what I should, yet never can, remember:
> No garden appears, no path, no hoar-green bush
> Of Lad's-love, or Old Man, no child beside,
> Neither father nor mother, nor any playmate;
> Only an avenue, dark, nameless, without end.[4]

This bucolic, semi-Georgian melancholy affected a generation. But they were not looking back or remembering. Almost neurasthenically, they were looking forward – and still seeing 'only an avenue, dark, nameless, without end'.

In the December 1918 General Election the centrist coalition Government which had been in power for the previous two years was returned with a huge majority. Inevitably so perhaps, since the incumbent Liberal Prime Minister, David Lloyd George had been barnstorming the country promising 'to make Britain a fit country for heroes to live in'. But for possibly the first time in British history there was a very real doubt about who those heroes really were. Lloyd George was undoubtedly appealing to, and inviting the rest of the electorate to think of, the hundreds of thousands of returning ex-servicemen. But in constituency after constituency the *Henry V* spirit was strangely absent, and the young Oswald Mosley, seeking election as the Coalition Unionist candidate for the Harrow division of Middlesex, was not alone in his scepticism. Essentially he believed, as his son has reported,[5] that the 'elderly men who had not been in the war were [seeking to make] a country profitable to themselves' – and so did a great number of his contemporaries.

The world had changed. Erstwhile 'heroes' now seemed hollow men; the bright, carefree, schoolboyish optimism of the prewar years had been subsumed in the greyer, more dogged quest for a new and wider national identity. The numbing experience of war had changed – or aged – a generation. For thousand upon thousand of them – the 'men', the 'Tommies', the 'other ranks', those whose was never to reason why – the coming of peace entailed little more than turning in their khakis, once more donning 'civvies' and, older, wiser and sadder, doing their best to pick up the threads of life:

> Stratford seemed to a-changed as much as I had! The streets weren't *tidy* no more – well there weren't the blokes to do it – and there was queues everywhere: queues of women waiting for food, queues of wounded soldiers from Clopton House waiting for God knows what, there was even a queue for bloaters at the corner o' Meer Street! Who should I meet on Meer Street but Jack Wright.
>
> 'Ullo,' he says.
>
> I asked him if he knowed of any work? He shook his head.
>
> 'You'se a-goin to be a gentleman, George,' he says, 'for the rest of your life. Ey!' he says, 'I 'ear that nancy boy Taylor's copped it. Best thing as could 'appen if you asks me.'

I couldn't hit him; I could never do no more bricklaying neither. Ah. I could only do what was on the floor, I couldn't go up in the air, or bend, come down the ladder. Nobody would take me on to do the bottom; you'd got to take your share, go up with the rest . . .[6]

But for a lesser, although still not-inconsiderable number of others – the improbably-promoted, the officers and gentlemen and the wilting survivors of a corps of schoolboy-captains – the problems were, if anything, more complex. The war had taken them to their limits, and frequently shown them wanting. Battle had proved bewildering, far more demanding than OTC practice or even the rough-and-tumble of the dormitories. Now peace was making further demands.

First produced almost exactly ten years after the Armistice, R. C. Sherriff's play *Journey's End* was perhaps the most acute exploration of the roots of their failure – although it is not irrelevant to note that Siegfried Sassoon's rather bitter *Memoirs of a Fox-Hunting Man* appeared the same year and Robert Graves's *Goodbye to All That* was first published a few months later, in 1929. Sherriff had himself been a Captain in the East Surreys, and in the course of what remains a classically well-made play managed to give an unrelentingly accurate account of the failure of a whole generation. There are no Raymonds or Julians in *Journey's End*. Instead, as its very title suggests, the play charts the cowardice and moral disintegration which characterized the last days of many more ordinary members of the officer-class in the muddy squalor of the trenches.

Preparing for an expected enemy attack one evening (Sherriff specifies that the entire action of his play takes place on Monday, 18 March 1918) twenty-one-year-old Dennis Stanhope, the commanding officer of an Allied infantry company, also has to deal with an enemy within when he is cornered by one of his fellow-officers claiming neuralgia and thus 'a ticket home'. Stanhope at first produces a re-volver, but then appeals to basic decency:

STANHOPE: If you went – and left Osborne and Trotter and Raleigh and all those men up there to do your work – could you ever look a man straight in the face again – in all your life! You may be wounded. Then you can go home and feel proud – and if you're killed you – you won't have to stand this hell any more. I might have fired just now. If I had you would have been dead now. But you're still alive – with a straight fighting chance of coming through. Take the chance, old chap, and stand in with Osborne and Trotter and Raleigh. Don't you think it's worth standing in with men like that? – when you know they all feel like you do – in their hearts – and just go on sticking it because they know it's – it's the only thing a decent man can do. What about it?[7]

It is certainly the only thing Stanhope can do; for, as we have already seen, the trench life of that officer-class was largely regulated by the ethos of the public school and its notions of decency and fair play. It could hardly have been otherwise when so many of those officers were themselves little more than schoolboys. Sherriff makes this point well by centring the action of *Journey's End* around the arrival of Second Lieutenant Raleigh.

'Well-built' and 'healthy-looking', he apparently comes straight from the Yvo Charteris and 'Bim' Tennant mould, for he too is – as Sherriff explicitly notes in his stage directions – still a 'boy of about eighteen'. No more than a few months have elapsed since Raleigh was 'only a kid' at school, hero-worshipping Dennis Stanhope who 'was one of the big fellows', wicket-keeper in the school cricket team, 'a jolly good bat, too', and captain of the rugger XV. Tragically, he cannot now accept that things are different:

STANHOPE: D'you understand an order? Give me that letter!
RALEIGH: But I tell you – there's nothing – [STANHOPE *clutches* RALEIGH's *wrist and tears the letter from his hand.*] Dennis – I'm –
STANHOPE: Don't 'Dennis' me! Stanhope's my name! You're not at school! Go and inspect your rifles! [RALEIGH *rises in amazement at the foot of the steps.*][8]

Was Stanhope a hero? Was Raleigh? Or even the cowardly Hibbert? And were they and their likes really the new inhabitants of Lloyd George's Britain? . . .

The questions would have risen unbidden in the minds of those who saw the first production of *Journey's End*, which opened at the Apollo Theatre on 9 December 1928. For many of them, indeed, the show must have provided an uncomfortable evening's entertainment. Lured there by the critics in order to see the extraordinary performance of a young actor called Laurence Oliver who had been cast in the role of Stanhope, they would not necessarily have expected the play to challenge their world-view. The Apollo was after all normally the home of safe, undemanding plays like Frederic Lonsdale's *The Fake* (1924) and cheery revues with titles such as *By the Way* and *Is Zat So?*.

But in just the same way that the conundrum posed by the preacher John Ball at the time of the Peasants' Revolt – 'When Adam delved and Eve span, who then was the gentleman?' – had continued to preoccupy medieval England, *Journey's End* proved that the issues which had confronted the survivors of Passchendaele, Ypres and the Somme on their return to Britain were going to be equally long-lasting.

Had they not destroyed the very life they were fighting for? Were not the real heroes dead and buried in some foreign field? And if so, who were *they*? Lucky, fortunate or (as it often seemed to them) merely fraudulent survivors, what was to be their role in that land fit for heroes?

Pathetically, they case around in search of an answer. They cadged, pulled rank or used the classified advertisements in national newspapers to advertise what were by then outmoded virtues:

INFANTRY OFFICER (23) seeks POST as private secretary. Public school education. Highest references.

OFFICER, well educated capable organiser and administrator, wide secretarial experience, keen, energetic, tactful, good horseman, experienced athlete, desires post as secretary or secretary-manager; home or abroad; excellent references.[9]

Some – a few – were successful, and adjusted to life in this new world where their sort of bravery went for nothing. Others – fewer admittedly, but still an appreciable number – were not so lucky, and lingered in an unhappy classless limbo, insisting on being called 'Colonel' or 'Major' even as they whiled away the hours on corner stools in the bars and roadhouses of the twenties and thirties. A small minority fell still further and ended up on the streets:

Men who had fought in the trenches, now unwanted, and left to starve, were all huddled together [. . .] The Major told me he had been caught out by one of the many crooks who were battening on to old soldiers. They offered shares in businesses, producing false books and when the money had been paid over they just disappeared. All his money had gone. However, he was to see one of his old junior officers that day and he was hoping to get a break. After an argument, I persuaded him to accept a few cigarettes and a shilling to carry him over.[10]

The inequity and indignity of all this was to have a radical effect on the life of one man in particular. On Armistice night Oswald Mosley had limped into one of London's most fashionable hotels. He later recalled his feelings:

> Smooth, smug people, who had never fought or suffered, seemed to the eyes of youth − at that moment age-old with sadness, weariness and bitterness − to be eating, drinking, laughing on the graves of our companions. I stood aside from the delirious throng, silent and alone, ravaged by memory. Driving purpose had begun; there must be no more war. I dedicated myself to politics, with an instinctive resolution which later came to expression in my speeches: 'Through and beyond the failure of men and of parties, we of the war generation are marching on and we shall march on until our end is achieved and our sacrifice atoned.'[11]

'I still laugh at the idea of Oswald Mosley as an "English gentleman",' his widow has written,[12] 'although of course he was one, from a long line of squires in Lancashire and Staffordshire [. . .] As a boy and young man he loved hunting above all.'

Many people today would happily laugh with Lady Mosley, for Sir Oswald did not earn his place in the history books by being one of the century's gentlemen. In retrospect he seems to have muscled his way in as quite the reverse: arrogant, black-shirted, chin jutting, right arm outstretched; the very image of the thug, the bully-boy, the cad. Seen in context, however, the picture is far more interesting. For the opprobrium Mosley attracted − the simplistic descriptions of him as an arch anti-semite or 'the British Hitler' − came late in his life. The *New Statesman*'s famous castigation of Mosley as 'the only Englishman today who is beyond the pale', for instance, only appeared in May 1979, when he was eighty-two years of age. Half a century earlier, it had all been a very different story.

By all accounts the young Oswald Mosley who watched the Armistice-night revelry in what was surely the Savoy was then a full-blown Hero, and a gentleman in both the easier, grand, old-fashioned manner and the newer, more casual style. 'He had wonderful *manners*,' recalls his widow,[13] the erstwhile Diana Mitford. Others who knew him in the 1920s have taken a similar line, praising everything from his sporting prowess to his oratory and bearing. According to the diary of Lady Violet Bonham Carter it was no less a figure than H. H. Asquith (her father) who proclaimed that Mosley 'had made the most brilliant speech he had almost ever heard'; while a few years later Egon Wertheimer, a German journalist, noted that he was 'a young man with the face of the ruling class of Great Britain but with the gait of a Douglas Fairbanks'.

He was born on 16 November 1896, the eldest son of the heir to a Staffordshire baronetcy, and for twenty years his life followed what must now seem an all-too-familiar pattern. Never particularly close to his father, the young Mosley was groomed to take his place as a gentleman in all the usual places – on the hunting field, at preparatory school and then at Winchester College. And although 'he hated both schools unashamedly and with an intensity which went on into old age',[14] at Winchester at least he showed something of the Tom Brown spirit.

He rejected both 'learning and homosexuality' – 'at the time I had no capacity for the former and I never had any taste for the latter'[15] – and was by his own admission 'half-witted' during his schooldays. Reverting to type, this latter-day Tom (and, quite coincidentally, from his early childhood Mosley was familiarly known as 'Tom') turned instead to the sports pitches and the gymnasium. He played for Winchester's cricket XI, and excelled in both boxing and fencing. He was Public Schools' fencing champion at the age of fifteen, winning both the foil and sabre competitions; and, although boxing soon lost its appeal, his interest in hunting and fencing continued long into adult life.

Lady Mosley has recalled:

> When he got into Parliament and realized he couldn't do politics seriously if he went constantly to Leicestershire, where he kept his horses, it was a real wrench to give [hunting] up and sell the horses, which he did. He went back to fencing in his early thirties and was in the English team. He always said some of his happiest times were in *Salles d'Armes* all over the place.[16]

Tellingly, perhaps, in the light of his future life, at the age of seventeen Mosley progressed from Winchester to the Royal Military Academy at Sandhurst rather than to Oxford or Cambridge. This was in January 1914. By that September, because of the outbreak of war, he had been gazetted as an officer in the 16th Lancers, and by the end of the year seen active service during a secondment to No.6 Squadron of the fledgling Royal Flying Corps. He was back with the 16th Lancers in

1915, but invalided out of the army during the second Battle of Ypres because of an aggravated injury to his leg. Two operations to repair the damage left him for the rest of his life with his right leg an inch and a half shorter than his left. 'I had entered the war in the category Al, and left it in the category C3, fit for office work only,' he wrote later.[17]

But back in London in 1917 and 1918 that didn't much matter. Sporting a clipped black moustache, the suave, limping Oswald Mosley, 'nice rather than good-looking', and now employed at the Foreign Office and in the Ministry of Munitions, was soon pulled into smart society circles. He was 'taken up' by the leading hostesses of the day, and apparently revelled in his reputation as something of a womanizer. As late as 1923 F. E. Smith was to describe him as 'the perfumed popinjay of scented boudoirs'. (Understandably stung, Mosley let it be known that he did not mind the reference to boudoirs; being called a popinjay, however, was almost actionable since it seemed to impugn his performance therein.) Certainly, he enjoyed intimate assignations with women like Catherine D'Erlanger and the exotic Maxine Elliott (she 'looked like a Roman Empress should have looked') every bit as much as the hours he spent at the fashionable luncheon and tea-tables of the likes of Lady Cunard, Lady Colefax and Lady Astor. Why, after all, did any young man attend those elaborate *salons*, but for the chance they offered to (in Mosley's phrase) 'flush the covers'?

Newly elected to Parliament – he had been offered candidacies by both the Conservative and Liberal parties – by the end of the decade Mosley was widely regarded as one of the coming men, almost the reincarnation of Raymond Asquith and the prewar heroes. And when in March 1920 it was announced that he had become engaged to Lady Cynthia Curzon the picture seemed complete. For 'Cimmie' was not only 'the personification of the society girl, tall, willowy, with a slightly bored expression' (as she was gushingly described in a contemporary newspaper feature) she was also the second daughter of George Nathaniel Curzon, by then serving in the first of what would be two spells as Foreign Secretary.

The wedding, which took place at the Chapel Royal in St James's Palace on 11 May and was preceded by an elaborate lunch at the Ritz, was one of the social events of the year. By all accounts it bettered even Raymond's. King George V and Queen Mary, King Albert and

Queen Elizabeth of the Belgians and the Conservative leader Andrew Bonar Law were among the guests. Crowds, twelve deep in Pall Mall, turned out to watch the comings and goings. The next day's newspapers were full of photographs of the occasion – stiff, formal groups in which Mosley himself is frequently the only untitled figure – and descriptions of the thousands of pounds-worth of wedding presents which the couple received. The closely-printed lists of the guests at the Chapel Royal and the huge reception that Lord Curzon hosted at the Foreign Secretary's official residence which the newspapers also published resembled nothing so much as a who's who of postwar London society.

Almost effortlessly, it seemed, Oswald Mosley, the son of an obscure country squire, had emerged as one of the leaders of the new *beau monde*. Weekend after weekend he and Cimmie were feted at innumerable country houses. *Snap! Sir Oswald and Lady Mosley arrive at Cliveden!* Season after season they were photographed together at Ascot, Henley, Lord's and countless charitable functions before flying off to such chic foreign resorts as Venice and Deauville. *Snap, snap! There they were again, arm in arm at Croydon aerodrome.* They owned an opulent town house in Smith Square, Westminister and a succession of country homes of their own, culminating in the Tudor manor house at Denham in Buckinghamshire which Tom purchased in 1926. The gossip and society columns continued to print accounts of Mosley's 'jazzy' private life – how he would leave the House of Commons late in the evening and then, with Cimmie on his arm, frequent the most fashionable nightclubs until the early hours – but no one minded that. Rather pruriently perhaps, they were more interested in how the pair could afford it all. The gadabout MP had to be a millionaire, it was generally concluded; even a multi-millionaire.

The reality was more prosaic. It is true that, on the death of his father in 1928, Mosley did inherit an estate then valued at around a quarter of a million pounds, but most of it had long-since been made over to leaseholders on 999-year leases – one less 9, he used to say, and he really would have been a multi-millionaire. In the years before 1928 he was a merely a comparatively wealthy man with an income on a par with that of many others of his class and background. Six weeks before his marriage his future father-in-law gave a very accurate assessment of Mosley's finances in a letter to his wife:

It turns out he is quite independent – he has practically severed himself from his father who is a spendthrift and a ne'er-do-well. The estate is in the hands of trustees who will give him £8,000–£10,000 a year straight away and he will ultimately have a clear £20,000 p.a.[18]

Lady Cynthia had an annual allowance from a family trust of roughly the same amount, so it is fair to picture the Mosleys surviving quite comfortably on an income of something like £15,000–£20,000 a year during the early and middle 1920s.

It was clearly quite sufficient, for despite his obscure origins Mosley had passed muster. In a very literal sense he was an officer and a gentleman, albeit a gentleman of the new school. Indeed he was almost too good to be true, combining the attributes of the old school – a baronetcy and huntin', shootin' and fishin' in the shires – with the preoccupations of the new, postwar world. For all that Curzon, his father-in-law, was 'political' in a rather grand patrician sense, no-one could imagine *him* putting up with the drudgery of back-bench life; nor in their wildest dreams could they see him shimmying round the dance-floor of the Embassy Club.

'Very young, tall, slim, dark [with] rather a big nose, little black moustache, rather a Jewish appearance',[19] Mosley was in constant demand as everything from polo player to public speaker. Lord Curzon himself had to concede that by the early 1920s his son-in-law had 'already made something of a mark'. Others were going much further and even beginning to talk of him as a future prime minister . . .

Oswald Ernald Mosley himself would have argued that he was no more than another man who happened to be in the right place at the right time, and to a large extent that was true. But at this stage in his life at least, there did seem to be (in his own phrase again) a *ganzheit* or 'wholeness' about him. His background, upbringing, war record, marriage and burgeoning career seemed to have produced something very close to 'the complete man'.

But there was more to his *ganzheit* than that. For, despite the privileged superficiality of much of his life – 'He was born with a golden spoon in his mouth – it cost £100 in doctor's fees to bring him into the world,' his father once complained – the 'driving purpose' which he had first felt in 1918 never left him. He continued to be dedicated to politics and in particular to an increasingly personal vision of a world in which he and his fellow fighting men would see their 'sacrifice atoned'. The years he had spent in the army had marked him deeply; but it seems that this vision derived at least as much from an almost Curzonian sense of duty and obligation.

And, inevitably perhaps, Mosley also appears to have fallen in with the general belief that he had a special role to fulfil and was somehow marked out for greatness. Certainly, like some latter-day prophet, from about 1920 he began keeping his own counsel. The Conservative politician Robert (later Lord) Boothby knew him well and was later to write that at this time Mosley was a 'Byron rather than Mussolini'.[20] Characteristically, Boothby went on to develop the metaphor: 'He was certainly a powerful swimmer and [during a visit to Venice in 1925] used to disappear at intervals into the lagoon to commune with himself.' There was more than an element of truth in the comparison. Mosley's biographer Robert Skidelsky has more recently described him as a 'young crusader' in the early twenties, while as early as 1919 a parliamentary colleague had noted that he was 'a lonely, detached figure'.

He was certainly not cut out for – or maybe just saw himself above – the doctrinaire party wranglings of Parliament. On winning his seat he had accepted the Conservative-Unionist whip, but more often remained his own man, unwilling to trim his own beliefs to the demands of Lloyd George and the 'hard-faced men who looked as if they had done well out of the war'. He still believed in the concept of a 'land fit for heroes', but his plans for its realization rapidly began to diverge from the Government's vaguer, more expedient notions of national recovery.

Mosley's, expressed from the comparitive freedom of the back benches, were bold, broad and imaginative – if little more than an intelligent expression of the dreams of tens of thousands of men who had lounged in the trenches dreaming of what would happen 'when this lousy war is over'. Crucially, they were isolationist, favouring a situation in which Britain should stand alone, going to war only if actually attacked, and referring any other dispute to the recently-established League of Nations:

> My recurrent theme was that we should conserve our resources for the benefit of our own people and the development of our own country and Empire, and should refrain from extraneous adventures which exhausted our means and jeopardised those ends. This line I followed consistently until it brought me to the final clash in 1939.[21]

The emphases would differ – with Mosley becoming, if anything more pan-European – but they were views he would re-affirm for the remainder of his life.

In the early twenties, however, they inevitably brought him into conflict with his own party, and the difference of opinion only intensified with Lloyd George's decision to use teams of ex-servicemen to 're-conquer' Ireland, then virtually under the control of Sinn Fein nationalists and the newly-formed Irish Republican Army. Almost alone on the Government benches, Mosley was violently against every aspect of the deployment of these 'Black and Tans' (as they became known because of their distinctive uniforms) in what was virtually a guerrilla war. He was a gentleman; he did not see how their beating of suspects with thin steel rods – or, more bizarrely, how their use of a Chinese form of torture which involved putting hot boiled eggs under the armpits of prisoners – could be considered acceptable behaviour.

There was only one honourable way out. Lloyd George's handling of the 'Irish Question' and more specifically the issue of the Black and Tans left Mosley with no alternative. Accordingly, on 3 November 1920 he resigned the Government whip and, together with Lord Henry Cavendish Bentinck, 'crossed the floor' of the House of Commons to throw in his lot with the Liberal opposition rump, then rather disparagingly known as the 'Wee Frees'. Notions of duty and honour were involved. Mosley was doing what he considered to be the only possible thing. He later explained that he 'preferred to face my enemies rather than be surrounded by them. It was better to confront what appeared to me as a charge of howling dervishes than to stand in the middle of it'.[22] He never went as far as taking the Liberal whip; nevertheless, his actions on 3 November were to shape the rest of his life. Never again would he be comfortable within the traditional party system. Something new was needed, he realized – a 'confederation of reasonable men'.

Since the spring of 1919 he had been trying to bring that about, working with the New Members' Parliamentary Committee (predominantly a group of the so-called 'Babes' who had won seats for the first time in the 1918 election) in an attempt to form a new centre group. But because of self-interest and a variety of other reasons the National party, which would have honestly represented the nation's ex-servicemen, never got off the ground. Simultaneously, he was also president of a body calling itself the League of Youth and Social Progress. But above all he was disillusioned with the status quo:

> Some people imagine that it is possible to pass through an earthquake and still find the old familiar landmarks standing. But it is mere blindness to reality to ignore the basic fact that the world of politics, for better or for worse, is new. *The war destroyed the old party issues, and with them the old parties . . . The party system must, of course, return in the very near future, but it will be a new Party system . . .*[23]

A new party system did emerge in the 1920s, but not necessarily along the lines which Mosley predicted. In the 1922 General Election the Labour party more than doubled its share of the vote. Prior to the dissolution it had had sixty-three MPs; in the new Parliament that number had risen to 142. Less than two years – and another General Election – later it held the balance of power with no less than 191 seats, and in January 1924 Ramsay MacDonald was appointed Britain's first Labour Prime Minister.

Mosley could not fail to see which way the wind was blowing. In both 1922 and 1923 he had fought and won his Harrow seat as an Independent candidate – actually increasing his majority in 1922 – but his unofficial position among the Liberals was becoming quite untenable. Accordingly, on 27 March 1924, he formally applied for membership of the Labour party. He wrote to MacDonald: 'You stand forth as the leader of the forces of progress in their assault upon the powers of reaction . . . I ask leave to range myself beneath your standard.' That leave was quickly given. Joyously accepting his application, the new Prime Minister replied:

> My dear Mosley,
> Although I have welcomed you into the Party by word of mouth, I would like to tell you in writing how pleased I am that you have seen your way to join us, and to express the hope that you will find comfort in our ranks and a wide field in which you can show your usefulness. I am very sorry to observe in some newspapers that you are being subjected to the kind of personal attack with which we are all very familiar. I know it will not disturb you in the least, and I assure you it will only make your welcome all the more hearty as far as we are concerned.

But it wasn't just newspapers which were attacking Mosley. Indeed, the *Harrow Observer*'s castigation of its errant MP as a 'will-o'-wisp' was mild in comparison to some of the more personal abuse to which he was subjected. In society circles his defection to Labour, his abandonment of the 'powers of reaction' for the 'forces of progress', was seen as 'class betrayal'; gentlemen simply did not do that sort of thing. The reactions of Lord Curzon, by then Leader of the House of Lords and Lord President of the Council to this latest twist in his son-in-law's career have seemingly gone unrecorded. Ironically, however, those of Leon Trotsky have not. In 1935 he recalled in his diary that Mosley was 'the aristocratic coxcomb who joined the Labour party as a short cut to a career'.

Ten years earlier, many would have agreed with him. To say the least, Mosley's Left-ward progress did seem opportunistic and almost cynically time-serving. With the enthusiastic support of his titled wife, the one-time Tory gentleman of the shires was now ranging himself with the likes of the Clydeside union leader Jimmy Maxton and such die-hard socialists as Hugh Dalton and Herbert Morrison. It was at best an uneasy alliance; for, if he was castigated by his own class, Mosley was also distrusted by Dalton, Morrison and much of the parliamentary Labour party. However, in a chilling prelude of things to come, Egon Wertheimer suggested that, within the Labour party, Mosley had at last found his true constituency. Writing for the German socialist newspaper *Vorwärts*, he described Mosley's appearance at a Labour party rally at the Empire Hall in April 1924:

> There stood Oswald Mosley ... a new recruit to the Socialist movement at his first London meeting. He was introduced to the audience, and even at that time, I remember, the song 'For he's a jolly good fellow', greeted the young man from two thousand throats ...

The critic Richard Usborne surely had a sneaking, ambivalent affection for his subject when he wrote that

> Bulldog Drummond is the Monarch of Muscle, the Sultan of Swat. He is the huge, ugly, cheerful, apparently brainless hunk of a man, who slaps you on the back with a hand the size of a leg of mutton, picks you up, gives you several tankards of beer to drink, and then takes you off in a Sports Bentley to help him gate-crash on the Moated Grange.[24]

Drummond affected people like that for, despite his hulking amorality, you could not help liking him – nor realizing the moment you met him that he too was a gentleman. And it is inconceivable that his creator, Sapper (the pen-name of Lieutenant-Colonel Herman Cyril McNeile) ever intended anything else. In scarcely fifteen pages at the very beginning of his first adventure, *Bulldog Drummond* (originally published in 1920 and rarely, if ever, out of print since) and in a few other later biographical references he makes it very clear that Drummond came out of the same top drawer as another of his characters. In an earlier war-novel, *Mufti* (1919), he had described how, before the war, a proto-Drummond by the name of Derek Vane was

> what is generally described as a typical Englishman. That is to say, he regarded his own country ... whenever he thought about it at all ... as being the supreme country in the world. He didn't force his opinion down anyone's throat; it was simply so. If the other fellow didn't agree, the funeral was his, not Vane's. He had to the full what the uninitiated regard as conceit; on matters connected with literature, or art, or music, his knowledge was microscopic. Moreover, he regarded with suspicion anyone who talked intelligently on such subjects. On the other hand he had been in the eleven at Eton, and was a scratch golfer. He had a fine seat on a horse and rode straight; he could play a passable game of polo, and was a good shot . . .[25]

For Vane – given the foregoing, it is tempting to wonder whether that homophonic surname was entirely coincidental – read Drummond, only more so. Before the war he too had been educated at public school. Now he was a gentleman of some leisure. If he didn't exactly take *The Times*, he certainly read the *Sportsman* and was an active member of the United Sports Club – you know, that place on the south-west corner of St James's Square. He was an expert at jujitsu and a first-class shot. Somewhere (surely not in St James's Square!) he had also learnt how to kill a man with his bare hands in no more than a second. He consumed vast quantities of beer, but still appreciated any cocktail that was put before him. He occasionally smoked a pipe, but was also continually lighting cigarettes which he kept in a silver case – 'Turkish that side – Virginian the other'. And although he was inevitably 'a bit of an expert with a Rolls', he habitually drove a 30 hp two-seater sports car which 'could touch ninety with ease'.

Now, in December 1918, Captain Hugh Drummond, DSO, MC, late of His Majesty's Royal Loamshires was living at 60A Half Moon Street in the West End of London. His telephone – still something of a rarity in itself in 1918 – had the number MAYfair 1234. He was around twenty-three years of age (a surprise, that; somehow Drummond comes over as much older) and distantly connected to the aristocracy. He was looked after by a 'square-jawed ex-batman' called James Denny. He bathed every morning, and thrived on the hearty kidney-and-bacon breakfasts served up by Mrs Denny.

So far, so good: Drummond even had a 'little place' of his own on the river Thames at Goring. P. G. Wodehouse could not have done better. There were, however, differences between Bulldog Drummond and the typical Wodehouse hero, most notably in the matter of physique. Characters like Bertie Wooster and the Hon. Galahad Threepwood were slim and svelte; the former at his best in white tie and tails, the latter more at home amid the country delights of Blandings in Shropshire. They were both tall, albeit chinless, paragons of the upper class. Drummond on the other hand was

> slightly under six feet in height [and] broad in proportion. His best friend would not have called him good-looking, but he was the fortunate possessor of that cheerful type of ugliness which inspires immediate confidence in its owner. His nose had never quite recovered from the final one year in the Public Schools Heavy Weights; his mouth was not small. In fact, to be strictly accurate, only his eyes redeemed his face from being what is known in the vernacular as the Frozen Limit.
>
> Deep-set and steady, with eye-lashes that many a woman had envied, they showed the man for what he was – a sportsman and a gentleman. And the combination of the two is an unbeatable production.[26]

Only Sapper, perhaps, could have got away with the addition of that last sentence. Of course it was true; as we have already seen, by 1918 Oswald Mosley was fast making his name, not least as a polo-player and international fencer, while batches of John Buchan's characters were already tramping across the Scottish grouse moors. ('You have got yourself into the wrong ditch, my friend, and you had better climb out,' are the first words Richard Hannay utters in *The Thirty-Nine Steps*.) But there was something more about Hugh 'Bulldog' Drummond; one further attribute which also set him apart from

Wooster, Threepwood and the rest of the 'silly asses' whom he himself tended to write off as 'daisies' or 'priceless beans':

> It was a characteristic of the man that he did not hesitate; having once made up his mind to go through with a thing, he was in the habit of going and looking neither to the right hand nor to the left. Which, incidentally, was how he got his DSO; but that, as Kipling would say, is another story.[27]

Like Mosley, Drummond was fired by an inner purpose, and driven in whatever he did by a conviction that it was 'all done for the best' or with the best of intentions. Not, of course, that he would himself have seen things like that. For, *unlike* Mosley, Drummond was no thinker and had a horror of culture which more than equalled Ernest Hemingway's. You would never have caught *him* reciting Swinburne, as Raffles was wont to do. And while Buchan's Richard Hannay could demonstrate an intimate knowledge of *Pilgrim's Progress* (Richard Usborne has noted that it is 'the code-book and *locus classicus* through much of *Mr Standfast*'), you could put money on the fact that Drummond had never so much as opened it. Nor did he have either Hannay's 'fly-paper' memory for poetry or his fluency in something like twelve languages. Even French caused Drummond problems – never more so than on the occasion when he had to explain away a crashed car to an uncompromising Parisian *gendarme*:

> '*Vous comprenez: c'est defendu d'arriver en Paris sans des passeports?*'
> '*Parfaitement, mon Colonel,*' continued Hugh unmoved. '*Mais vous comprenez que nous avons craché dans un field des turnipes – non: des rognons . . .* What the hell are you laughing at, Jerry?'
> '*Oignons,* old boy,' spluttered the latter. '*Rognons* are kidneys.'
> 'What the dickens does that matter?' demanded Hugh. '*Vous comprenez, mon Colonel, n'est-ce-pas? Vive la France! En-bas les Boches! Nous avons craché.*'
> The *gendarme* shrugged his shoulders with a hopeless gesture and seemed on the point of bursting into tears. Of course this large Englishman was mad; why otherwise should he spit in the kidneys?[28]

Almost symbolically, this philistinism sets Drummond apart from the 'Lost Generation'. Hardly an Asquith (though are there not traces of Julian Grenfell in his physical make-up?) he was nevertheless very much a product of his times and the epitome of a new kind of gentleman. For the beefy hero of some of the most popular adventure stories published in the 1920s and early 1930s always had at least one foot in the real world. As Sapper was also at pains to point out, at the beginning at least Drummond too was essentially just another casualty of the Great War. Implausible though it now seems, during the last few weeks of 1918 even Captain Hugh Drummond, DSO, MC, was casting around for a new role in life:

> Demobilized officer, finding peace incredibly tedious, would welcome diversion. Legitimate, if possible; but crime, if of a comparatively humorous description, no objection. Excitement essential. Would be prepared to consider permanent job if suitably impressed by applicant for his services. Reply at once Box X10.[29]

Drummond was lucky. Unlike many ex-officers, he found his peacetime 'diversion' very quickly. The morning after that newspaper advertisement appeared, no less than forty-five replies were neatly stacked on his breakfast table. Within another eight hours the demobilized Captain – yes, he too clung to his rank; even his enemies gritted their teeth and addressed him as 'Captain Drummond' – was taking tea at the Carlton and being introduced to the man he would 'probably have to kill' . . .

Never a writer to waste time or weary his readers with irrelevant verbiage, Sapper had related all that in hardly more than thirty pages. He was a consummate but careless storyteller. (Was it the United Sports Club, the Junior Sports Club or the Senior Sports Club to which Drummond belonged? He scarcely seemed to care.) Details hardly mattered, for by page thirty of *Bulldog Drummond* Sapper had long-since won the loyalty and attention of those readers. Even today, it is difficult to put the book down or fail to succumb to any of the later novels and short stories which chronicle Drummond's subsequent career. They all have a wit and verve which transcend time.

More significantly, their sheer narrative efficiency also frequently masks what can only be described as an underlying moral turpitude. For although Hugh Drummond might have been a gentleman, even when ranged against Richard Hannay, Sandy Arbuthnot, Edward Leithen and everyone else whom Buchan, Dornford Yates and the rest put in the postwar catalogue, he showed alarming new tendencies. Inviting himself down to a house called The Larches he had Denny pack just 'the bare necessities for the night'. The Larches was no further from civilization than Godalming in Surrey; Drummond needed no more than a toothbrush and a pair of pyjamas – yet among the neat folds of the latter Denny still concealed a 'wicked little automatic'.

There was a reason, of course. Sapper had already warned us that in Godalming Drummond had a rendezvous with a mass-murderer, the man whom he would 'probably have to kill'. What's more, as Drummond explained to Denny – every bit as patiently as Holmes did to Watson and Raffles to Bunny – the mass-murderer in question was

> *the* most dangerous man in England – the IT of ITS. This gentleman goes by the name of Peterson and he owns a daughter [and] it appears that some unpleasing conspiracy is being hatched by IT, the IT of ITS, and the doubtful daughter.

But it wasn't just that he was a mass-murderer, or even 'the IT of ITS'. For Carl Peterson with his oh-so-slightly-foreign-sounding name and ice-cold mien was also the first in a whole gallery of unseemly, unsavoury and fundamentally *un-English* villains against whom Drummond found himself pitted. *En-bas les Boches!* . . . It was as if the Great War had never ended. Time and again throughout the twenties and thirties he ended up isolated in a moral No Man's Land, a lone champion of the Breed confronting unspeakably unscrupulous foreigners intent on destroying England As He Knew It.

But, officially at least, the war had ended; and unlike Derek Vane, for whom the enemy was at least readily identifiable and the rules of war (such as they were) clearly laid down, in his postwar career Drummond had no more than his wits and those leg-of-mutton fists to continue the battle. The latter were to prove of greater use to him, adept as they were at handling an assortment of pistols, revolvers, sjamboks, bull-whips and blunt instruments. For as we have seen, in virtually every one of the Bulldog Drummond stories our hero is quite literally forced to stand up and fight for what he believes in.

Drummond himself always remained pretty sanguine about the carnage he left in his wake; given his head, he would happily 'push a fellah's face' for no other reason than that he'd 'got spots and things'. He was accustomed to brush it all off as no more than a part of 'the game' or, more grandly, 'The Great Game' (echoes of Kipling here, together with Newbolt's 'Vitae Lampada' and, surely, the schoolboyish ethos of the trenches). But he still fought in deadly earnest; and people still got killed. By and large though, the casualties tended to be hunchbacks, dwarfs and other 'inferior beings', rather than members of the Breed or anyone remotely resembling them. They were central Europeans (like Peterson), Negroes or, even more frequently Jews.

And today this is where the trouble starts, even if contemporary critics' castigations of Drummond's anti-semitism, chauvinism, snobbery and callousness are – like denigrations of the 'racist' attitudes and avowedly middle-class values implicit in the children's novels of Enid Blyton – ultimately anachronistic and irrelevant. For, crucially, they ignore the fact that Drummond, like Blyton's Famous Five and Noddy, was no more than a reflection of the values of his times.

No one had yet started talking seriously about *übermenschen* and the 'master race', but even in 1920 the germ of the idea was abroad. It is arguably implicit in the postwar notion of The Hero and the rather older idea that the gentlemen members of the Breed (and there were no others) were all white, middle-class, Protestant Englishmen with clear complexions. We have already seen that Raymond Asquith had complained to his stepmother that the student body at Balliol, to which he had matriculated in 1897, was 'for the most part composed of niggers and Scotchmen'. Even then he was by no means alone in displaying such xenophobia. The private letters and popular fiction of the period contain countless other examples. But the mere fact that Asquith was able to lump together 'niggers' and 'Scotchmen' (and even in the 1890s both were pejorative terms) should give some measure of the extent of his class-based prejudice. If it does not, a slightly earlier letter should. In the summer of 1897 Raymond told his father that he was competing for his scholarship against 'a very large number of diseased and hideous people' – one even had 'a black beard and flaxen undergrowth over the rest of his face'.

Jews were a different matter, however. For generations they had represented something dimly sinister in the European consciousness – Ahasuerus the Wandering Jew and Shakespeare's Shylock cast long shadows – but now, in the immediate aftermath of the Great War, feelings were becoming more focused. The Boche had been defeated; but many an English gentleman, caught in that No Man's Land between his traditional incarnation as the 'verray parfit English knight' and his more recent role as the khaki-clad warrior, remained on the *qui vive*, ever alert for further threats to England, Home and Beauty. And as the 'land fit for heroes to live in' failed to materialize it became all too easy for him to subscribe to conspiracy theories and neurotically begin casting around for an 'enemy within'. The Jew fitted the bill exactly; and, for all that its author was a non-combatant American Anglophile, the fractured, nightmarish imagery of T. S. Eliot's poem 'Burbank with a Baedeker: Bleinstein with a Cigar' (1920) exactly caught the postwar mood:

> The rats are underneath the piles.
> The Jew is underneath the lot.
> Money in furs . . .

Its hysteria and insecurity are exactly echoed in the opening pages of John Buchan's slightly earlier novel *The Thirty-Nine Steps* (1915). That too is concerned with a threat to the status quo, and the whole plot turns on some information which Richard Hannay receives – coincidentally from another American:

> The Jew is everywhere, but you have to go far down the backstairs to find him. Take any big Teutonic business concern. If you have dealings with it the first man you meet is Prince *von und zu* Something, an elegant young man who talks Eton-and-Harrow English. But he cuts no ice. If your busines is big, you get behind him and find a prognathous Westphalian with a retreating brow and the manners of a hog. He is the German businessman that gives your English papers the shakes. But if you're on the biggest kind of job and are bound to get to the real boss, ten to one you are brought up against a little white-faced Jew in a bathchair with an eye like a rattlesnake. Yes, sir, he is the man who is ruling the world just now . . .[30]

Even here, however, we should be careful, for it is a mistake to tar either Eliot or Buchan with the label 'anti-semitic' as the term is understood in a post-holocaust world. Regrettably insensitive as both may have been – Sapper too – in the first four decades of this century there was little or nothing for them to feel vicariously guilty about; and the xenophobic anti-semitism which they shared with Asquith and his contemporaries was no more sinister than, say the 'anti-Irish' feeling in today's Englishman-Irishman-Scotsman jokes. It too thrived on exaggeration and caricature – ultimately, Eliot's cigar-smoking, top-hatted capitalists and Buchan's white-faced wheelchair-bound cripple have all the cardboard menace of the Demon King – while its perpetrators can, by the standards of their time, be seen as almost liberal. Ironically, Eliot numbered several Jews among his closest friends, most notably Leonard Woolf – and it is not without significance that Woolf himself once said: 'I think T. S. Eliot was slightly anti-semitic [but only] in the sort of vague way which is not uncommon.'[31] It was the same with Buchan. Although (as Janet Adam Smith had pointed out) in his writings the very word 'Jew' is almost always an approximate synonym for 'vulgar wealth', he maintained long-lasting friendships with a number of prominent Jews including Lionel Phillips – to whom he dedicated *Prester John* – and the Zionist leader Chaim Weizmann.

None of this, however, should blind us to the fact that a deeply-rooted anti-semitism did exist at this period. It was bolstered by the listlessness and lingering bellicosity of the postwar world, but it was not in any way 'vague', nor as detachedly liberal and affectedly literary as Eliot's or Buchan's. In the printed record, it surfaces most noticeably in the writings of G. K. Chesterton and Hillaire Belloc, both of them immensely influential critics and commentators in the 1920s.

Chesterton, with his belief in 'the mob', the international brotherhood of the innately good, his inneffable beer-drinking Englishness but increasingly-fervent Catholicism (he saw no contradiction) was especially prone to blame the nation's and even his own family's problems on what he called 'the tribe'. He was, for example, convinced that Jewish interests, especially those of Godfrey and Sir Rufus Isaacs were behind the treatment of his brother Cecil in the Marconi scandal during the war and at least partly responsible for Cecil's premature death in 1918. 'Grief had unbalanced him', a recent critic has written, seeking not so much to condone as explain the paranoia which is increasingly apparent in the vast output of his final years.

All the same it remains inescapably true that throughout his life Chesterton, otherwise the most affable of men, refused to believe that 'the Jew' – any Jew – could ever be a real traveller along the rolling English road. Far more sinister than 'the horrid French', he was the real enemy within. And as we shall see, far more than the pantomimic effusions of Sapper or Buchan, it was to be the ostensibly-sensible opinions of the likes of Chesterton, and their quiet denunciations of the Jewish control of business and finance, which were to prevail.

All that, however, lay in the future. For the present, the new gentlemen of England – the hero-gentlemen, the survivors, the Mosleys of the early 1920s, the survivors – were struggling to maintain control in a radically different world … and, like Bulldog Drummond, using every means at their disposal to maintain the integrity of the Breed. But it had already started to become an uphill task.

CHAPTER SIX

Every Other Inch a Gentleman

*I think I would have liked to have known him in
'The Green Hat' period. When he was young,
and full of dash, and neither quite a gentleman,
and neither not, and he really did make quite a
splash.*

– Michael J. Arlen on his father

As his biographer Clive Ellis has pointed out, 'it was very hard to ignore Charles Burgess Fry at any stage in his life. Physically dominating and mentally arresting, he had to be the focal point in any gathering.'[1] That compulsion was to remain with him until his death in 1956 at the age of eighty-four. The Sussex and England cricketer who so delighted the crowds at Hove, Lord's and later at Hampshire's ground in Southampton during the early years of the century had officially hung up his pads at the beginning of the 1920s, as he approached his fiftieth birthday. It was, however, hardly a retirement, for by then he had found far wider wickets to conquer.

His earlier pre-eminence at the crease had given him a certain social cachet, and like W. G. Grace (who had been more than an encouragement when he was just beginning to make his mark in the first-class game) Fry was determined to exploit it to the full. Indeed, comparisons between the careers of the two men are illuminating. Both were in a certain sense sportsmen born before their time and, more interestingly, gate-crashers in an alien world. Grace set the precedents; but it was Fry who made the running.

Maybe he should not have gone so fast or so far, for opinion is still divided on whether Fry was ultimately the gentleman he claimed to be or merely a jumped-up player. Although they were originally sent out in the twenties, the jury has still not returned a definitive verdict. Paying tribute in an essay published in the *Manchester Guardian* shortly after Fry's death, Neville Cardus at least appeared to be in no doubt:

> Fry must be counted among the most fully developed and representative Englishmen of his period; and the question arises whether, had fortune allowed him to concentrate on the things of the mind, not distracted by the lure of cricket, a lure intensified by his increasing mastery of the game, he would not have reached a high altitude in politics or critical literature. But he belonged – and it was his glory – to an age not obsessed by specialism; he was one of the last of the English tradition of the amateur, the connoisseur, and, in the most delightful sense of the word, the dilettante.

Given the circumstances and the constraining conventions of obituary-form, Cardus's attitude is not entirely surprising, nor even is that of the *News Chronicle* which, with apparent sincerity, went as far as to describe Fry a 'a perfect human being'. However, it was a sign of changing times that neither could ignore the fact that, perfect or not, this 'most fully developed and representative Englishman' had sprung not from the leisured-cum-aristocratic backgrounds which had produced the likes of George Curzon and Raymond Asquith, but from much humbler origins.

Born in April 1872, 'C.B.' – as he was known from childhood – was the son of a Scotland Yard police official and spent his early life in the suburbs of south London, living at various times in Croydon and the village of Chislehurst in Kent. Recalling this period some fifty years later in his somewhat awkward autobiography *Life Worth Living*, Fry described an almost modern childhood. Until the age of thirteen he attended a local preparatory school, played football and cricket with other ordinary boys and spent many hours tramping alone across Chislehurst Common and fishing for roach in the nearby Keston ponds. Only his chance meetings with Napoleon III's widow, the Empress Eugenie ('She was pale, and walked just as a little boy would expect an Empress to walk') and her son, the Prince Imperial who then lived in exile at Camden Place in Chislehurst, hinted at the existence of a wider world beyond.

Within a very few years, however, the young C.B. had begun to make his mark in that world. In 1885 he progressed from the obscurity of his Kentish prep school to full-blown public school life at Repton, and there a characteristic doggedness soon made itself apparent:

> My first week I was bottom from one of my form. My second week I was second from top. I was top every other week of the term; but I was third after the examinations because I got very low marks in mathematics. All the same, I was top in classics, and I do not believe any boy has ever worked harder.[2]

The hard work never stopped. Before he left Repton he had been head boy of his house for three consecutive years. He had won school prizes for Greek verse, Latin verse, Latin prose and French composition. He had been one of the finalists in the school singing competition, and received high praise for his performance in the title role of Molière's *Le Malade Imaginaire*. Nor had he neglected the *corpore sano* side of things. Describing his schooldays in *Life Worth Living*, Fry recalled little more than that he was made a member of the Under Sixteen house team in his first term at Repton, and much enjoyed football. But by the late 1880s the pages of the school magazine *The Reptonian* were telling a different story. The thirteen-year-old Charles Burgess Fry had run the 100 yard sprint in 12.0 seconds and the 220 in 28.8 seconds, they recorded. Two years later they announced that Fry had set an Under Sixteen record of 17 ft. 5 in. in the long jump and won the senior hundred-yard race. By 1890 he was clearing a very creditable 5 ft. 6 in. in the high jump and setting a schools long-jump record that would be beaten only by the future Olympic sprinter, Harold Abrahams.

Off the athletics field too Fry's sporting achievements were equally impressive. He swam, and on one occasion came equal first in a school diving competition. By the age of fifteen he was a member of Repton's strong First Soccer XI, and within a couple of years was also playing for an élite amateur side, the Casuals, as well as turning out in occasional FA Cup matches. Curiously though, his talents as a cricketer did not fully develop until quite late in his school career. He did not win a place in the Repton First XI until 1888. Within two years, however – doubtless because of more hard work – he had found his form: he was playing for the Public Schools against the Gentlemen of Surrey, making a half-century in one innings and taking seven wickets in a single match.

By 1891, then, C.B. was marked out for greatness. Oxford beckoned and, seemingly without so much as breaking sweat, he came top in the entrance examinations for Trinity and Wadham colleges and won the first Classical scholarship that Wadham ever awarded. That autumn he arrived at the university trailing clouds of glory, his name three places above that of F. E. Smith, later the Earl of Birkenhead and a Lord Chancellor of England, on Wadham's 1891 entrance list.

At Repton and at home in Kent he was fêted as the local boy made good; one of Us who had beaten a titled, aristocratic Them at their own game. There was a certain truth in that. He had got himself to Oxford – but, as he quickly discovered, Wadham was hardly Balliol. Fry had joined a college which was neither academically nor socially distinguished. Even if he did not know it before he arrived, he would very rapidly have been apprised of the conundrum that more fortunately-placed Oxford undergraduates had been asking one other since the early 1880s: 'Why is the Wadham boat like Noah's Ark?' By 1891 everybody knew the answer: 'Because it moves slowly upon the face of the waters and is filled with all manner of beasts.'

The 1891 intake were to change all that. And among them Fry was more than capable of holding his own, even against the likes of the mercurial Smith (called 'Galloper' by his friends) and another exact Wadham contemporary, John (later Sir John) Simon who was to serve as Home Secretary during the First World War and, following in Smith's footsteps, as Lord Chancellor during the Second. Indeed, the artist William Rothenstein, a fellow-student and friend of them all, reckoned that C.B. had the best brain of any undergraduate during his time at Oxford.

Socially too, Fry did much to restore Wadham's tarnished image. Pursuing his interest in the stage, he joined the Oxford University Dramatic Society and appeared in a production of *The Merchant of Venice* alongside the son of Sir Henry Irving. On a rather different level, he and F. E. Smith founded the Wadham Cat Club, whose members set themselves the task of paying unauthorized nocturnal visits to the precincts of every other college, and apparently succeeded. By all accounts he was a 'good fellow'. Certainly it was as much because of his sporting prowess, chiselled good looks and classical build (in his prime he was 5 ft. 10½ in. in height and weighed a little over twelve stone) as his academic ability that Fry was dubbed 'the Almighty' within months of his arrival. The sobriquet stuck; and during his final year letters simply addressed to 'Lord Oxford' still found their way to his oak-panelled rooms overlooking Wadham's front quad.

And yet beneath the glittering surface Fry was never really satisfied. In *Life Worth Living* he implies that, despite his superficial success, he always remained something of an outsider. He went out of his way to mention that 'when I packed a small trunk and went up to Oxford, I had no allowance from home [and] about £3 in my pocket' – and that, he added, at a time when 'one really needed £250 a year at Oxford to be comfortable'.[3] (It is an interesting comment on fast-changing values to note that George Nathaniel Curzon had complained nearly twenty years previously that, while many of his contemporaries at Balliol had five-figure incomes, he himself was forced to live on an allowance from his father of less than £1,000 a year.)

Deep down, of course, Fry was right. He was not at Wadham because of what he called 'ancient wealth'. He was the representative of a new egalitarianism; a meritocrat who had muscled his way in but was still being made to pay for the privilege. He tried to be proud of that too, but again it didn't really work. 'My vacations,' he wrote, 'instead of being available for reading (and it is during the vacations that one can really read), were occupied in tutorships and in modest efforts at saleable literature in order to meet my University expenses.'[4]

Life cannot have been easy for him, and for this reason perhaps Fry's Oxford career was riddled with inconsistencies. He was argumentative and orally adept, for instance, but never so much as spoke at the fashionable, dinner-jacketed Union. He gained an outstanding First in Classical Moderations at the end of his first year – but then, like many an 'individual' before and since, 'ploughed' his Finals and went down with only a fourth-class degree.

In all probability he suffered some form of nervous breakdown at this period; but even that does not wholly explain what amounted to a spectacular fall from grace. Undoubtedly he had been playing hard – at various times he had been Captain of Oxford's First XIs for both cricket and football, and President of the University Athletic Club – but so had a fair number of other students, possibly the majority. Very few of them, however, were brought before a special sitting of the University Vice Chancellor's Court.

Fry was, and accounts of how he got to be there throw a fascinating light on the personality of the strange beast of Wadham. In 1895 the *Oxford Chronicle* reported that

Charles Burgess Fry, undergraduate of Wadham College, was summoned for wilfully extinguishing five street lamps in High St on March 15. – He pleaded guilty. – P.C. Higgins said he saw defendant climb two of the lamp posts and extinguish the lights at 11.45. He stopped the defendant and said, 'Mr Fry, I believe.' Defendant replied that that was so. There were three other lamps out further up the street. – Defendant had nothing to say in defence. – The Vice Chancellor said the Bench were very sorry to see a young man of the defendant's ability and youthful promise brought up for these school-boyish tricks. He would be fined 40s and costs 7s.6d. or 14 days' imprisonment.[5]

Not unnaturally, Fry chose to pay the fine (although 'severely tempted to subject the Vice Chancellor's Court to the absurdity of the second alternative') and, officially at least, the incident was soon forgotten. However, it is hardly over-emphasizing matters to say that it remained one of the seminal events in his life. Albeit unconsciously, he even seems to have conceded as much himself. For although he was never completely open in his autobiographical writings – his tone was too hectoring, too relentlessly avuncular – it obviously rankled, since he devoted nearly three pages to an account of the incident and its repercussions in *Life Worth Living*.

Reading them now, along with the fractured prose of the *Chronicle* court reporter, one is left with the impression that Fry was up to more than 'school-boyish tricks' when he accepted a challenge from F. E. Smith and 'essayed the not difficult feat' of putting out those gas lights in the High. He was, for instance, 'entirely sober and quite well-behaved' at the time. Witnesses also confirmed that he caused no real damage; indeed, part of Smith's wager was that he should also re-light the lamps.

Why then did he do it? Fry himself could advance no coherent defence for his actions; but in retrospect it seems at least possible that the middle-class meritocrat was over-compensating for his background; attempting to prove himself by consciously emulating the drunken exploits of generation after generation of more monied undergraduates. And the fact that – as we shall see – much of his later career was to be devoted to the assiduous promotion of himself and his solid middle-class belief in the virtues of the discipline and hard work which had made 'Lord Oxford' as good as his masters only lends credence to such a view.

*

In 1895, however, all that lay in the future. We have already seen that Fry's background was suburban, if not exactly humble or impecunious. Now, with no private income to support him, he was faced by the necessity of earning a living. His undoubted sporting prowess was about his only real credential. Characteristically stubbornly, however, he refused to exploit it and instead chose to remain an amateur, a Gentleman in a world increasingly dominated by professional Players. There was no particular reason for his having done so. Several professionals were already members of the Sussex County Cricket Club which he joined in 1895 and several more were playing for Southampton Football Club when he signed there in 1900. Indeed, Fry was one of the very last amateurs to play in an FA Cup Final when his Southampton side went down 2–1 to Sheffield United in 1902.

There was only one way in which he could subsidize his far-from-lazy summers of sport. Like many more ordinary Oxbridge graduates who had ploughed their Finals and were uncushioned by private incomes, the Almighty Fry was forced into teaching. His biographers have found little to say about his two-year career as an assistant master at Charterhouse, and Fry himself skips over it in a single paragraph in *Life Worth Living*. The job was clearly not at all to his taste, but in the late 1890s there was simply no alternative. Although he still persevered with it, his occasional journalism and attempts at producing 'saleable literature' were not yet paying anything like enough to live on – certainly not now that he was batting at the same crease and, for at least three months of the year, moving in the same circles as his fellow Sussex all-rounder and exact contemporary, Prince Ranjitsinjhi and the other wealthy Gentlemen who turned out for county elevens.

But within a very few years both his finances and the whole tenor of his life were to change. At about the time he began playing for Sussex, Fry first visited the T.S. *Mercury*, a nautical training school based on the river Hamble in Hampshire which was then owned and run by Charles Hoare, a member of the London banking family, and his mistress, Beatrice Holme Sumner. He clearly liked what he saw and, notwithstanding the fact that she had borne two children by Hoare, soon announced his engagement to Beatrice.

Whether or not the couple's wedding in June 1898 was, as it now seems, essentially a marriage of convenience, contracted at least in part to defuse the scandal which would ensue if the previous Hoare-

Sumner liaison became known, it certainly proved advantageous for all concerned, not least the twenty-six-year-old Fry. At a stroke it solved the majority of his financial problems, for from that summer the wealthy Hoare began 'sponsoring' his career and continued to do so until his death in 1908 – in other words throughout the greater part of what has become known as Fry's 'vintage' period.

The details of that can be briefly sketched, for in *Wisden*'s terms of runs per over, first-class centuries and most-successful partnerships, it need not unduly concern us. Nevertheless, it should be borne in mind that at the same time as he was becoming increasingly involved with promoting himself as a national and political saviour – the side of his career which is of greater relevance here – Fry was also playing classic, beautiful cricket. As early as 1901 he was more than living up to *Cricket* magazine's description of him as 'about the best batsman in England'. He scored more than 3,000 runs that season and hit centuries in six successive innings. In 1904 he was made captain of Sussex and in 1905 scored a staggering total of 560 runs in a period of just six days. Four years later he left Sussex and joined the Hampshire Cricket Club, thus severing a long-lasting partnership with Ranji (who had by then become the Jam Sahib of Nawanagar). Then in 1912 he finally accepted the captaincy of the England team . . .

At all levels there was an inevitability about this, for even before 1912 C.B. was already fulfilling a *soi-disant* role as England's prefect, geeing the nation along for all the world like the captain of a school First XI addressing a surly, indifferent Lower Fifth. Like the self-invented Michael Arlen (in reality an Armenian by the name of Dikran Kouyoumdjian) who wore sharp suits, brandished a cigarette-holder and bought a Rolls-Royce on the profits of vastly popular novels like *The Green Hat* (1924), he had all the trappings of superficial success. But ultimately he knew that they were illusory and that he would always remain (as Michael J. Arlen has described his father) 'neither quite a gentleman and neither not'. Thus, just as at Repton and Oxford he had *needed* to run faster, jump higher, bat better and put out the lights in the High, now he needed to pronounce, pontificate, editorialize, drop names and shout louder than anyone else. It was all part of his need to compensate for a salaried, suburban background.

Opportunities were not slow in coming. But given the coincidence of dates, Fry's statement that he gave up teaching in the summer of 1898 – at precisely the time he married Beatrice – because he had suddenly discovered that he 'could earn by journalism three times the income for the expenditure of a tenth of the time' sounds distinctly disingenuous. Even though it is now impossible to quantify the extent of Hoare's sponsorship, it seems far more likely that it was only because of his backing that Fry was able to leave Charterhouse and become 'involved in contributing to the *Athletic News*, the *Daily Express*, the *Daily Chronicle*, *Lloyd's News*, the one-time successful boys' magazine *The Captain*, the *Strand Magazine* and, finally, in conducting a magazine' himself.[6]

Such a scenario makes both personal and financial sense. Cushioned from the dull necessity of earning a living, within four years of leaving Oxford to his own satisfaction at least Fry had proved himself every bit the equal of his fellow-undergraduates and their 'ancient wealth'. Now he was up among them, a 'man of letters', a thinker, one of the chosen few. But even if we accept that it was prowess on the field which was largely responsible for his association with the *Athletic News* and indeed the *Daily Express* (for which he began writing on football and cricket in 1900) there does seem to have been something of the 'old-boy network' in operation in his connection with venerable institutions such as *The Captain* and the *Strand Magazine*.

Not that Fry worried. Pragmatic and self-serving (in 1923 the *Oxford Chronicle* found it impossible to rate the ex-captain of England 'higher than a superior carpet-bagger') he seems rather to have realized early on that magazines such as *The Captain* could prove exactly the bridgehead he was looking for. 'The prints' gave him a platform from which he could berate, bludgeon and occasionally entertain the British public with his views on subjects which only seldom had anything to do with cricket. *Fry's Magazine* in particular, the one he began 'conducting' in 1904, was exactly what its name implied; a monthly in which for reasons of vanity or mere expediency the editor's own column frequently ran to more than 10,000 words. Originally entitled 'Straight Talk', and then successively (and perhaps tellingly) renamed 'The Sportsman's View Point', 'Expert Opinion' and 'To My Mind', it presented C.B.'s views on everything from sport to aeroplanes, men's fashion, Esperanto and the importance of drill to a readership which at its peak numbered something like 100,000.

Quite what those views amounted to soon took concrete form, for well before *Fry's Magazine* finally folded in September 1914 the T.S.

Mercury had supplanted it and even cricket as the mainstay of Fry's life. Indeed, it is hardly irrelevant to note that he chose to call the chapter of his autobiography which deals with his involvement with the *Mercury* 'A Life's Work', nor that in its first paragraph Fry recalled a conversation with his old friend F. E. Smith, by then Lord Birkenhead:

> Once, standing in the *Mercury* rose garden at Hamble, Lord Birkenhead said to me, 'This is a lovely place and a fine show, C.B. But for you it has been a backwater.'
> 'The question remains,' I replied, 'whether it is better to be successful or . . . happy.'[7]

As we have already seen, Fry's 'happy' association with the *Mercury* went back as far as 1898. But it was only after Charles Hoare's death in 1908 that C.B. emerged as the 'Honorary Director' of the institution. He assumed duties 'such as would make the Headmaster of Eton retire immediately', and began shamelessly exploiting his friendship with the likes of Birkenhead and Winston Churchill, then First Lord of the Admiralty, in a single-minded campaign to make the *Mercury* a school of which even the 1864 Clarendon Commissioners would hardy have approved. He was indefatigable, and very soon its whole ethos and curriculum were accurately reflecting his own not-quite-gentlemanly view of society; with the imperatives of discipline, order and knowing ones place, together with an almost fetishistic devotion to work and service, displacing any concession to pastoral care and liberalism.

Understandably, C. B. Fry is not now recognized as a great educationist; equally understandably, the T.S. *Mercury* has long-since closed. But *Life Worth Living* does include a statement of what might loosely be called its most famous director's theory of education. Taken more generally, this also amounts to a glimpse of the world as it appeared to Fry in the years between about 1920 and 1939. It is worthy quoting at some length:

> In a world which is trying to call itself democratic, and in days when a main idea is that all our Services should be careers open to talent, my own conclusion in this respect may be of interest. It is not true that breeding, environment, and the atmosphere of home count for nothing. It is true that in the Royal Navy the broad gold stripe and curl of an Admiral are in the ditty-box of every seaman boy who

joins the Service. But it is also true that whereas out of the boys at a good Public School – say, Repton or Uppingham – up to the age of 16 you can find at least 40 per cent capable of making first-rate officers, on the other hand, out of a similar number of boys who come from the council schools and the environment of wage-earning homes you will not find more than 10 or 12 per cent. This may be an unpopular opinion, and it would not do for the platform of a prospective Member of Parliament, but it is nonetheless factual. The ultra-democratic proposition which inclines to suggest the general equality of youth as material for the responsibility of an officer is all very well on paper, but in real life it does not work.[8]

That was written in 1939. By then Fry had 'spent thirty years of [his] life in trying to produce the best results obtainable from boys of any and every sort' – but by then too he and just about everyone else was also beginning to see where the cult of the *Übermenschen* could lead. His Edwardian Liberalism was long dead; now he was unapologetic and indeed proud of what he and the *Mercury* had been able to do for the boy whom he – surely somewhat improbably – characterized as 'the well-behaved fifth son of the farm labourer':

> You give me a hundred boys for a month, and give me also a seaman gunner to drill them on parade, and I guarantee that the whole lot will be far better citizens in every capacity than they were at the start.
>
> That is one reason why I have never been able to understand the objection of our free democracy to compulsory military service. Such compulsory service for, say, a year ought to be the university of the ordinary young man.[9]

Concluding his account of that thirty-year involvement with the T.S. *Mercury*, Fry quoted a one-time Bishop of Winchester as saying that it 'is the best thing that ever came out of cricket'. Fry himself undoubtedly agreed with that; in contrast to his enthusiastic celebration of the *Mercury*'s rather dubious achievements, in *Life Worth Living* he is curiously deadpan and even reticent about his feats at the crease. Half a century on, however, there is something at best patronising and at worst unnatural about the book's ponderous descriptions of his concern for the labourer's son and 'the boy of the wage-earning classes'. Indeed, there have long been persistent, if unsubstantiated, rumours that the *Mercury*'s regime of discipline and obedience only cloaked Fry's own more prurient predilections.

Those too need not unduly detain us; for what is more noticeable today about *Life Worth Living* is the fact that, even though it was written and published in 1939 (when it was subtitled 'Some Phases of an Englishman' and began with a patriotic introduction describing the 'Origins of an Englishman') Fry persisted in using the book to laud the authoritarian stance taken by European dictators:

> Although nominally I am the head of the establishment, my wife and I have always acted as two persons in one – like the consuls at Rome; which shows that the Romans knew something *even before the days of Mussolini.*[10]

That was perhaps going a bit far; but as we have already seen, C.B. was hardly alone in expressing a disgruntlement with the way in which things had panned out in Britain (or as he would say, in England) as the political euphoria of 1918 and 1919 evaporated during the early 1920s. If he was a hero – and he was not entirely alone in believing that he was – why did he find his native land becoming more and more impossible to live in, his belief in the value of discipline, hard work and sheer persistence being so consistently derided? Could it be that, suddenly, Italy and Germany were emerging as more thoroughly 'English' than England itself?

Judged on his own terms, the answer can only be Yes; but it is important to note that at that time others too were coming to the same conclusion. As late as 1927 even Winston Churchill had called Mussolini 'the expression of Roman genius, the great lawgiver among mankind, [who] has shown every nation that may be harried by Socialism or Communism that there is a way out.' Later still, he had turned his attention to Germany and, not without some misgivings, ventured to hope that ultimately Hitler would be seen as having 'enriched the story of mankind'.

Churchill, of course, was later to recant of such views. Fry did not; and there is an awful inevitability in the way that, even in 1939, a sunny chapter towards the end of *Life Worth Living* was entitled 'Adolf Hitler'. In extraordinarily sanguine terms it relates the story of Fry's first contact with the Führer and the Third Reich. Even that had come comparatively late – in the spring of 1934 – but five years on Fry could still sum up the chapter with the words:

> Such were my impressions and my conclusions when last I saw Herr

Adolf Hitler. Whatever may have happened since, I see no reason to withdraw any of them. '*Fas est ab hoste doceri.*'[11]

Inevitably, Fry's German connections were a direct result of what was by 1934 his twenty-five-year association with the training ship *Mercury*. As he recalled, in the spring of that year he had been lunching at the Junior Army and Navy Club when he was drawn into a conversation about relative merits of German youth movements and the English Scouts. It was a subject close to his heart since 'the German Scouts [members of the Hitler Youth Movement] were strong on discipline, whereas the English Scouts were strong on goodwill'. What was more, the *Hitlerjugend*

> underwent a formal discipline foreign to our Scout methods, which made the Nazi system much more of a training and less of a game; a distinct point of superiority on the German side. I do not believe in training without discipline [. . .] The Nazi ideal of education definitely places health and character in front of mere intellectual training, and lays formal stress on physical drill, athletics, and games; and includes all this formality in its Youth Scheme. In fact the German Youth Scheme is a definitely coherent State method of producing the citizens it wants. We have not any such definite State methods.[12]

In due course, Fry was invited to visit Germany in an attempt to arrange some sort of ongoing contact between the young people of the two nations. He accepted with alacrity (mollifying any doubts he may have had by insisting on 'running the whole show at my own expense') and predictably found much to his taste:

> The men one met were mostly young and keen. They wasted no time about irrelevancies, were always impersonal and objective, free from the egoism of self-importance, direct and clear-headed. If something were mooted to be done there were no delays [. . .] There was a complete absence of the lounge-lizard type of youth, who looks as though he would break in two in the middle, so frequently seen in the entertainment resorts of London. Nor did one see the kind of girl who looks as if she were presenting herself to the late hours of the night as the whole object of her existence. Indeed, Berlin of 1934 gave me the feeling of a world swept clean by a fresh wind which had left it stimulated, energetic, and ready to work without losing its capacity to enjoy itself.[13]

112

The Führer made an equally good impression: 'What struck me about him as he advanced was his alertness. When we met he bowed formally, but with the kind of fine ease with which I have seen Baron von Cramm bow to Queen Mary at Wimbledon.' Not unnaturally, the two men got on well, and saw eye-to-eye on many subjects:

> His first point was that the whole object of the Youth Movement in Germany was to bring up the next generation as first-rate citizens of the National-Socialist State [. . .] it was quite impossible for Germany to exist without a strong army, and naturally he hoped that the Youth Movement would make first-rate material for the armies of Germany when the country was again capable of assembling her forces on a scale proper to her [. . .] Herr Hitler listened very carefully to my statement of my idea of *rapprochement* of the youth of the two countries, and I found him approving the line of exploration which I had advocated.[14]

Well might Hitler have approved, one is tempted to add – while at the same time wishing that the reactions of Winston Churchill to his erstwhile friend's scheme for the formation of what in 1940 would have become a British 'Churchilljugend' had also been preserved. As it is, we have only Fry's word that, despite his blandishments, even J. A. Spender, 'the well-known writer, journalist, and publicist, former editor of the *Westminster Gazette*' (and, Fry might have added, the uncle of the poet Stephen Spender and a venerable Liberal free-thinker in his own right) would have nothing to do with the project.

By 1939 that hardly mattered. Every bit as much as J. A. Spender (b. 1862) by then C. B. Fry seemed a figure from another age, his plan for Anglo-German training-with-discipline just another eccentric whimsy. Already in his late sixties, strutting rather imperiously in his pseudo-Naval *Mercury* uniform and a monocle, C.B. cut a Blimpish, slightly ridiculous figure. Except in the Long Room at Lord's and in the memories of the elder generation, his cricketing career was long forgotten. *Fry's Magazine* had not appeared for a quarter of a century; and the League of Nations (and for that matter the Liberal party) in which he had invested so much energy was in tatters. For all his high hopes, Fry had not changed the world nor even made a significant or lasting impression on the England he loved so much.

And yet 'the Almighty' had not fallen. He was not reviled, held in contempt or even so much as laughed at. Like, say, G. K. Chesterton or – for very different reasons – such postwar figures as Dylan Thomas and Lady Docker, he was tolerated and even to some extent loved; an amiable eccentric who enlivened national life. Eleven thousand copies of *Life Worth Living* were sold during the first few months of the war; a second edition was printed and would also doubtless have sold out had it not been destroyed when the premises of Eyre & Spottiswoode, along with those of many other publishers, were blitzed on the night of 29 December 1940. No, if Fry was punished at all it was by not being taken seriously. To the general public he was after all only a cricketer; and cricket was after all only a game . . .

Among the Establishment, however, it seems that reactions to him were rather more mixed. For if Fry himself always remained morbidly conscious of the social inadequacy of his background – that lack of 'ancient wealth' continued to rankle – so too were members of what two centuries earlier had been called 'the Quality'. To them, nothing he said or did mattered very much since he was not a 'real' gentleman and always remained fractionally beyond the pale, a seat or two below the salt. In public school parlance, he was no 'cad' or 'bounder'; but on the other hand no one could ever quite bring himself to see Fry as anything other than an 'oik'. Hence, although there is no suggestion that he was ever made less than welcome at Lord's and even in the wider purlieus of clubland – *noblesse oblige* and all that – by the same token there is no evidence that he ever received from the Quality any more than the odd pat on the head.

It is noticeable for instance that, despite his own trumpeting of his many and various services to the nation and a lifetime of hard work, Fry was never honoured by a grateful country, unlike many of his cricketing contemporaries. In 1937, in recognition of *his* services to the game – his captaincy of Middlesex and England, his chairmanship of the MCC selection committee and capable editing of *The Cricketer* – Pelham Warner, Fry's partner in so many Gentlemen and Players matches during the early years of the century, was knighted. So too (although admittedly not until much later) were younger players such as George 'Gubby' Allen and Don Bradman. Beyond a curious suggestion, that he should accept the rather unstable throne of Albania – he did not know, but the post was also offered to Aubrey Herbert[15] – Fry got nothing.

This may easily have been because of no more than a feeling that he had got a bit above himself – a bit, well *uppity* – and for that reason was best dealt with, just like a spoilt child in the nursery, by being ignored. More contentiously, however, it is tempting to argue that Fry's very strutting and fretting in what amounted to a lumpen-parody of the Establishment's own innately-held attitudes and beliefs also had something to do with it. For, without for one moment suggesting any kind of upper-class conspiracy, one can certainly imagine sections of it deliberately keeping him at arm's length, particularly in the latter half of the twenties and during the early thirties – the period when, in his new off-field career, Fry was giving very public voice to precisely the views they were then beginning to see the wisdom of airing only in private.

Right-wing, elitist and authoritarian, we have already seen that for three-quarters of a century at least those views had been quite deliberately fostered in successive generations of gentlemen. Now – as we shall presently see – they were coming under serious attack, and at precisely the time when Fry, the crass outsider, was taking it upon himself to extol them in the crudest terms. No wonder then that the Quality closed ranks! No wonder that C.B. found himself left out in the cold; taking what must, even to him, have been an increasingly-meaningless salute at sundown every evening ten, fifteen, twenty and twenty-five years after he took over the T.S. *Mercury* with such high hopes. But back in London the gentlemen among whom he so desperately wanted to count himself were now fighting for their very existence.

By the early 1930s it had become crucially important to know who one's friends were. Bastions were already crumbling, and at the highest level men were muttering that something had to be done.

CHAPTER SEVEN

'Something Must be Done!'

Old men who never cheated, never doubted,
Communicated monthly, sit and stare
At the new suburb stretched beyond the run-way
Where a young man lands hatless from the
air.

– John Betjeman,
'Death of King George V', 1937

Set as it was on the bank of the river Torrens, the Oval at Adelaide, South Australia might almost have been an English county cricket ground – Worcester or Taunton perhaps; Canterbury even. With the spire of the nearby Anglican cathedral of St Peter dominating the skyline above a bank of trees and its modest, white-painted stands, it suggested decency, traditional sportsmanship, age-old notions of fair play and the small-town values of Adelaide itself. At the Oval, 'the game' had always been the thing. Certainly, there was none of the fierce partisanship which so frequently errupted on the Hill in Sydney. Nevertheless it was at the Adelaide Oval that the rules of 'the game' were to be rewritten over the course of one weekend.

Inauspiciously perhaps, it was on Friday 13 January 1933 that Douglas Jardine led an MCC XI on to the pitch at the beginning of the third of five Test matches which the English team had travelled half way around the world to play against the old enemy, Australia. The Australian sun was shining fiercely, baking the hard, tinder-dry wicket, and some 39,300 people were crowded into the stands and open enclosures.

Jardine knew that there was everything to play for. So far in the current series honours were even. England had notched up an easy, ten-wicket victory in the first Test at Sydney six weeks previously. In Melbourne over the New Year holiday, Australia had squared things, winning the second Test by 111 runs. But England's 1932–33 tour of Australia was only the latest round in a continuing battle. Throughout the greater part of the previous decade the 'home country' had dismally failed to put the Australians to the sword. In the Test series of 1920–21, and then 1924–25 Australia had won every time. Never before had a side achieved such domination.

More recently, it was true, England had taken the 1926 series when, after four drawn games, they had beaten the tourists in the final Test at the Kennington Oval in London. Two years later, led by A. P. F. Foster, they had also trounced Australia on their home ground and retained the Ashes by four matches to one on a 1928–29 tour. But bitter memories of the return visit of the Australians in 1930 still remained. On that occasion a young batsman by the name of D. G. Bradman had hit 254 runs – at that time the highest individual score ever made in an English Test – during the second Test at Lord's. As if that was not enough, the virtually unknown New South Walian had then gone on to score no less than 334 in the third Test and a 'modest' though still worrying 232 in the fourth.

Australia had taken the series and in the intervening years Donald Bradman – dubbed 'the Don' by C. B. Fry and later more formally created Sir Don – had become an antipodean hero. In Australia the small-town boy made good – a Fry then without even C.B.'s dubious claims to gentility – was fêted wherever he went. A sponsor provided him with a car; a cinema was named after him. Although he was only in his early twenties, even in England an evening newspaper had serialized what purported to be his autobiography. Now, he was spear-heading the Australian attack in the 1932–33 Test series. And although injury had kept him out of the first Test at Sydney, in the second he had served notice of a return to form by scoring 103 not out in Australia's second innings.

Thus, as the teams took lunch at Adelaide on that fateful Friday, Jardine realized that something had to be done. He had won the toss and, on what had looked like a perfect wicket, opted to bat. But what was by all accounts one of the worst English batting performances of that period can only have increased his desperation: within ninety minutes four wickets had been lost for only thirty runs.

By the end of the first day's play, things were little better. England had scored just 236 and were seven wickets down. Following a rally by the middle- and lower-order batsmen, the next morning they were all out for a respectable but still disappointing total of 341 – and facing the prospect of dismissing an increasingly-confident Australian XI in which D. G. Bradman was coming in at No. 3. *Something had to be done!*

As far as Jardine was concerned, his Australian opponents were all – Bradman included, Bradman especially! – little more than colonial jackaroos, hardly members of the same species as the mixed band of public school gentlemen and seasoned players whom he had led off the Orient liner *Orontes* when it docked at Fremantle on 18 October the previous year. It was almost as if he had been despatched at the head of a task-force to put down an outbreak of uppishness on the North-West Frontier or quell a little local difficulty among the Hottentots. He had previously batted with distinction for both Winchester College (where he was captain of the First XI in 1919) and Oxford University where, as a student of New College, he had been awarded Blues in the 1920, 1921 and 1923 seasons – an injury had kept him off the field for much of the summer of 1922. He had gone on to play for Surrey and was a member of the England side which had toured Australia five years previously. But he was relatively new to the captaincy and strangely insecure. Now, everything was boiling over, and Jardine's every word and gesture signalled the disdain he felt for his opponents.

Tall, with a hawkish, patrician nose and a cultivated 'aristocratic' (some were already saying arrogant) manner, he habitually dressed for dinner, sported a brightly-coloured Harlequins' cap on the field and evinced a fondness for cravats. (In the team photograph of the 1932–33 tour he is wearing one; all the other players are in open-necked shirts.) Together with his general taciturnity and single-mindedness of purpose, none of this did much to endear him to the Australian public or their outspokenly democratic Press. Wearing a black homburg hat, a jazzy I Zingari tie and a 'lucky' sprig of white heather, he had been in his element during a Press conference on the deck of the *Orontes* shortly before she set sail from Tilbury. Notions of England, home and beauty seemed to be at the forefront of his mind as he assured his fellow-countrymen that he and 'his boys' would 'do our utmost to bring those Ashes back'.

Now, as that twenty-strong MCC party (if one includes the two

118

joint-managers and a full-time baggageman) began the second half of their punishing seven-and-a-half month, 30,000-mile trip, exactly what 'D.R.J.' had meant was already becoming clear. Quite simply, it appeared that Jardine was prepared to bend the rules, break the rules or even make totally new ones in his attempt to bring those Ashes back.

What he told his bowlers in the dressing-room before they went out to face the Australians on Saturday 14 January 1933 has not been recorded; but one of their number, the Old Etonian Gubby Allen, had good cause to remember a conversation with his captain which had taken place in the dressing-room at Melbourne, two weeks previously. A gentleman in both immediate and absolute terms, in a letter home written shortly before the start of the Adelaide Test Allen described how:

> D.R.J. came to me and said the following: 'I had a talk with the boys, Larwood and Voce, last night and they say it is quite absurd you not bowling "bouncers": they say it is only because you are keen on your popularity.' Well! I burst and said that if it had been a question only of popularity I could have bowled 'bouncers' years ago. I concluded by saying if he didn't like the way I bowled he still had time to leave me out not only in this match but until he came to his senses: it also would give me time to complete a full statement of our conversation for the benefit of the MCC Committee. He said 'Well! I am afraid you will have to do.'[1]

Allen did 'do' – taking in what had suddenly become his old-fashioned way, two wickets for forty-one runs in that second Test. Noticeably however, neither then nor in subsequent matches did he change his style. At Melbourne and again at Adelaide he continued to operate as an orthodox fast bowler, delivering what commentators at the time called full-length 'off-theory' balls. Douglas Jardine still got his 'bouncers', however; 'the boys' saw to that.

Even before the start of the first Test, during a number of warm-up matches against State sides, Australians both on and off the field had noticed that, with the exception of Allen, the English fast bowlers were playing a new kind of game. 'Is it cricket?' one magazine had asked bluntly. It was a pertinent question, for the ex-miner Harold Larwood, the disconcerting left-hander Bill Voce and, to a slightly lesser extent, Bill Bowes had no truck with Allen's preference for 'off-theory'. Rather, they went in for 'leg-theory' or (in a more modern phrase) 'bodyline' bowling. The technicalities are complex, but in essence they preferred to bowl towards the leg stump – and hence the batsman – and pitched their deliveries so that the balls frequently fell short of the crease and reared up unpredictably in close proximity to the batsman's body.

Put even more simply, 'the boys' were blatantly intimidating the opposing team; for as Ian Botham, a contemporary player who has both bowled and received bouncers in the first-class game, has described: 'Whenever a ball is going to miss you in cricket it's just a blur on either side, but when it's going to hit you, it's about the size of a football in front of your nose.'[2]

'I felt a lot safer in the Press box, for the bowling looked very dangerous stuff,' noted Jack Hobbs after a pre-Test match at Melbourne during which 'bodyline' bowling had been used for the first time in Australia. Then at the end of his career, but only a few years previously England's closest equivalent to a Bradman, Hobbs was covering the whole MCC tour for the London *Star*. Without at that time necessarily condemning 'leg-theory', he merely noted that he 'found it amusing' – adding, significantly, that 'your feelings are very different when just watching'.[3]

Hobbs was again safely out of the way in the Press box when play in the third Test resumed at Adelaide on the morning of Saturday 14 January. Having been dismissed for 341 in their first innings, the MCC XI had now taken the field, and Jardine was preparing to unleash his boys on Bradman and the Australian batsmen. The crowd was even bigger than it had been the previous day; an unheard-of 50,000 people were ringing the pitch when the England 'skipper', as expected, asked his two best fast bowlers, Larwood and Allen, to open the attack.

Ironically it was Allen who drew first blood, dismissing Fingleton, the young New South Wales opener, for a duck – and bringing Bradman on to the field. Before long, however, Larwood had drawn a more literal type of blood. As 'bouncers' went, the last ball of his second over had not been particularly vicious, but it bounced in such a way that it rose and struck the Australian No. 2 – by chance their captain Billy Woodfull – directly above the heart.

Predictably, the crowd erupted; the incident was identical – same batsman, same bowler – to one which had occurred in the pre-Test knock-up at Melbourne. And a graphic Press photograph of the unfortunate Woodfull's obvious discomfiture then had already gone round the world.

Out at the wicket, however, tempers were cooler. Although both it and Larwood had sailed close to the wind, by all accounts the ball had been a legitimate one, and players of both sides hurried to aid the winded Woodfull. It was only Jardine who turned to Larwood and, well within the earshot of Bradman, said: 'Well bowled, Harold.'

Quite why the England captain chose to say those words then, and his intentions in saying them at all have been debated ever since. Was Jardine merely attempting to reassure Harold Larwood, understandably rattled by the crowd's reaction as the fair-minded Gubby Allen believed? Or was he, as his detractors had it, giving credit where credit was due, as he saw his strategy coming into play?

With the hindsight of half a century, cricketing analysts and commentators have, if anything, veered towards the latter view. Certainly Jardine's subsequent actions – and the contemporary *reactions* of those intimately involved – seem to bear them out. The former, amounting to the evidence for the prosecution, are the more easily summarized.

As we have seen, Woodfull had been hit by the last ball of Larwood's second over. When play restarted Allen resumed the bowling, but only for one over. After that, the ball was passed back to Larwood. Woodfull was again at the wicket, his face understandably enough 'as white as a sheet of notepaper' as Larwood began his run-up.

'*One, two, three, four, five* . . .' the crowd never reached ten in their habitual 'counting out'; Larwood never reached the bowling crease – for, midway through his run-up, Jardine stopped him and made a calculated alteration to the field. With the peremptoriness which came so easily to him, he positioned virtually all his team in a tight semi-circle at short leg, close up around the batsman, thus almost literally confining Woodfull in what was called the 'leg trap'.

Jardine was quite entitled to do such a thing, of course;[4] but his decision to do it at that particular moment caused nothing short of a sensation. Everyone realized that it was intended to intimidate the still shaken Woodfull and licence Larwood to go in for the kill with some full-blown leg-theory bowling – he might then have been facing the Australian captain, but the highly-dangerous Bradman was after all at the other end of the wicket. Play was again interrupted for a minute or two as all sections of the crowd expressed their contempt for Jardine and his tactics in a torrent of booing and abuse.

Tension remained high for the rest of the day. Genuinely fearing that the enraged crowd might 'come over the fence' at any moment, an English fielder asked the umpire to leave him one of the stumps so that he had something with which to defend himself. 'Not on your life,' replied the umpire, 'I'll need all three myself!' Equally worried about a pitch invasion, the Adelaide authorities kept a detachment of mounted policemen outside the ground until the close of play.

Thankfully, however, nothing happened that Saturday afternoon to inflame the situation further. And when stumps were drawn and the vast crowd at last streamed home, Australia were 109 for four wickets, still 232 runs behind England in their first innings. It was true that Larwood had knocked the unfortunate Woodfull's bat from his hands with his second ball in the new over, but the Australian captain had survived and was eventually dismissed (by Allen) for a respectable twenty-two some time after Bradman had been caught in the leg trap (by Allen once more, but off a ball of Larwood's) for a mere eight. It even looked as though Jardine's controversial strategy was paying off. He had 'got' Bradman, and got him cheaply; and that had always been his aim. Bill Bowes has recalled how, after he had bowled Bradman for a duck in the Melbourne Test, he noticed 'the usually sphinx-like' Jardine celebrating 'with his hands above his head, going round doing a sort of Indian war-dance in his extreme delight'.[5]

At Adelaide, however, that delight was to be short-lived. For on the Saturday evening a storm erupted which was ultimately to be of far greater significance than even an invasion of the pitch. In an attempt to calm things down, Pelham Warner, one of the joint-managers of the England side, had gone to the Australian dressing-room, if not exactly to apologize for, then certainly to enquire after the seriousness of, Woodfull's injury. But the Australian captain was in no mood for condolences, and said so in no uncertain terms:

> I don't want to speak to you, Mr Warner. Of two teams out there, one is playing cricket, the other is making no effort to play the game of cricket. It is too great a game for spoiling by the tactics your team are adopting. I don't approve of them and never will. If they are persevered with it may be better if I do not play the game. The matter is in your hands. I have nothing further to say. Good afternoon.[6]

Unfortunately for all concerned, Woodfull's words were overheard and subsequently leaked to the Press – some say by Bradman, some by Fingleton, both of whom had contracts with Australian newspapers. Ultimately, however, the means by which the story got out are irrelevant: all that matters is that on the following Monday morning, in a pre-television age in which there were not even ball-by-ball radio commentaries of Test matches and newspapers were the primary source of information, lurid accounts of the Australians' simmering resentment of 'leg theory' or 'bodyline' bowling displaced the expected match reports and themselves became headline news.

Poor Warner! Then sixty years of age, he was a lonely survivor of the game's 'golden age'. In that halcyon era before the Great War he had captained the Rugby First XI – shades of Tom Brown again – played for Oxford University and first come to public notice in a 1901 Gentlemen *v*. Players match during which he and his partner C. B. Fry had added a dazzling 101 to the Gentlemen's score. He had gone on to captain both Middlesex and England, led two previous MCC tours of Australia and was now the very embodiment of the English cricketing Establishment – chairman of the MCC selection committee, editor of *The Cricketer* magazine and cricket correspondent of the *Morning Post*. As we have already seen, he was to be knighted for his services to the game in 1937.

But, a weak although fundamentally decent man – 'neatly dressed, gently spoken [and] always optimistic', as *The Times* was to note after his death almost exactly thirty years later – on the field and off 'Plum' had more in common with Allen, the urbane Old Etonian, than the abrasively 'modern' Jardine. He played the game, any 'game', by the rules. Secure in the old dispensation, he was at ease with his place in the scheme of things. At home in the committee rooms at Lord's and the contemplative quiet of his clubs (Buck's, the East India and inevitably the Sports, the real-life version of Bulldog Drummond's bolt-hole in St James's Square) he cut a poor figure in the international spotlight. Instinctively and inevitably opposed to 'bodyline' and all it stood for – 'That is not bowling. Indeed it is not cricket,' he had thundered in *The Cricketer* when Bowes had tried a bit of leg-theory in England the previous summer – he also found himself in an impossible position. After a lifetime in the game, he had been accused by an opposing captain of running a team which was 'making no effort to play the game of cricket'. In effect, he was being charged with cheating. It was the lowest moment in his career.

'They turned their backs on me! They wouldn't speak to me!' he kept repeating, back in the safety of the tourists' dressing-room that Saturday evening. 'They turned their backs on me!'

For England, however, worse was still to come. When play resumed on the Monday morning the atmosphere at the Oval was at least as tense as it had been the previous Saturday evening. The rights and wrongs of 'bodyline' and 'leg-theory' were about the only topics of conversation in every quarter of the ground. But out at the wicket Australia doggedly played on, albeit with their lower-order batsmen walking to the crease heavily and ostentatiously padded with 'body armour'. Slowly, they took their overnight score of 109 up to 150 and then 200, at which point a new ball was due. Jardine gave it to his fast bowlers Allen and Larwood (Voce was not bowling, owing to an ankle injury) in order that they could reap maximum benefit from the still-perfect pitch. Allen again struck first: Grimmett was caught for ten when the score stood at 212. But only six further runs had been added before the Australian vice-captain Bertie Oldfield was knocked unconscious when a delivery of Larwood's struck him on the side of the head. He was so badly injured, in fact, that the official score-card listed him as 'absent hurt' for the remainder of the match.

From that moment on, the outcome of the game was academic. Indeed, it hardly now matters that after a further three days' play England went on to win by a margin of 338 runs, although the score-card itself is not without some historic interest:

AUSTRALIA v. ENGLAND
(Third Test)
At Adelaide, 13–19 January 1933
ENGLAND

H Sutcliffe c Wall b O'Reilly 9	c sub (L P J O'Brien) b Wall.. 7
D R Jardine (*capt*) b Wall..................... 3	lbw b Ironmonger 56
W R Hammond c Oldfield b Wall........ 2	(5) b Bradman....................85
L E G Ames (*vice-capt*) b Ironmonger ... 3	(7) b O'Reilly....................69
M Leyland b O'Reilly 83	(6) c Wall b Ironmonger 42
R E S Wyatt c Richardson b Grimmett...78	(3) c Wall b O'Reilly 49
E Paynter c Fingleton b Wall...............77	(10) not out 1
G O B Allen lbw b Grimmett 15	(4) lbw b Grimmett.............15
H Verity c Richardson b Wall..............45	(8) lbw b O'Reilly 40
W Voce b Ball 8	(11) b O'Reilly...................... 8
H Larwood not out 3	(9) c Bradman b Ironmonger 8
B 1, l-b, 7, n-b 7 15	B 17, l-b, 11, n-b 4 32
——	——
341	412

1/4, 2/16, 3/16, 4/30, 5/186, 6/196, 7/228, 8/324, 9/336, 10/341

1/7, 2/91, 3/123, 4/154, 5/245, 6/296, 7/394, 8/395, 9/403, 10/412.

Bowling: *First Innings* – Wall 34.1-10-72-5; O'Reilly 50-19-82-2; Ironmonger 20-6-50-1; Grimmett 28-6-94-2; McCabe 14-3-28-0, *Second Innings* – Wall 29-6-75-1; O'Reilly 50.3-21-79-4; Ironmonger 57-21-87-3; Grimmett 35-9-74-1; McCabe 16-0-42-0; Bradman 4-0-23-1

AUSTRALIA

J H W Fingleton c Ames b Allen	0	b Larwood	0
W M Woodfull (*capt*) b Allen	22	not out	73
D G Bradman c Allen b Larwood	8	(4) c and b Verity	66
S J McCabe c Jardine b Larwood	8	(5) c Leyland b Allen	7
W H Ponsford b Voce	85	(3) c Jardine b Larwood	3
V Y Richardson b Allen	28	c Allen b Larwood	21
W A S Oldfield (*vice-capt*) retired hurt	41	absent hurt	
C V Grimmett c Voce b Allen	10	(7) b Allen	6
T W Wall b Hammond	6	(8) b Allen	0
W J O'Reilly b Larwood	0	(9) b Larwood	5
H Ironmonger not out	0	(10) b Allen	0
B 2, 1-b, 11, n-b 1	14	B 4, l-b 2, w 1, n-b 5	12
	222		**193**

1/1, 2/18, 3/34, 4/51, 5/131, 6/194, 7/212, 8/222, 9/222

1/3, 2/12, 3/100, 4/116, 5/171, 6/183, 7/183, 8/192, 9/193.

Bowling: *First Innings* – Larwood 25-6-55-3; Allen 23-4-71-4; Hammond 17.4-4-30-1; Voce 14-5-21-1; Verity 16-7-31-0, *Second Innings* – Larwood 19-3-71-4; Allen 17.2-5-50-4; Hammond 9-3-27-0; Voce 4-1-7-0; Verity 20-12-26-1.

England won by 338 runs

There were even suggestions that the match and the whole Test series should be summarily abandoned. Certainly, the Australians' downright anger knew no bounds, as can perhaps be judged from the fact that even the august members of the South Australia Cricket Association were observed outside their pavilion, 'standing on the steps and yelling' their disapproval. That might not have been considered cricket either, as an Australian satirical magazine of the period, the *Bulletin*, suggested in a nicely-timed piece of sharp invective which sent a plague on both the dressing-rooms:

> At 'Ome, of course, we Play the Game,
>   The crowd behave decorously;
> They never criticize or blame,
>   But say 'Bravo!' sonorously;

125

'Played, sir!' they chirp, or cry 'Well run!'
But barrack, haw! – it isn't done.[7]

By then, however, 'the Game' had become subsumed in a wider argument about sportsmanship, integrity and fair play – an argument which Jardine characteristically did little to settle at the traditional close-of-play Press conference. 'What I have to say is not worth listening to', he said. 'Those of you who had seats got your money's worth – and then some. Thank you.'

Even if Jardine could have brought himself to change the habits of a lifetime and been more conciliatory, more communicative even, it is unlikely that he would then have been able to save the situation. Well before the match was over, the Australians had appealed to Warner and his joint-manager, R. C. N. Palairet, to ban 'bodyline' bowling: and, on receiving a sorrowful reply that really, the managers had no control over what happened on the field they had taken the decision to appeal directly to the MCC, at that time still the governing body of English cricket. Accordingly, on Wednesday 18 January, while the third Test was still in progress, a cable was despatched from the Australian Board of Control to Lord's, and copies released to the Press. Such an action was in itself unprecedented; and the wording of the cable only indicated how far a game of cricket had already gone in souring international relations. It read:

'BODYLINE' BOWLING HAS ASSUMED SUCH PROPORTIONS AS TO MENACE THE BEST INTERESTS OF THE DAY, MAKING PROTECTION OF THE BODY BY THE BATSMAN THE MAIN CONSIDERATION.

THIS IS CAUSING INTENSELY BITTER FEELING BETWEEN THE PLAYERS AS WELL AS INJURY. IN OUR OPINION IT IS UNSPORTSMANLIKE.

UNLESS STOPPED AT ONCE IT IS LIKELY TO UPSET THE FRIENDLY RELATIONS EXISTING BETWEEN AUSTRALIA AND ENGLAND.

Piqued and prickly at suggestions that their men were, or could even be *considered*, 'unsportsmanlike' the MCC responded in kind, and fired off a cable of their own. It too was short and to the point – although rather longer in pomposity than the ABC's. 'We, Marylebone Cricket Club, deplore your cable. We deprecate your opinion that there has been unsportsmanlike play . . .' it began. That too also went to the been unsportsmanlike play . . .' it began. That too also went to the newspapers, with the result that, even before the end of the third Test, a war of words had begun. In Britain, the *Star* told its readers about 'the cheapest possible insults [which] are daily levelled at Jardine and the English team'. The *Daily Herald* opined that the Australians' cable was just an example of 'undignified snivelling'; while *The Times* contented itself with the comment that it was quite 'unthinkable' for Jardine to countenance anything that 'was not cricket'.

Unwittingly, the Australians had touched a raw nerve; and as the remaining two matches dragged on at Brisbane and Sydney (England won both, with margins of six and eight wickets respectively, to take the series – and the Ashes – by four matches to one) and cables continued to fly backwards and forwards across the world, in England serious questions were being asked. Not for the first time, cricket had become a metaphor, and the cricket field a microcosmic model of society. Before the war, *The Times* would have been quite right; it would have been 'unthinkable' for an English cricket team to do anything other than 'Play the Game'. Now, though, the issues were more blurred.

On the face of it Jardine and his team were 'gentlemen'. Many had, like Allen and D.R.J. himself, been to public schools; and all, it seems, still honestly believed that they were doing nothing to compromise the old Corinthian traditions of the game. In their own statement, issued in Adelaide at the end of the third Test, they had written that they were, and always had been, 'utterly loyal to their captain, under whose leadership they hope to achieve *an honourable victory*' [my italics]. Even now, there seems no reason to doubt the sincerity of those words. For if the notion of honour and even the connotations attached to the word 'cricket' have become rather tarnished in the intervening sixty years, in the early 1930s they still had some value.

That Jardine and his team did play close to the limits is self-evident – but also ultimately unimportant. What is far more relevant is the fact that they were touring Australia as 'sporting ambassadors', the representatives of the MCC; and as Laurence Le Quesne has pointed out in his study of the whole bodyline controversy, in the early 1930s the MCC was still one of the central pillars of the English Establishment. At the time of the 1932–33 tour its Main Committee 'included half a dozen members of the peerage and four other titled gentlemen – a Speaker of the House of Commons, a Chairman of the Unionist party and ex-Governor of Bengal, a Cabinet minister and a Lord Mayor of London.'[8]

In this respect the MCC touring party really were playing for England. But it was a very different England from the one for which players such as Warner and Fry had been batting little more than a quarter of a century previously. We have already seen something of the fundamental social changes which had come about in the immediate aftermath of the Great War. Not all of them were directly attributable to it, of course; but the division in the ranks of the 1932–33 touring party, exemplified by the differences between Allen and Jardine on the one hand and the more fundamental class split between them and 'the boys' on the other, only served to highlight the more fundamental divisions coming to the fore in English society.

Les Ames, Jardine's vice-captain, was later to give a trivial but illuminating example of the ways in which this fragmentation manifested itself in Australia. In an interview with E. W. Swanton he recalled that Jardine had said to him: 'Leslie, you know as well as I do that our chance of winning this series depends on Larwood and Voce, and that they're both very fond of their beer. Well, I want you to see that they go quietly before and during the Tests.' Ames did his best, whilst realizing that he was hardly qualified for the job: 'The trouble was that what was nothing to them was too much for me.'[9]

It was not just that Gubby Allen was a polished, sophisticated Old Etonian, very much a gentleman of the old school, while Harold Larwood was the beer-swilling son of a coal miner. Rather it was the fact that they were now together in the same team, apt if uneasy ambassadors for a country which was then attempting to accustom itself to just the same social mix. (And a team which was equally aptly, if ineptly, captained by a man whose response to change was a chilling retreat to the absolutes and certainties of an ancien régime.) By 1932 two Labour governments had come and gone – they in themselves had set alarm bells ringing – but Ramsay MacDonald remained Prime Minister, albeit at the head of a National administration. Good middle-class boys were still being inculcated with the belief that 'Mr Ramsay Mac', was no better than that arch-fiend

'Boney' – in Peter Vansittart's family it was even said that he 'was liable to be hanged, very properly'[10] but it was clear that he and his kind were there to stay.

At the same time, the General Strike of the early summer of 1926 was still a vivid memory. Then, it seemed, there was everything still to play for. The Allens and Jardines of the time had by and large been unswerving in their loyalty to Stanley Baldwin and the then Conservative government's attempt to cow the real-life Larwoods, the coal miners whose strike had precipitated events. All but about fifty of the undergraduates at Oxford University had rallied round and enthusiastically volunteered to drive ambulances and buses or act as special constables. Nevertheless, the fact that the strike had happened at all and that a rump of young men who 'should have known better' had actually supported the strikers only stiffened the resolve of the upper echelons as they sought to maintain control and preserve a traditional hegemony.

Most of the student activists had acted, like the young W. H. Auden (then up at Oxford and one of the 'Oxford 50'), 'out of sheer contrariness'; but retribution was swift, and their acts of 'class betrayal' punished with Jardinean peremptoriness. Auden, for instance, had been driving a car for the TUC, ferrying trades union leaders around London. Once, he wrote in *Forewords and Afterwords*, he took R. H. Tawney to his house in Mecklenburgh Square, Bloomsbury. Then, since:

> a first cousin of mine, married to a stockbroker, lived a few doors away [. . .] I paid a call. The three of us were just sitting down to lunch when her husband asked me if I had come up to London to be a Special Constable. 'No,' I said, 'I am driving a car for the TUC.' Whereupon, to my utter astonishment, he ordered me to leave the house.[11]

Back in Britain in the early spring of 1933 attempting to preserve a convenient status quo was thus absorbing the greater part of the still-considerable energies of the Establishment, and all the more so since by then it seemed to have become something of a rear-guard action. For if accounts of the rackety antipodean progress of the England cricket team were filling the back pages of mass-market newspapers, those who were privileged enough to be on the inside track found themselves confronted by a problem which was potentially of immensely greater importance.

Quite simply, it looked as if David was going off the rails. Blond, blue-eyed, charming and above all approachable, the Prince of Wales had made a very favourable impression on London society when he began what was to turn out to be a life-long association with the rich and famous during the summer on 1914. Now though, he appeared to be displaying alarming new tendencies. There were rumours – *'I've danced with a man who's danced with a girl who's danced with the Prince of Wales'* – and although they had been circulating for the best part of a decade they *were* only rumours; but as his father, King George V grew noticeably weaker, they began to proliferate.

My dear, you'll never guess, but I gather he's been singing the 'Red Flag' with some dreadful Welsh miners! . . . Rum sort of lad . . . Last I heard, there'd been some sort of private chinwag with that Ramsay Mac . . . Fellow's young . . . Remember those frightful shoes he used to wear . . . It's all that woman's doing, you mark my words – Mrs Dudley Ward indeed! . . . Still, cave, cave, keep it under your hat, know what I mean? No real problem yet-awhile . . . Wild oats . . .

There was undoubtedly an element of truth in all this. David[12] had been acting in a manner quite unlike that of any previous Prince of Wales. There were certainly only fleeting similarities – a shared fondness for women, gambling and the high-life – between his behaviour in the late 1920s and early 1930s and the more concentrated dissoluteness of his predecessor in the early Marlborough House days almost half a century previously. And to the Establishment, then still chiefly composed of John Betjeman's 'Old men who never cheated, never doubted,/Communicated monthly' and their likes, his open flaunting of convention – appearing in public without a hat, wearing suede shoes, and his brazen, *brazen!* squiring of the vivacious Mrs Dudley Ward – was if anything even worse than his grandfather's comparatively discreet philandering. As early as 1929 Captain (later Sir Alan) Lascelles had left David's staff because he could simply stand no more of him, preferring King George V, to whom he was later appointed Assistant Secretary, and his more ordered ménage. (The mutual antipathy between an unrepentant David and the cultivated, ultra-Establishment Lascelles, however, lingered on: in her biography, *Edward VIII* Frances Donaldson notes that even 'in the later years of his life when the Duke of Windsor spoke of Sir Alan Lascelles, he made the name sound like a whip'.)

Times had changed. In an otherwise remarkably prescient address to the House of Commons shortly after the Prince's birth in June 1894, the Labour MP Keir Hardie had recalled King Edward VII's early life and predicted that 'from childhood, this boy will be surrounded by sycophants and flatterers and will be taught to believe himself of superior creation. A line will be drawn between him and the people he might be called upon to rule.'[13] If only that had been the case! Lascelles and his likes might have been forgiven for thinking. Unfortunately for them, however, things had turned out rather differently, and from an early age David had embodied the free spirit of the new, post-Victorian century.

Mindful of his father's isolated redundancy in the long years until he ascended the throne at the age of sixty, even the normally dull and conventional King George V (at that time the Duke of York) had been at some pains to give his eldest son what then passed for a 'normal' education. No 'line' was drawn to prevent David's meeting ordinary (though naturally well-born) children of his own age, for instance. At the age of twelve he had even been sent as a cadet to the Osborne Naval College – from which he was to progress a few years later to the Royal Naval College at Dartmouth and then, albeit for a rather unsatisfactory eight terms, to Magdelen College, Oxford.

'If my association with the village boys at Sandringham and the cadets of the Naval Colleges had done anything for me, it was to make me desperately anxious to be treated exactly like any other boy of my age,' David was later to write.[14] That of course was not entirely possible. We have already seen that the concept of duty was early on instilled into him. Now he was reminded of it with a vengeance, for in 1910 the newly-crowned George V abruptly reverted to type and instructed his sixteen-year-old son to 'remember to conduct yourself at all times with dignity and set a good example to others. You must be obedient and respectful and kind to everyone.'[15]

Those are not the words which any teenager cares to hear, least of all one who has tasted a kind of freedom; and David duly rebelled. As the twenty-year-old Prince of Wales, he furiously scribbled in his diary about how bored and angry he had been during the State visit of the King and Queen of Denmark in 1914:

> We stood about in the picture gallery till 11.15 talking to the guests
> ... What rot & a waste of time, money & energy all these State
> visits are!! This is my only remark on all this unreal show &
> ceremony!![16]

Although he might not have realized it then, in later life David
concluded that, despite everything, he remained 'a man brought up in
a special way, as a Prince trained in the manners and maxims of the
nineteenth century for a life that had all but disappeared by the end of
his youth'.[17] And if there was one occurrence which more than anything else both put an end to that life and showed up its essential
falsity, it was of course the war.

'In the normal course of events I would have enlisted and been sent
overseas, where, in all probability, I should have been killed or certainly wounded within a year,' David wrote[18] with an honesty and
candour which makes his account of the Great War and its immediate
aftermath the most compelling and revealing section of his extraordinary autobiography, *A King's Story*. In the special circumstances
which applied to him, however, there was no normal course of events
and he had to put up with the next best thing.

He was allowed to go to France, but only after the King and Lord
Kitchener had decided that he would never see front-line action. He
served with the headquarters staff in the Guards Division – 'I knew
most of the officers: from childhood dancing classes, from Oxford,
from country house shooting parties, from hunting, and from the
West End' – but on at least one occasion he managed to get himself
up to the trenches and see for himself.

It was to prove a shattering experience (his chauffeur was killed by
flying shrapnel) and, taken together with his experience of the relative
informality of the headquarters regime, it was to have a profound
effect on the rest of his life. In this, of course, he was hardly unique.
But for the adjective 'Royal' in its first sentence, the following passage
– again taken from *A King's Story* – could have been written by
Oswald Mosley or virtually any other survivor of the Great War. As
things were to turn out, however, it remains of crucial importance in
understanding David's subsequent actions:

> More than being a mere product of my Royal upbringing, I was also a
> product of the war, with ideas of my own, a little on the cynical side
> maybe, but sure that I knew the answers. My father, on the other

hand, was wholly steeped in the Victorian and Edwardian traditions that had been the order under which he had lived the best and most vigorous years of his life.[19]

That was undoubtedly true for – as the more outspoken members of the Establishment were quick to point out – the comparison between father and son could hardly have been more marked. Even David could see that King George (and indeed his consort, Queen Mary):

> had the Victorian's sense of probity, moral responsibility and love of domesticity. He believed in God, in the invincibility of the Royal Navy, and the essential rightness of whatever was British [. . .] He disapproved of Soviet Russia, painted fingernails, women who smoked in public, cocktails, frivolous hats, American jazz, and the growing habit of going away for weekends.[20]

As if that was not enough, he also retired to bed at precisely 11.10pm every evening. On the other hand, David 'believed, among other things, in private enterprise, a strong Navy, the long week-end, a balanced budget [and was sure that] the failure of the free play of the market brought distress to the working classes [and] impeded the rational development of housing.'[21]

It is difficult now to assess whether it was merely this revolutionary, pseudo-socialist, even Keynesian attitude which excited his critics, or whether there were shades of Grundyism behind it all. For it has to be said that budgetary propriety and the maintenance of the gold standard were hardly uppermost in David's mind at this time. As he also admitted, throughout the twenties and early thirties he (and of course Mrs Dudley Ward) had almost nightly 'recourse to one or another of the gay nightclubs, which had by then become fashionable and almost respectable. There were the Café de Paris, Ciro's, the Kit-Kat Club, and the one I went to most, the Embassy Club in Old Bond Street [. . .] a brightly lit, expensive, and altogether respectable, even staid, restaurant with an elegant international clientele.'[22]

It is easy to imagine that for virtually the whole of the 1920s David did little, and went hardly anywhere else. Picking up on the sniffy disapproval of sections of the Establishment at the time, many of his modern-day detractors have concluded as much. But to do so is to be overly harsh on a man who at least tried to come to terms with the times through which he was living. He was undoubtedly right when he later observed that the decade immediately following the Great War was 'the last time in this tortured century that a man could enjoy himself in good conscience; the last time that Princes could circulate easily and without embarrassment through all levels of society'. Even then – only then, perhaps – he knew which way the wind was blowing. There had been an occasion when, shortly after the Armistice, David and his younger brother, the new Duke of York (and later King George VI) had accompanied the King to a parade of some 15,000 disabled soldiers at Hyde Park in London. And although David's account (based on diary notes) was not written up until thirty years later, it still reveals an unexpectedly sharp appreciation of the mood of the times:

The men, all in plain clothes, were drawn up in divisional formation. At first glance everything appeared in order, the men at attention, the bands playing, and so forth. Most of the men wore on their lapels the 'Silver Badge', signifying their honourable discharge for wounds or other disabilities. But there was something in the air, a sullen unresponsiveness all three of us felt instinctively. My father, steady as a rock, rode down the front line. Suddenly there was a commotion at the rear; and, as if by a prearranged signal, hitherto concealed banners with slogans were defiantly unfurled. With cries of 'Where is this land fit for heroes?' – a hurling back of Lloyd George's famous election slogan – the men broke ranks and made straight for the King, who was cut off from me and my brother by a solid mass. For a moment I feared he would be borne to the ground. Then I saw, with relief, that those who were closest were only trying to shake his hand [. . .]

Fortunately the police were able to extricate us, but the mob was still milling around in the Park as we rode back to the Palace. After my father dismounted, he looked at me, remarking, 'Those men were in a funny temper.' And shaking his head, as if to rid himself of an unpleasant memory, he strode indoors.

For a while the exact meaning of all this turmoil puzzled those at the Palace; isolated as they were to some extent from the harsh impact of events by the protecting cushion of Cabinet Ministers, much that was then going on seemed remote and unreal. This and other episodes could be conveniently explained away as the unfortunate, but probably inevitable, result of the post-war let-down that the natural good sense of the British people would presently bring under control. *But I had seen enough to convince myself that the trouble went far deeper, that the social unrest was related to the slaughter and misery that the first 'people's war' had inflicted upon the whole population.*[23]

To the almost audible irritation of his detractors, David really did have a social conscience. It might have been naïve – he was undoubtedly a 'middle-brow', untroubled by intellect – but it was there all the same. And all the evidence suggests that he does seem to have felt a real and almost mystical communion with the tens of thousands of returning ex-servicemen. It was this which antagonized the Establishment and led to his impatience with it – specifically (as he was later to recall) with the 'authority of the law, of the church, of the monarch to a certain extent. And universities and maybe the top brass of the army and navy.'[24] Although this is again naïve, and a very simplistic, personalized view of exactly who composed the Establishment – as Lady Donaldson has pointed out, it takes no account of the City, the Civil Service or, crucially, the 'old boy network' which linked it all together – it still identifies a formidable list of opponents. For even if someone like Alan Lascelles could reasonably have been described as a Liberal, the vested interests of the majority of his more dyed-in-the-wool coevals would have prevented their going very far out of their way to bring about that 'land fit for heroes to live in'.

David, on the other hand, was quite literally prepared to go to inordinate lengths to see fair play:

> Many an evening I slipped down to the East End to look in on one or more [newly-established college or public-school missions] where I mingled with the boys, watched them boxing, or joined them in a game of darts. And it was from the dedicated men who had given up lives of leisure to run these places that I learned most about the poor.[25]

More publicly, in 1928 he had also become Patron of the National Council for Social Service and immersed himself in its work for the unemployed. Unexceptional and indeed expected though such social concern is today on the part of a member of the Royal family, in the early 1930s even David's frequent tours of unemployment black-spots in Scotland, Wales and the north of England drew ambivalent comments. When he paid a three-day visit to north Wales in May 1934 *The Times*'s anonymous correspondent was not alone in explicitly stating that things had come to a pretty pass. Dutifully dogging the Royal progress he described how, from Caernarvon, David had been driven to Rhosgadhan nominally to see the new village hall and social centre, which the unemployed men have built almost unaided [. . .] The quarries here are on Crown lands and are exploited by a company normally employing 500 men; only 80 are now drawing wages.

It was really a relief to get back to the colour and movement of the brilliant scene awaiting in the courtyard of Caernarvon Castle. Mr Lloyd George received the Prince at the foot of the steps leading to the main entrance . . .[26]

It would be interesting now to know why the journalist wrote that the visit to Rhosgadhan was only 'nominally' in order that David might see the new village hall; what other, underlying purpose could there have been? By the same token, it seems unlikely that David, with his professed impatience with pomp and ceremony, would have found it 'really a relief' to get back to Caernarvon Castle. The words say it all, particularly since they appeared in *The Times* – 'the Thunderer' – then among the most august bastions of the Establishment.

Indeed, reading them today, let alone his own account of events, one is tempted to have sympathy for David; to accept that he was indeed 'the boy Prince', unversed in the ways of the world despite being a well-travelled, superficially-sophisticated man of forty. But to do so is to fall into one of the deepest man-traps of historical and biographical analysis. For, despite their various spats, it is clear that essentially David and the Establishment were always on the same side. He was over-idealistic in his interpretation of his role; but only in the same way that they were over-reactionary in their expectations of him. He was after all second only to his father, the King, as a living symbol of the Establishment. They needed him just as much as he needed them – and, at least in the pre-Mrs Simpson days, neither he nor they was as stupid as to forget that for a second.

David was back in Wales two years later, in 1936, this time to see for himself the even grimmer conditions at Ebbw Vale. Not unnaturally, they affected him deeply, and he demanded, suggested or merely hinted (interpretations vary) that 'something must be done'. As always, his words were widely reported; and once more the Establishment's eyebrows were raised – 'certain Government circles were not pleased' – but this time needlessly so.

David himself was later to comment that on this occasion he was to all intents and purposes misquoted. Although his words were taken to mean that 'the Government had neglected to do all that it might have done', he wrote in *A King's Story*, that was not what he intended to say at all. Rather, he was calling for the introduction of some scheme which would 'repair the ravages of the dreadful inertia that had gripped the region'. In retrospect the semantics are unimportant. Indeed the imperative tone of his original words – *'Something must be done!'* – and what even he said they meant amount to virtually the same thing: the siren-call and elixir of the thirties Establishment. It too is best expressed by imperatives, for they most closely embody the desperate sloganizing of the time: *Galvanize that inertia! . . . Hard work! . . . Discipline! . . .*

Sadly, it was true that, like many of the Establishment he so derided, David still valued a society in which the trains ran on time. Chats with 'Mr Ramsay Mac' and darts matches with the boys of Whitechapel were one thing; but as he very well knew, on another level he was fighting for his very existence.

In July 1919 his 'Uncle Nicky', the Russian Tsar Nicholas II and the whole of his immediate family had been shot by the Bolsheviks in a cellar at Ekaterinberg. Nor was that an isolated family tragedy. During the reign of David's father King George V (1910–35) no less than five Emperors, eight Kings and eighteen ruling dynasties were killed, deposed or otherwise disposed of. Though probably sincere, in the final analysis David's simplistic 'socialism' amounted to no more than self-interested trimming. If he occasionally got the balance wrong, the equally self-interested members of the Establishment would have been reassured by his considered response to the General Strike:

> What was unique about the strike of 1926 was the reaction of the upper and middle classes. They regarded it as a blow aimed at the constitutional foundations of English life. In response to the Government's appeal thousands left their business desks and their suburban homes or emerged from their landed estates, their clubs and their leisure, determined to restore the essential services of the nation. The people I knew felt they were putting down something that was terribly wrong, something contrary to British traditions. And they put on a first-class show.[27]

Something had to be done indeed! Although ironically it is the actions of the likes of W. H. Auden and the Oxbridge supporters of the 1926 strikers which have retrospectively received most attention, it can now be seen that within the Establishment both that crisis and the more general postwar drift towards egalitarian socialism were also polarizing attitudes. Not for the only time, David was quite wrong when he wrote in 1951 that the General Strike had been 'a dangerous social crisis [which] had been overcome in the traditional English way, without bloodshed or reprisals and leaving no lasting scars'.[28] Such complacency did not survive the 1930s; then, like C. B. Fry and Douglas Jardine, even David was forced to come clean. And by the end of the decade it had become abundantly clear what his 'something' was.

CHAPTER EIGHT

'Cut is the Branch . . .'

'Unless you lived through it, Peter, you cannot understand.'
'Oh, I lived through it, Anthony,' I said, suddenly angry. 'I know more about the thirties
probably than you will ever know. I remember my father driving himself mad with drink, because
he couldn't get a job. I remember losing my education, my world, everything. I know all about the
thirties . . .'

— Peter Wright, interrogating Anthony Blunt, *Spycatcher*, 1987

Towards their end at any rate, the 1930s probably were – as W. H. Auden famously described them – 'a low dishonest decade'. Certainly, as that decade drew to its close there were a lot of weasel words and, at all levels of society, not a few weasels. With all the advantages of hindsight (an overall historical perspective, access to recently-released documents as well as to latterly-published diaries and letters) it appears that fudge, appeasement, 'accommodation' and duplicity were very much in the air.

At the time, however, things looked very much more simple. It wasn't just the 'Auden Set' and what was left of Bloomsbury which saw the country as standing virtually alone against the tide of Right-wing authoritarianism which had already engulfed Italy, Spain and Germany. British men had rushed to join the International Brigade formed by the Republican Popular Front in Spain after a military coup, lead by Francisco Franco in 1936 and subsequently backed by Italian troops and the German *Luftwaffe*, developed into full-scale civil war. Tales of their experiences there, such as George Orwell's *Homage to Catalonia* (first published in 1938) and Arthur Koestler's *Spanish Testament* (1937), as well as poems such as Auden's 'Spain' (1937) had been eagerly read and also done their bit to shift the popular political and moral climate a few degrees to the Left.

It has to be said, however, that as far as Britain was concerned the Spanish Civil War remained no place for gentlemen. It has been calculated that, out of the 2,762 Britons who volunteered for service on the 'Spanish front', more than eighty per cent were from working-class backgrounds.

It was true that, as volunteer ambulance-drivers, John Cornford and Julian Bell (a Cambridge Apostle) had rekindled something of the spirit of Julian Grenfell, Raymond Asquith and the 'lovely lads'. Going into battle, Cornford 'had a bandage round his head [. . .] and looked like Lord Byron'.[1] (He was killed during the battle for Brunette at the end of 1936, one day after his twenty-first birthday; Bell in 1937, aged twenty-nine.) But there was a certain phoniness about the socialism and/or communism which they and their likes peddled in the quads and streets of Cambridge; Bell had after all beagled seven days a fortnight throughout his time at King's. It was something which quickly struck the young Denis Healey who went up to Balliol College, Oxford in 1936, shortly after Cornford's death:

> Coming from a grammar school in Yorkshire, I found the element of romantic savagery in such middle-class young communists somewhat distasteful. Their Byronic posturing seemed to spring more from the need to sublimate some purely personal or class neurosis, than from the harsh realities which confronted the rest of us. I particularly resented their affectation of the glottal stop, which they regarded as essential to the proletarian image. 'Ours is a Par'y of a new type', they would say.[2]

Like Orwell's friend, the Left-wing Eton-and-Trinity baronet Sir Richard Rees who also drove ambulances – and, for that matter, like other Cambridge contemporaries such as Guy Burgess and Anthony Blunt – these middle-class communists are not yet part of this story. Far more important are a handful of very different individuals whom we have already encountered. We have seen that C. B. Fry brooded over the decade, by yet more hard work – radio broadcasts, endless articles and what we would now call personal appearances – having transformed himself into a faintly gung-ho paterfamilias of the soft Right. But even he, for all his self-aggrandizement, was no more than a minor irritant, a persistent burr scratching the side of public consciousness. Despite his ambitions to galvanize the Boy Scout movement, inject a new discipline into the Navy and ally Britain's children with the *Hitlerjugend*, he did not really matter. When all was said and done, he was yesterday's man. Oswald Mosley, on the other hand, wasn't; and in the 1930s Oswald Mosley *mattered*.

Leon Trotsky and the British Establishment seemed to have summed him up when they had respectively concluded that he was an 'aristocratic coxcomb' who had joined the Labour party in 1924 as a calculated act of 'class betrayal', or in the words of Lady St Aubrey in Amabel Williams-Ellis's novel *The Wall of Glass* (1927) because 'he thought there would be less competition'.[3] Within a few years, however, both judgements had been overtaken by events.

Mosley had risen fast, initially within – but for all but a few months of the 1930s outside – the Labour party, and quickly proved (to those who did not know already) that he was far from being a mere coxcomb, and was motivated by instincts which had little or nothing to do with class betrayal. Indeed, it would be possible to argue that such 'treachery' was always anathema to him.

Abandoning his previous position as candidate for Harrow, back in the spring of 1924 he had let it be known that he was interested in re-entering Parliament for another constituency. The Labour party selection committee in the Birmingham district of Ladywood swiftly asked him to be theirs, and within six months the fall of Ramsay MacDonald's first Labour government (on 8 October) gave him his chance. Mosley did not win the seat when the votes were counted after the general election three weeks later; but the fact that he lost by a margin of only seventy-seven (and that after a recount; initially he was judged to have won with a majority of two) even though he was standing against Neville Chamberlain, a member of the dynasty which had held Birmingham as a family fiefdom for the previous half-century as well as a nationally-known politician, gave him a certain Pyrrhic triumph.

Not unduly disheartened then, Mosley watched from the sidelines as Stanley Baldwin formed his first administration, and prepared himself for the call – acquiring during the late 1920s an encyclopaedic knowledge of economic reality. Robert Skidelsky has written that 'by 1930 he had a firmer grasp of what needed to be done than any other politician in Britain';[4] while Lady Mosley (who first got to know him at around this time) says that 'one cannot sufficiently emphasize how hard he worked'.[5] He might have been out of office, away from the green leather benches of power and influence in the House of Commons, but these were crucial years.

In fact he was not out of office for long. In December 1926 there was a by-election in the neighbouring constituency of Smethwick.

Mosley was selected as the Labour candidate and, after an acrimonious campaign, won the seat with a majority of 6,582. Back in Parliament at the beginning of 1927, he quickly hit his stride. For the first time, perhaps, all the elements of his personality came together. As he saw it, he now 'had complete confidence in [his] own capacity to solve any problem confronting the nation'[6] and, of course, still retained that wider, deeper sense of Messianic mission we have already noticed.

Others, however, remained determinedly unimpressed. Within five months of Mosley's return to Westminster, Leslie Hore-Belisha was none-too-privately grinding his teeth:

> Dark, aquiline, flashing; tall, thin, assured; defiance in his eye, contempt in his forward chin, [Mosley's] features are cast in a mould of disdain. His very smile is a shrug. His voice is pitched in a tragedian's key. His sentences are trailed away. He is the only man in the House of Commons who has made an Art of himself.[7]

As Skidelsky comments, Mosley would have taken that as 'high praise'. Physically and intellectually, both inside and outside Parliament, he was simply impossible to ignore, as his friend Ramsay MacDonald – once again Prime Minister – realized. He had toyed with the idea of making Mosley Foreign Secretary (almost unprecedented promotion for someone with no ministerial experience) but when his administration was announced the Honourable Member for Smethwick was confirmed in the more junior post of Chancellor of the Duchy of Lancaster. He was in the Government – outside the Cabinet, it was true, but with an office and staff of his own at the Treasury.

Initially, Mosley flung himself into his new job, immersing himself in the minutiae of pensions plans and public works, and within a year had emerged as what amounted to 'Minister for Unemployment'. It was, he knew, a key position. He was at the sharp end of policy-making in a Government which could still, however reluctantly, however belatedly, have brought about the postwar equity in which he still believed. But somehow, with the likes of MacDonald and Thomas at the helm, it kept getting blown off course. Nothing was *happening!* Within hardly more than a year Mosley had become frustrated, if not downright bored, by the processes of bureaucracy. He had all the answers, but no one was prepared to listen: 'In government I was met with urgent and menacing facts in which theory availed me little [he wrote. I had to act, and quickly, yet to retain my sense of direction and final objective.'[8]

It is easy – all too easy – now to make mountains out of what Mosley meant by that reference to his 'final objective'; his own displacement of MacDonald, authoritarian rule, dictatorial powers, world domination . . . all these have been advanced or implicitly suggested by his detractors. (Mosley himself was later to comment that 'modern biography delights to deal in trivial scandal rather than large events'.) Yet an analysis of the facts, rather than a reliance on his latterly-gained and even-more-latterly talked-up reputation as a divisive, fascist rabble-rouser, provides an alternative interpretation.

During the 1929 Christmas recess, on his own initiative Mosley had written a long paper (the so-called 'Mosley Memorandum') in which, as well as describing what he perceived to be the Government's failings, he went on to advocate future policy in fields such as economic reconstruction, employment and finance and credit policy. Explicitly calling for State intervention, it was respectfully read but then summarily dismissed by the mandarins of Whitehall. Nor were MacDonald and the majority of the Cabinet impressed. In particular Philip Snowden, the Chancellor of the Exchequer cavilled at its demand for £200 million, a sum which Mosley believed would give work to 300,000 men for up to three years.

Depressed and still further disheartened by his colleagues' lack of imagination and will, Mosely took the only course open to him. On 20 May 1930 he resigned from the Government, intent on putting his plans for national recovery before a wider audience. For although the Memorandum failed to galvanize the elder statesmen of Cabinet, it had been enthusiastically received by sections of the Press. A younger generation of politicians was also won over. Ostensibly unlikely allies such as Harold Macmillan, Robert Boothby, Sir Archibald Sinclair and even Leslie Hore-Belisha united in admiration both of Mosley himself and his ideas. Harold Nicolson remembered hearing Macmillan (then out of Parliament) forecast the election of a Mosley government – in which, naturally enough, Macmillan himself would be offered a seat in the Cabinet.[9]

Although in retrospect there is a certain irony in the degree of support which Mosley attracted from young turks such as these in both the Liberal and Conservative parties, it is also of vital significance. It again demonstrates the degree to which, throughout his life,

Sir Oswald was the mouthpiece of his class and generation. Macmillan's prophecy was less than accurate; but the Eton-educated gentleman and future prime minister had also served as a Captain in the Great War and been as shaken as Mosley by his experiences in France. Instinctively he felt himself to be on the same side, fighting in a battle at once bigger and more important than the superficial squabbling of the House of Commons. It was the same with Boothby (another old Etonian) who described Mosley as 'the first of my generation to strike a blow against the old men who have for so long battened themselves and their obsolete *laissez-faire* on the body politic'.

Freed from the obligations of office, it was with these coevals that Mosley now began to ally himself. A back-bencher once more, he was still, however, a member of the Parliamentary Labour party – although it very soon became apparent that even that was a position which was very rapidly becoming untenable. As early as January 1930 his father-in-law, Lord Curzon had been heard saying that Mosley was 'anxious to leave the Labour party and reconcile himself with his old friends'.[10]

The break finally came something more than a year later. After the publication of another of his prophet-in-the-wilderness calls to arms (this time entitled the 'Mosley Manifesto') Mosley was unceremoniously expelled from the Labour party for 'gross disloyalty' on 10 March 1931. It was a pre-emptive strike on the part of the party bosses, and made in the nick of time since it had become known that Mosley, Cimmie (who, preferring to be known as plain Mrs Mosley, sat as the Labour Member for Stoke-on-Trent) and half a dozen other disaffected PLP back-benchers had already decided to resign the party whip. Over the previous month, indeed, all but Mosley – then inconveniently bed-ridden with what turned out to be pleurisy – had actually got round to doing so.

Suddenly, there was neither need nor excuse for them to continue in the Labour party. During the previous December the motor-magnate Sir William Morris (later Lord Nuffield) had read Mosley's Manifesto, seen in it a way for Britain to climb out of its 'slough of despond' and promptly given its Hero-author a cheque for £50,000. It was a gesture of faith; the money was to be used to establish a new political party, the New Party, which – with Mosley significantly cast as its '*real* leader' (my italics) – would fight for the implementation of the Manifesto's proposals.

Punch was not entirely alone in divining which way the wind was blowing. With remarkable prescience, in December 1930 it had published a cartoon entitled 'Moslini'. It showed a uniformed, strutting *Duce*, and beside him a formally-dressed Mosley rather incongruously carrying a trade union style banner bearing the words: 'THE MOSLEY MANIFESTO. WANTED: A NATIONAL CABINET OF FIVE'. Beneath it, the caption read: 'The Duce (*to Sir Oswald Mosley*): "*Five* dictators! Why worry about the other four?"' [11]

Oswald Mosley was never a dictator; nor did he ever intend to become one. As at every other crossroads in his career, his emergence as leader of the New Party and subsequently of its direct descendant, the British Union of Fascists, was largely a matter of his having been in the right place at the right time. For if he hadn't been there, someone else would; and the restrospective opprobrium to which he has been subjected should not blind us to the fact that, in many ways in Britain at least he has been made the scapegoat of a generation. He dared to go further, to say what others were merely thinking; and he paid the price. (Characteristically too, he took it like a man, standing by what he said and listening courteously to the views of political and ideological opponents until the very end of his life. Would he have let me interview him? I asked Lady Mosley in 1989. 'Oh yes, very definitely,' she said. 'He would debate with anyone. He would have enjoyed it.') [12]

We have already noticed the development of a general identification with the State (and hence their own wellbeing) among the British upper and middle classes in the years immediately following the Great War. Implicit too in C. B. Fry's proselytizing on behalf of Hitler's Germany in the early 1930s was the idea that this was in no way an isolated British phenomenon. Indeed, a xenophobic concern with national identity and the restoration of central authority was shared by members of the *haute bourgeoisie* right across Europe. Coming to terms with the peace, they felt as threatened by its attendant spectres of economic depression, inflation, social unrest, communism and even revolution as they had been, for rather different reasons, by the war.

In Italy it was the upper and middle classes who were the first to rally round the axe-and-rods symbol of Mussolini's *Fascisti* – and that, tellingly, as early as 1919. They were to remain the *Duce*'s most faithful supporters for the next quarter of a century. Similarly in

Spain, despite Primo de Rivera's original plans for a specific mobilization of the working classes, under Franco the Falange found its true
constituency among the bourgeosie, as for that matter did the Ro-
manian Iron Guard movement. In Germany too, as the Berlin stories
of Christopher Isherwood and the letters and writings of many other
eye-witnesses make clear, it was the respectable middle class's complacency and nostalgic yearning for a return to the days of Bismarck's
Second Reich, rather than the later rabble-rousing of the Brownshirts
(*Sturmabteilung*) or the choreographed hysteria of the *Hitlerjugend*,
which paved the way for Nazism. In *Mein Kampf* (1923) Hitler had
after all held out the prospect of something very close to Lloyd
George's 'land fit for heroes to live in' when he eulogized the Second
Reich as 'a Reich [that] was born for the sons and grandsons – a
reward for immortal heroism'.

Isherwood was there; he saw it happen. And in the closing pages of
his second *Berlin Diary* (covering the winter of 1932–33) which itself
concludes his book *Goodbye to Berlin*, he described how his landlady,
'Fräulein Schroeder' had been sucked into the madness, almost in
spite of herself:

> Poor Frl. Schroeder is inconsolable: 'I shall never find another
> gentleman like you, Herr Issyvoo – always so punctual with the rent
> . . . I'm sure I don't know what makes you want to leave Berlin, all of
> a sudden, like this . . .'
> It's no use trying to explain to her, or talking politics. Already she is
> adapting herself, as she will adapt herself to every new régime. This
> morning I even heard her talking reverently about 'Der Führer' to the
> porter's wife. If anybody were to remind her that, at the elections last
> November, she voted communist, she would probably deny it hotly,
> and in perfect good faith. She is merely acclimatizing herself, in
> accordance with a natural law, like an animal which changes its coat
> for the winter. Thousands of people like Frl. Schroeder are acclimatizing
> themselves.[13]

Of course the *Sturmabteilung* were there – Isherwood had seen them in
action too – but in Germany as elsewhere, and especially in Britain,
fascism grew in the rich mulch of fading gentility, frustration and
disappointed ideals which underlay the superficial optimism of the
1920s. Thus when Oswald Mosley began specifically articulating the
vague sentiments which were already preoccupying the thoughts of a
generation he found few among those whom, in the broadest sense,

1. *The Bad Old Days*: two oppidans brawl on the staircase
to the Upper School at Eton in the days before Dr
Arnold, the Earl of Clarendon and a host of other
reformers transformed the public schools into more
seemly breeding-grounds for 'gentlemen'.

2. *A New Start*: the spacious quadrangle at Christ's Hospital School (1902) – big enough for even the most elaborate O.T.C. parades.

3. '*A Most Superior Person*': the lofty, patrician disdain of George Nathaniel Curzon is well caught in a caricature by Harry Furniss.

4. *One of Us?*: Grey-bearded and rotund, an elderly W. G. Grace at the crease for the benefit of the camera.

5. *Letting the Side Down*: Horatio Bottomley MP (second left) arrives at Bow Street Police Court on the first day of his trial.

6. *Fathers and Families I*: even when it was painted, John Singer Sargent's portrait of Lord Ribblesdale (1902) celebrated the fast-disappearing 'Victorian' notion of the English gentleman.

7. *Fathers and Families II*: Pensive and preoccupied, the 25-year-old Raymond Asquith was already casting around for a useful role when this family snap was taken in 1903.

8. *Fathers and Families III*: Julian Grenfell was the only member of the coterie who really adapted to service life. This photograph was taken shortly before his death in 1915. Note the DSO ribbon on his uniform.

9. *Famous British Writers I*: R. C. Sherriff, the author of *Journey's End* (1928), was one of the several ex-officers featured in a series of Wills's cigarette cards issued in the 1930s.

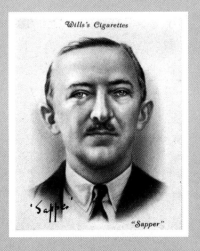

10. *Famous British Writers II*: 'Sapper' (Lt.-Col. Herman McNeile, MC). There was an inherent streak of fascism in Drummond and a strong physical resemblance between Sapper and the young Mosley.

11. *Waiting in the Wings I*: the young Oswald Mosley, son-in-law of Lord Curzon, poses in his office. Notice the fascist emblem on the windowsill behind him.

12. *Waiting in the Wings II*: Happier in uniform than cricketing whites, C. B. Fry admired both Hitler and Mussolini. But Britain resisted making him captain of a 'National XI'.

13. *The God that Failed*: Mosley marches with his supporters in 1936. The thugs who surrounded him in the East End were only the most public manifestation of the Mosleyite sympathies shared by members of every section of society.

14. *Building the Future*: Muffled against the cold of a partially-rebuilt Theatre Royal, Drury Lane, a weary Noël Coward watches rehearsals for *Pacific 1860* with designer Gladys Calthrop in 1946.

15. *This Happy Breed I*: The film star Leslie Howard became an unlikely but effective propagandist for the New Britain – in all probability he was killed by the Germans in 1943. This portrait was unfinished at the time of his death.

16. *This Happy Breed II*: Jobs for the boys ... ironically it was the Labour Party which benefitted most from Churchill's 'One Nation'. Posters featuring confident, classless faces such as this won them the 1945 General Election.

NO MORE DOLE QUEUES....SO IT'S

LABOUR

FOR SECURITY

VOTE LABOUR FOR SELF-RESPECTING JOBS

17. *This Happy Breed III*: Down-to-earth and working-class, the Stoke City, Blackpool and England footballer Stanley Matthews became a national hero in the late 1940s – and was knighted in 1965.

18. *Doing it Their Own Way I*: Not yet *personae non gratae*, Sir Bernard and Lady Docker pose with her son Lance Callingham in 1956.

19. *Doing it Their Own Way II*: Witty, good-looking, intelligent and well-connected, the Old Etonian Guy Burgess could, should and *would* have been among the heroes of his generation. Unfortunately, he backed the wrong side.

20. *Every Inch a Gentleman?*: If we must have spies, let them be like James Bond, an Old Etonian and an *Englishman* . . . Sean Connery as Bond in an early 1960s publicity shot.

Lord Curzon might have counted as 'his old friends' who could disagree with him – and fewer still who would.

In their hearts, no one who really *mattered* in the Britain of the early thirties – or perhaps more accurately no one who *thought* he really mattered in the Britain of the early thirties – would have felt anything other than the flutter of patriotic pride on reading the combative epitaph which Mosley composed shortly after the acrimonious but still unexpected collapse of the New Party in the autumn of 1931. Superficially, the tone is that of Henry V on St Crispin's day; but is there not also something of the arrogance of Coriolanus?

> Better the great adventure, better the great attempt for England's sake, better defeat, disaster, better far the end of that trivial thing called a political career, than stifling in a uniform of blue and gold, strutting and posturing on the stage of little England, amid the scenery of decadence, until history, in turning over an heroic page of the human story, writes of us the contemptuous postscript: 'These were the men to whom was entrusted the Empire of Great Britain, and whose idleness, ignorance and cowardice left it a Spain.' We shall win; or at least we shall return upon our shields.

In London drawing-rooms fine words still counted for something, and Mosley remained the hero of the hour. Nothing he did was wrong. Even before the formal establishment of the British Union of Fascists, his ur-fascism only mirrored the attitudes of his 'friends'. In polite society no one saw anything wrong or unnatural in his devotion to 'little England' and the greater Empire; quite the reverse. Throughout the first half of the 1930s, as Brian Masters has described,[14] the dining-rooms of Lady Astor, Lady Cunard, Lady Londonderry and that mesmeric hangover from Edwardian times, Mrs Ronnie Greville rang with impatient cries for the removal of the increasingly washed-out Prime Minister, Ramsay MacDonald. *Something must be done!* . . . Beneath the starched napery, the tables themselves became sounding-boards for fascism and the policies of Hitler. At least he was doing things, and from 1933 the successes of his National Socialist Germany along with the 'efficiency' of Mussolini's Italy were loudly championed.

There was nothing furtive or guilty about all this – why, David himself, the Prince of Wales, was reputed to be louder than most in his singing of the dictators' praises! In short, a whole section of the population was beginning to see Hitler and Mussolini as something like a pair of brisk, efficient public school housemasters administering national cold showers and the occasional caning on a this-hurts-me-more-than-you principle. Thus, given the continuing prevalence of that old Eton-England axis, supporting them from afar was almost a public duty, and actively courting the attentions of the 'square, breezy' German ambassador, Joachim von Ribbentrop no more than 'doing one's bit' for England and a new *entente cordiale*. Certainly his company was eagerly sought, as the American-born Henry 'Chips' Channon observed: 'In the midst of our talk Ribbentrop rang up, the arch-Hitler spy of Europe. Emerald [Cunard] flattered him for a few minutes and then asked him to join her at the Opera tomorrow.'[15]

Behind its sloganizing rhetoric, the communist *Daily Worker* was not so far off the mark when it told its readers that if they went to Mosley's big BUF rally at Olympia in June 1934 they would see 'hundreds of Rolls-Royces and fine cars – showing the class who want more fascist action against the workers – to maintain their dividends'.[16]

Up and down the country too, a Mosley-ite message was being preached in the most unlikely quarters. In his unambiguously-titled book *Hitler* (1931) Percy Wyndham Lewis had heaved ambivalent sighs over the 'hefty young street-fighting warriors' who would later bring the Führer to power. Elsewhere, Henry Williamson was attempting to deify (a not entirely unco-operative) T. E. Lawrence, by whose 'taken thought' Williamson had done the Biblically-impossible and 'added a cubit to his stature'. The island was full of noises; and in her novel *The Prime of Miss Jean Brodie* (published in 1961 but with the main action very firmly set in the Edinburgh of the early 1930s) Muriel Spark exactly caught the manner in which the authoritarian clamour quite naturally intruded into even the most banal of situations. Back at the Marcia Blaine Academy after the long vacation of 1931, Miss Brodie tells her girls:

> I have spent most of my summer holidays in Italy once more, and a week in London, and I have brought back a great many pictures which we can pin on the wall. Here is a Cimabue. Here is a larger formation of Mussolini's fascisti, it is a better view of them than that of last year's picture. They are doing splendid things as I shall tell you later. I went with my friends for an audience with the Pope. My friends kissed his ring but I thought it proper only to bend over it. I wore a long black

gown with a lace mantilla, and looked magnificent. In London my friends who are well-to-do – their small girl has two nurses, or nannies as they say in England – took me to visit A. A. Milne. In the hall was hung a reproduction of Botticelli's *Primavera* which means the Birth of Spring. I wore my silk dress with the large red poppies which is just right for my colouring. Mussolini is one of the greatest men in the world, far more so than Ramsay MacDonald, and his fascisti . . .[17]

A later, fictional example, perhaps – but vividly illustrative of the mood of the times in which Oswald Mosley, as he himself put it in his autobiography, decided to 'become a fascist'. Nor was Jean Brodie all that atypical; in 1937 Evelyn Waugh was to note that there always had been

a natural connection between the teaching profession and a taste for totalitarian government; prolonged association with the immature – fanatical urchins competing for caps and blazers of distinguishing colours – the dangerous pleasures of over-simple exposition, the scars of the endless losing battle for order and uniformity which rages in every class-room, dispose even the most independent minds to shirt-dipping and saluting.[18]

Quite how long this taste for totalitarianism and overt or covert admiration for Hitler in particular persisted is now difficult if not impossible to ascertain. Certainly, in books such as John Parker's *King of Fools* (1988) much has recently been made – though very little conclusively *proved* – of the Prince of Wales's allegedly long-lasting Nazi sympathies. Again, it is worth noting that when Rudolf Hess, who had been Hitler's deputy since 1933 and one of the chief architects of the *Führerprinzip*, parachuted into Scotland on 10 May 1941 he claimed that he had come to liaise with a pro-German peace movement and organize a *putsch* to oust Churchill and end the war. It is inconceivable that Churchill and the Government did not know of this – shortly after his capture Hess was interrogated by Lord Simon, the Lord Chancellor – but, significantly, although powers already existed for such a course of action, there was no wholesale round-up of pro-German 'peaceniks' in the summer of 1941 to compare with the '18B' corralling of known fascists in May 1940.

Conspiracy theorists would disagree, but it now seems likely that by mid 1941 – when the Blitz had finally revealed the true nature of

German intentions – Hess was deluding himself, and any pro-German sentiment had to all intents and purposes evaporated. (Ironically, however, it now appears that Lord Halifax, Foreign Secretary in Churchill's National government, was all along one of the last appeasers and unofficially suing for a negotiated peace as late as the summer of 1940.)

That such sentiment had existed, albeit among a small section of the population, and was still sincerely held less than five years previously is, however, incontestable. The recently-rediscovered membership book of the semi-secret Right Club more than bears this out. Its handwritten pages offer proof that even in the summer of 1939 businessmen, members of the aristocracy (most notably the Duke of Wellington) and other influential people were more than vaguely pro-German. More interestingly, so too were a dozen members of the House of Commons. The Right Club's membership lists for 1939 include the names of Captain Archibald Ramsay and three men who were close allies of the Government itself in 1940; Colonel Harold Mitchell, then a parliamentary private secretary, Major Sir Albert Edmondson and Colonel Charles Kerr (created Lord Teviot that year) who were both National coalition whips.

In the face of all this it is important to remember that before the war and even in the first half of 1939 merely becoming a fascist had only the vaguely-comic connotations of today becoming a Euro-Communist, say, or a genuine Social Democrat. Mosley did not see himself, and nor was he ever taken, as a predecessor of General Pinochet or Hendrik Verwoerd. Indeed, it cannot be overstated that until the final months of the 1930s, when the totalitarian excesses and blatant expansionism of Nazism had become apparent, fascism *per se* remained a perfectly respectable political creed to all but a hard core of communist and Jewish agitators. Had they but world enough, and time, the coyness of Boothby, Macmillan, Hore-Belisha and the remainder of Mosley's political friends might even have been overcome. As it was, Mosley was left to go it very much alone – and in attempting to formulate a specifically English version of what was essentially a peculiarly un-English philosophy, he made the crucial, but perhaps understandable, mistake of going too far, too fast. As we have seen, throughout the metamorphosis of the New Labour Group, first into the New Party and then the British Union of Fascists, he had enjoyed a considerable degree of both popular and behind-the-scenes, influential support. Standing as an (unsuccessful) New Party candidate in the General Election of 1931, he polled 10,543 votes, while the remaining twenty-two New Party hopefuls received an average of less than 1,100 votes apiece. Now though, as the New Party emerged in its true colours as the BUF ('We had to reform our organization, but not our policy')[19] that support began to ebb away.

On a high, intellectual level, Mosley's anti-semitism had something to do with it, and left a nasty taste in the mouth. But as the thirties progressed, his seeming ambivalence to what was seen to be happening in Germany and Italy became increasingly important. Was he or wasn't he pro-German? Above and beyond the grass-roots violence which his meetings and rallies increasingly attracted, the subtleties of his pro-European, anti-war stance got lost in a public mood of increasing belligerence. There was a dim realization that this was no time for 'clever Dicks'; a sense that Mosley had crossed an invisible line; a groundswell of feeling that somehow the erstwhile hero's aping of Mussolini and his failure to distance himself absolutely from Hitler and the territorial imperatives of Nazism was no longer appropriate – no longer, well, *English*.

In the very early 1930s even Cimmie had had doubts about her husband's plans for a 'mobilization of ex-servicemen for the achievements of peace'; while Harold Nicolson and some of the New Party stalwarts who were at least prepared to be BUF fellow-travellers – quite literally in so far as several of them joined Mosley on a fact-finding trip to Rome – were later to cavil at his fulsome praise of the *Duce*. 'The great Italian represents the first emergence of the modern man to power,' Mosley had written to the *Daily Mail*. 'Englishmen who have long suffered from statesmanship in skirts can pay him no less, and need pay him no more, tribute than to say, "Here at least is a man." '[20]

Privately, Nicolson in particular found that sort of thing hard to take, and noted in his diary: 'Tom cannot keep his mind off shock troops, the arrest of MacDonald and J. H. Thomas, their internment in the Isle of Man and the roll of drums around Westminster. He is a romantic. That is a great failing.'[21] (Here, as elsewhere, the full manuscript of Nicolson's diary gives a more vivid picture of his feelings than the published abridgement which, in the passage quoted above for instance, omits the references to MacDonald, Thomas and the Isle of Man.) Publicly, too, as 1932 became 1933 and 1933 became 1934, questions were beginning to be asked.

It is impossible now to say when the Rubicon was crossed; impossible too to explain how hitherto so shrewd a politician as Mosley could have so misread the public mood. For although it is both simplistic and wrong to suggest that he was doing anything other than following to its conclusion the logical path which had led him to leave the Conservative party not so many years before, until very recently accounts of his career in the mid thirties have been almost uniformly condemnatory. The very mention of his name has been enough to provoke apoplectic rage, and still is: the BBC received in excess of 200 complaints when it announced that Lady Mosley was to be the castaway on *Desert Island Discs* in November 1989, nearly a decade after her husband's death.

In no small measure this hostility was (and continues to be) fuelled by Mosley's own fiercely antagonistic stance. It did no good to anyone, for instance when, in October 1936, three years after Cimmie's sudden death from peritonitis, he married the beautiful, vivacious Diana Guinness (neé Mitford) in Berlin, and more particularly in Hermann Goebbels's drawing-room, with Hitler as one of the invited guests. Lady Mosley has since explained that the couple were to have been married in Paris, since 'we wanted it kept quiet, and if we had been married in a registry office in England it [would have been] written up three weeks previously. It's like having banns published in church. Therefore it would have been known by the journalists. So that was impossible.[22]

That is rather disingenuous but, like so much of the writing of both Mosley and Diana then and now, also guilelessly true. If the couple had married in England, or even at the British embassy in Paris, his precarious position and her recent divorce *would* have attracted attention; as it was, the wedding went entirely unnoticed. If, however, marrying in Berlin served immediate ends, it also left Mosley a hostage to fortune, and has ever since been a continual distraction from his more urgent message. In the anxious months between what was then simply referred to as 'Munich' and the outbreak of war in September 1939 in particular it did much to foster the notion of Mosley as 'the English Hitler' or 'the Führer's puppet', when in actual fact nothing could have been further from the truth.

As distinct from Diana who tended to idolize Hitler (although to a far lesser extent than did her sister Unity) Mosley was never a close ally of the German Führer. Socially and politically, he had little time for him, and indeed met him on only two occasions – a fact which even his friends have found difficult to believe: 'When I told Frank [Lord] Longford that, he was amazed,' Lady Mosley has recalled. 'He thought they saw each other constantly.'[23]

Lord Longford can be forgiven for his mistake; but in retrospect it is clear that there were profound differences between the two leaders. Underneath everything, Mosley always remained the English squire, ineffably seigneurial and, albeit in what now seems a grotesque parody of the role, essentially a gentleman. Lady Mosley says that 'masterful is the wrong word; but he was much more independent [than Hitler]'. His

> followers adored him and looked up to him and thought him perfection, really, and thought that he could lead them, as it were, into a promised land.
>
> With Hitler it was a bit different. It was as if *he* relied on them; he needed them to buoy him up, you know. He had a very soft side to his nature, really, so that people terribly felt they would like to help him; and that tremendously, I think, applied to women who already had the vote in Germany. I think it probably was the women's vote that put him in. There was something almost vulnerable – it sounds mad to say that of somebody who was considered such a mad dictator – about him which made men want to help him and made women want to cherish him [. . .] Mosley hadn't got that at all.[24]

Notwithstanding any of this, the confusion still remained; and erstwhile friends and parliamentary allies like Longford were not alone in asking whether Mosley had finally gone too far. For as the thirties progressed, the sinister-sounding sobriquet 'Mosler' seemed to sum him up far better than the comic-opera 'Moslini'. It wasn't just that, in both facial appearance and their styles of platform demagogy, there was a slight similarity between the English baronet and the German Chancellor. There were more obvious parallels too. Hitler had his Munich rallies; Mosley his mass-gatherings at the Royal Albert Hall, Olympia, Oxford and elsewhere. Hitler had his *Sturmabteilung*, the Brownshirts; Mosley his Blackshirts – what could have been clearer than all that?

In vain did the Mosleys attempt to distance themselves, preaching their specifically English fascism in which the Nation, the Empire and European peace were given paramountcy. But Mosler/Moslini had gained too great a hold over the popular imagination, and no one was prepared to listen any more to plain Sir Oswald. Hence, few if any uncommitted Englishmen in the mid 1930s would have given much credence to the rational – and indeed National – explanation which Lady Mosley still gives of her husband's decision to adopt the black shirt as the BUF party uniform. Far from being a reference or hymn to the brownshirt uniform of Hitler's SA, she says, it

> had a very practical advantage, which was that it was extremely cheap. I think it cost two shillings or something, and it meant that whatever class of life you came from – and you know how class-ridden the English are – they were all in black shirts with just ordinary grey trousers [...] It was very valuable, because *whether you were a multi-millionaire or unemployed it made no difference.*[25]

With the benefit of hindsight, this too is certainly plausible. Dressing everyone the same is only a first step towards treating them the same; and an unbiased assessment of Mosley's views in the 1930s (or indeed at any stage of his career) does reveal his sincere, albeit rather traditionally patronizing, Squire-Brownish belief in the One Nation and concern for the common weal. Once again, however, it has to be said that, at the time, the BUF's adoption of the black shirt was at the very least misunderstood and more generally seen as nothing less than inflammatory. Confronted by what so often seemed to be no more than a threatening, black-shirted 'gang of roughs' – in common with Diana's brother Tom, Mosley's more refined supporters tended to eschew the black shirt – unlike the thousands of Frl. Schroeders in Berlin, ordinary British people refused to 'acclimatize' and shied away from out-and-out fascism. No matter that deep down what Mosley was saying, up to and including what can only be described as his outright anti-semitism, was no more than a projection and extrapolation of its own beliefs, middle-class England indulged in a comfortable piece of Orwellian double-think and managed to persuade itself that Mosley represented a serious danger to the precious status quo.

In this, it has to be said, it was at the very least aided by an increasingly partisan Press. Only Lord Rothermere's papers continued to give Mosley wholehearted support, with the *Evening News* going as far as sending free tickets for BUF rallies to readers who wrote in describing 'Why I Like the Blackshirts'. For the most part Mosley himself was either damned with faint praise or ignored altogether by what does look suspiciously like a media plot: incredibly, from 1934 until 1968 he never once appeared on BBC radio or television, for instance.

Indeed, it is only now that much of what Mosley and Diana spent half a century reiterating about the existence of an organized campaign to disrupt and discredit the activities of the BUF is being heard, and proved correct. In his autobiography, for example, Mosley was much later to thunder that:

> The view that the mass of the British workers rise in their wrath against men and opinions [of which] they disapprove and will do violent and brutal things is simply invented nonsense. Such events are bogus from start to finish, for they are manufactured by the Communist Party. If a man is alone, a score of these roughs will make him appear a public enemy by surrounding him and kicking him, or a public hero by encircling him and cheering him. If police protect him, the communists say he cannot come among the people without protection; this impression is the object of the whole exercise.[26]

Well, he would think that, wouldn't he, one might have been tempted to conclude, even as late as 1968 when the book was first published. In the same way, it would have been (and in some circles it still is) easy to see no more than rabid anti-communism behind Lady Mosley's more recent assertion that the violence which erupted during the BUF rally at Olympia in London on 1 June 1934 (and at which she admits she was not present) was 'absolutely organized by the Left. The *Daily Worker* for three weeks before published maps of how to get to Olympia. It was highly organized.'[27] But, as Mosley's biographer points out in a fascinatingly-detailed account of the Olympia rally, things were not as simple as that.

To start with, Olympia was not typical of the scores and scores of rallies and meetings held up and down the country between 1934 and 1938 at which the BUF sought to exploit Mosley's personal popularity and oratorical skills. Tellingly, those 'hundreds of Rolls-Royces' had brought the cream of London society (and more than a few Conservative MPs) to Earl's Court. Blackshirts and Communists alike realized that it was to be very much a set-piece occasion. Violence did flare, heads were broken and, famously, a woman Blackshirt did have her face slashed with a razor; but it is even more difficult now than it was during the first week of June 1934, when questions were asked in Parliament and letters written to all manner of newspapers, to determine exactly who was to blame. The Blackshirt 'roughs' were certainly in attendance, and did deal severely with hecklers. But on the other hand it has to be remembered that there were around 12,000 people present, and according to contemporary police reports only about thirty were ejected. That figure was subsequently revised upwards. Significantly, however, the duty officer's report that the meeting passed off 'without any serious violence' has never been challenged.

Nevertheless, even when it is shorn of its society connections, Olympia can be seen as having set a pattern. At later rallies, at Oxford (on 25 May 1936) and elsewhere, beneath the uneasy, borrowed panoply of the demagogues, Mosley preached a (comparatively) quiet, very English fascism, praised the Empire and deployed logic, subtlety and all his considerable rhetorical skills . . . while everywhere around him the chairs were flying. Lady Mosley was present when her husband addressed a meeting at the Carfax Assembly Rooms in Oxford, and recalls:

> There again, [the communists] were determined to stop him speaking. What was interesting was that when [the Blackshirts] had put those people out of the doors – including Frank Pakenham [later Lord Longford] and [Richard] Crossman and one or two others and a certain number of undergraduates and a good many men from the Cowley works – the hall still seemed to be packed with people, and he made a speech of an hour and then took questions for another hour in total calm and great interest and enormous applause.

Other eyewitnesses have testified that, at least to begin with, this was indeed the case. Frank Pakenham and Dick Crossman had – like their fellow-socialists Philip Toynbee and Patrick Gordon Walker – attended the meeting as no more than curious individuals. Mosley, one feels, would have actually welcomed – and had ready answers to – their questions. The *Daily Worker* 'reds', however, had little interest in donnish dialectic. Intent on trouble, they opted for deep cover and for a long time held their fire:

> What they did at Oxford was to open newspapers, pretending to read. So [Mosley] said, 'I'm very glad to see the young gentlemen are catching up on their lessons, because I hear they're very backward this year', or something – a tiny little sarcasm; whereupon the fight began. That sort of says it all [. . .] *They* lifted up those iron chairs and bashed our stewards with them.[28]

After that, Lady Mosley admits, it was 'six of one and half a dozen of the other, really; just a fight.' In popular memory, however, 'Oxford', like 'Olympia' and 'the battle of Cable Street' in the east end of London (4 October 1936) has been invested with greater significance. On the Left it has long since come to symbolize all the vicious, unprovoked attacks which Mosley and his black-shirted fascist thugs made on the working class or Jewish underdogs of England. But now even that convenient, sentimental view with its shades of Spain and attempt to take the moral high ground by an appeal to 'English' notions of decency and fair play is being challenged. The statistics just do not bear it out.

Not unnaturally, Mosley's rallies and the growth of the British Union of Fascists had early on attracted the attention of the authorities. The police and the Special Branch in particular kept an assiduous eye on what was happening, monitoring activity in both the fascist and opposition camps, and their reports to the Home Office (now held at the Public Record Office) give what must be regarded as the best impartial picture of events. They have recently been analysed by Stephen Cullen at Nuffield College, Oxford, and others; and, if anything, the picture that emerges suggests that Mosley was more accurate than has previously been accepted in his assertion that the notoriety which the BUF rallies attracted was largely due to the communists. Even Lady Mosley's opinion that the violence which so often accompanied them was 'six of one and half a dozen of the other' now seems unnecessarily coy.

Between the beginning of January 1934 and 24 September 1938 reports were made on some 402 fascist meetings (not by any means all which took place, but a figure which in itself says something about the prevalence of fascism at the time). They reveal that a total of 198 anti-fascists were arrested, as against seventy-two fascists (and ninety-two 'others'); that fascist meetings were many times more likely to be attacked than those of the Left, and that in the ensuing violence the fascist 'roughs' came off very much the worse. One hundred and nineteen of them were injured in the sixty-month period covered by the Home Office reports. They were attacked with 'bottles, knuckle-dusters, bricks, loaded rubber tubing, stones and a sword'. By contrast, the Blackshirts (normally armed with no more than lengths of electrician's tape wound round their knuckles) were judged responsible for only seventeen injuries (and seven further assaults) over the same period.[29]

After the passage of so many years, however, such figures are ultimately only of interest to the historian. No amount of statistical proof or tendentious persiflage will now serve to rehabilitate Mosley. As early as 1939 when he was only forty-three – and by political standards, young – he had realized that to all intents and purposes the game was up. More recently, Lady Mosley has also acknowledged this:

> I think really, probably [it all started to go wrong] because of the war; that's what finished it, really. I think when the war began [Mosley] thought – he imagined – that they would close [the BUF] down, and that he would be forbidden to speak. He was quite prepared for that. If he had been, he would have obeyed absolutely. His whole record shows that; he never disobeyed the police.[30]

As it turned out, things did not happen with that degree of neatness or convenience. By the autumn of 1939, with the country on a war footing and an Emergency Powers Act on the statute book which licensed the Government to make Orders in Council controlling everything pertaining to the 'Defence of the Realm', it became impossible to ignore – or even request the co-operation of – Mosley. Thus, on 23 May 1940 he was arrested under Defence Regulation 18B (1A). This had been promulgated only hours earlier with the specific intention of detaining the members of any association which was either unduly friendly to an enemy power or whose officers were deemed by the Home Secretary to 'have or have had associations with' that country's leaders or to sympathize with its 'system of government'. Quite simply Regulation 18B (1A) was a catch-all measure aimed at preventing the British Union of Fascists or 'the fascists' in general building the foundations of a fifth column. Mosley was far from being its only target: Diana was arrested a month after her husband, and by the end of June very nearly 750 card-carrying members of the BUF had also been detained.

Most of those were subsequently released, but Mosley himself was not. Initially he was interned for more than eighteen months in Brixton Prison – although in conditions very different from those imagined by a *Sunday Pictorial* writer who quite fancifully and indeed maliciously described the 'No. 1 "Guest" at the big house on Brixton Hill' as living the life of Riley:

Every morning his paid batman delivers three newspapers at the door of his master's cell. Breakfast, dinner and tea arrive by car. After his midday meal [Mosley] fortifies himself with alternative bottles of red and white wine daily. He calls occasionally for a bottle of champagne [...] He selects a different smartly cut lounge suit every week. His shirts and silk underwear are laundered in Mayfair.[31]

Diana – who had given birth to a son, Max, only a matter of weeks before her arrest – was at this time faring even worse in Holloway Prison, where both baths and food were erratic. Mosley was eventually allowed to join her there, and the couple lived together as cell-mates in a previously disused wing. And, despite well-attested reports that, left to themselves, Winston Churchill and other members of the Government who counted Mosley as a personal friend (or, as in Churchill's case, Diana a blood relation) would have acted sooner, there they stayed until November 1943 when they were finally released but still kept under house arrest.

> Cut is the branch that might have grown full straight,
> And burned is Apollo's laurel-bough,
> That sometime grew within this learnèd man.[32]

Although the second half of the 1930s spawned its own crop of Jeremiahs – sitting in a New York 'dive' drafting his poem 'September 1, 1939', W. H. Auden was one of the last – in reality the threnodies of the decade had been sung much earlier. A full twenty years previously, the able, unoccupied mothers of 'golden boys' and 'lovely lads' had tried to assuage the grief they felt at the death in France, Mesopotamia or elsewhere of those doting sons by arranging, with all the care they had previously lavished on pressed flowers, the private printing of elaborate *encomiae* celebrating the vigour and promise of 'the branch that might have grown full straight'.

Now, the 'loveliest' of those lads, the man who was in so many ways the epitome of his generation, had also fallen; but apart from the ever-loyal Diana there was no one to lament what might have been. Significantly, however, other than in the pages of the *Sunday Pictorial* and an equally-hostile *Daily Mirror*, Mosley's arrest, detention and effective political demise occasioned precious little rejoicing or triumphalism in the Britain of 1940, either.

The nation and its leaders were, after all, then grappling with graver problems than what Robert Skidelsky has quite fairly contextualized as the fate of 'a few fascists in his majesty's gaols'. Thus it was against the background of a welter of regulations and apprehension, as the nation drew together and geared itself up to fight for all it held most dear, that the 'officer and gentleman', the very totem to which it had looked up for almost exactly three-quarters of a century, was discovered to have had feet of clay. The ironies were deep, complex – and potentially disastrous. At the very moment in which gentlemanly, public-school notions of team-spirit and decency – *Play up, play up, and play the game!* – should have been most helpful, their deeper resonances had been heard. And, as we shall see, it was from about 1940 that new notions developed. Indeed, the sheer backs-to-the-wall, all-pull-together stringencies of life that year, the hardship symbolized by Henry Moore's drawings of huddled proletarian masses sleeping on the platforms of London's underground stations during the Blitz (we choose not to remember the more salubrious sanctuary available to the rich in the basements of the Dorchester and other hotels) presaged something of the new order.

Certainly, it was then that a sort of selective public amnesia allowed Mosley himself to slip into a timeless limbo which would continue for the rest of his life. It was as if the whole story of his rise – neatly caricaturing as it did the mesmeric hold which a self-created oligarchy of gentlemen had exercised over the nation – had become too painful, too shaming to dwell upon.

It had been a close call; but like some fallen hero in an ancient Greek tragedy, the suddenly pathetic, limping figure at the centre of it all was at least allowed the dignity of exile. Although after the war he remained semi-active on the fringes of British politics, standing in parliamentary by-elections until as late as 1966 and publishing a steady stream of books and articles which began with his characteristically forthright analysis of the problems of postwar Europe, *The Alternative* (1947) and reached its apogee with the appearance of his no-less-combative (and very well-reviewed) autobiography, unequivocally entitled *My Life*, in 1968 he had been marginalized. Living in Ireland and, more permanently, at Orsay, outside Paris he was away from the centre of things.

Ironically, however, at his new home, the Temple de la Gloire in Orsay, he was for many years a friend and near neighbour of David, that other exile, who had accepted the title of Duke of Windsor following his abdication in 1936. And although Lady Mosley now plays them down, there are many parallels between the two households. In one lived Britain's 'rightful' King, in the other the man who, for a few brief, glittering years had been fêted as its Prime Minister-in-waiting, the coming man. And yet, in less than two decades, both had attracted a uniquely bitter and lasting obloquy. To ask why is to touch the rawest of nerves and attempt to address the central problem confronting any observer of the immense social changes of the interwar years: where did it all go wrong?

On the face of it, no one, least of all the venerable David Lloyd George, would have credited it. That in far less than two decades his 'land fit for heroes to live in' should have been fought over by those heroes themselves and a none-too-select band of their champions armed with bottles, coshes, knuckle-dusters and the like seemed too cruel an irony. And yet, even in 1919, there was no chance that that promised land would ever be redeemed. As the survivors of Passchendaele and the Somme knew only too well, by then there were precious few real heroes left, and those who did remain had abandoned the heroic certainties of Henry Newbolt and Victorian England among the mud and slaughter. In their terms, as early as 1930 and 1931 even Mosley was offering too little, too late. Even the later 'Mosley Manifesto' was no more than another of the blandishments of a bankrupt government and a toadying Establishment. Something new was needed.

Although he himself was still in no more than early middle-age, by then even Mosley with his war record and 'smartly cut lounge suits' had become yesterday's man. Able and, in the best sense, plausible, he had taken too much for granted, and pushed the aspirations of his generation one stage farther than was right or prudent. In 1920 he had been one of the figureheads of postwar England; quite literally an officer and a gentleman. Within hardly more than a decade he had thrown all that away, as it seems now – and yet, on a wider canvas, his failure is only symbolic of the more general failure of that whole depleted generation of gentlemen to come to grips with the fast-changing realities of their postwar world.

By the end of the 1930s they had finally missed their chance. By then, their own sons were coming of age and beginning to question their inheritance. They too had been to public school and passed on to

Oxford or (more particularly) to Cambridge. In that simplistic sense then, they too were gentlemen, much though they might have derided the term. But, not in the least constrained by the memory of Dr Jowitt's homilies about public duty, they were to prove wayward and disputative heirs. Donald Duart Maclean, for example, *should* have been another Raymond Asquith or Julian Grenfell. Though not an Etonian, he had grown up in the shadow of the great and the good. Like H. H. Asquith and Julian's father Willie (later Lord Desborough), until his death in 1932 Maclean's father, Sir Donald, had also been a Member of Parliament and even – albeit very briefly – a Cabinet minister. As we shall see, however, Donald was to achieve public eminence way beyond the confines of Westminster.

CHAPTER NINE

The Yeomen of England

Here in this pretty world Gallantry took its
last bow.
Here was the last ever to be seen of Knights
and their Ladies Fair, of Master and of Slave . . .
   – Prologue to Gone With The Wind, 1939

❖

Sunday, 3 September 1939 was bright and unseasonably warm. 'Queen's weather', the older generation could have been forgiven for thinking, as they let their eyes drift away from the newspapers' urgent headlines to the cerulean blue of the sky. But by lunchtime Britain was at war, even though Neville Chamberlain's words – *I have to tell you now that no such undertaking has been received . . .* – distant and disembodied in the hastily-arranged live wireless broadcast from the Cabinet Room at 10 Downing Street shortly after 11.15 a.m., failed to do more than spread a momentary chill through the Indian summer.

Both houses of Parliament were sitting, the air-raid sirens sounded in London, but otherwise life seemed to go on as normal. The Duke and Duchess of Kent still walked their dog in Belgrave Square, while Earl Jellicoe and Viscount and Viscountess Bearsted arrived at the Dorchester Hotel from the country. Out of town, it was announced that 'the Hon. Mrs Ronald Greville' had once again taken up residence at Polesden Lacy, near Dorking in Surrey; and in Aldershot, Captain Con Wilson married his fiancée Audrey by special licence.

. . . and that consequently this country is at war with Germany. There was an air of unreality about it all; the headlines – 'FOOD RATION-ING PLAN READY'; 'HOW TO APPLY FOR A COMMISSION'; 'RAID

WARNINGS IN LONDON' – and in those early days even the little private tragedies:

JOURNALIST KILLED IN BLACKOUT
Car in Collision
Mr Geoffrey Swaffer, brother of Mr Hannen Swaffer and himself a well-known journalist, was killed during London's blackout early on Saturday when the car in which he was a passenger collided with a tram in Kennington Park-road, S.E.
Mr Swaffer, who was 39, was on the staff of the *Daily Express*.[1]

Long expected, the Prime Minister's radio announcement that Appeasement had failed – *You can imagine what a bitter blow it is to me . . .* – and the unthinkable come to pass nevertheless soon had apocalyptic consequences. And the military manoeuvrings and other strategic necessities – 'HOSPITAL DUTY AT ONCE: Doctors and Nurses Should Report' – the details of which filled the inside pages of every paper for a week or more, rapidly began to have a sobering effect on every stratum of society.

Like Captain Wilson's, many other weddings were hastily brought forward: every one of those listed in the *Daily Telegraph*'s social column on Monday, 4 September was described as having taken place 'quietly', or 'quietly owing to the international situation'. It was also noted that, at the marriage of Mr E. C. F. Nutting and Lady Rosemary Eliot at Hungarton, Leicestershire the previous Saturday, Mr John Nutting was able to discharge his duties as best man only because he was 'on sick leave from his regiment'. More ominously, that same edition of the *Telegraph* contained the Southern Railway's announcement that 'the normal week-day train service will operate today, subject to any minor alterations that may be found necessary'.

Despite the fine weather and that nice Mr Chamberlain, as early as Monday, 4 September it had become apparent that the war with Germany was going to have an effect on the social fabric of Britain which would be every bit as devastating as the blitzkrieg that the *Luftwaffe* had long threatened to unleash on all the nation's major ports and cities.

Buildings could be repaired, or at least shored up; but, as had long been recognized at the very highest level, social order was altogether more unstable. And well before the 'Phoney War' ended, the bombs started falling and people began to get hurt, it was officially recognized that a let-them-eat-cakes mentality was no longer enough. To win the war in what even the King (since the upsets of 1936, David's younger brother Bertie, who ruled as George VI) had called 'this grave hour, perhaps the most fateful in our history', something new was needed. As early as June 1940 Chamberlain's successor as Prime Minister, Winston Churchill had explicitly said as much in what would become one of his best-known speeches:

> The Battle of Britain is about to begin. Upon this battle depends the survival of Christian civilization; upon it depends our own British life and the long continuity of our institutions and our Empire. The whole fury and might of the enemy must very soon be turned on us. Hitler knows that he will have to break us in this island or lose the war. If we can stand up to him, all Europe may be free, and the life of the world may move forward into broad sunlit uplands. But if we fail, then the whole world, including the United States, including all that we have known and cared for, will sink into the abyss of a new Dark Age made more sinister and perhaps more protracted by the lights of perverted science. Let us therefore brace ourselves to our duty, and so bear ourselves that if the British Empire and its Commonwealth last for a thousand years, men will still say, This was their finest hour.[2]

These were fine words and, quite understandably, they have subsequently become part of the national consciousness. But with their distant echoes of Henry V's somewhat similar rallying of his troops, their specific invocation of the concept of duty – that word again – and their allusions to British 'institutions' and the Empire they *could* have been misunderstood. As we have seen, barely a year before they were uttered Oswald Mosley had been deploying a similarly 'Churchillian' rhetoric and invoking identical notions of England, Empire, home and beauty, even if he stopped short of promising what sounds suspiciously like a new 'land fit for heroes' set somewhat bizzarely amid those incongruously Audenesque 'broad sunlit uplands'.

In an earlier and equally famous speech, Churchill too had admitted that he had nothing to offer – and, by implication, was asking for no less – than 'blood, toil, tears and sweat'.[3] But to what end? Quite patently it was not in any attempt to shore up the existing social fabric whose class base had anyway been severely dented by Mosley and the British Union of Fascists, and (though no one knew it at the time) whose very foundations were already being undermined by the subversive activities of Philby, Burgess, Maclean, Blunt and other 'moles' who were, in the most literal sense, 'class traitors'.

Rather, Churchill was offering and/or demanding something very different. And although he was himself ineradicably part of the 'upper ten thousand', educated at Harrow and, as a descendant of John Churchill, first Duke of Marlborough, hitherto a central member of the social and political ruling élite, he too was breaking ranks to do it. It is difficult now to so much as suggest that Churchill, 'the greatest Englishman of them all', could have been guilty of that same class treachery, but that is what it amounted to.

His attitude is most clearly demonstrated by the tone of his speeches. For he was implicitly saying that old divisions would have to be broken down if 'we' were to defeat 'the whole fury and might of the enemy' and break through into those 'broad sunlit uplands'. His repeated use of that inclusive 'we', together with words such as 'us' and 'ourselves' in his address to the nation on 18 June 1940 can hardly have been accidental. No Prime Minister had ever spoken like that before: indeed, it is worth noting that in his 'Cabinet Room' speech the previous year, Chamberlain had used 'we' to refer variously to the Nation and the Government, while keeping a slightly patronizing, patrician 'you' up his sleeve:

> We and France are today, in fulfilment of our obligations, going to the aid of Poland, who is so bravely resisting this wicked and unprovoked attack on her people. We have a clear conscience. We have done all that any country could do to establish peace [. . .] And now that we have resolved to finish it, I know that you will all play your part with calmness and courage.

Thus, in little more than nine months, Us and Them had become redundant concepts. (If, indeed, they had not vanished overnight. Reporting London's first air-raid warning, the *Daily Telegraph* of 4 September 1939 had noted that in the House of Commons shelter 'there were no distinctions of class or function. Tea-room girls and barmaids found themselves standing next to famous politicians.')

Standing alone against the spectre of 'a new Dark Age', suddenly we were all one nation. Disraeli would have approved of the principle, if not the pragmatic realpolitik which underlay it. For what Churchill was really calling for amounted to more than blood, toil, tears and sweat. Time and again, his speeches during 1940 – when Britain was threatened as never before by the very real prospect of invasion and domination – contained implicit demands for social reconciliation. If 'we' could only pull together, he seemed to be saying, we would win together – and then stay together, democratic equals, the classless coevals of those 'broad sunlit uplands'.

It was a bold, almost revolutionary, message; but one which was understood by the overwhelming majority of its recipients. Churchill was at the head of a broadly-supported Coalition government, and in his popular incarnation as the classlessly siren-suited 'Winnie', really did seem to be giving a lead (even if what to all intents and purposes we would now call a piece of social engineering was also being furthered by the iron hand of an all-embracing, hastily-promulgated Defence of the Realm Act). Arriving at 10 Downing Street to photograph the Prime Minister and Mrs Churchill in September 1940, Cecil Beaton noticed 'the presents sent to the Prime Minister from fans, with letters thanking him for what he was doing for the nation'.[4]

In short, and purely in the national interest, Churchill and the Government were attempting to demolish the fences of protocol and precedence which had for so many years protected the Gentlemen from the Players. The sub-text of speech after speech and the implication of innumerable official pronouncements ensured that everyone realized that they were all equal now. 'For the duration', there was to be no such thing as a gentleman – nor, as plans were laid during that duration for free education and Welfare State orange juice to be supplied to the alluringly sunlit uplands, did the gentleman seem to have much of a place in the eventual thereafter. Everyone, be he a member of that ironic and awkward *new* élite 'the Few', the knights of the air whom even Churchill hymned as the champions of their native land ('Never has so much been owed by so many to so few') or the lowliest clerk or teacher was henceforth to regard himself as an Englishman.

Irrespective of the inherent ironies, W. S. Gilbert too might have approved. He would have been churlish to have done otherwise, for what at any other time would have seemed like unconscionable intervention in the scheme of things not only saved the day but also served to bring about the most radical change in attitudes for more than three-quarters of a century; a necessary realignment of British society which in turn spawned a whole new breed of 'gentlemen'.

However, the fact that the country was at war when it occurred both clouds and clarifies the change. Would it then have happened otherwise? Yes, in all probability it would. Things had gone too far. In the late 1930s the centre was palpably not holding; some form of realignment was imminent. Somehow though, one feels that, even without Defence Regulation 18B(1A), Oswald Mosley would still have been brought up short. Ultimately his was not the way. There could never have been an 'army of the unemployed'. There *would* never have been internment camps on the Isle of Man for turbulent politicians. Things just didn't happen like that. Deep down, everyone knew it just wasn't *English*.

But those 'in the know' knew other things too. Hardy more than a year into his premiership, even Churchill was going through a rough time. On 6 June 1941, his long-time friend Henry 'Chips' Channon was noting in his diary that 'on all sides one hears increasing criticism of Churchill. He is undergoing a noticeable slump in popularity and many of his enemies, long silenced by his personal popularity, are once more vocal. Crete has been a great blow to him.'[5] We should not lay too much weight on this. From the context it is clear that the ambitious and never-completely-reliable Channon was anyway more concerned with the Prime Minister's political fortunes: Crete had fallen less than a week previously. Nevertheless, Channon's gossipy ambivalence does serve to highlight the scale of the task which Churchill was undertaking and the stark – but now-too-often overlooked – fact that 'we' were not always behind him.

Ideologically as well as politically, winning the war had become a *sine qua non*; a stubborn imperative in the face of which everything else paled. In just the same way as he had earlier been prepared to countenance the seemingly-inevitable destruction of London in the long-promised Blitz (and would later sanction the more comprehensive razing of Dresden) so too was Churchill prepared to use every means at his disposal to win the war on the 'Home Front'. No quarter could be given there, either. Nothing could be left to chance for it was always apparent to the authorities – although understandably not publicized – that there were those among 'us' who, while not actively revolutionary, continued to believe that the struggle nought availeth.

Their existence and the extent of the disaffection which it represented is perhaps best demonstrated by the increasing Allied concern with the morale of American bomber-crews stationed at East Anglian air bases from 1942.[6]

On 23 May 1944, for example, after nearly 400 B-17 and B-24 aircraft (each of which had a normal crew of eleven men) had put down at neutral airfields in Sweden and Switzerland, William Corcoran, the United States Consul in the Swedish port of Göteborg, had written to his superior in Stockholm:

> Sir,
> It is my conviction that the morale of the escaped young fliers with whom I have had contact warrants serious consideration and surveillance [. . .]
> The suggestion is heard that it is easy to land quickly in neutral territory while on a bombing raid and thereby escape further hardship and danger. One navigator recently told me that this means of getting out of the war with impunity was openly discussed among bomber-crews in Great Britain.

Although his views were subsequently challenged, Corcoran was hardly alone in suggesting that appreciable numbers of airmen were to all intents and purposes deserting in the most crucial months of the war in the air. Indeed, there is a persistent rumour that station commanders gave escorting fighter pilots off-the-record (and therefore unattributable) briefings in which they were led to 'understand' that it would be appropriate for them to shoot down any Allied bomber they observed heading towards neutral territory without an obvious reason.

Coming as it did at a time when the chances of survival of a member of any bomber-crew were rated less than those of a Great War infantryman (50,000 US airmen were killed in Europe in just two years) this breakdown in morale is now perhaps understandable, particularly since the American airmen had been born as citizens of a nation still nominally wedded to the non-interventionist Monroe Doctrine of 1823. And indeed 'the morale problem' had dogged US military command well before Corcoran's letter found its way to Washington. In December 1943 diplomatic sources in Stockholm had reported on the commitment of American aircrews who had legitimately put down on neutral soil and subsequently been interned in the Swedish town of Falun, and duly commended 'the impression they give of bold, dynamic strength, accompanied by a friendly good nature'. But by then rumours of a less-than-bold, war-weary homesick-ness were already circulating in Berne, the Swiss capital. And by March 1944 – still a full two months before Corcoran wrote his letter – the tone of even the Stockholm reports had become altogether less positive:

> Swedish comments [. . .] continue to be fairly good natured. Less good natured was some of the gossip and insinuation reflecting adversely on the conduct and courage of the American aviators which members of the legation staff heard privately.

Back in Britain, these were words which Sir Arthur Harris, Commander-in-Chief, Bomber Command, Churchill and the Government could well have done without. For although Churchill's own praise for 'the Few', specifically the Spitfire and Hurricane fighter pilots of the Battle of Britain, has gone down as a eulogy of the entire Royal Air Force, it now seems clear that within the RAF too there were those who begged leave to doubt. Well before the American squadrons flew in, Harris had certainly been dealing with a very similar problem.

He chose to see it in terms of a collapse of resolve, 'a lack of moral fibre', or 'LMF' as it was even then officially abbreviated. Well before 1942 he had accepted that British and Commonwealth airmen could be (in his own words) 'weaklings' or 'waiverers'. How many of these there were and the real extent of their 'weakness' remains un-clear. However, recently discovered documents show that Harris was prepared to go to extreme lengths to prevent what he called the 'contagion' spreading. Until late in 1944 any airman 'diagnosed' as lacking moral fibre was summarily reduced in rank to Aircraftsman, second class (AC2) and segregated from his colleagues. Until the political implications of the practice became clear in 1944, his papers and service records were also stamped in red 'LMF' or 'W' (for 'waiverer') and he was assured that this was a mark of Cain he would carry until the end of his life.

'We weren't all Guy Gibsons; we weren't all Leonard Cheshires', one Second World War RAF officer has recently admitted. It would have been extraordinary if they had been – but only as extraordinary as the fact that, to a far greater extent than the aircrews, the great mass of the British public *was* won over by Churchill's rhetoric and did willingly accept its role in the new Britain. Give or take one or two halfhearted attempts at rebellion – in September 1940 the Communist MP Phil Piratin led a group of 100 or so dissatisfied East Enders to the front door of the Savoy hotel in a protest about the inequity of airraid shelter provisions – there was no 'LMF' on the 'Home Front'.

Even the Royal family was doing its bit. On 25 August 1942 it was announced that the King's younger brother, the Duke of Kent had been killed in an air crash while on his way to visit RAF personnel in Iceland. As if that was not enough, much was also made of the fact that after his funeral at Windsor, while driving back to her wartime quarters at Badminton House in Gloucestershire, Queen Mary had stopped her limousine and insisted on giving a lift to an RAF sergeant and a young American Air Force parachutist.

Everyone seemed quite happy under the enforced egalitarianism – even if blatant propaganda and the widespread dissemination of stories such as Queen Mary's gave them little real choice. Ministry of Information films and Pathé Gazette newsreels painted a relentlessly positive picture of a united and determined 'us' (though with hindsight we might now feel that Pathé's portrait of 'The Spirit of the RAF' did protest too much). Their every word subject to the imprimatur of the censor, newspapers and 'the wireless' also toed the line, sparing readers and listeners facts, figures and opinions which might have disturbed 'the common weal'.

There was an implicit consensus that this was the right thing to do. (It certainly raised fewer moral problems than the self-denying ordinance under which little more than five years previously the whole of the British media had agreed to turn a blind eye to the Prince of Wales's association with Mrs Simpson.) Like Queen Mary, individuals and organizations were all keen to 'do their bit' and present the picture of a nation perfectly at one with itself and proud to be 'pulling together'. It was as if 'we' were all fee-paying members of Churchill House, playing up and playing the game; the more active among us actually out there at the crease, the rest of us either loyally pacing the boundaries, cheering on the first team ('the Few'; 'our boys') or back home washing the kit (knitting scarves and sweaters).

On the wireless it was suddenly deemed appropriate for listeners to the BBC's Home Service to hear the accented voice of Wilfred Pickles reading the news and the bluff Yorkshire vowels of J. B. Priestley delivering his personal 'Postscript'. It was explained to a nation more attuned to the perfectly modulated tones of Alvar Liddell and Frank Gillard that this was in the interests of national security – no German fifth columnist could ever 'take off' such accents – but at a deeper level it was another useful reinforcement of the one-nation ideal. Merely listening to Pickles and Priestley, one knew they weren't wearing dinner jackets!

Above and beyond all the other media, however, it was the cinema which best exemplified the new and still very fragile mood of national unity. And with what in a pre-television age really was ubiquity – the very same 'pictures' were seen in West End Empires and every provincial fleapit – it was uniquely well placed to do so.

But it is important to realize that it was not entirely because of some official *dictat* or the fear of the censor's blue pencil that it came to act as an agent of social cohesion. Some films – Olivier's *Henry V*, Noël Coward and David Lean's *In Which We Serve* – were certainly made with 'the help, guidance and co-operation' of the Government and the military; but others – the majority – were not. Looking at all of them today, however, it is difficult to tell the difference. Underlying films as different as *Henry V*, Bernard Miles and Charles Saunders's *Tawny Pipit*, Michael Powell and Emeric Pressburger's quirkily independent allegory *A Canterbury Tale* (1944) and for that matter even William Wyler's mawkish *Mrs Miniver* (1942) in which Greer Garson suffered her way through a Hollywood version of the Blitz is the same idea of 'Englishness' which had fired Raffles and even Oswald Mosley. With their overt patriotism (*Henry V*) and images of thatched cottages, country villages and rolling fields (best exemplified by the downland setting of *Tawny Pipit* and *A Canterbury Tale*'s pilgrimage through Kent, 'the garden of England') it was also a notion of 'Englishness' which exactly chimed with that of their audiences – a fact which was confirmed early in the war when Mass Observation asked a cross section of the population to describe what they were fighting for.

Despite the fact that 'up to 1939 Britain had hardly established a recognizable school or style of cinema',[7] within a year or two of the outbreak of hostilities the film industry was more than 'doing its bit'. Film after film gave the impression that it had been made both by and for people who were – like the torpedoed crew of HMS *Torrin* in *In Which We Serve* – all in the same boat. But, more interestingly, several of the key films of this period also served to further Churchill's one-nation ideal.

Tawny Pipit was one such. On the surface it tells the faintly-ludicrous tale of how a convalescent member of the Few, Jimmy Bancroft, DSO, DFC, who had previously 'got mixed up with some German fighters and come home with a pair of broken legs and a shoulder-blade in about ten pieces', and his nurse-fiancée save a nest of rare bird's eggs. But there are deeper resonances, for the couple's battle against an egg-stealing 'fifth columnist' in the Association of British Ornithologists is joined by the squire, the vicar and all the more ordinary inhabitants of the idyllically English village of Lipsbury Lea. Later, a Government minister (conveniently once the squire's fag at Marlborough) and the army also rally round. No one is left under any misapprehensions; the pair of tawny pipits are more than just rare birds, and their eggs are more than just eggs. The earthy, aitch-dropping Corporal Philpotts makes that clear when, in a crowded mess hut, he explains to his superior officer:

> These eggs are yours and mine and 'is – and 'is, and 'is and 'is – and Major Watson's and the Colonel's. They belong to England, sir.

Working on a larger canvas, Noël Coward's *This Happy Breed* was another explicit and rather sentimental celebration of Englishness. Its very title was, after all, a quotation from the most famous speech in Shakespeare's *Richard II*. But, like the strains of Coward's song 'London Pride' with which it ends, the film hymns an essentially suburban Englishness, a world away from both Lipsbury Lea and the élite sophistication of the West End and the clubland of St James's. Every scene revels in the 'niceness' and ordinariness of lower-middle-class London life in the years leading up to the outbreak of war. No problem is too big to be solved by the brewing of a fresh cup of tea, the purchase of a new hat, or the promise of a trip to the Lyon's Corner House.

Shakespeare's John of Gaunt, the Duke of Lancaster, might not have had the likes of Coward's imaginary families, the Mitchells and the Gibbonses, in mind when he praised the inhabitants of 'this royal throne of kings, this sceptred isle' in *Richard II*.[8] He was speaking of 'royal kings,/Feared by their breed and famous by their birth,/ Renownèd for their deeds'. But, Coward seems to be saying, Bob Mitchell and Frank Gibbons were kings in their own way too – just as he was, in his way, a new Gaunt, 'a prophet new inspired'.

On the face of it, it sounds absurd: Coward – the arch-sophisticate, the author of such brittle comedies as *Hay Fever* (1925), *Private Lives* (1930) and *Blithe Spirit* (1941), he of the clipped delivery; that darling of the dressing-gown set – paving the way for Aneurin Bevan and Welfare State gentility! But Shakespeare at least knew better – *What must the king do now?* – and so, by a neat change of circumstances, did things turn out. For, despite his Shaftesbury Avenue airs and 'gay apparel', Coward was actually a child of the south London suburbs. With neither a public school or university education, deep-down he was more similar to Bob Mitchell or Frank Gibbons than the Elyot Chase he himself had played in the original production of *Private Lives*.

From time to time it showed, and never more than in the early 1940s. Thus, in *This Happy Breed* and – as we shall see – to an even greater extent in *In Which We Serve*, he came into his own, and emerged as the ablest mass-propagandist of the one-nation ideal. Olivier had rewritten Shakespeare and, at the almost-unprecedented cost of £500,000, come up with a version of *Henry V* that was both an artistic and a patriotic triumph. Coward, however, set his sights lower and merely *reinterpreted* an existing tradition of naïve, unthinking Englishness which, after all, was largely rooted in the world of Falstaff, Prince Hal and John of Gaunt:

> *This royal throne of kings, this scept'red isle,*
> *This earth of majesty, this seat of Mars,*
> *This other Eden, demi-paradise,*
> *This fortress built by Nature for herself*
> *Against infection and the hand of war,*
> *This happy breed of men, this little world,*
> *This precious stone set in the silver sea,*
> *Which serves it in the office of a wall,*
> *Or as a moat defensive to a house,*
> *Against the envy of less happier lands . . .*

For all its sentimentality, the success of *This Happy Breed* lay in the way in which Coward managed to give such lofty apostrophizing the common touch. Frank and Bob might not have been able to quote a line of Shakespeare between them, but they had a native 'nous'; if not gentlemen they were at least 'honourable men' whose devotion to 'this land of such dear souls, this dear, dear land' was beyond reproach. Thus the film pleased everybody. Coincidentally – or was it only that? – Coward had completed an earlier, stage version of the script a few months before the outbreak of war ('there is a note that [it] was finished at exactly eleven-thirty a.m. on June 29th'[9]) but when it was filmed by David Lean *This Happy Breed* still seemed to sum up the moment. It erected Frank and Ethel Gibbons, their family, friends and neighbours as the backbone of the nation – good-natured, full of common sense, worth their weight in gold, the salt of the earth and national 'treasures' – only because they had previously proved their worth. They would see us through this duration precisely because they and their likes had endured all manner of 'durations' in the past.

There was no mere gratuitousness in the sequence in which Bob Mitchell and his lady-friend pointedly walked past a ranting Oswald Mosley lookalike addressing a fascist rally at Speakers' Corner. Ostensibly they might have been heading for the Corner House, but in cinematographic, semiological terms they were highlighting, and very literally turning their backs on, the follies of the past.

The script of *This Happy Breed* was hardly 'vintage' Coward – a line like 'Japan! Who worries about Japan?' echoes but fails to equal 'Very flat, Norfolk' – but that had long-since ceased to matter. On one level at least, the medium had already given way to the message. On quite another, however, the medium was itself continuing to play an important role. The actress Celia Johnson (cast at the last minute as Robert Newton's long-suffering wife, Ethel) later recalled that – not insignificantly – *This Happy Breed* was made in colour. It was, in fact, one of the earliest British colour features. Consequently the shooting 'took hours. One used to wait, and wait, and wait'[10] – but in 1942 that too hardly mattered.

All the same, the technical longueurs endured by Miss Johnson must have been as nothing when compared with the privations suffered by those working on another of the colour features of the period, Powell and Pressburger's lengthy and immensely more ambitious *Life and Death of Colonel Blimp* (1942–44). At times almost self-consciously a great film; as its title suggests, from the start this eschews *Tawny Pipit*'s sentimentality and *This Happy Breed*'s terraced-house, lower-middle-class realism in favour of something more elusive and 'artistic'.

Since April 1934 Colonel (Horatio) Blimp had been a familiar character in the *Evening Standard* (and later the *Manchester Guardian* and

Daily Herald) cartoons of David Low. Seemingly named after the 'blimp' airships which had been used as observation balloons in the Great War, he was quite literally a windbag. Clad only in a towel, so that he resembled a paunchy little Caesar, his walrus moustache a-quiver, he would address the nation – '*Gad, sir* . . .' – from a West End Turkish bath. (Low always claimed that he had met the 'real' Blimp at a gentlemen's baths near Charing Cross.) But although he was intended to epitomize the most reactionary, dyed-in-the-wool Tory backwoodsman, the bloated, pompous, crusty officer-gentleman for whom all change was anathema and progress *per se* regrettable, as C. S. Lewis later realized, Blimp quickly became more than that:

> It may well be that the future historian, asked to point to the most characteristic expression of the English temper in the period between the two wars will reply without hesitation, 'Colonel Blimp.'[11]

Certainly, by 1939 his name (and the abstract nouns 'Blimpishness' and 'Blimpery') had long-since passed into the language: 'Blimp' made its first appearance in the *Universal English Dictionary* as early as 1937. By then too Blimp and his real-life counterparts were already figures of fun. Dame Lucy Houston, whom even the staid *Dictionary of National Biography* describes as 'a strident, perhaps sincere, patriot, who painted her rooms in red, white and blue – her racing colours', was one such. No one quite knew where she stood; although after Low hinted that the stout 'Blimpess' had a fondness for Mussolini, she tartly informed the editor of the *Evening Standard* that she 'would rather wear a black shirt than a dirty one stained with the blood of Englishmen'.[12] Convinced as early as 1932 of the inevitability of war (with whom?), she offered to give the London County Council £200,000 to provide some form of air defence for the metropolis. It was politely declined – but Dame Lucy still had the last laugh. After her death in 1936, it was discovered that she had died intestate; no relatives came forward and her entire fortune of some £2.5 million went to the State.

With their appropriation of Blimp in 1942 and the public announcement of his 'death', Powell and Pressburger could thus reasonably have expected to have been seen to be 'doing their bit'. As it turned out, however, *The Life and Death of Colonel Blimp* was much criticized for its moral ambivalence; Churchill hated it, and it was heavily censored before being shown abroad. Given the climate of the time it is not difficult to see why. It was bad enough that for an hour or more the film teetered on the brink of frothy Viennese operetta. Then, out of a Straussian welter of Biedermeier uniforms and turn-of-the-century diplomacy, its hero Clive Wynne-Candy emerged . . . but he was not Low's Blimp at all.

Like some English *Rosenkavalier*, as played by Roger Livesey he was the perfect, unreconstructed, turn-of-the-century gentleman. He even fought a duel to save the honour of England. He was an Old Harrovian, svelte and charming, as well as a quondam schools fencing champion. By the time the story had advanced into the late 1930s he had also become Brigadier-General Clive Wynne-Candy, VC, DSO. He had undoubtedly aged, but for all his parade-ground bluster, his moustaches, his clubby, curmudgeonly sophistication and the fact that this 'simple English gentleman' preferred 'ridin', huntin' and polo' to the opera, he was still hardly Low's figure of fun. If anything he had acquired a certain nobility. Underneath everything he was a fundamentally decent liberal – a Raymond in old age – an old soldier of the old school; an Englishman.

And yet this was the man whose death the posters promised! Not for the first time, the patriotic instincts of Powell and the Hungarian – *Hungarian!* – Emeric Pressburger were called into question. Just what did they think they were doing? Only a couple of years previously they had been criticized for the rather limp sentiments which seemed to lie behind their film *49th Parallel* (1941). Part-financed by the Ministry of Information (which only made things worse) this had told the story of a quiet, almost ineffectual Englishman's pursuit of an escaped German U-boat crew in Canada. It wasn't that he (Leslie Howard) didn't get his men; that would have been unthinkable. Rather, controversy centred around the fact that he seemed so 'amateurish' when compared with the steely, single-minded *Mein Kampf*-quoting German commander (Eric Portman).

Now Powell and Pressburger were at it again. Not content with letting Blimp/Wynne-Candy fraternize with another German through most of the film, in its final few minutes they had gone as far as to make *him*, the icily charming, heel-clicking Theo Kretschmar-Schuldorff, into a sort of anti-hero! Albeit with the best of intentions, it certainly seemed to be Theo who 'killed' Colonel Blimp:

'Well, am I dead [*asks Wynne-Candy*]? Does my knowledge count for nothing, eh? Experience? Skill? You tell me.'

'It is a different knowledge they need now, Clive [*Theo explains*]. The enemy is different, so you have to be different too [. . .] If you let yourself be defeated by them, just because you are too fair to hit back the same way they hit at you, there won't be any methods but Nazi methods. If you preach the rules of the game while they use every foul and filthy trick against you, they'll laugh at you! They'll think you're weak, decadent. I thought so myself in 1919.'

'I heard all that in the last war. They fought foul then, and who won it?'

'I don't think you won it. We lost it, but you lost something too. You forgot to learn the moral. Because victory was yours, you failed to learn your lesson twenty years ago, and now you have to pay the school fees again. Some of you will learn quicker than the others; some will never learn it because you've been educated to be a gentleman and a sportsman in peace and in war. But Clive − dear old Clive − this is not a gentleman's war. This time you are fighting for your very existence against the most devilish idea ever created by a human brain − *Nazi-ism!* − and if you lose there won't be a return match next year, perhaps not even for a hundred years.'

On one level at least, the English gentleman − that paragon concocted and perfected by Dr Arnold and a mid-nineteenth-century generation of public school men, exemplified by George Nathanial Curzon and hymned by everyone from Henry Newbolt and A. E. Hornung to Rupert Brooke and C. B. Fry − died the moment Anton Walbrook, playing a German with an unpronounceable name and an accent to match, first said those words. The blinkered patriots of 1944 certainly thought so.

On quite another level, however, that impassioned final speech of Theo's can be seen as marking the moment of the gentleman's rebirth as one of 'us'. For, unlike Blimp, Brigadier-General Clive Wynne-Candy, VC, DSO does not die. Far from it, in the film's final frames he rises again as a Home Guard leader, his experience respected, his qualifications recognized. Bombs had reduced his comfortable, servanted London home to rubble, but that too only served to symbolize the fact that he was now in the same boat as the rest of us.

For all of Powell and Pressburger's undoubted intelligence and scepticism (postwar, they were to go on to make some of the greatest British films of the late Forties, *The Red Shoes* and *The Small Back Room* among them), both *49th Parallel* and *The Life and Death of*

178

Colonel Blimp should have been recognized as having their hearts in the right place. Viewed today, they are certainly almost impossible to take in the wrong way. For all its merits, however, *Blimp* in particular remains a curiosity. The nation has never taken it to its heart in quite the way in which from the first it embraced Noël Coward's more popular 'classic' on that same 'in-the-same-boat' theme, *In Which We Serve* (1942).

There is a certain inevitability about that, for Coward was nothing if not adept at giving audiences what they wanted. Thus, the work which was to be his major contribution to the war effort is essentially a simple film. Like *This Happy Breed*'s, its blacks are blacker and its white whiter – and curiously the film was made in black-and-white – than those of *The Life and Death of Colonel Blimp*. Nor does *In Which We Serve* have any truck with Powell and Pressburger's ambivalent even-handedness. Toeing a pronounced party, propagandist line, Coward has no time for Germans, even good Germans. They simply do not appear in his very inward-looking story. They are the unseen pilots of 'enemy aircraft' and the equally-invisible crews of the distant vessels which torpedo the plucky little destroyer HMS *Torrin* somewhere off Crete in 1941. In the dialogue they are 'Fritz' – and the Italians fare no better. This characteristic of keeping the enemy at arm's length even colours 'off-duty' moments. Walking on the south Downs while planes engage in a dog-fight overhead, the Captain is told by his wife (Celia Johnson) that they are 'toys having a mock battle to keep us amused'.

There is no apology for this since *In Which We Serve* was made as a piece of overt propaganda. Coward based part of the story on the experiences of his friend Lord Louis Mountbatten and his ship, HMS *Kelly*. What's more, he shamelessly traded on his connections with Mountbatten in order to ensure the film's technical accuracy, as Mountbatten himself later recalled:

> 'It's got to be genuine, it can't be counterfeit,' [Coward] said. 'Otherwise it would be immediately detected.' I agreed, provided that it couldn't be traced back in any way to the *Kelly* – and above all to me [. . .]
>
> I did my best to help him, and in fact he produced a film which as far as I was concerned was exactly like life at sea. All the survivors of the *Kelly* agreed that it was quite staggering to find how true to life the whole film had been.[13]

Mountbatten was able to arrange for Coward and his co-director David Lean to receive the fullest co-operation from the Royal Navy during the production of the film – he had after all been appointed Chief of Combined Operations in 1942. He also seems to have been genuinely excited at the idea of a film in which 'the heroine of the story is the ship, certainly not the Captain or even the other men'.

Despite his genuine affection and admiration for Mountbatten, however, Coward could not work up much enthusiasm for the scheme. He went through the motions; the finished version of the film even begins with a voice solemnly intoning the sentence 'This is the story of a ship'. But, although we are then treated to a stirring montage of shots chronicling the various stages of her construction, as an entity or 'heroine' the *Torrin* very quickly disappears from the story. She is merely the *locus in quo*; the set rather than a character. On his mother's side, Coward frequently claimed to come from a naval family – 'Admirals and Captains' – but he was just not interested in ships *qua* ships. As he had already shown in his stage extravaganza *Cavalcade* (1931; and was to do again in the 1961 musical *Sail Away*) he was far more concerned with their passengers and crews. Their chance and passing acquaintanceships – yes, their brief encounters – the rough with the smooth, the boy with the girl, the Captain with the ordinary seaman, were the very stuff of his drama. And so it was with *In Which We Serve*. Mountbatten has claimed that he was responsible for the film's comprehensive, slice-of-life approach:

> 'You must definitely make it about more than just the Captain,' I said. 'You must have a chief petty officer, like a chief bosun's mate. You must have a junior rating like an ordinary seaman. You must have their families, and they must be involved together.14

With *This Happy Breed* still fresh in our memories, however, we may beg leave to doubt Mountbatten's artistic involvement, for *In Which We Serve* is pure Coward – and it has to be regarded as such since he was its writer, producer, star and co-director, as well as the composer of its main theme and incidental music. Surprisingly, however, it does not buckle under this egotistical, almost megalomaniac masthead. Despite the neo-Wildean brilliance of *Private Lives* and *Blithe Spirit*, it still remains among his greatest works.

We know we are on familiar territory right from that moment when, in one of the first of many flashbacks, Captain Kinross (Coward himself) calls his company together for the first time and, meta-phorically at least, mucks in with them:

> 'Break ranks and gather round. Can you hear me all right in the back? Good. You all know that it's the custom of the Service for the Captain to address the ship's company on commissioning day to give them its policy and tell them the ship's programme [. . .] Well, there are enough old ship-mates to tell the others what my policy's always been. Reynolds, Adams, Blake, Coombe, Parkinson – what sort of a ship do I want the *Torrin* to be?'
> 'A happy ship, sir.'
> 'That's right.'
> 'An efficient ship, sir.'
> 'Correct. A happy and efficient ship. A *very* happy and a *very* efficient ship. Some of you might think I'm a bit ambitious wanting both, but in my experience you can't have one without the other. A ship can't be happy unless she's efficient, and she certainly won't be efficient unless she's happy.
> Now for our programme . . .'

Implicitly, and with characteristic economy, the very middle-class Kinross ('Captain "D"') is welding this crew of Mitchells and Gibbonses into a team, a happy breed. He invites them to break ranks and mingle together. He knows their names. Chief petty officers, junior ratings and the likes of Adams, Blake and Parkinson are treated in exactly the same, fundamentally decent way. And when, within half an hour of the film's opening, the *Torrin* is abandoned for a life-raft the symbolism gets heavy, almost overpowering. A representative selection of her company are adrift in the raft, and the flashback sequences interrupt their struggle for survival with memories of their past lives.

The threatening present and a somewhat sentimentally-remembered past are thus carefully orchestrated to produce an image of homo-geneity as virtually every scene reveals more of the spirit of Churchill's 'new Englishness'. At one point Captain Kinross and Ordinary Seaman 'Shorty' Blake (John Mills) even discover they have some-thing other than their present oil-soaked predicament in common. Travelling down to Torquay for a brief honeymoon after their 'quiet' wedding, the new Mr and Mrs Blake had unexpectedly run into Captain and Mrs Kinross on the train. Even Churchill could not banish class differences overnight, and the introductions were made with a naturalistic awkwardness; but then friendliness or at least communality flickered. Mrs Kinross recognized Blake: 'He practically saved my life when I came on board the other day. My foot slipped on the gangway and I nearly as anything fell overboard. D'you remember?' Moments later, we are made aware that the Kinrosses had also spent their honeymoon at Torquay.

Little moments like this pepper the film. There is the juxtaposition of three separate Christmases, with glasses being raised as very similar toasts are proposed in an upper-middle, a lower-middle and a working-class home; there's the cutting between off-duty moments in the ward room and on the mess-deck of the *Torrin*, and a final sequence in which Captain Kinross says an individual goodbye to each of his surviving 'shipmates' in a vast transit-shed in Alexandria. Polite pleasantries are all he or they can muster. They speak them, quietly, then shake hands and part – equals now in the face of an uncertain future:

> 'Goodbye, sir. The very best of luck.'
> 'Thanks, Roach. Goodbye.'
> 'The very best of luck, sir.'
> 'Thanks, Moon. Goodbye.'

Over-sentimental as it seems today, in 1942's terms at least that final scene encapsulated the whole spirit of the film. It did constitute what we would now term a 'downbeat' ending. (It also served as the focus of yet more unnecessarily-nervy Government criticism. Why, Coward was asked, had he produced a film in which one of His Majesty's ships was seen to sink in wartime? 'When else do ships sink so frequently?' he replied.) On the other hand, like everything else about *In Which We Serve*, its under-played simplicity and quiet dignity only exemplified that new Englishness which had replaced the low dishonest ranting of the mid thirties.

Everything else – only retrospectively perhaps, is it possible to appreciate quite how far every last detail of the film reflected the changes which society was undergoing. Even the opening titles told their own story. It was true that there was a special credit reading 'Officers' Uniforms: Forster & Sons Ltd' – Raymond would have gone there; some things never changed – but in far bigger print, filling the whole screen, a list of the principal players hinted at the *dramatis personae* of the future. Rank and Degree be damned! The characters were announced in strict accordance to their contributions:

Captain E. V. Kinross, RN ... NOËL COWARD
Ordinary Seaman Blake ... JOHN MILLS
Chief Petty Officer Hardy ... BERNARD MILES

For those who had eyes to see, the mere mixing of officers and men would have told its own story. The message was clear enough, and not dictated by any actor's or agent's vanity. This was the new dispensation. Shakespeare's worst fears had come to pass. Unexpectedly, the Bard seemed to have been dethroned by the man who would later be called 'the Master'. Degree had indeed been 'shak'd', and the string untuned. Even in the last months of the war, however, there were still enough real-life Colonel Blimps around – men fully conversant with the niceties of rank and title and imbued with a public school-man's knowledge of the more ti-tum-ti-tum bits of Shakespeare – to deliver dire warnings about 'what dischord follows'. They would definitely have noticed the scandalous *lèse-majesté* of another of the opening credits of *In Which We Serve*:

NAVAL ADVISORS
Able Seaman T. W. J. LAWLOR

Lt. Commander I. T. CLARK, RN, OBE
Lieutenant C. R. E. COMPTON, RN

Such was Noël Coward's cachet in the early and mid forties, such were the stakes invested in *In Which We Serve* – all the Service goodwill but, in the light of Olivier's half-million, only a modest £200,000 in cash – it was deemed appropriate for King George VI and Queen Elizabeth to take an interest in its production. Accordingly they paid a well-publicized visit to the studios at Denham in Buckinghamshire (the King wearing the full-dress uniform of an Admiral of the Fleet) where Coward, John Mills, Bernard Miles and the 'crew' of HMS *Torrin* were doing their bit in a specially-constructed water tank. Photographers were on hand to record the event, and what amounted to this early Royal imprimatur considerably aided the success of the film when it was released a few months later. More significantly, it also legitimized the quasi-documentary style of film-making with which British cinema was becoming synonymous.

Tastes had changed. Less than half a decade previously, in 1939, film-goers had been queuing to see the most successful picture of the year, David Selznick's epic depiction of life in America's Old South, *Gone With The Wind*. Now they were clamouring for much smaller scale, introverted films which were more like the GPO Film Unit's *Night Mail* (1936) than Sam Goldwyn's (or for that matter David Selznick's) idea of cinema: something 'that starts with an earthquake and works its way up to a climax' – the burning of Atlanta, perhaps. Whether they *were* actually asking for them or just making the best of what was available is ultimately unimportant, for as we have seen the mood of the industry itself had changed. And quite how fundamental that change was is best exemplified by the wartime career of Leslie Howard.

Although he had little enthusiasm for the role, Howard had played the part of Ashley Wilkes in *Gone With the Wind*. It was a piece of inspired or wilfully bizarre casting; cine-buffs and even those who were party to the original decision continue to disagree. Without question, Howard was up to the part. He had been acting since 1917 when he played the small role of Jerry in an English touring production of *Peg o' My Heart*. Ten years later he had attained real star status on Broadway when he appeared in Michael Arlen's stage adaptation of his novel *The Green Hat* and then played the eponymous hero in a now-forgotten play with the unpromising title *Her Cardboard Lover*. By 1939 he had also played Hamlet in New York and made some twenty films in Hollywood.

But he was an Englishman, born in 1893, brought up in the south London suburbs (coincidentally only a couple of miles away from Noël Coward) and educated at Dulwich College. More to the point, this naturally quiet, unassuming, rather tweedy, pipe-smoking and (off-screen) bespectacled gent was also happily married with two teen-age children. It was small wonder then that he confided to Selznick, 'I don't really think I can do much with Wilkes', the rather flashy Confederate gentleman-owner of a substantial Southern estate called Twelve Oaks.

He did, of course. Wilkes was no competition for Rhett Butler (Clark Gable) but – with an accent which combined the deep south and an unmistakable public-school drawl – he and Howard more than passed muster. For English audiences in particular he came to personify the 'land of Cavaliers and Cotton fields' which Margaret Mitchell's novel had so graphically depicted, and which, as we have already seen, the England of the early 1930s sometimes disturbingly resembled. Typically, though, Howard himself privately despised Wilkes and all he stood for, calling him 'a dreadful milksop, totally spineless and negative'.[15] And certainly, there was little of him in the Leslie Howard who returned to Britain in August 1939 after a decade in which he had spent far more time and latterly become far better known in New York and Hollywood than in London.

He had seen the storm-clouds gathering and, although he was by then beyond the age for military service – 'an old fossil of forty-six' in 1939, he had been a cavalry lieutenant in the Great War until he was invalided out with shell-shock – he wanted to do his bit. On the *Gone With the Wind* set Selznick had told him, 'Just be yourself'. He had been – and by returning home he was again doing no more and no less than that.

But what could he actually do, other than learning how to operate a stirrup-pump in case the *Luftwaffe* bombed the village in Surrey in which he had bought a house? No films were being made in Britain in the early months of the war. Howard lobbied tirelessly, writing memoranda urging the Ministry of Information to put more effort into propaganda work in southern Europe; but until the summer of 1940 when he began broadcasting to America and was (briefly) considered as a replacement for his friend J. B. Priestley in the weekly 'Postscript' slot ('If the BBC makes this switch-over then it will certainly achieve a triumph of contrast', *Picture Post* noted ambiguously)[16] there seemed to be nothing for him.

Then, slowly, film-making restarted, as we have already seen. *Pimpernel Smith* (1941), which Howard devised, directed, produced and starred in, was actually made back-to-back with *49th Parallel* at Denham. Howard had high hopes that it would somehow act as a morale-boosting fillip, but like *49th Parallel* and *The Life and Death of Colonel Blimp*, it was too arch, too elusive.

Undeterred, he pressed on, quietly, doggedly, methodically. 'He despised the razzmatazz that went with [film-making], but had a very professional attitude and deep instinct for what really counted with the public,' his co-star Rosamund John recalled.[17] Ironically, however, it was not his talent as an actor-director so much as his ineffable Englishness which was in demand. We have seen how on occasions the two could combine, as in his portrayal of Philip Armstrong Scott in *49th Parallel*; from now on the latter was to be predominant. The transformation was sealed by his next film, *The First of the Few* (1942), a biography of R. J. Mitchell, the designer of the Spitfire, which became something of an RAF equivalent of *In Which We Serve*. Once again Howard insisted on being involved at every level, as producer, director and star. And after the film was released he inevitably became associated with and was even seen as personifying the patriotic spirit of the Few, of Mitchell (whom, with no particular regard for the facts, the film depicts as working himself to death to get the plane completed) and of the Spitfire itself.

Thus, it was hardly a surprise when the Ministry of Information and the British Council picked this dry, lined, bookish, pipe-smoking man in his late forties to represent Britain on a morale-boosting lecture tour of Spain and Portugal, planned for 1943. At every level he seemed the ideal choice, as a 'Private and Confidential' letter Howard received from the then Foreign Secretary Anthony Eden in April 1943 reveals:

> . . . it is very important just now to fly the British flag in Spain and to give encouragement to our many friends there, who are to be found in all classes. [. . .]
>
> I hear that the preliminary arrangements for your trip have already gone quite far and I think it would be a great pity to interrupt them at this stage. *I am sure you can do a lot of good for us in Spain and Portugal.*[18]

He needed no further persuasion, and flew to Lisbon on 28 April 1943 to begin a round of lectures and receptions. He spoke about film-making in wartime, delivered a set-piece lecture entitled 'An Actor's Approach to Hamlet', and on 8 May left for Madrid where his name was already 'a household word'. There the pattern was much the same, even if the pressures were rather greater. Howard was paraded at Embassy parties, lunches and Press receptions, at cocktail parties and film premières, his talk about film (*Pimpernel Smith* in particular) and the *Hamlet* lecture, delivered to a celebrity audience at the British Institute on 19 May, hardly interrupting the punishing social whirl. The latter, however, upset the German Embassy who saw it (correctly) as subtle Allied propaganda and succeeded in persuading the Spanish authorities to keep all mention of it out of the media.

The next day Howard returned to Lisbon, for a screening of *The*

First of the Few and a few days' rest at Estoril. Then, early in the morning of 1 June 1943, he boarded a KLM airliner at Lisbon airport for the seven-hour flight home. It never arrived. At around 12.50 it was intercepted by a squadron of German Ju88 fighters. Raked by cannon and machine-gun bullets, the plane disintegrated and plunged into the sea a couple of hundred miles north of Cape Vilano in the Bay of Biscay. Neither Howard's nor any of the other passengers' bodies was ever recovered.

The attack made headline news. At the time, the Germans reacted with statements claiming that Howard's plane had been escorted by Allied fighters, that it was itself heavily armed, and even that it was a legitimate target. More recently, however, Howard's son Ronald and other writers[19] have begged leave to doubt that the eight Bordeaux-based Ju88s which shot it down were on a normal mission and have made plausible claims that there was a Madrid-based plan for the *Luftwaffe* to 'get' Howard.

Was he, as has been suggested, an unofficial British agent, bringing reports back to Eden about the steadfastness or otherwise of the Spanish intellectuals he had met? Was he, like the other passengers on the plane, merely another casualty in a plan to 'get' Churchill who at the time was about to fly back to Britain from a military conference in Algiers? Churchill himself seemed to veer towards this latter view. In *The Hinge of Fate* he was to write:

> As my presence in North Africa had been fully reported, the Germans were exceptionally vigilant, and this led to a tragedy which much distressed me. The regular commercial aircraft was about to start from the Lisbon airfield when a thickset man smoking a cigar walked up and was thought to be a passenger on it. The German agents therefore signalled that I was on board.[20]

The mysterious thickset, cigar-smoking man was actually Alfred Chenhalls, Howard's friend and business partner. But although from a distance he did bear a passing resemblance to the Prime Minister, it is unlikely that German intelligence really mistook him for Churchill; and, given the fact that they were also aware that Churchill's planes were habitually guarded by a squadron of British fighters, even more unlikely that they should have chosen to engage him over the Bay of Biscay.

Thus, bizarre as it at first appears, it seems that Howard was indeed the target; a conclusion which is reinforced by the German Embassy's antipathy to his presence in Madrid and some earlier threats by William Joyce ('Lord Haw-Haw') that 'this sarcastic British actor' would be liquidated 'along with the Churchill clique'.[21] The Germans apparently appreciated just how far, on-screen and off, this languid, 'leisurely' figure had come to personify his new England. He had made the adjustment from matinée idol to useful member of society. Along with *Tawny Pipit*'s public-spirited Jimmy Bancroft (Niall Mac Ginnis), Noël Coward's Captain Kinross and even Roger Livesey's Clive Wynne-Candy, he had gained one of the earliest passports to the broad sunlit uplands. In the saloon-bar parlance of the time he had become 'one of nature's gentlemen', and for that reason alone neither we nor Churchill could afford to lose him.

CHAPTER 10

Straitened Circumstances

We must all *have new clothes – my family is
down to the lowest ebb.*
† Letter from George VI to Clement Attlee, 1945

It was, they said, the 'service vote' which cost Winston Churchill and
the Conservative party the 1945 General Election. They were right;
and, wise after the event, the commentators nodded sagely and agreed
that they should have seen disaster coming.

But no one, or virtually no one, did. Shortly after the results were
announced King George VI admitted privately that the Labour victory had come as 'a great surprise to one and all', while only the
Duke of Devonshire, Lord Templewood, Aneurin Bevan and Em-
manuel Shinwell were later to be credited with correctly predicting
the extent of the landslide. Churchill himself certainly seems to have
had no inkling of what was going to happen. In an unguarded
moment during the campaign he had even confided to Ernest Bevin
his belief that the Conservatives 'know they can't win without me' –
and that was *after* Sir Arthur Harris had warned him that eighty per
cent of the Royal Air Force would be voting against him (and the
other twenty per cent not voting at all).

Imperceptibly but vitally, the national mood had changed in the
early summer of 1945, even in the few brief weeks since VE Day.
Almost unanimously, the Press was still writing of the Prime Minister
in the same laudatory, Greatest Living Englishman manner that it had

used at the time of Dunkirk, five years before. As Anthony Howard noted as long ago as 1963, with the exception of the *Daily Mirror*, the old *Daily Herald* and the then *Manchester Guardian*, 'it persisted in seeing the election as some kind of Roman triumph for a conquering hero'.[1] The trouble was that no one else did, or at any rate not in sufficient numbers to make any significant difference. As the nation emerged from its air-raid shelters, took down the heavy blackout curtains and screwed up its eyes to face the suddenly brilliant lights of peace it was in no mood for another bout of the land-fit-for-heroes triumphalism which had been so much a feature of 1919. Churchill was in a minority of one when he told his doctor, Lord Moran: 'I feel very lonely without a war.'

He was, quite literally, yesterday's man; but the legacy of what he had done lived on. Back in 1941 his Government's acceptance of virtually all the recommendations of Sir William Beveridge's committee of inquiry into Social Insurance and Allied Services had by itself ensured that the forties would be remembered as the 'we' decade. He had started a hare in 1940: now he or his successors had little option but to run with it. Chickens were coming home to roost. Now, although rationing meant reduced means and straitened circumstances, 'we' were still there. The 'one nation' was, as we shall see, already beginning to fracture; but Jack would never again accept that he was not as good as his master.

In this sense 'we' were all natural Labour voters. Clement Attlee and the Labour party wooed us, not so much with visions of another 'land fit for heroes', as with promises of a continuation of the caring, sharing co-operative England of *This Happy Breed*. 'The Conservatives did not – as is often suggested – merely misjudge their electoral tactics,' Anthony Howard went on. And in an essay which took its title from a remark made by Sir Hartley Shawcross, the new Attorney-General, in 1946 – 'We are the masters at the moment – and not only for the moment, but for a very long time to come' – he continued with the most perceptive judgement of 'our' mood:

> The 1945 voter was not so much casting his ballot in judgement of
> the past five years as in denunciation of the ten before that. The
> dole queue was more evocative than El Alamein, the lack of roofs
> at home more important than any 'national' non-party edifice, the

peace that might be lost far more influential than the war that had nearly been won.

Putting that war behind them, the members of Clement Attlee's new Labour government, so decisively elected on 5 July 1945 (although, because of the difficulties of collecting and counting that overseas service vote, the results were not announced until three weeks later) thus seemed set to continue and build on Churchill's egalitarianism. 'We', 'us' and 'ours' were what mattered now, or so it looked on the evening of 26 July after the results had been announced.

It was certainly a bad time for the surviving Colonel Blimps and Tory backwoodsmen. Opportunistic *arriviste* as he was, 'Chips' Channon felt this as much as anyone. There is a skin-of-my-teeth feel to his account of the climax of the 1945 election campaign, compounded as it is in his diaries by a series of personal (but still in retrospect, meaningful) epiphanies:

28 July 1945
On 10 July I was operated on at the London Clinic for hernia and for ten days was prostrate, too ill and angry to reflect seriously on the disastrous Election results. I am stunned and shocked by the country's treachery, and extremely surprised by my own survival [. . .]

I predict the Socialist régime will soon come to grief: I give it three years, and then we shall be returned to power [. . .]

This morning Puffin Asquith rang up to announce the death of his valiant old mother, Lady Oxford [H. H. Asquith's widow, and Raymond's stepmother, Margot]. She was 81, and had long been ill. She was one of the most remarkable, though irritating, women I ever met [. . .]

1 August
I went to Westminster to see the new Parliament assemble, and never have I seen such a dreary lot of people. I took my place on the Opposition side, the Chamber was packed and uncomfortable, and there was an air of tenseness and even bitterness. Winston staged his entry well, and was given the most rousing cheer of his career, and the Conservatives sang 'For He's a Jolly Good Fellow'. Perhaps this was an error in taste, though the Socialists went one further, and burst into the 'Red Flag' singing it lustily.[2]

The previous week had offered other moments of poignant symbolism, too. Mr and Mrs Attlee's arrival at Buckingham Palace on the twenty-sixth in their own Standard 10 saloon only minutes after Churchill's departure in a chauffeur-driven Rolls-Royce following his final audience with the King was perhaps the most graphic. But even that had only been one of many: a few hours earlier there had been the spectacle of jubilant crowds laughing, dancing and even lighting bonfires in the Mall. And it wasn't only in Chips Channon's ears that the very sound of them, as they stood outside the Palace, baying and chanting 'We Want Attlee! We Want Attlee!' at exactly the same spot from which, only a couple of months previously, they had repeatedly cheered the faraway balcony appearance of the King, the rest of the Royal family and Mr Churchill, sounded just like the rattle of the tumbril.

For all that the quiet, unassuming and entirely uncharismatic Attlee was about the most unlikely political leader of modern times, he had presided over the most profound electoral *volte face* in nearly half a century. Almost in spite of himself, he had engineered a rout – or merely ridden a wave – the proportions of which surprised even those close to the centre of things at Labour party headquarters, and elsewhere. The King recalled that Attlee himself was 'looking very surprised indeed' when he arrived at Buckingham Palace to kiss hands. Other observers noted that even the normally-voluble Ernest Bevin was temporarily 'speechless'.

Well he might have been, for the figures spoke for themselves. Labour had gained no less than 227 seats in the new postwar Parliament; the Conservatives alone had lost 203, while the Liberals had been reduced to a rump of just twelve – for many, Margot Oxford's death on 28 July seemed like a timely release. Swingometers were still things of the future, but it did not take a psephologist to understand that the poll had highlighted a seismic change in popular feeling. What took longer to sink in were the deeper implications, for it was not just the numbers of bodies on the Government and Opposition camps which had altered. Almost wilfully, it seemed, the electorate had voted in favour of new brooms. Fifty or so well-known Conservatives, among them no less than twenty-nine wartime ministers, had lost their seats. The most notable were Leslie Hore-Belisha (Minister of National Insurance), Leo Amery (Secretary of State for India), Churchill's own unofficial *aide-de-camp* Brendan Bracken (First Lord of the Admiralty), and Harold Macmillan. Into their places on the green leather benches – or, more accurately, the red leather benches of the House of Lords into which the Commons had decamped after a direct hit on their own chamber – there came . . . who?

Looked at in retrospect again, it is very easy to say that Labour's '45 intake contained some of the best politicians of the century. But Hugh Gaitskell, Richard Crossman and three men who have since been permanently translated to the Upper House, the quondam Prime Ministers Harold Wilson and James Callaghan and the then twenty-seven-year-old Major Woodrow Wyatt were the leavening in a very heavy dough. Three hundred and ninety-three members took the Labour whip when Parliament finally got going at the beginning of August. Unprecedentedly, however, no fewer than 253 – substantially more than one third of the membership of the whole House – were new boys with no Parliamentary experience.

As reports came in that the red flag had been raised in British military compounds around the world in celebration of Attlee's triumph, it did seem that 'we' had got our way. 'Chips' Channon might have talked about a 'Socialist régime', Churchill might have muttered about 'gau-leiters' in his angry bewilderment, and in clubland they might have been talking of England as a kingdom 'under enemy occupation', but it was what we wanted. Or, at any rate, what most of us wanted. Even as the results were being announced on 26 July – Anthony Howard again reported – something like a fifth column was being launched in the dining-room of the Savoy Hotel. There, on that very night, a woman diner was heard to observe: 'But this is terrible – *they've* elected a Labour Government, and *the country* will never stand for that.'

It is a pity that the name of that woman diner has gone unrecorded, for the complexity of her response deserves further analysis. In its sure but subtle differentiation between *them* (the *mobile vulgus*, the Labour-voting common herd) and *the country* (she and her kind) it pinpoints an interesting phenemenon. It suggests that, while she might have been prepared to go along with Mr Churchill and the rest of us when we were 'up against it' in 1940, she now wanted nothing at all to do with our mass ascent to the broad sunlit uplands.

Nor was she alone. Before the end of the summer of 1945, London society had doggedly begun to pick up the pieces and started all over again as if nothing had happened since the warm summer of 1939. It didn't take very long, since for some people nothing very much *had* happened.

On the evening of 7 March 1944, for instance, as the Allied forces prepared for a final push in Europe, Chips Channon marked his forty-seventh birthday with a party in the fabulously ornate dining-room of his London house, 5 Belgrave Square. Thirty of his friends ate salmon, oysters, dressed crab and minced chicken amid what Harold Nicolson had earlier called the 'baroque and rococo and what-ho and oh-no-no' but the snobbish Channon preferred to describe as an 'atmosphere of splendour'. Later – after the brandy – 'the King of Greece gracefully proposed my health!'

'No raid disturbed our revels, and we all wished that Hitler could have seen so luxurious a festival in London at the height of the war,'[3] Channon noted in his diary that night. But if a certain arrogance and tastelessness now seems to underlie those words and indeed the whole idea of throwing such a party at such a time, worse was to follow within a couple of years, for Channon – husband of the wealthy Lady Honor Guinness – faced up to the problems of the new peace with all the concern with which he had faced the war. On 19 September 1945, he noted in his diary, 'Terry [Rattigan] came to lunch, and afterwards we took off our coats and settled down comfortably while he read me the script of his play which took till six. I adored it, and made many comments, suggestions and criticisms.'[4] (They were obviously appreciated by the thirty-four-year-old playwright – unlike some of the bi-sexual socialite's other suggestions – for a grateful Rattigan later dedicated that play, The Winslow Boy, to Channon's son Paul.)

Two years later (and by then divorced) the Chicago-born Conservative MP took up his pen again, this time to describe a lifestyle which still had far more in common with that of Raffles and the grandest chams of Edwardian England than the demob world of Bob Mitchell, Frank Gibbons and 'Shorty' Blake. This was at exactly the time when Attlee's President of the Board of Trade, the prim, puritanical (or in Channon's words, 'honest, if demented') Sir Stafford Cripps was attempting to accustom 'us' to Austerity. Channon, however, was having none of it. Cripps might have been the living image of Austerity – he seldom ate more than the 'three scraped carrots, some salad and an orange' he had one lunchtime at Belgrave Square[5] – Chips, by contrast, was keeping a different flag flying:

5 November 1947
My mornings are what Lady Brownlow calls 'quelque chose'. I am

called early, pummelled by a sergeant; then a breakfast tray appears – eggs, coffee and prunes, and I lie back – revel in the beauty of my room; three telephones tinkle simultaneously, messages are brought in; letters opened, newspapers glanced at . . . Soon it is mid-day and I rise, regretfully. Today was typical of this routine.[6]

Channon was perhaps more assiduous than most in his attempts to recreate the *ancien régime*. His particular 'rococo and what-ho' existence certainly seems signally inappropriate to a time in which a considerable number of his fellow-Londoners (and even some of his Southend-on-Sea constituents) were living amid 'vistas of rotting nineteenth-century houses, their sides shored up with baulks of timber, their windows patched with cardboard and their roofs with corrugated iron, their crazy garden walls sagging in all directions'.[7] Nevertheless, he was by no means alone. Despite the Austerity which meant that bread, meat and other basic commodities continued to be even more tightly rationed than they had been during the war; despite the very special fiscal austerity which our Socialist 'masters' were imposing on the upper classes – it was at this period that many began opening their stately homes to the public in a desperate attempt to make ends meet and pay the taxes – 'polite society' at least was making a determined effort to pretend that there had never been such a thing as a war.

A dance-hall with a unique red plush-egalitarian ambience during the war, the Royal Opera House, Covent Garden quickly regained its exclusivity when it reopened for business in February 1946 with a lavish production of *The Sleeping Beauty*. The King and Queen, the Princesses Elizabeth and Margaret Rose and Queen Mary were in the Royal Box on the opening night, the Queen and Queen Mary wearing pearls and diamond tiaras to emphasize the importance of the occasion. Four months later the Royal family was also present for the running of the first postwar Derby. A quarter of a million people cheered their drive down the Epsom course, and more than £1,000,000 was placed in bets.

Queen Mary had long since returned from the country to her bomb-damaged but hastily patched up home, Marlborough House in the Mall; and the dustsheets were also being removed in the other great London town houses which had survived the Blitz. Lord and Lady Kemsley were soon reinstalled at Chandos House in Queen Anne Street, Mayfair – one of the very finest – where the panelling and Adam chimneypieces had been restored under the supervision of

Sir Kenneth Clark. Lady Londonderry too lost no time in coming back to Londonderry House.

Evening dress was once again *de rigueur* at the Savoy as well as at any self-respecting dinner party, and West End theatres were doing record business. The blackout had ended in April, and although shows continued to 'go up' early because of transport difficulties, by the autumn of 1945 Tommy Trinder was filling the London Palladium every night. Ivor Novello was appearing in his own musical *Perchance to Dream* at the Hippodrome, and Lupino Lane was doin' the Lambeth Walk nine times a week in *Me and My Girl* (Mats, Wed., Thurs. and Sat.) at the Victoria Palace. But unsurprisingly perhaps, Noël Coward was still the toast of the town:

> APOLLO. (Ger. 2663.) 6.45. Weds., Sats., 2.30 Noel Coward's *Private Lives*.
> DUCHESS. (Tem. 8243.) 6.30. Weds., Sats., 2.30. Noel Coward's *Blithe Spirit*. 5th Yr.[8]

On the surface and in the gossip columns it seems as though everything was very rapidly getting back to normal after the 'duration'. The essential fabric of society appeared to be being patched up far more quickly than the tens of thousands of damaged properties. Despite Shawcross's bluster, it looked as though the old Establishment was in all essentials unmoved by Attlee and Austerity. Back in 1963 Anthony Howard quite rightly pointed out that, even in the mid forties, the House of Lords retained sufficient self-confidence to vote down two of the Government's flagship proposals (bills dealing with the nationalization of the steel industry and the abolition of capital punishment) within a matter of months. It was true, too, that even in the teeth of Government opposition, the public schools were beginning to enjoy something of a boom.

Most symbolically of all perhaps, cricket was also bouncing back. At the start of the 1945 season the MCC had actually sanctioned an increase in the number of games to which it gave first-class status. Later in the year came the 'Victory Tests' against Australia (the fourth of which was played at a Lord's which scores of German prisoners of war had been paid three-farthings ($\frac{1}{4}$p) an hour to renovate). There was also a special match in which England took on the combined might of the dominions. England lost by forty-five runs, but that hardly mattered. A total of 1,241 runs was scored during the three days of play, Wally Hammond hit a six (one of no less than sixteen in the match) straight into the Long Room, and at the close of play even Pelham Warner had to concede that it had been 'one of the finest matches played at Lord's'.

Despite all this, with the improved perspective of a further quarter-century we can see that Howard's assertion that, far from ushering in revolution, the 1945 Attlee Government actually 'brought about the greatest restoration of traditional social values since 1660' is not entirely true. On a strictly pragmatic, political level the Government was demonstrably incapable of living up to the heady rhetoric of 1945, but its very existence – so inevitable yet so unexpected – still had profound social consequences. For all the let-them-eat-cakes sang-froid of a man like Chips Channon, there was too a new irreverence. Londoners at the time talked a lot about the scent of the willow herbs which were flourishing on every bomb site; it was as if this new spirit was also in the air. It certainly got everywhere. It pervaded the minds of the once-loyal Londoners who suddenly declared themselves independent in the 1948 Ealing comedy *Passport to Pimlico*. It led to a strike by the waiters and kitchen staff at the Savoy, the Ritz, Simpson's-in-the-Strand and several other hotels. It even penetrated the grand dining-rooms of London SW where the conversation and, my dear, the *company* suddenly seemed to lack something of its former sparkle.

No less a self-propagandist than Chips Channon, Cecil Beaton described a party – 'a quiet and small affair of eight people'; just Churchill, Brendan Bracken, Field Marshal Alexander and one or two others – which was hosted by Lady Cholmondeley at her home in Kensington Palace Gardens in December 1945. Beaton should have been in his element. He too was at the top of his tree – he had designed John Gielgud's revival of Wilde's *Lady Windermere's Fan* which had opened to great acclaim at the Theatre Royal, Haymarket three months previously – but there is a waspishness about his response to the evening which makes it absolutely of the period. Five years previously, no one could possibly have written:

In silence I watched Churchill holding, in his feminine hands with the pointed nails and fingers, a glass of champagne too near his face so that the exploding bubbles tickled him and, like a baby, he screwed up his nose and eyes to display an almost toothless mouth. He wore cracked patent-leather shoes, and his stomach was high-pitched under an immaculate shirt, and his heavy gold watch-chain was like my father's.[9]

Though they were of course not published until much later (the first volume of Beaton's diaries did not appear until 1961) such words do much to vitiate the blind, almost offensive, insouciance of the likes of Chips Channon. Nor are they entirely wayward and atypical. From time to time other straws were caught up on that willow herb-scented wind. Among the most telling are those which were hardly recognized at the time but can now been seen to have a curious, almost symbolic significance.

Thus, it hardly made headline news in 1945 when it was discovered that the Guards Club's premises in Charles Street, once the London *pied-à-terre* of Mrs Ronnie Greville, in which the drawing-room was ornamented with eighteen-carat gold scroll-work, was riddled with dry rot. (Nor for that matter did anyone really notice that in her will Mrs Greville had been public-spirited enough to leave Polesden Lacey, her country home, to the National Trust – to 'us' in effect.) Similarly, not much attention was paid at the time to the auctioning off of the contents of the old German Embassy in Carlton House Terrace. Now, though, the fact that the ornate mahogany desk at which Ambassador von Ribbentrop used to work was knocked down for just £590 (and to, of all people, a theatrical producer!) is not entirely devoid of interest. Most telling of all, however, is the fact that at a time when belt-tightening was the order of the day and builders stretched to their limits, one or two newspapers had the temerity to ask polite but pointed questions about how Winston Churchill, the new Leader of the Opposition, had been able to arrange for the prompt and elaborate refurbishment of his recently-acquired home at 28 Hyde Park Gate.

The times *were* changing. Glittering though they were, Channon's parties, Lady Cholmondeley's dinners and their likes had become isolated, one-off events. With a bottle of champagne costing £3 or more, pineapples at 7/6d each, grapes at 6s a pound and other so-called 'luxury fruits' so scarce as to be virtually unobtainable, they were simply too expensive. No one could afford that sort of entertaining on anything other than special occasions. (And even then something more basic usually sufficed. In 1947 the up-market *Vogue* ran an article on 'Party Food' which included recipes for cauliflower soup, creamed haddock, stuffed marrow and baked beans. Three years later, in June 1950, it was reported that a London restaurant was even serving bison. The 400 lb animal had been raised by the Duke of Bedford at Woburn Abbey; now 'some of it would be served as steaks, other bits would be stewed'.) Good food had become a treat, even something of a Proustian madeleine – which is perhaps why, at an official reception at the Russian Embassy in February 1946, the tables of smoked salmon and caviar were stripped bare within half an hour.

Suddenly, the erstwhile gentleman with Channon's tastes but not necessarily his wife's money was finding himself cabin'd, cribb'd and confined by a new economic reality. In 1938 the pound which in 1914 had bought one pound's-worth of goods or services obtained only sixty-four pence-worth – that had been enough, but over just the next decade its purchasing power was halved again. In 1948 the 1914 pound was worth only 32.9p, sterling having collapsed during the Second World War almost as calamitously as it had in the First. Indeed, a graph of the changing value of the pound in the last one hundred years (*see chart*) also provides a graphic analysis of the changing fortunes of the English gentleman.

By sheer coincidence, the 1880 pound had been worth almost exactly the same as the 1914 pound. Between those two dates, however, in the heady days of Lord Curzon and the Souls and the long afternoon of the Edwardian era, its purchasing power had actually risen. In 1896 the 100-pence 1914 pound was worth no less than 140 pence. Year to year there had been a succession of alpine highs and lows – the Boer War triggered a sudden crash in 1900 – but the entire 1880–1914 period was characterized by an above-the-line bullishness.

Then came the Great War and a spectacular collapse, with the pound tumbling to an unprecedented low of just forty pence in 1920. It never really recovered; albeit that the following fifteen years saw a modest rally with the 1933 pound worth an almost-respectable seventy-one pence. But 'Munich' and the political uncertainties which presaged the outbreak of a second war put paid even to that. Nothing was ever the same again, for this time there was to be no postwar recovery. In 1958 that 1914 pound was worth 22.9p; in 1968, 17.5p; and in 1978 a mere 5.8p – by 1988 it was worth hardly anything at all.

For the English gentleman quite as much as the pound in his pocket, from 1933 on it was to be downhill all the way:

199

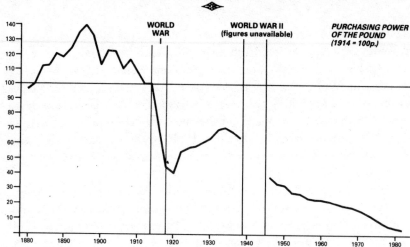

It took some getting used to. Accustomed to buying his shirts in Jermyn Street, he now found that he could not afford them. And adding insult to injury, there were comparatively few servants around to wash, starch and prolong the life of his old ones. That too all came down to money. The days were long gone when, as in the years before 1914, a full-time maid could be had for around 10/- (50p) a week. Even the interwar years in which a gentleman of fairly modest means (say £6,000 or £7,000 a year) could afford a 'gentleman' of his own were receding fast.

In March 1947 the plight of the Marquess of Salisbury was reported in the newspapers. The so-called 'servant problem' had even affected Hatfield House, and the eighty-seven-year-old peer was forced to do his own washing-up. 'But,' he admitted, 'I broke so much china that Lady Salisbury has taken me off washing and allocated me to drying only.' Like everything else, Jeeveses were in particularly short supply during the Austerity years of the late forties.

Unlike most other commodities, however, they were not rationed or on the 'coupons' which were as much a part of life as queues in 1947 and 1948. (With a double irony, a 1947 Government announcement had even said: 'Take care of your 1947-48 clothing book. To save paper it will have to last you two years'!) More than anything else, perhaps, it was the ubiquity of those coupons which imposed the egalitarianism of the time.

No one was exempt. In 1945 Cecil Beaton had had to cut corners so that not one of the elaborate costumes he had designed for Gielgud's production of *Lady Windermere's Fan* took more than its official

200

allowance of twenty-four. (That, however, was comparatively generous: Beaton himself had, like everyone else, an annual, *total* allocation of twenty.) Coupons had become the danegeld of the new dispensation. In the autumn of 1947 it was officially announced that 'Princess Elizabeth will be given 100 coupons for her wedding. Brides-maids will get twenty-three coupons each. Pages ten coupons each'. As if that was not enough, to much dark Tory muttering it was also decreed that at the ceremony itself (which took place on 20 November) formal dress would be optional.

It was thus an Austerity wedding, but hardly the less magnificent for that. It was of its age – and, with fitting irony, it was none other than Chips Channon whose actions finally put both it and that age into context. Greatly to his chagrin he had not been 'commanded' (as he put it) and could only watch the proceedings from the Parliamentary enclosure in Westminster Abbey. On the other hand he had sent a present. He called it a 'faux Fabergé' silver box. Others probably called it 'ersatz' – that ineffably forties word which still conjures up images of snoek and powdered eggs. But at least one newspaper cut through all the persiflage and saw the bibelot for what it was: 'imitation'.

Five days after the wedding, the indefatigable Chips gave a 'big dinner' at 5 Belgrave Square in honour of the Royal couple. Unfortunately, they could not be there in person, and so for once even the great cham was forced to make do with imitations:

> Noël Coward arrived first, wearing what he called the 'Coward emeralds', and everyone was in gala dress – white ties and the women dripping with jewels. I never saw a lovelier sight. The Queen of Spain arrived punctually and I was on the doorstep to meet her. Five minutes later the Queen of Romania drove up with her sister in a taxi . . .[10]

Channon himself admitted that he ' "laced" the cocktails with Benzedrine, which I find always makes a party go'. It seemed to work since the last guests lingered until 4.00 a.m. It was, though (their host later confided to his diary) too bad that Queen Frederika of Greece had been unable to make it: 'Three Queens – it would have been like a hand at poker. But a pair is not bad.' The absence of 'Queen Freddie' notwithstanding, the evening remained 'a great, great success'. Twenty-four hours later Channon could still think of nothing else. 'London rings with tales of my party', he wrote, adding a little later: 'But I am haunted by Queen Helen [of Romania]'s remark to me "When I am back behind the Iron Curtain I shall wonder whether this is all a dream"'.[11] She was not alone. Another of Channon's guests had been the novelist and playwright Somerset Maugham. At one point in the evening he had whispered: 'This is the apogee of your career'. There were two ways to take that – Maugham was famous for his barbed and mordant wit – and though Chips naturally remembered to record the comment in his diary, he seems to have been well aware of its ambivalent acuity too, for with a startling (and almost unique) honesty that very evening he added: 'In a way it was'.

It must have pained him to write that, but by the end of 1947 even Channon's vaunting ambition was failing to keep pace with the times. As a rich American of no particular background (his grandfather had founded a Great Lakes shipping line) the Henry Channon III who first set foot in England in 1918 had never been more than an 'ersatz' gentleman. Politically too he had always been a lightweight; the highest office he ever held was a parliamentary private secretaryship to R. A. Butler (1938–41). But in the thirties he had been amusing; and his marriage to the eldest daughter of the Earl of Iveagh and subsequent election to Parliament (in a seat previously held by both his father- and mother-in-law) had given him the entré to the *beau monde* he so desired.

Now though, with all that 'rococo and what-ho' and his much talked-about ruby-and-diamond buttons, he was beginning to cut a rather ridiculous figure. Hanging on to the coat-tails of the titled and famous – he was himself desperate to be given a peerage – he failed to notice that his prewar brand of white-tied snobbishness was no longer appropriate. Austerity had spawned a 'New Look', and there was simply no room for an increasingly caricatured 'gentleman' like Channon in Attlee's new Britain. In the strictly literal sense he had never been a member of this happy breed; nor now could he ever become one.

He was to live for another eleven years, keeping up his diary all the while – its last entry, written almost exactly ten years after the description of his 'big dinner', characteristically begins with the words: 'I gave a cocktail party for King Umberto [of Italy] who appeared punctually . . .' He never achieved that peerage, but in 1957, barely a year before his death, he was given the consolation prize of a knighthood. Somehow, however, even that came too late.

*

For those perceptive enough to notice, it was a mark of how far Henry Channon and his like had slipped from the real centre of things that, less than a decade after Chips accepted his knighthood, another man received a similar honour in recognition of his achievements which had begun, like Channon's, in the the mid thirties and reached their climax at the dawn of the new Elizabethan era, twenty years later.

Stanley Matthews was created a Knight Bachelor in 1965, shortly after his fiftieth birthday and his retirement from a thirty-five-year career as a First Division footballer.

There had been 'star' footballers before. Sydney Puddefoot, for one, had first turned out for West Ham United in 1912 and, after spells at other clubs and five England caps, rejoined 'the Hammers' before retiring at the end of the 1932–33 season. In 1947 other prewar 'greats' such as Wilf Mannion, Frank Swift and Tommy Lawton were still Saturday-night heroes among the fans of Middlesbrough, Manchester City and Chelsea respectively. But Matthews had a wider constituency, and precisely because of his genuineness – or ordinariness: like Attlee, he never drove anything more flashy than a standard family saloon – he came to personify all that we were aspiring to in the immediate postwar years.

Born at Hanley, Stoke-on-Trent in 1915, 'Stan' was English, working-class and quintessentially one of us. (As indeed he still remains. On the eve of his seventy-fifth birthday at the beginning of 1990, he commented: 'I don't like to go through the front doors. I like to go the back way. I was brought up that way.')[12] The son of a professional boxer, he had no more than a basic secondary education at Wellington Road School, Hanley – but, as two generations of fathers told their sons, he still went on to play for England no less than fifty-four times! What was more, even at the peak of his career, in the late forties and early fifties, he earned no more than about £1,000 a year. (By contrast, Chips Channon had noted as early as September 1935 that it was 'very difficult to spend less than £200 a morning when one goes out shopping'.) He really was one of us.

In retrospect, though, it is tempting to say that it wasn't his athletic prowess – those broad, swerving, dodging, feinting sweeps down the wing that he made for Stoke City (1930–47) and then Blackpool – so much as his singlemindedness which so caught public attention. He embodied football, but he was also an example to us all:

203

Every morning I used to get up at about six o'clock – I still do – and do exercises. When I was in Blackpool I used to run on the beach before training, and every Monday I didn't eat. I just sort of had a clean out, just had fruit juice, and I felt better.

I trained hard. I did a lot of exercises, a lot of skipping exercises and a lot of breathing exercises. I felt so good. I felt I wanted to play for ever.[13]

Football had always been 'the people's game' – 'our' game – and never more so than in 1947. In that year a Great Britain team took on The Rest of Europe at Hampden Park, Glasgow. The national side had never previously lost in front of a home crowd; now though, faced by the combined talents of two Danes, two Swedes, a Belgian, a Czech, a Dutchman, a Frenchman, an Irishman and a Swiss, all that we stood for was at stake. Particularly so since the home team was a blend of all that was good about the prewar years (Matthews, Swift, Mannion and Lawton) together with some younger, postwar blood. Billy Liddell – like Matthews, from an impeccably working-class background – had actually been an RAF fighter pilot. George Hardwick, the captain had also been in the air force and now, with his neat moustache, looked more like a matinée idol than a Middlesbrough clogger. Slightly older, Billy Hughes was an eerie reincarnation of C. B. Fry; a dedicated, teetotal athlete who wrote 'Yours in sport' whenever he was asked for an autograph.

The match was fixed for 10 May 1947.[14] It was a bright, warm Saturday afternoon. Hampden Park was all but full, and the crowd as excited and expectant as that at any prewar Test match when the teams came out. In the cheaply-printed, Austerity-standard programme the full Great Britain line-up revealed a strong England bias:

Swift – Manchester City and England
Hardwick (capt.) – Middlesbrough and England
Hughes – Birmingham City and Wales
Macaulay – Brentford and Scotland
Vernon – West Bromwich Albion and Ireland
Burgess – Tottenham Hotspur and Wales
Matthews – Stoke City and England
Mannion – Middlesbrough and England
Lawton – Chelsea and England
Steel – Morton and Scotland
Liddell – Liverpool and Scotland

For the first twenty minutes it was a close-run thing. Buoyed up by memories of their recent 2–0 victory over the Dutch national side, The Rest of Europe withstood the combined assault of Hardwick's team and the partisan (though peaceful) barracking of the home crowd. But then Matthews – *Matthews!* It had to be Matthews – broke free, and tickled and teased the ball down the wing, and shot!

Oooooh! . . . Da Rui, the French goalkeeper, intercepted well. But, for the home crowd at least, Matthews had as good as scored. Our Stan was a goalmaker – a sturdy Warwick to the transient kings, the dependable 'one' in the textbook's old 'one-two' – but now he was showing his mettle, *our mettle*. Thus, it came as no surprise that we drew first blood. Only minutes later Mannion was there; fair hair flying, through sheer skill outwitting, *out-classing* everything that Europe could throw at him – *Too late, Parola! Enjoy the trip, Ludl?* – to put the ball squarely into Da Rui's net.

One-nil! Europe soon equalized – with an 'easy' goal from the Swedish centre-forward, Gunnar Nordahl; but from there on it seemed an unequal match. Mannion scored again from a penalty; within seconds Steel had put another one away; then Tommy Lawton tipped in a fourth.

Half-time. Already it was four-one – *four-one!* – to us. For those following the match it was already all over bar the (inevitable) shouting. It hardly mattered that there was a second half, nor that two further Great Britain goals were scored; the first an embarrassing own goal by Parola, the second the result of a classic pass from Matthews – *Matthews again!* – to Lawton.

For everyone in Britain it was a classic victory. On one sunny Saturday afternoon it really seemed that all the privations of Austerity, and all the pious words of Mr Attlee and Sir Stafford Cripps had had some point. *Six-one!* We were winning – and, fittingly somehow, Chips Channon missed it all. Equally fitting was the fact that he was away in India – 'the guest of the Viceroy' – paying 'gay visits to dark Princes' and generally taking his fill of the very last days of Empire.

205

CHAPTER ELEVEN

The New Look

I've been offered titles, but I think they get
one into disreputable company.
– George Bernard Shaw on his ninetieth birthday, 26 July 1946.

❧

Six-one! . . . As the cheers died away and the crowds streamed home from Hampden Park at teatime on that sunny Saturday afternoon in May 1947, it seemed like a vindication of all we had been through. The sinking of the *Torrin*, Clive Wynne-Candy's rejection, our own personal privations: *Yes, sir, we have no bananas; no, madam, no nylon stockings; no, positively no linen sheets;* Horizon? Encounter? *You must be joking, guv! Don't you know there's a war on?*

The victory proved particularly hollow, however. In November 1953 a Hungarian side was to destroy England's home invincibility for ever by knocking in six goals at Wembley. *Six*! How that hurt! Best try to forget that they 'might have scored ten'.[1] Best try to forget, too, that by 1953 Attlee's bold experiment was also long forgotten.

With the purest of intentions, he tried to squeeze the rich until – in a more recent phrase – 'the pips squeak'. To a remarkable extent he succeeded. Newspaper gossip and society columns were full of accounts of peers and members of the landed gentry who were suddenly 'down on their uppers'. Throughout the late 1940s and early 1950s there was a steady stream of stories about Lord This or Viscount That who was selling up or (more typically) opening his ancestral pile to the public – ostensibly to share it with us, more

206

pragmatically because he was in desperate need of our 2/6d. entry fee.

Apsley House at Hyde Park Corner, the London home of the 'Iron Duke' and every subsequent Duke of Wellington, was handed over to the nation in 1947. The same year the new National Coal Board established a regional headquarters at Himley Hall, Staffordshire, previously the seat of the Earls of Dudley. Only months later, following the death of Emerald Cunard in her suite at the Dorchester Hotel, rumours circulated that, despite that exalted *locus mortis*, even the celebrated prewar hostess had been near-destitute, the renowned 'Cunard emeralds' long-since sold off and replaced by worthless paste copies. How were the mighty fallen!

It was certainly true that, within yards of Churchill's new home in Hyde Park Gate, Sir Roderick Jones was keeping a cow named Flora Bella in his back garden to provide milk for his family. More seriously, it was also true that in 1948, only three years after inheriting his title on the death of his father, the new Earl Lloyd George had emigrated to America, muttering darkly: 'The British Government is the most inefficient since the Stuarts.'

Things hadn't worked out quite according to plan. Squeezing the rich was one thing, throttling them to death quite another – and quite definitely not what Attlee and his Government had set out to do. That, though, was what was happening. Degree had been fundamentally shak'd and the nation was gradually becoming aware of the consequences. In our demob suits and cut-down hand-me-downs we were still ostensibly one nation, but one which for the first time lacked an officer class – an HMS *Torrin* without our Captain Kinross. He hadn't exactly been evicted from the Big House as the clergy had been 400 years previously, but deprived of the props and appurtenances of life, the traditional English gentleman suddenly both appeared and, more interestingly, *believed himself to be* redundant. True, the higher reaches of the civil service, the City, the judiciary and the Church, the higher ranks in the army and all the influential Court positions were still held by the public school-educated sons of 'good families' (and were to remain so for another quarter of a century). But somehow the pavements of Jermyn Street were less crowded, less and less champagne was being consumed in places like the Drones' Club.

To true socialists like Attlee and Sir Stafford Cripps, that might have been no bad thing. There was a problem, however, for soon the lack of real leadership began to show as all manner of false prophets and new messiahs sought to fill the vacuum – something which had not been dreamt of in the new-utopian philosophy.

All that wartime talk of us and what we would do had raised aspirations. No longer were many of us prepared to remain on the pavement, our noses pressed to the glass of the sweet-shop window while 'the toffs', 'the gentry', call them what you will, enjoyed the party inside. We wanted a part of it. Though they were never more than a fringe, basement-flat movement, the members of a group calling itself The Front Line Generation went as far as to publish a ten-point manifesto which explicitly mentioned this new proletarian uppishness. *Inter alia*, it announced their commitment

> To preverve and extend the wartime spirit of comradeship, born in the danger and suffering, on all fronts, fields, offices and factories.
> To combat snobbery, cruelty, exploitation, warmongering, and bureaucracy wherever they are found to exist.
> To propagate by books, press, meetings, discussion and social groups the aims of our 'Front Line Generation'.
> To assist ex-Servicemen and workers in obtaining suitable occupations in which they can best serve the community, and to encourage their participation in local and national government with the ultimate aim of forming a Front Line Generation Government.[2]

Courtesy of that nice Mr Attlee, we were all soon engaged in much the same struggle. Despite the coupons, controls, licences, permits and 'red tape' which continued to proscribe most forms of private enterprise, almost in spite of themselves, the Labour government's bold plans for the nationalization of almost every strategic industry (coal-mining and iron- and steel-making) and most of the essential services (gas, electricity, road haulage and the railways) only served to raise the expectations of the individual. Quite as much as the rabble-rousing rhetoric of Labour's own 1945 election manifesto, *Let Us Face the Future* – 'No more dole queues in order to let the Czars of Big Business remain kings in their own castles' – the very names of the new *British* Railway Board, *National* Coal Board and *National* Health Service implied that we all now had a stake in things. And with, it has to be said, a thoroughly un-socialist disregard for that future, there were those among us who wanted as big a stake as possible.

Soon there arose in London and every other major city an entrepreneurial under-class of *lumpen*-gentlemen, cocks of the walk who had none of the seigneurial instincts of the Curzon generation. Quite the reverse. Their equivalents had long since emerged throughout 'free Europe', right across 'the West'. Berlin had had the *stenz*, Budapest the *yass*; Paris was still virtually controlled by *oisifs* and *voyous*. Now, in the late 1940s, the 'spivs' erupted on to the streets of London.

The derivation of the term was and remains uncertain. One theory held that it was connected to an old Welsh gypsy word. Another, rather more plausibly, suggested that it originated in the race-course slang of the twenties. No less a man than Lord Rosebery put his money on that – and when it came to racing Rosebery was hardly without experience.

Etymological considerations notwithstanding, in the late forties the spiv became a national figure. He was caricatured on the rapidly disappearing music-hall stage by Sid Field and on the wireless by Arthur English who was even billed as 'The Prince of the Wide Boys'. His every 'outrage' was further chronicled in Arthur Helliwell's hugely popular weekly column in the *People*. It was impossible not to notice him, or to forget him. Writing as recently as 1963, the novelist and critic Colin MacInnes remained able to put him into graphic perspective:

> I remember a pub (run by a former army comrade) where whisky in bottles, intended for export, was obtainable. I knew a man who had Service contacts and could arrange for petrol, though this was dicey because army petrol was coloured puce. As for the spiv, he was a rogue, but for women who wanted impossible nylons, or that legendary object of desire, the new LP record, or the fabulous ballpoint pen that cost 34s. 10d. in the shops (now 6d.), the spiv seemed a kind of Robin Hood.[3]

Like most of MacInnes's journalism, that has the ring of truth. That was exactly how the spiv had been perceived fifteen years earlier. In popular parlance (and in the pages of the *People*) he was the lad with access to bananas which had 'fallen off the back of a lorry', or the man with a friend who had mysteriously 'acquired' a couple of cases of Scotch. He was 'Honest Ed' who knocked out used cars from somewhere round the back of Great Portland Street, or the bloke in the pub with a suitcase full of 'black market' nylons. He always had a pencil moustache and wore 'sharp' suits with chalk stripes and wide lapels, topping off the whole ensemble with a rakishly-tipped trilby hat, corespondent shoes and an unspeakably loud tie.

The likes of Field and English (as well as more recent performers such as the late James Beck, who created the spivvish Pte. Walker in the BBC Television comedy series *Dad's Army* which was first screened in the 1970s) got a lot of mileage out of the new 'Robin Hood'. So too did cartoonists such as Osbert Lancaster. But even there, in going for the easy laugh they were missing the wider point, for the spiv was only the street-corner manifestation of a wider phenomenon.

He dressed as he did in an attempt to prove that he was a cut above the rest of us, a 'regular toff', a 'real gent' – further parallels here with the ostentatious raffishness of the Marlborough House Set. In most cases however that proved a futile gesture. He and most of his kind remained (in another more recent phrase) 'East End boys made bad'. With very few exceptions, they were no more than petty criminals or 'chancers'. But it is important to note that there were those exceptions, for if the majority of spivs were content to remain in the seedier pubs around Denmark Street, Rathbone Place and every suburban dog-track, a few went far further, right into the heart of the Establishment. One or two even came to embody the deep-seated national desire to be up there, doing it, making it and – in a very real sense – coining it.

There was, for instance, Sidney (or later Sydney) Stanley, the last incarnation of a man who had previously operated under the names Solomon Kohsyzcky, Sid Wulkan and Schlomo Rechtand. Opinions were sharply divided about Stanley. To begin with he had seemed to be no more than just another upstart barrow-bow in a 'flash' Italian suit:

> Sidney Stanley was in some ways one of the funniest men one's ever met. He really was a music-hall comedian, there is no doubt about it. He was quick as lightning. He certainly had no visible means of support.[4]

> Sidney Stanley was a larger-than-life character. Very well-off, very friendly, living in Park Lane, very sympathetic to the Labour Party.[5]

Later, however, when it became clear that, through his activities as a 'contact man' or 'fixer' (the euphemisms varied, and Stanley engagingly and characteristically disassociated himself from them all), Stanley had come perilously close to bringing down the Government, both he and the brand of ambitious *spivvery* which he represented were grudgingly taken more seriously.

For a man of obscure 'central European' origins (it later transpired that he had been born in Poland) he had indeed come a long way. In 1927 he had been declared bankrupt. In 1947 he was still undischarged – but by the time that the Prime Minister recommended to Parliament in October 1948 that there should be some investigation into alleged 'irregularities' at the Board of Trade, the extent of his 'penetration' of the hitherto private corridors of power had become alarmingly apparent.

Stanley was, in essence, no more than a 'Mr Fixit'. He made a living – and one substantial enough to support that Park Lane flat – by doing no more than cultivating an acquaintance with Mr A. and then using (and embroidering on) that to 'help' Mr B. further his business interests. Mr B. was naturally asked to defray the costs of all the necessary wheeling and dealing, and cheques of £5,000 or even £10,000 regularly came Stanley's way.

But Stanley was not interested in trading in gallons of black market petrol or even the used cars into whose tanks that puce-dyed petrol might be surreptitiously syphoned; by 1948 he was playing in the big league. He was never quite believed when he dropped Ernest Bevin's name into the conversation, or when – as was later alleged – he told one of his Mr B.s to 'hold himself in readiness' for phone calls from Hugh Dalton and Sir Stafford Cripps. On the other hand, it was becoming all too apparent that he really did have an impressive list Mr A.s. Most of them were politicians: there was George Gibson, a director of the Bank of England: there was Charles Key, Minister of Works; and, best of all in that pinched and permit-ridden era, there was John Belcher, Parliamentary Secretary to the Board of Trade.

For anyone like Stanley, Belcher was a star catch; and Stanley looked after him well, albeit in an Austerity sort of way. He gave the junior – but none the less powerful – minister a gold cigarette-case. He paid for a birthday dinner, advanced the money for a family holiday at Margate and also provided tickets to London dog-tracks. (Accusations of more regularized graft and corruption, in which

Stanley was said to be paying Belcher £50 a week and presenting Mrs Belcher, whom he allegedly knew as 'Lulu', with occasional 'gifts' of £100, were later proved to be without foundation.)

Belcher was the natural victim for a man such as Stanley. A one-time Great Western Railway clerk who had been swept into Parliament by the Labour landslide of 1945, he lacked the knowledge of the inside-track possessed by Attlee, Cripps, Dalton and other more senior members of the Government, many of them veterans of Churchill's wartime National administration. Nothing in his life had prepared him for his new role as ruler and maker. Thirty years earlier he would have been lucky to have been elected to Parliament; there would certainly have been no way in which he could have expected to have been a member of the Government. Now, pitched into power, he was frankly out of his depth:

> Belcher was a very poor man. [He] lived in a war-damaged semi-detached house in Enfield. He let out his rooms to another MP and to a young couple. He himself had three children, so they were all together in this small house. When he first met Sidney Stanley he had a patch on his suit because he had a cigarette burn on it and couldn't afford to replace the suit. Sidney Stanley simply said: 'I'll replace your suit. You're a politician, you simply can't walk around looking like this.'[6]

Belcher allowed him to replace the suit. It now seems almost inconceivably naïve of him to have done so, but in the circumstances Stanley had the upper hand. He was, in Belcher's own words, 'interesting, amusing, generous'; just the kind or urbane, sophisticated and, yes, wealthy and well-connected fellow a Government minister *should* have as a friend. It is unlikely that Belcher had ever previously encountered anyone like him. Thus, blinking in the unaccustomed light, the new minister enjoyed Stanley's friendly blandishments – while failing to notice that he was a member of an administration which in the most literal sense might have looked a little threadbare, but which still professed the highest moral standards.

Attlee's announcement of an inquiry into what had been going on in and around the Board of Trade was therefore inevitable. Headed by Mr Justice Lynskey and imbued with powers to compel the attendance of witnesses and hear evidence under oath, it was not, however, a court of law. Its purpose, Attlee stressed, was to establish what had happened, not to assign guilt. All the same, the tribunal which convened at Church House, Westminster in the autumn of 1948 rapidly came to be seen as an official inquiry into the state of the nation, or at least of those who were at its head. There were long queues for admission to the public gallery, and Lynskey's 50,000-word report became an immediate bestseller when it was published (at just 1/6*d.*; 7½p) in January 1949.

More restrained in tone than the report of Lord Denning's inquiry into the 'Profumo affair' of 1963, it made fairly dull reading. There was no sex, no scandal; just an immensely detailed account of the way in which permits and licences had been obtained by, among others, an importer of amusement-arcade machinery, a firm wishing to export twenty million paper sacks, and a football-pool promoter. In a way, it summed up the period. It was a dry, grey, Crippsian tract which implicitly sought to establish a new morality.

Belcher, like George Gibson, had been unwise, even silly, it concluded. The ministers had put themselves in a compromising situation through their association with Stanley; Gibson in particular had consorted with him specifically in order to bring 'some material advantage to himself'. Gifts and favours had indeed been received; and although they were not exposed to the very public obloquy heaped on several later offenders against the arcane rules of the House of Commons and the elastic standards of public life, the guilty men – who were not, of course, technically guilty at all – paid the price.

Gibson resigned from a number of directorships, just as he had already left the Board of Governors of the Bank of England. 'Surprised and grieved' by Lynskey's conclusions, John Belcher left ministerial office, applied for and received the stewardship of the Chiltern Hundreds – shouldn't that have been the Chiltern Thousands? the wags were asking – bowed low as he took his leave of the House of Commons and returned to his job on the railways.

Sidney Stanley, meanwhile, having confessed to journalists that he would not be bothering with Lynskey's report – it was too long to read in bed, he said – carried on regardless. He sold his story to the papers, ironically it was the *People* which paid him a reputed £10,000, and laughed off the suggestion that he was in any way to blame for what had happened. Within hardly more than a year, however, he had been forgotten. Very few people noticed when he left Britain in 1950 to begin another new career, wheeling and dealing in Israel.

As scandals go the Belcher/Stanley affair was not up to much, and in the long term the Lynskey tribunal which had so dominated the papers in the final weeks of 1948 didn't change much, either. Attlee had been right to set it up, everyone was agreed about that; at the time it had cleared the air, although it now reads as little more than an elaborate (and unwitting) exercise in navel-contemplation.

Everything about it is redolent of the period: even the cheap, coarse paper on which it was printed and which is itself now literally crumbling away. The dry, sweet smell it exudes also seems to bring to mind those postwar years in which dogged, rather dull but indisputably hard-working men strove against all the odds to bring about a just and equitable New World. Appropriately enough, in his own way John Belcher summed them up. Looking back, James Cross, his parliamentary private secretary at the time, has concluded:

> I don't think [Belcher] would ever have been one of what they now call the great Officers of State, but he would have made a very good minister in a reasonable-sized department and could have had a long and successful political career.[7]

In its passing details too Lynskey's report also revealed quite how far removed Attlee's New World was from Churchill's broad sunlit uplands. Publicly at least, Churchill never envisaged an England peopled by contact men, fixers, spivs and Government ministers with patches on their trousers. Nor was our finest hour meant to fade so quickly into a seemingly-endless winter of fuel shortages, rationing, permits, licences and controls in which football pools and one-arm bandits assumed national importance. The bright new certainties offered by the propaganda films of 1942 and 1943, had long since faded. Their usefulness over, Frank Gibbons and Bob Mitchell were now probably claiming National Assistance (the dole); Clive Wynne-Candy had been stood down and pensioned off, while Captain Kinross had been succeeded as master of the *Torrin* by the carrot-eating Stafford Cripps.

Yes, everyone knew that half a millennium previously, at the height of the Peasants' Revolt, the preacher John Ball had posed the question, 'When Adam delved and Eve span/Who then was the gentleman?' Now the question seemed relevant again. Yes, everyone knew that there were still 'grey men' controlling the City, belted earls in the House of Lords, a battalion of Old Etonians in the House of

Commons, adolescent playboy Viscounts at Oxbridge and a whole new generation of postwar 'gentlemen' beginning their public school careers. But somehow they no longer counted. They had lost confidence in themselves – and in so far as we no longer bothered to turn out and gawp as we had done only thirty years previously when one of them decided to marry or christen his child, we had also lost confidence in them.

Was there really no middle ground then, no one to whom we could look up; nothing between the new-monied, essentially American Belgrave Square *beau monde* of Chips Channon and the Denmark Street *demi-monde* of Sidney Stanley and the spivs?

No was the short answer to that; not really. And the very fact that the plinth was empty was itself not accidental. We have seen that from the moment it came to power in July 1945 the Labour Government had set out to squeeze the rich. Despite (and because of) what was possibly the worst economic crisis of the century, it was to continue to do so for the rest of the decade. They were simply the only people who had anything to give.

Attlee was boxed into a corner. On the one hand the Treasury insisted on an 'export drive' to narrow the trade gap caused by a cataclysmic fall in the value of the pound during the war – although this necessarily led to prolonged shortages at home. On the other, it had no alternative but to continue to finance an extravagant programme of public spending. Manifesto commitments to introduce new social policies (in themselves intended to enforce a new egalitarianism) had to be honoured. The armed forces also had to be paid. In December 1946 there were 1,500,000 under arms; by early 1948 the figure had been reduced by more than a third – but that still left 940,000 men for whom the Government was responsible. What was more, as the Opposition never tired of pointing out, they were a double burden. Instead of sitting around waiting for demobilization, the majority could have been wage-earning, tax-paying members of the home workforce, doing their bit for the export drive . . .

Well-meaning if not always well advised, the Government got what should have been its biggest break at the end of 1947 when, after typically well-meaningly disclosing the drift of his Budget to a journalist before announcing it in the House of Commons, the Chancellor of the Exchequer Hugh Dalton resigned and was succeeded by Sir Stafford Cripps.

Like some lesser, pocket Churchill, at the time Cripps came un-expectedly close to reuniting the nation. He was popular – more popular than Dalton anyway – and although he can hardly be said to have had the common touch, the austere 'lawyer's lawyer' got his message across. It was, after all a very simple message: 'There is only a certain-sized cake, and if a lot of people want a larger slice they can only get it by taking it from others.'[8]

That was the true meaning of Austerity. And more than anyone perhaps – certainly more than poor John Belcher – Cripps can stand as Austerity's gentleman. A successful and by all accounts coldly efficient barrister, 'more at home with a judge than with a jury',[9] he was the nephew of Beatrice Webb and, equally importantly, a devout member of the Church of England who really believed in the rightness of what Labour was doing. Despite a very upper-middle-class upbring-ing – his father, another lawyer, became the first Baron Parmoor in 1914 and Lord President of the Council in the 1924 Labour Govern-ment – in his youth he had even been something of a fireband. 'The ruling classes will go to almost any length to defeat parliamentary action,' the newly-knighted Cripps had warned in 1931. In the past he had written a stream of worthy books and pamphlets with titles such as *Towards Christian Democracy*. He had even asked the question *Can Socialism Come by Constitutional Methods?* (1931). Now he was given a unique opportunity to find out as he began putting theory into prac-tice.

He worked hard but, like most prophets, though initially popular, the austere, eccentric, tight-lipped Cripps was soon being pilloried. Naturally enough perhaps, Chips Channon had never been one of his admirers, and in 1951 was noting in his diary:

> In the [House of Commons] lobby I passed Cripps and the air chilled. I felt as if I had breathed the dark, fetid atmosphere of beyond the tomb. He always gives me that impression. Later he went to the dining-room with [John] Strachey, and death and the devil supped together.[10]

Vegetarian frugality might have been to Cripps's taste, but even as the winter of 1947 slowly thawed into the late spring of 1948 the rest of us were already beginning to look for more substantial fare. Cripps did not – could not – succeed in refashioning the nation in his own image. So far as *he* could – so far, indeed, as it was practical –

Churchill had tried that during the war. Now it was too late. The raucous VE night celebrations and the unexpected election of the Labour Government in 1945 were to have signalled the end of a 'duration', a return to normality. Two years on, no one expected that things would be even worse. Austerity be blowed! Cripps was a Roundhead; we wanted to be victorious Cavaliers. Cripps was content with carrots; but another knight, Sir Bernard Docker, was already demonstrating that there was plenty of cake around.

If the spivs and Sidney Stanleys of the late 1940s had looked up to anyone it would have been him. Ironically, however, Bernard Dudley Frank Docker was born out of his time. A more gracious deity would have allowed him to have been a member of King Edward VII's Marlborough House Set. Their bullish extravagance would have suited him; Austerity did not. An old Harrovian, he had been knighted in 1939 and first came to prominence at the beginning of what even Dalton called 'the *annus horrendus*' that was 1947. Fifty years of age and chairman of the Daimler car company, that January he sailed out of the bleakest winter Britain had ever known for a South American cruise on his own 860-ton yacht, the s.s. *Shemara* which was reported to have a crew of thirty-five. That was bad enough; but although Docker couldn't have known it at the time (and even if he did, it would probably have made no difference) the voyage was to mark the start of a longer, fifteen-year journey across the headlines in which he would be hailed, harangued and ridiculed for doing no more than had come naturally to a man of his class and means no more than forty years previously.

The problem was that he did it all so publicly. In comparative terms he was probably no richer than the industrialists who had bought themselves into 'Tum-Tum''s favour half a century earlier. He went to many of the same places too – Ascot and the Ritz were particular favourites – but instead of entering by a side door and entertaining in a private room, it was more Sir Bernard's style to pose for photographers on the front step.

That was exactly what he did at Caxton Hall, Westminster on 3 February 1949 after his marriage to Nora Collins, the widow of Sir William Collins, a wealthy former chairman of the Cerebos Salt company. *Snap!* It made an unforgettable picture: a 'captain of industry' arm-in-arm with his new wife. It made good copy too – for not only was the new Lady Docker wearing a full-length mink coat, it soon emerged that she had at one time been a 'hostess' at the Café de Paris.

Once again there were parallels with Marlborough House days. Old heads shook sagely when they remembered not just the Prince of Wales's liaison with Lily Langtry, but also how a Gaiety Girl called Rosie Boote had become The Most Honourable The Marchioness of Headfort, and how the music-hall star Vesta Tilley had married the Conservative MP Sir Walter de Frece.

But there were crucial differences too. For all that he was the chairman of Daimler and the Birmingham Small Arms Company (BSA), the multi-million pound conglomerate of which it formed a part, like the spivs Docker was still 'in trade'. And although there were superficial similarities between his extravagance and, say, Chips Channon's, that still made a difference. In historic terms he was not quite a gentleman; and yet the very fact that he worked for his living – and was thus virtually one of us – ensured him a place in national affection never granted to the likes of Channon. Tacitly at least, he emerged as an early prototype of what we might call the New Gentleman – and with the vivacious and stupendously snobbish Nora at his side he accepted the mantle with what can only be called unseemly enthusiasm.

Risible though many of his – and more particularly *her* – exploits now seem, at the time they held us all in thrall. To start with, while we put up with a seemingly eternal regime of rationing and yet more coupons, the doings of 'the Dockers' suggested that there was life after Austerity. Later, when it was our turn and we'd 'never had it so good', their difficulties only seemed to emphasize our good fortune. For whatever reason, throughout the late forties, the fifties and much of the 1960s, they were seldom out of the headlines.

They were hardly back from their honeymoon in the south of France when it was revealed that they had bought Hays Lodge in Mayfair, the house in which General Eisenhower had lived from 1943 when he was appointed Supreme Commander of the Allied armies, as their London home. Only a few hundred yards from the Ritz, it was a convenient base for Nora in particular. Soon, she was everywhere, gracing and dwarfing the social scene with her presence, her clothes and above all, her cars. At the 1951 London Motor Show she took delivery of a custom-made Daimler. The number-plate bore her initials. The car itself and every fitting – headlamps, door-handles and even the vanity-mirror – was gold-plated. Even the seats were up-holstered in hand-woven gold brocade. It was a gift from her husband. 'The car is without price. Sir Bernard wanted the British public and overseas visitors to see something really choice,' said a Daimler spokes-man.

Further 'choice' vehicles were to follow. 1953's was a 'Silver Flash' two-seater upholstered in red crocodile leather – which, as fashion pundits were quick to note, exactly matched Lady Docker's handbag. It was small wonder that when any of these cars was parked in London, Prattley, the Dockers' chauffeur had to ensure that a police guard was posted.

Small wonder, too, that 'Lady D' became the darling of the papa-razzi, despite the fact that she was fast approaching fifty years of age. *Snap!* There she was at Ascot, almost literally elbowing the teenage film star Elizabeth Taylor out of the limelight. *Snap!* She was off for a short holiday on her husband's yacht, the *Shemara* at Monte Carlo. *Snap!* Wearing a fur stole ('It's white fox dyed blue') she was at Lord's and supporting Harrow in the annual Eton and Harrow cricket match, because of family ties. It was explained that not only was Sir Bernard an old Harrovian, Lady Docker's own son Lance Callingham was a pupil at the school. *Snap!* Along with Sir Bernard she was having 'an internal spring-clean' at a Hertfordshire health farm. *Snap!* She was at it again, this time hob-nobbing with the likes of Noël Coward, Prince Aly Khan and the Duchess of Argyll at Princess Margaret's charity production of Edgar Wallace's thriller, *The Frog*.

There seemed to be no stopping her. At the end of 1954 she threw a party at Claridge's purely because she wanted 'to thank all those people who have amused and entertained me so much during the past year'. Some 200 of them turned up to drink champagne and receive her gratitude, among them show-business stars ranging from Norman Wisdom (*Snap!*) to Michael Redgrave and Margaret Leighton (*Snap, snap!*). Wearing a £350 dress (*Snap!*) she became the World Women's Marbles Champion in March 1955 when she fortuitously defeated a number of factory girls in a match at Castleford in Yorkshire. Later that year she and Sir Bernard were back at Monte Carlo and noticed at a party at the exclusive Sporting Club – among the other guests, fittingly enough, were Mr and Mrs Aristotle Onassis.

By then, however, things were starting to get desperate. People were beginning to laugh, or worse; and in January 1956 Sir Bernard resorted to holding a Press conference at the Savoy (where else?) to defend his and Lady Docker's lifestyle.

'It's our money we are spending,' he declared – but was it? A full three years previously, at the end of January 1953, Docker and some of the crew of the *Shemara* had been charged with evading currency regulations – in effect with bringing money into the country after cruises in the Mediterranean. He denied the charge and was indeed acquitted on all major counts. 'I feel we have been virtually vindicated,' Lady Docker told reporters, after her husband had been fined a mere £50 for minor, technical infringements of the law. Earlier, her tone had been somewhat more strident: 'I will take the rap for anything my husband is supposed to have done. He is the most perfect husband any woman could possibly have, and I think I am the luckiest woman in the world.'

Lucky or not, the court case marked the beginning of the end for both Lady Docker and her 'most perfect' husband. The New Aristocrats had outstayed their welcome. From about 1953 their position had started to become increasingly precarious. As we have seen, however, they hung on for another three years or so, at or near the top. In April 1956 they had even been among the invited guests at the 'fairytale' wedding of Prince Rainier of Monaco and the film star Grace Kelly. The eyes of the world were upon them as they left Monaco Cathedral in stiff morning dress – *Snap!* some 600 photographers had been assigned to cover the event – but there was already something faintly ridiculous about the way in which they were disporting themselves in that tiny principality little more than half a square mile in area.

The Dockers' wedding present to the new Princess was a gold powder-compact. It was among the last gifts they ever gave, for shortly after their return the cloud of hubris which had ever hovered above their heads descended with a vengeance. At the end of May Sir Bernard was abruptly sacked from his chairmanships of BSA and Daimler – some said because of the reported £8,000 of company money which had been spent on the clothes Nora wore at the opening of a Daimler showroom in Paris. The Docker's own fairytale was over.

'I could hardly have got more publicity if I had cut someone's throat,' Sir Bernard complained. But despite a vigorous campaign in which he went as far as to buy three minutes of air time on the newly established commercial television network and appealed directly to his shareholders for their support, those same shareholders upheld his dismissal at a special meeting on 1 August.

Lady Docker was tearful as she emerged to face a crowd of journalists and the inevitable photographers. Before she was driven away (in, it was noted, a new Bentley) it was as much as she could do to tell them: 'If I have done anything to harm the company, I am very sorry. But I did it to help my husband.'

Snap! . . . Thereafter, the Press photographs and gossip column paragraphs began to tell a very different story. For all their pretensions, the Dockers were now fair game, figures of fun. Luckily for them, Sir Bernard was shortly able to announce that they had 'all the money we shall want for our rather expensive life, and we shall be able to leave Lance as much as we want to'.

Nevertheless, in 1958 it was gleefully reported that Prince Rainier had named Sir Bernard and Lady Docker *personae non gratae* in Monaco after Nora had apparently torn up the country's flag during an evening at the Monaco Casino. The Dockers' own accounts of the incident were eagerly sought – 'Prince Rainier can go and jump in the sea. Monte Carlo is a dump, and anyway I've already banned myself,' said Nora; and Sir Bernard loyally confirmed that they were 'not going back to that dreary little country' – but the whole tone of the reporting made it clear that the nation was no longer behind them.

Apparently unperturbed, they lingered on for some time. Before long, however, Nora was beginning to sell her jewellery. A sapphire-and-diamond necklace which had originally come from Cartier was sent for auction at Christie's at the beginning of 1958. 'Nora has never been very fond of sapphires. She prefers rubies and emeralds,' Sir Bernard explained – although a year later it emerged that his wife was not *that* averse to sapphires. While she was opening a Southampton hair salon, her car (by then a Rolls-Royce) had been broken into – Where was Prattley? Where were the police guards? – and some £150,000-worth of jewels stolen. Through more tears, Lady Docker explained that the sapphires alone were 'as big as half-crown pieces'.

Worse was to follow. One by one the Dockers' possessions were sold off as the couple valiantly struggled to keep up appearances. At an auction Valerie Hobson, the actress-wife of John Profumo picked up a fur coat which had once belonged to Nora for just £80. Later, it was discovered that Sir Bernard was disposing of gold cigarette-box and a cigar-piercer, along with a silver champagne-cooler and cocktail-shaker – but, he stressed, he was 'certainly not' giving up smoking and drinking.

In April 1967 the Dockers moved to Jersey in the Channel Islands. 'Income tax is only four shillings in the pound and there are no death duties,' Sir Bernard said. But by then the braggadocio fooled no one; and the unkindest cut of all came the following summer when it was announced that the property tycoon Harry Hyams was negotiating the purchase of the *Shemara*. 'She is much too large for us now,' Nora explained, while her husband pocketed a cheque reputed to be for some £270,000. 'We are not the rich people we were once,' Sir Bernard explained a few weeks later from the comparatively modest surroundings of the Great Western Hotel, Paddington where he and Lady Docker were staying during a flying visit to London. They were out – but not down. The 1960s ended with the indefatigable Nora (by then sixty-two) clawing her way back into the public eye by doing what by then she did best: reliving past glories. She had fallen out with her Jersey neighbours and, in terms strikingly reminiscent of her self-exile from Monaco more than a decade earlier, lambasted them as 'the most frightfully boring, dreadful people that have ever been born'. *Snap!* She and Sir Bernard were selling up, she said, and 'with the money we get for the house, we will buy a yacht and then we'll be on the move. We'll pull up anchor and float away'.

They were seldom heard of again until, on 22 May 1978, it was announced that Sir Bernard had died at the age of eighty-one.

What is it about the Dockers? . . . Imagine 'Housewives' Choice' playing unheeded in the background, say it with the plaintive twang of Eth in 'The Glums' and you are immediately back in the world of the early fifties. But, a quarter of a century after their tragi-comic two-decade spree, and with only a slight change of tense, we might well ask the same question: What was it about the Dockers?

Their tastelessness (those gold-plated Daimlers), their tactlessness (those mink coats, foreign holidays, champagne parties at Claridge's during a time of Austerity) and their general disregard of all rules and restrictions had something to do with it; but there was more. To start with at least, Bernard and Nora (could there ever have been two more perfectly-suitable names?) appeared to represent all that was worth

222

working for in the postwar world. Untroubled by degree and inherited rank, they seemed to be personifications of the free Churchillian spirit, the natural legislators of the broad sunlit uplands.

As time went on, however, their glamour came to look as tarnished as everyone else's. A little belatedly perhaps, the BSA shareholders got it right in 1956 when they dispensed with Sir Bernard's services. Well before then the world had moved on. It was not without significance that by then we had a new sovereign and that Winston Churchill was back in Downing Street. Finally, it seemed, we were in the ascendancy, the New Elizabethans.

Now, of course, hindsight tells a different story. Far from being a latter-day Edwardian, Bernard Docker was born before his time. He should have been born hereafter. Even with Nora on his arm, *especially* with Nora on his arm, he would have found the perfect niche among the jazzily-dressed junk-bond sellers, market-makers, commodity brokers, international traders, yuppies, dinkies and dealers in any City wine bar at any time in the mid eighties. Had he only timed it right and peaked then (or in the Wilsonian mid sixties) he could even have found himself translated to the House of Lords.

How Nora would have loved that! And how the old socialist Clem Attlee would have winced . . . or perhaps not. *O tempora, O mores!*, in 1955 the ex Prime Minister accepted an earldom and became the first Lord Attlee.

CHAPTER TWELVE

'Sex, Snobbery and Sadism'

Every hero becomes a bore at last.
– Emerson, *Representative Men*

❧

Try as we might, at the beginning of June 1951 it was simply impossible to ignore stories that an Old Etonian and an Old Greshamian, both of them Cambridge graduates (one of them an Apostle!) and senior Foreign Office officials, had gone absent without leave. Rumours had been rife in 'intelligence circles' for a week or more; but then on 7 June the *Daily Express* and *Daily Herald* simultaneously went public about the 'missing diplomats'. A banner headline in the former proclaimed: 'YARD HUNTS TWO BRITONS'.

Dramatic though they were, however, those first articles barely scratched the surface of a story which ran and ran, and has continued to run for almost forty years, scattering all manner of further stories, articles, books, plays, films and theories in its wake.[1] Thankfully, none of these need unduly concern us here. Indeed, from the moment when, shortly before midnight on Friday, 25 May 1951, they boarded a cross-channel ferry at Southampton and formally went missing, the two men cease to have any real relevance to this story: in a complicated way, even as the s.s. *Falaise* headed out into the Solent, Guy Francis de Moncy Burgess and Donald Duart Maclean had ceased to be gentlemen.

No one said as much at the time; but somehow, ineffably, it

happened. There was no fuss,[2] perhaps because to the majority of us it was all very straightforward. Tipped off by the flag-waving *Express* that the upper-class spies were heading for the USSR and in all probability had 'important papers with them', we regarded them as traitors pure and simple.

For the members of what was even then becoming known as the Establishment however, things were not quite so simple. E. M. Forster's Whiggish belief that it was somehow less dishonourable to betray one's country than one's friend still held sway, and many even managed to remain personally loyal to Burgess and Maclean while still appreciating that at a deeper, more atavistic level their friends had finally gone beyond the pale. W. H. Auden, for example, when taxed with the idea that Burgess (an acquaintance rather than a real friend) had apparently wanted to hole up at his (Auden's) house in Ischia after helping Maclean to defect, unequivocally proclaimed: 'Had Mr Burgess really proposed visiting me in Ischia, I should have invited him [. . .] It would be dishonourable of me to deny a friendship because the party in question has become publicly notorious.'[3]

Matters were even more complicated for the Government. For quite some time Foreign Office mandarins had known very well what was going on. In his recent biography of Maclean, Robert Cecil not only establishes that, by the morning of Friday, 25 May the Foreign Secretary (at that time Herbert Morrison) knew of Maclean's treachery, he also goes on to suggest that it had been proved more than a month previously.[4] Maclean had certainly been placed under surveillance – even if, in accordance with the genteel niceties of a bygone age, it effectively ended once the men from M.I.5 had tailed him from his room at the Foreign Office to Charing Cross Station and seen him board the 5.19 p.m. train home every evening. His role as 'Homer' in a transatlantic spying operation in which British and American atomic know-how was being systematically passed to the Russians had also been confirmed. And yet no one did anything!

Looking back it is not difficult to see why. On the one hand there were sound political reasons for keeping everything 'under wraps' for as long as possible. Too hasty a declaration would certainly have severely tried the already-strained patience of the American intelligence community. All the same, the authorities' fatal vacillation also seems to have had quite as much to do with the fact that no one was willing to believe what they were hearing. 'We saw a lot of Donald and [his wife] Melinda when we were in Washington,' Lady Jackling, widow of the diplomat Sir Roger Jackling, has recalled. 'We ran into them all the time; so when we heard, it was *unbelievable*. Donald was such good company.'[5]

There is seemingly no other explanation for the decision, taken at Cabinet level on the very Friday he disappeared, that Maclean should be apprehended and questioned – but not until the following Monday morning. What's more, its underlying insouciance, the implicit belief that, just like anyone else, M.I.5 and even spies 'knocked off' for the weekend at 5.00 p.m. on a Friday, is vividly illustrative of the quandary in which the Government found itself. There was simply no precedent for what Maclean had done; mere 'class-treachery' was only the half of it. Therefore there was nothing in the form-book or school rules to tell it what to do. So, severely shaken, it prevaricated and, publicly at least, did nothing, blithely hoping that the problem would go away – which of course it did, if not in quite the way it had hoped.

Despite all the evidence, Maclean, whose father had after all been a Privy Councillor and Cabinet minister, somehow still remained 'one of us'. He came from an immaculate family background, and was ostensibly such a pillar of his class that the accusations were almost impossible to credit. Hence, what should have been telltale signs of weakness or downright dissidence were for a long time either not noticed or indulged as no more than eccentricity.

It was the same with Burgess; for all his faults he still belonged to the right clubs. Not only were there no suggestions that he was anything worse than a 'pretty rum fellow' before that fateful Friday in May 1951, with his Old Etonian bow-ties, his love of Gilbert and Sullivan, his passion for *Hymns Ancient and Modern* and the novels of Jane Austen (a complete pocket edition of which was among the very few articles he packed prior to his defection) he even seemed to many people to be a paradigm, if increasingly parodic, English gentleman of the mid twentieth century.

He was born in 1911, the son of a Royal Navy commander, and had initially been sent to Eton. But then, in the hope that he would emulate his father's service career, it was agreed that he should transfer to the Britannia Royal Naval College at Dartmouth. Poor eyesight (and very probably the death of his father in 1924 and his mother's subsequent re-marriage) put paid to that and, exceptionally, Burgess was allowed to return to Eton to complete his schooling. He was an able scholar, and although not considered suitable to be a member of Pop, he certainly impressed one member of the Eton staff:

> It is refreshing to find one who is really well-read and who can become enthusiastic or have something to say about most things from Vermeer to Meredith. He is also a lively and amusing person, generous, I think, and very good-natured. He should do very well.[6]

He went up to Cambridge in 1930, to read history on an open scholarship from Trinity College, and seemed set for greatness. He passed part one of the history Tripos with distinction in 1931 and did almost as well in his 'part twos' a year later. Even his blackballing by Pop must have faded into insignificance when, at the end of 1932,[7] Burgess was elected to membership of the Apostles, having been proposed by Anthony Blunt. In public at least, the undoubtedly good-looking, intellectually brilliant, personally charming and generally 'good-natured' old Etonian appeared to be nothing less than another eerie reincarnation of Raymond, Julian, Bim or Rupert; a golden boy, a 'lovely lad' who had somehow pitched up at Trinity rather than Balliol.

Privately, however, various other, less attractive sides of his character had already become apparent. It was, of course, at about this time that Blunt (four years his senior, and elected to a Trinity Fellowship in 1932) recruited him to the communist cause. Both men were homosexual – and occasional lovers – and indeed it has more than once been conjectured that their sexual deviancy and rebellion lay somewhere behind their political deviancy.[8] Unlike the discreet, if effeminate, Blunt, however, Burgess scarcely bothered to conceal his (then illegal) proclivities. Robert Birley, his Eton history teacher, would never have found in Blunt's rooms at Cambridge the 'extraordinary array of explicit and extremely unpleasant pornographic literature' which he discovered in Burgess's when he arrived unexpectedly early for tea one afternoon in the summer of 1931. Nor was Blunt actively involved in the 'higher sodomy' of the Apostles which had reached its peak a quarter of a century earlier (when the society was effectively run by Lytton Strachey [elected 1902] and J. M. Keynes [1903]) but was then enjoying something of a resurgence. It is difficult to imagine him, but all too easy to picture Burgess, enjoying the sybaritic excesses of which members of the society were accused throughout the 1930s:

Hugh Sykes Davies was once asked: 'Is it true that at your Saturday meetings the youngest member is stripped, made to lie face down on the floor and you use his back and buttocks as a table?' 'No,' he replied, tongue in cheek, 'we place him face downwards and he balances the main dish on his penis.'[9]

Such waywardness took its toll, for when Burgess sat his Finals in 1933 he collapsed at his desk in the examination room (in floods of tears, according to Miriam Rothschild) and received only an aegrotat degree. He blamed nervous exhaustion, others discreetly but rather less charitably pointed to a growing laziness and his heavy social commitments.

Whatever the truth, this very public failure was a shattering blow and set the course for the rest of his life. Despite the intercession of friends (notably Sir George Trevelyan, himself a former Apostle and at the time Cambridge's Regius Professor of Modern History) the golden boy was not given what had once seemed an inevitable Fellowship, and went down from Trinity like many another new graduate with no clear idea of what he wanted to do.

All that really mattered was that it was something interesting, and something which would pay enough to keep him in the manner to which he had all-too-rapidly become accustomed. If nothing else, Trinity had acquainted him with the finer things of life – and Burgess was never one to drop a useful acquaintance. At various times over the next eight years he was to have flats in Chester Square, Belgravia (visitors admired its white walls, red curtains and blue cushions and counterpane), in Bentinck Street on the northern fringe of Mayfair and in Lower Bond Street. In addition, there was his hectic social life. Within a few years of coming down from Cambridge he became a member of the Reform Club, while his 'below the line' activities on the flourishing but underground prewar homosexual scene were not without their own expense.[10] Above all, however, the new job had to be something which would give him (and of course his Soviet controller) access to the 'inside-track'. It took some finding. But after several false starts – a spell working for Mrs Charles Rothschild, the mother of his friend Victor (later Lord) Rothschild; an unhappy four weeks as a trainee sub-editor on *The Times* – and with more help from the doughty Trevelyan, in 1936 Guy Burgess finally arrived at Broadcasting House.

Life there was not quite as glamorous as he had hoped, however;[11]

and in consequence, perhaps, his career at the BBC did not last very long. By 1940 he had jumped ship and was doing what he described as 'highly confidential' work for the War Office. He was to combine this with further work for the BBC until 1944 when he was invited to join the Foreign Office in a permanent, full-time capacity. Not unsurprisingly, he accepted with alacrity, and his new career as a diplomat reached its zenith when he was appointed Second Secretary at the British Embassy in Washington in 1950.

Even at the BBC, however, Burgess's job as a talks producer had put him fairly close to the centre of things. He was responsible for, among other programmes, the influential parliamentary review *The Week in Westminster*, and he certainly met politicians by the score. Although not entirely popular with the BBC establishment, he seemed to be in his element. John Green, a Broadcasting House colleague, has recalled:

> He had literally no principles at all. None at all. He was intellectually wicked. He was filthy dirty. He used to leave toffee papers and chocolate in his drawers and then we had a plague of mice. He chewed garlic all the time [. . .] But he was a very good producer. He wasn't at all like a spy. He was a snob. If I said I had been talking to someone in the Carlton Club he knew who I was talking about and wanted to know more. But that was because he was a gossip.[12]

By around 1936–37 Donald Maclean too was in his element. An altogether colder fish than Burgess, in 1934 he had come down from Cambridge wreathed in glory. (Tellingly, he had gone up to the earnest, unfashionable Trinity Hall rather than its more fashionable neighbour.) He took a First in modern languages and then sat the Foreign Office entrance examination. In that too he did spectacularly well. Marked out as a 'high flier', in the autumn of 1935 he started work in the diplomatic service, specifically in the London-based League of Nations and Western Department which dealt with matters concerning the rapidly-ossifying League as well as Spain and Portugal, Switzerland and the Netherlands. Off duty too, the once gauche son of Sir Donald Maclean had metamorphosed into a suave, elegant and very eligible man about town. He was beginning to make his mark in Liberal circles, adorning the right sort of dinner party, squiring the right sort of girl to society dances and, occasionally, nipping off to raffish if not downright Bohemian nightspots.

There had been one or two questions raised at his Foreign Office interview about the communism which he had so publicly espoused as a student, but in view of his background no one took it too seriously. Nor apparently, in those days before any formal vetting was deemed necessary, did anyone notice a long-standing insecurity in Maclean's make-up, a weakness which led the ostensibly ideal diplomat to indulge in bouts of heavy drinking and, on occasion, guilt-ridden homosexual forays.

It wasn't even as if any of this had been 'hushed up'. The evidence was there for all to see. While still a student, Maclean had been accorded the rare honour of a profile in the Cambridge undergraduate magazine, *Granta*. Even more pretentious than most student journalism then and now, this anonymous article was couched in the form of a dialogue between a Questioner (*Q*), Maclean (*DM*) and the 'three dear little fellows' who apparently lived in his head. Most recognizable to the normal run of Maclean's friends and social contacts perhaps, there was 'Fred':

> *Fred*: Well the point is this. Everybody ought to work. That's what I'm here for. I want to get on. Take Shakespeare or Henry Ford – they knew what was what. I belong to eleven societies and three lunch clubs. I once read a paper on Lessing's *Laokoon* (in German, of course). I hope to get a First. It's all due to *hard work*. Any questions. None – well, that's all right. I'm afraid I must go and see a man about a thesis. Goodbye.

Contrasting sharply with 'Fred', there was a rather Burgess-like 'Jack' who seemed to embody everything that the 'Brideshead generation' had stood for at Oxford in the mid twenties:

> *Jack*: Hullo, chaps. I was just having a steak at The George. Awfully good fellows there – and damn' fine waitresses, too. (*He winks*) . . .
> *Q*: May I ask you how you spend your day?
> *Jack*: Oh, I just crack around, you know. Buy a few club-ties here, and smash up a flick there. Bloody marvellous.
> *Q*: Have you no ambitions, Jack?
> *Jack*: Rather. My heart's set on getting into the Hawks. They are such wizard blokes. Besides, the blazer is topping – it looks grand with a Crusader's tie and Sixty-Club trousers.

As if that was not enough, there was also 'Cecil'. *Granta*'s nameless 'questioner' should be congratulated for recognizing and so succintly capturing this aspect of Maclean. A bisexual dilettante in comparison with Burgess, on occasions he could still exhibit a homosexual fayness strongly reminiscent of Oscar Wilde, Bosie, the love-that-dares-not-speak-its-name and the *fin-de-siècle* Aesthetes. Even in 1933 'Cecil' embodied it all:

> *Cecil*: Oh my dear, you did startle me. I was just slipping into my velvet trousers when I heard you call. What *is* the fuss? Has anyone shaved off your hair, or destroyed the Picasso?
> *DM*: No, nothing like that, Cecil. I want to introduce you to the *Granta* representative.
> *Cecil*: Oh, how sweet! You must come to my next party. I am going to have *real* passion flowers, and everybody is going to dress up as a poem . . . *Do* come.[13]

Nothing in either Guy Burgess or Donald Maclean's life was to change very much in the years between their salad days in the late 1930s and their defection on 25 May 1951 (coincidentally, Maclean's thirty-eighth birthday). Quite the reverse: if anything, the character deficiencies which had worried the likes of John Green at the BBC and the *Granta* writer had only intensified with the passing years. Friends and acquaintances were more than ever struck by the instability and inadequacy of the two men. (Although their names are now irrevocably bracketed together, they were never in fact particularly good friends, and still less lovers: Burgess once commented that going to bed with Maclean 'would be like going to bed with a great white woman!')

By the end of the 1940s, Robert Cecil remembers, Maclean was regularly 'drinking himself silly' (although it should perhaps be added that Sir Roger and Lady Jackling never noticed this side of his character). The strain of being 'Cecil', 'Jack' and 'Fred' simultaneously was beginning to tell, and in 1950 the Foreign Office had gone so far as to send the man who was by then the Head of Chancery at its embassy in Cairo for psychiatric treatment. After a period of observation his problems were ascribed to overwork, marital problems and repressed homosexuality. But though they were apprised of all this, his employers seem to have assumed that it was all pretty normal, part of the usual fabric of life for a man in his position. No alarm bells rang, and Donald Maclean simply returned to work, albeit that to friends like Cyril Connolly he was still 'looking rather creased and yellow, casual but diffident'.[14] Fellow-diplomats also noticed a change in the one-time socialite:

> I was struck by Donald's shabby dress and moroseness. He wore an untidy, worn, brownish tweed coat and a crumpled trilby hat, when we were wearing Anthony Eden homburgs. He walked, untalkative, with his hands thrust deep into the coat pockets and his shoulders hunched.[15]

Where Guy Burgess was concerned, the alarm bells had been ringing with monotonous regularity. But again no one did anything. Friends recall his reckless driving, his heavy smoking and even heavier drinking and a general *loucheness*: 'He was at his most congenial on someone else's sofa, drinking someone else's whisky, telling tales to discredit the famous.'[16] The full flavour of his milieu is, however, best conveyed by Goronwy Rees's description of a party thrown by Burgess at the Lower Bond Street flat in 1950. Anthony Blunt was there; so too, among others, were a Cabinet minister, a couple of high-ups from the security service, 'a distinguished homosexual writer of impeccable social origins' and even a German diplomat, 'also homosexual'. In addition,

> There were two very tough working-class young men who had very obviously been picked up off the streets. The drink flowed faster, one of the young men hit another over the head with a bottle, another left with the distinguished writer.[17]

Burgess was leaving to take up his post at the British Embassy in Washington the following day. He was less than keen on the prospect, but it had been pointed out that this was a last chance. Not for the first time the Foreign Office was falling over itself in what amounted to an attempt to save 'dear old Guy' from himself – and that despite the opposition of officials such as George Carey-Foster:

> From my position as Head of the [Foreign Office] Security Department he was a pain in the neck almost from the first day that I met him. Charming he could be, but had my recommendation in 1949 that he be dismissed from the service been accepted, the Foreign Office would have been saved considerable embarrassment.[18]

Gentlemanly forbearance is probably the best way of describing it. No one did anything because (with one or two honourable exceptions such as Carey-Foster) no one thought anything needed to be done. There was, in any case, no mechanism for doing anything: to have reprimanded or even remonstrated with Burgess or Maclean would have been as difficult as pointing out to either of them that he had dressed wrongly for a party or neglected to button his flies. And the fact that neither would ever have been guilty of such solecisms only made matters more difficult.

Thus when they made their move in 1951 it had repercussions which spread far wider than Whitehall and the intelligence community. Auden's reaction was in many ways typical; but even that did not convey what can best be described as the *hurt* felt in Whitehall, Mayfair and clubland. Almost without trying, Burgess and Maclean had inflicted a grievous wound on their own kind. To put it bluntly – and behind panelled doors a lot of blunt talking was going on – they had shat on their own doorstep. Curiously, though, they were shits for running away, not for what they had previously done. It was implicit in the mood of the times that if they had stayed – and there was, of course, really no reason for Burgess to have gone – if Maclean had only faced it out man-to-man with the inquisitors on that Monday morning, socially at least, everything would have been all right. A deal could have been struck, something could have been worked out.

And in all probability it would have been. In those days, when Kim Philby was still regarded as a dependable (if again slightly eccentric) pillar of the Establishment, and lower-middle-class-grammar-school spies such as George Blake were unthinkable, there really was no alternative. A Cold War show-trial of Maclean would have been out of the question. A quiet interrogation, a cover-up and Maclean's subsequent resignation – probably 'for health reasons' – would have been the only safe option. (It might have been the best one too, since even the tacit suggestion that he had 'talked' would almost certainly have curtailed Philby's activities and, indirectly, served as an *a priori* block to the later actions of spies such as Blake.)

There would, inevitably, have been an element of you-scratch-my-back, don't-rock-the-boat-ism about it. Just the same considerations were after all paramount when, as late as 1964, Anthony Blunt, by then Professor Sir Anthony Blunt, Knight Commander of the Royal Victorian Order and Surveyor of the Queen's Pictures, was granted immunity from prosecution on the understanding that he 'told all'. He did, apparently; and his all – or nearly-all – was enough to ensure his survival for a quarter of a century, until times changed and on the afternoon of 15 November 1979 Mrs Margaret Thatcher felt constrained to inform the House of Commons about Blunt's true place in the scheme of things.

A quarter of a century earlier, her predecessor as First Lord of the Treasury, Clement Attlee had remained markedly more reticent. The disappearance of Burgess and Maclean elicited only the most tight-lipped of comments from officialdom. But by its very circumspection and peculiarly dotty attention to form, a statement eventually issued by the Foreign Office only seemed to deepen the mystery:

> Two members of the Foreign Office have been missing from their homes since May 25. One is Mr D. D. Maclean, the other Mr G. F. de M. Burgess. All possible enquiries are being made. It is known that they went to France a few days ago. Mr Maclean had a breakdown a year ago owing to overwork but was believed to have fully recovered. Owing to their being absent without leave, both have been suspended with effect from June 1.

If it was intended as a piece of damage limitation, the statement was published far too late. Coming as it did at exactly the time when stories of the spivs' violation of all that we had achieved were at their height and competing in the columns of every tabloid newspaper with accounts of Bernard and Nora Docker's latest trace-kicking, it only added another nail to the coffin of the One Nation. With its listing of fancy names – *Mr G. F. de M. Burgess indeed!* – and admission that Maclean hadn't been sacked in 1950 despite not being up to the job, it implicitly accepted that there were different classes, that Us and Them still existed. Something was rotten in the State of Denmark; and it was the State or at least its ruling élite which was adjudged to blame.

Those of us on the outside-track weren't to know how grievously it had been shaken by the defection of Burgess and Maclean, nor how seismic and long-lasting the consequences would be. (It is beyond the scope of this book to detail how that panicky, ill-planned departure led to the detection of Philby and then any number of armchair exposés of putative Third, Fourth, Fifth and even Sixth men: *post* Blunt, the names of Victor Rothschild, Sir Roger Hollis, the journalist and Labour MP Tom Driberg (Lord Bradwell) and most recently

John Cairncross have frequently been canvassed. Nor does it serve any real purpose.) Some notion of the extent of the soul-searching, however, came a full four-and-a-half years later when the House of Commons got around to debating a White Paper which contained the conclusions of an official inquiry into the whole Burgess and Maclean affair.

Making the best of what was by any standards a long, botched, embarrassing and very messy business, Harold Macmillan, the then Foreign Secretary, tried to reassure the House that lessons had been learnt. The inquiry had gone to great lengths, he said; and the 'first thought' of its members was 'not how much they could tell the public but what they could do to minimize the harm that had been done'. Unwisely as it turned out, Macmillan also went to extraordinary pains to stress that Burgess and Maclean had been the odd bad apples in an exceptionally rosy barrel. They had been acting on their own; they had not received any 'tip off'. Answering a question tabled by Lieutenant-Colonel Marcus Lipton, the Labour MP for Brixton, he continued:

in this connection the name of one man has been mentioned in the House of Commons, but not outside. I feel that all Honourable Members would expect me to mention him by name and to explain the position. He is Mr H. A. R. Philby, who was a temporary First Secretary in Washington from October 1949 to April 1951 . . .

Macmillan did indeed explain the position. He outlined how Philby had first met Burgess when they had both been undergraduates at Trinity in the early thirties; how it was known that he had had communist associates during and after his university days, and how, as temporary First Secretary in Washington, he had invited Burgess to lodge with him and his family during his time there. Philby had been 'asked to resign from the Foreign Service' in July 1951, Macmillan revealed. Since then his case had been 'the subject of close investigation' – but

no evidence has been found to show that he was responsible for warning Burgess or Maclean. While in Government service he carried out his duties ably and conscientiously. I have no reason to conclude that Mr Philby has at any time betrayed the interests of this country, or to identify him with the so-called 'Third Man', if indeed there was one.[19]

235

On that score at least, Macmillan's statement went a long way towards calming things (although it did nothing to stop the intense Press interest which culminated in the full-dress Press conference that Philby later held). Over and above the Foreign Secretary's emollient words, however, another debate was raging. This one had little to do with the specific whys and wherefores of the Burgess and Maclean case, despite the fact that it too was most eloquently voiced over the despatch boxes in the House of Commons on 7 November 1955. Far more illustrative of the mood of the times, it argued from the specific to the general and saw the spies as symptoms of the rottenness of the State. Speaking for Labour from the Opposition benches, for instance, Richard Crossman berated

> a curious perverted liberalism which tolerated as eccentricity inside the Foreign Office conduct which would have been condemned if anybody else had done the same thing outside the Foreign Office.

That was bad enough; everyone knew he wasn't really talking about the Foreign Office. But then Macmillan came back. Not for the first time – and certainly not for the last – he was wearing his heart on his sleeve when he said:

> Our Foreign Office regards this case as a personal wound, as when something of the kind strikes at a family, or a ship, or a regiment.[20]

Macmillan wasn't just talking about the Foreign Office, either. For what really *was* the last time he was talking about the One Nation, about families like the Mitchells and the Gibbonses, ships like the *Torrin* and regiments like the Grenadier Guards in which he had himself served in the Great War. But it was too late, and outside the House of Commons his words and the White Paper counted for little. Four years previously the stories in the *Express* and *Daily Herald* had initiated a bout of what can only be called 'spy fever'. Papers around the world – and not least in America – had taken up the hunt for 'the missing diplomats', and soon reports that they had been found were attracting as much attention as reports of 'sightings' of the Earl of Lucan or posthumous appearances by 'Elvis Presley' in the tabloid Press today. Every day brought new intelligence. Maclean had definitely been spotted at a New York bus station. No, he was living in

Buenos Aires, disguised as a woman. Rubbish – he and Burgess had been seen together in Brussels, in Bayonne, in Cannes, in Prague and Barcelona . . .

Nowhere were these stories read more avidly than in Britain – poor, rationed, Austerity Britain – where the disappearance of a couple of 'toffs' only seemed to complement the pervading atmosphere of seediness and decay. And, gradually, the real natures of those toffs emerged as journalists pieced together something of their lifestyles from interviews with Auden and anyone else they could think of who might have encountered them. The resulting copy did not make very edifying reading. The two men were reviled as 'society spivs' (surprisingly, no one at the time seems to have explicitly bracketed them with the likes of Sidney Stanley), corrupt maggots living off the decaying fat of a rotten body politic.

Much of this was true; they were corrupt, and so was the body. But that did nothing to abate the fever. The spy had become as central a part of the public's imagination as – coincidentally – he had been to W. H. Auden's, twenty-five years previously:

> Control of the passes was, he saw, the key
> To this new district, but who would get it?
> He, the trained spy, had walked into the trap
> For a bogus guide, seduced with the old tricks.[21]

And he was to retain that position for more than a decade. Indoors or out, wearing an Audenesque weatherproof or wielding a pocket-sized Leica, the spy came to personify Cold War Britain. That did little to ease Harold Macmillan's time at the Foreign Office nor, as we shall see, his later stint in Downing Street. Coincidentally though, it went a long way towards making Ian Fleming a very rich man.

James Bond was 'born', according to Fleming's biographer John Pearson, 'on the morning of the third Tuesday of January 1952, when Ian Fleming had just finished breakfast and had ten more weeks of his forty-three years as a bachelor still to run'.[22] At the time, Pearson adds, Fleming 'was wearing white shorts, a coloured beach shirt from Antonio's in Falmouth, and black hide sandals'. Pearson does not mention, however, that at the time, too, even Jamaica where Fleming had his home was only just recovering from the first shock of Burgess and Maclean's disappearance (indeed, neither man is so much as mentioned in his book).

It is going too far to say that Fleming had the two spies in mind when he sat down that January morning to write the first few pages of *Casino Royale*, the novel which would inaugurate the Bond canon. Commentators have previously preferred to see James Bond as a latter-day Bulldog Drummond and his career as a projection of events in Fleming's own, far-from-uneventful life. Nevertheless, the spy that was to emerge from book after book does now seem peculiarly similar to Guy Francis de Moncy Burgess. The parallels are not so apparent in the early novels, but they leap off the pages of *You Only Live Twice* (1964), not least in the obituary of Bond which 'M' has inserted in *The Times*:

COMMANDER JAMES BOND,
CMG, RNVR

James Bond was born of a Scottish father, Andrew Bond of Glencoe, and a Swiss mother, Monique Delacroix, from the Canton de Vaud [. . .] When he was eleven years of age, both his parents were killed in a climbing accident in the Aiguilles Roux above Chamonix, and the youth came under the guardianship of an aunt, Miss Charmian Bond [. . .] at the age of twelve or thereabouts, he passed satisfactorily into Eton, for which College he had been entered at birth by his father. It must be admitted that his career at Eton was brief and undistinguished and, after only two halves, as a result, it pains me to record, of some alleged trouble with one of the boys' maids, his aunt was requested to remove him. She managed to obtain his tranfer to Fettes, his father's old school [. . .] By the time he left, at the early age of seventeen, he had twice fought for the school as a light-weight and had, in addition, founded the first judo class at a British public school. By now it was 1941 and, by claiming an age of nineteen and with the help of an old Vickers colleague of his father, he entered a branch of what was subsequently to become the Ministry of Defence. To serve the confidential nature of his duties, he was accorded the rank of lieutenant in the Special Branch of the RNVR, and it is a measure of the satisfaction his services gave to his superiors that he ended the war with the rank of Commander [. . .] at the time of his lamented disappearance, he had risen to the rank of Principal Officer in the Civil Service.

The nature of Commander Bond's duties with the Ministry, which were, incidentally, recognized by the appointment of CMG in 1954, must remain confidential, nay secret [. . .]

James Bond was briefly married in 1962, to Teresa, only daughter of Marc-Ange Draco, of Marseilles. The marriage ended in tragic circumstances that were reported in the Press at the time. There was no issue of the marriage and James Bond leaves, so far as I am aware, no relative living.[23]

The comparison should not be pressed too far. But there are enough points of specific similarity in the lives of Bond and Burgess – Eton, paternal aspirations, the early death of a father – to be worth noting. In addition the two men shared a more general fondness for alcohol, cigarettes (Bond smoked in excess of sixty Morland Specials a day) and the good things of life. Not even 'death' could long divide them. Fleming finished *You Only Live Twice* and that obituary of the hero with whom he had become bored in the spring of 1963; less than six months later, on 19 August, Burgess died in Moscow.

Thus, though it is plainly fanciful to imagine that Fleming based Bond on Burgess, the comparison is instructive, if only to demonstrate quite how near Burgess had come to being the gentleman of his time. For as we shall see, Fleming specifically set out to make Bond such a paragon. In part he *was* the reincarnation of Drummond and Richard Hannay, as a contributor to the *Listener* was among the first to realize. 'Ian Fleming makes his bow as a kind of supersonic John Buchan,' he noted in a review of *Casino Royale*. And lest there were any doubt, a decade later the rather breathless prose of a 1964 brochure produced by Glidrose Productions, the company set up by Fleming to administer his Bond interests, hammered the point home:

007 JAMES BOND
HM SECRET SERVICE AGENT
and undoubtedly the most famous of them all.

Born for dangerous adventures, bred to take all hardship, pain and fearful threats with cold courage, trained till his six senses respond instantly to the menace of a situation, educated to be a gentleman – but one who can mix it with the best and the worst of them – he is the true hero of our day and age.[24]

In as large a measure, however, Bond was also conceived as a true Austerity gentleman although the technical razzmatazz and inevitable coarsening of his image in the film versions of the novels have rather obscured this point. The fact that, although Sean Connery was cast in the part, Fleming had wanted Bond played by that gentleman-of-all-trades David Niven in the first film, *Dr No* (1962) is also now forgotten. (So too is the very real possibility that any of those other essentially English actors, James Stewart, Rex Harrison and Trevor Howard, could have been given the role; all were originally considered.) But an examination of the books themselves, and in particular the first three, *Casino Royale* (published in hardback in April 1953), *Live and Let Die* (April 1954) and *Moonraker* (April 1955) shows this to be the case.

Though they have long-since found enduring success in the pulp paperback market, with a combined total of more than forty million sales worldwide, the Bond novels were originally written for a sophisticated readership. *The Times Literary Supplement* recognized this when it called *Casino Royale* 'both exciting and extremely civilized'. Thus Bond smokes 'a Balkan and Turkish mixture made for him by Morlands of Grosvenor Street', lives in a Chelsea flat, drives 'one of the last 4½-litre Bentleys with the supercharger by Amherst Villiers', wears Sea Island cotton shirts, snorkels in a Pirelli mask, dines at Blade's and kills with a .25 Beretta. Every mention of a brand name or real place is part of a conscious attempt to create a real, albeit guyed world in which the novels' target readers could immediately feel at home – if only they were not locked into the grey reality of Austerity. Slightly snootily, Fleming himself acknowledged this in a letter to the American CBS television network (which was considering a series featuring Bond) in 1957:

> In hard covers my books are written for and appeal principally to an 'A' readership but they have all been reprinted in paperbacks, both in England and in America and it appears that the 'B' and 'C' classes find them equally readable, although one might have thought that the sophistication of the background and the detail would be outside their experience and in part incomprehensible.[25]

Classes? . . . Was any one still talking about classes in 1957; anyone that is, other than Mr Mervyn Griffith Jones who, as late as 1960, in all seriousness asked an Old Bailey jury whether they would let their 'wives and servants' read D. H. Lawrence's novel *Lady Chatterley's Lover?* Fleming was rather overstating his case (maybe he thought he had to since he was writing to men whom many of his – yes! – *class* still thought of as semi-civilized 'colonials'). But, however badly he expressed it, he did have a point. Just like *The Life and Death of Colonel Blimp, In Which We Serve* and all those other wartime films – just like the Raffles stories of half a century earlier for that matter –

his books spoke directly to their times. They had the same vicarious fascination as the antics of the Dockers. They were cracking good stories in their own right, but 'the sophistication of the background and the detail' also played a part in their success – a fact borne out by a letter Fleming received from Hugh Gaitskell, the new Wykehamist leader of the Labour party. Writing to thank the author for an advance copy of *Dr No* in 1958, he admitted that he was 'a confirmed Fleming fan – or should it be addict?' And he went on:

> The combination of sex, violence, alcohol and – at intervals – good food and nice clothes is, to one who lives such a circumscribed life as I do, irresistible.[26]

Many a 'B' or 'C' class Labour voter would have said Amen to that, for when the early Bond novels went on sale in paperback they sold in tens and not infrequently hundreds of thousands. As a hardback first novel, *Casino Royale* had done well enough in 1953. All 4,750 copies of its first impression sold out within a month; within eighteen months a hastily reprinted second edition of 8,000 had also disappeared from the bookshops. By any standards those were respectable figures, but when Pan Books began issuing the Bond novels as paperbacks, the accountants began adding a nought, two noughts or on occasions even three, to the sales figures. *Casino Royale* was first published in paperback in April 1955 and in the remaining eight months of that year alone sold 41,000 copies. By the end of 1977 its paperback sales were 2,371,000. The same was true of virtually all the early Bond titles. *Moonraker*, which first appeared in soft cover in October 1956, sold 43,000 copies that year and by 1977 had cumulative sales of 2,282,000. *Live and Let Die* (1957) did even better, selling 50,000 copies in its first three months and, despite being out of print for a year, notching up a figure of 2,467,000 by 1977.

Clearly then, even at the time he was writing, Fleming was wrong: far from finding them 'incomprehensible', like Gaitskell the great mass of the reading public found the Bond novels 'irresistible'. Writing in the *New Statesman*, Paul Johnson might have described *Dr No* as an unattractive blend of 'sex, snobbery and sadism'; but that was exactly what the 'B's and 'C's wanted, what they had been starved of since 1945. Sex had been at a premium until the tabloids got wind of Burgess and their readers first encountered the 'Bond girls'. The

Dockers had offered snobbery. Sidney Stanley and like-minded spivs such as the slum-landlord Peter Rachman had purveyed a perverted, period sadism. Suddenly, everything had come together!

Burgess, Maclean, Bernard Docker, Sidney Stanley, John Belcher and now James Bond . . . by the end of the fifties the secret was out. Toppled from their pedestals of privilege and power, even the nobs had been seen to have feet of clay. *They were no better than the rest of us – a damn sight worse in some cases!* Churchill hadn't meant it to happen in quite that way, but as we stood together on the brink of the 1960s it seemed at least possible that a new, egalitarian One Nation was rising from the cold ashes of Austerity – albeit one in which the pedestals were ominously empty.

Nature abhors a vacuum . . . Spinoza's dictum came spinning down the centuries, and with Wagnerian inevitability smaller men were soon to be seen, tentatively trying their feet in dead men's shoes. As Macmillan's authority waned and the sixties took their own dizzying course, a new truth became self-evident: to be a 'gentleman' one did not need to be a gentleman. In the commercial breaks on Independent Television Cyril Lord was offering anyone the chance to outdo even the Dockers, for just the price of a fitted carpet. 'This is luxury you can afford!' screamed his adverts. Joseph (later Lord) Kagan did not even have to think about advertising. Following Gaitskell's premature (and unexpected) death in 1963 the new leader of the Labour party, Harold Wilson, was modelling his Gannex raincoats free of charge.

And then, of course, there was Wilson himself. No Gaitskellite Wykehamist he! State-educated, pipe-smoking, with a Yorkshire background, a Merseyside constituency and a holiday bungalow in the Scilly Isles, at the time Wilson really did seem to be the personification of Britain; one of Us. (No less than Wilson himself, the image-makers soft-pedalled the fact that this man of the people had not only been educated at Oxford, he had gone on to lecture there, and was elected a Fellow of University College at the age of just twenty-two.)

He was also a consummate politician. He was to run rings round Alec Douglas-Home, the erstwhile 14th Earl of Home, who 'emerged' as Harold Macmillan's successor: that 'elegant anachronism' he called him. But to those who had eyes to see, Wilson's mesmeric hold over the nation in the mid sixties (the comparisons can only be with Churchill and, more recently, Margaret Thatcher) had begun even before he became Prime Minister. In April 1964, six months before the

General Election, when he was no more than the plump, forty-seven-year-old Leader of the Opposition, he had been pictured presenting the then massively-popular Beatles with that year's Variety Club award.

Semiotically, it was a triumph; a Merseyside alliance heralding a promised 'hundred days of dynamic action' (which never quite got started) and new dawn for the common man. Only later was it learnt that Wilson had *proposed himself* for the job.

CHAPTER THIRTEEN

New Elizabethans

It is difficult to know the end of the world
when you reach it.
- Osbert Sitwell, *Laughter in the Next Room*, 1949.

◈

There are, and always were, many reasons why the English gentleman appeared to breathe his last in the 1960s. Not least among them was the fact that, while society was getting younger, he was already past retirement. Ian Fleming forebore from telling us, but (going from information in the *You Only Live Twice* obituary) even the James Bond who featured in his last novel *The Man with the Golden Gun* (1964) was fast approaching fifty. *Eheu fugaces, Postume, Postume,/Labuntur anni* – and the best joke of all was the fact that the new Prime Minister, Harold Macmillian was already pushing sixty-five when he moved into 10 Downing Street following Anthony Eden's resignation in 1957. A General Election later, it really was an old-age pensioner who led the nation into the bright new dawn of the sixties.

Much can – and already has – been said about the decade. In the present context, however, its significance lies in the fact that it saw the end of the natural span, the biblical three-score-years-and-ten, of many of the 'heroes' of this book. Tragically, many did not live to see it. Older than most, Raymond Asquith (d. 1916) would have been a venerable but credible eighty-one on 1 January 1960. Rather younger, Julian Grenfell (d. 1915) would have been seventy-one, Bim Tennant (d. 1916) and Chips Channon (d. 1958) a mere sixty-two. Among the survivors, 'David', the Duke of Windsor was sixty-six, Oswald Mosley and Sir Bernard Docker were both sixty-three, and Noël Coward just sixty.

All were, like Macmillan himself, to outlive the decade (David died in 1972, Coward in 1973, Docker in 1978, Mosley in 1982 and Macmillan in the last hours of 1986) but even before the sixties were over most were already 'weary, wayward, wandering ghosts', to use a phrase coined by Sir Colin Coote in his obituary of the Duke of Windsor.[1]

The world had passed them by. Indeed, in a very literal sense *their* world had virtually ceased to exist. We have already seen how postwar changes in taxation and social policy had practically killed off the traditional country estate. Now, fifteen years later, the position was still critical – but not, as we shall see, terminal. Similar economic exigencies were, however, at work in London. When Raymond Asquith was born in 1878 or, come to that, when Harold Macmillan was born in 1894 the capital had been a brick-and-stucco, predominantly eighteenth-century city, albeit with large areas of nineteenth-century depredation. Nor had very much changed by the time Macmillan came of age in 1915. Piccadilly, Park Lane and many of the squares of Mayfair were still lined with the London town houses of the aristocracy. One hundred years earlier, an American ambassador had noted that these aristocrats 'have *houses* in London [. . .] but their *homes* are in the country'. This was an important distinction and one which still held good at the beginning of the twentieth century when many of those gargantuan houses – to be in the first rank you really needed one with a dining-room which would seat at least twenty-four – remained little used except during the hectic twenty or so weeks of the Court and social season in the early summer.

By about 1920 few could any longer afford such profligacy. One by one the great eighteenth-century houses were sold off, to become offices, clubs and embassies, or simply pulled down. Devonshire House, which stood directly opposite the Ritz Hotel in Piccadilly, was one of the first to suffer this indignity. The 10th Duke of Devonshire rid himself of the vast (or, in comparison to Chatsworth, his Derbyshire country house, *vast-ish*) pedimented, red-brick pile in 1920 for the then unheard-of figure of £1,000,000. It was immediately demolished and replaced by Mayfair House, the 'prestige office block' and car-showroom which currently occupies the site.

Even before the *Luftwaffe* made short work of so much of Georgian London, a similar fate had befallen many of the other 'twenty-four-plus' aristocratic houses. Today scarcely half a dozen survive, the best examples perhaps being Lancaster House and Apsley House, the 'Number One, London' home of the Dukes of Wellington where the dining-table can seat fifty with ease. Nor did the hundreds of 'smaller' Georgian town houses in the streets and squares of Mayfair, Blooms-bury and Belgravia fare much better. Of these, a contemporary ar-chitectural historian reports,[2] less than fifty survive – not one of them now privately occupied. No. 44 Grosvenor Square remained the home of Lady Illingworth until she died in 1967. But then, within months, it too was 'disgracefully' demolished to make way for the new Britan-nia Hotel.

Thus, in the space of one man's lifetime, both London and the whole social fabric had changed out of all recognition. And it wasn't just the topography; there were other changes too which only went to emphasize how far traditional bastions of privilege were as tractable as the walls of Devonshire House when confronted by the bulldozers of the barbarians. The controversial Life Peers Bill which Macmillan introduced in the House of Commons in February 1958 seemed to its detractors actually to presage the end of the aristocracy itself. That was never its intention; even Macmillan would never have got such a measure on to the statute book. But die-hards (of both Right and Left) still saw its dilution of the traditional hereditary base of the House of Lords with men (and women!) appointed for life, as another straw in a domestic wind of change. To some extent they were right,[3] but the continuing existence after more than forty years of advocates of a more radical root-and-branch reform of the upper House is in itself a testament to the resilience of aristocratic influence.

A decade later another event, trifling in itself, was to assume almost equally totemic significance. It actually had more to do with Mr Wilson's 'white hot' technology than social engineering, but in the late 1960s the then General Post Office began a long overdue moderni-zation of the London telephone system. In 1915 there had been no more than 775,000 telephones in the whole of Britain (there are some twenty-five million now); at the Admiralty the Battle of Jutland was fought with the aid of just one wall-mounted instrument. Half a century later, however, the capital's telephone system was on the verge of collapse, and new technology in the form of all-figure, subscriber trunk dialling (STD) was brought in to ease the strain. It solved the problem, but almost incidentally wrought new chaos. Overnight, the traditional alpabetically-dialled exchanges were swept away and replaced by anonyomous three-digit codes. No longer could one be sure who one was dialling – or even who one was. Prefixing one's number with an exchange named MAYfair, BELgravia or GROsvenor (rather than a shyly pseudonymous exchange such as GULliver or DOMinion – both of them in East London) meant something. Now all that had gone: why, there was only a one-digit difference between a Mayfair number (491–) and one in Catford (461–), at the rougher end of Bromley, Macmillan's own south London constituency!

Oh, when degree is shak'd . . . Shakespeare had written. In the sixties it was, and with unprecedented vigour. It was in the sixties that all the birds unsettled by the social upheavals of the previous fifty years came home to roost. That restless, rather ridiculous decade – which in spirit anyway began in about 1956 and petered out in a welter of guilt and recrimination around the end of 1967 – saw the final and inexorable transfer of power from the likes of the patrician, Eton-educated Harold Macmillan, Prime Minister at its onset, to Harold Wilson's meritocratic but no-less-Oxbridge-dominated administration which was still clinging to office as Big Ben chimed in a new and even more disorienting decade. To pundits and revellers alike, the wonder that night was that Macmillan could have survived so long.

He was a showman, there was no doubt about that; Enoch Powell was truer than he knew when he called him an 'old actor-manger'. Friends and enemies alike also reached for theatrical metaphors when describing him as an 'old pro' and 'an old trouper'(Woodrow Wyatt); but occasionally the gloves came off and the Prime Minister was called 'a fraud' and far, far worse.

Just like James Bond, however, Macmillan was also a personification of his time. In a sixties sated by headlines and excess, he was the tabloid gentleman, slightly guyed, very much larger than life. Bernard Levin (no friend) was among the first to notice that during the sixties Britain was 'a nation unable to make up its mind whether to go forward or back',[4] and now perhaps we can see the two Old Etonians as its rival champions. Bond and Supermac: the one, unexpectedly hailed by the 'B's and 'C's, urging the schizophrenic nation on to further progress under the banner of technology and excess; the other donning plus fours and allying himself with the 'A's in a quixotic, backward-looking defence of grouse moors which had little or nothing in common with Chruchill's broad sunlit uplands.

Seen in this simplistic light it was a titanic struggle, and one which Bond (or perhaps Harold Wilson) was ultimately judged to have won on points. There was one problem, though – Bond was a fantasy figure, the creature of Ian Fleming's imagination; Macmillan was all too real. Indeed, no one could have invented him. He has of course made previous appearances in these pages – as a 'lovely lad' wounded in the Battle of the Somme, as an ambitious MP in the days before Munich – but it was only in the extraordinary years between 1957 and 1963 that (in a phrase he would himself have abhorred) the showman really 'got his act together'.

More than George Nathaniel Curzon, A. J. Raffles, Raymond Asquith, Richard Hannay, Oswald Mosley, Bulldog Drummond, Guy Burgess, James Bond or any of the other hero-gentlemen we have encountered, Maurice Harold Macmillan *was* the English gentleman throughout the first eighty-six years of the twentieth century. Another Eton and Balliol man, he was a former member of the Grenadier Guards, the husband of Lady Dorothy Cavendish (and thus an in-law of 'the Devonshires'), an affluent publisher in his own right, a sempiternal clubman (the Atheneum, Buck's, the Beefsteak, the Carlton, Pratt's and the Turf), a fly-fisherman and grouse-shooter of renown. Deaf to the charms of music, blind to the merits of literature more recent than the late novels of Anthony Trollope, he was in short the embodiment of Edwardian England at a time when everyone else – Bernard Docker, Harold Wilson – was trying hard to be a 'New Elizabethan'.

In consequence the Press either loved or hated him – in their terms, it made little difference: he was always good copy. Only hours after the new Queen had appointed him Prime Minister, the papers were gleefully noting that he had chosen to celebrate by taking Edward Heath, his new Chief Whip, off to the Turf Club for a champagne-and-oyster supper. Later he let it be known that he was having 'fun' (a favourite word) in Downing Street – nor were the burdens of the premiership prohibiting his constant rereading of the works of Thackeray, Trollope, Disraeli (with whose flashy political style his own statesmanship has more than once been compared) and Jane Austen. After the public and personal austerity of Attlee and Sir Stafford

Cripps and, more recently, the bland, diplomatic suavity of Sir Anthony Eden, the sketch-writers and political columnists had 'never had it so good'. To them Macmillan was quite the equal of *his* hero, Churchill; no far, far better.

During his regrettable second term as Prime Minister (1951–55) the elderly, ailing Churchill had seemed no more than a shrunken shadow of his siren-suited, cigar-smoking, 'V for Victory' wartime self. Now, Macmillan was daily reinventing the concept of the Lord of the Manor and taking it to neo-Wodehousean lengths. To begin with, it was all something of a joke, and one which seemingly reached its punchline with the Prime Minister's high-profile visit to the USSR in 1959. It was bad enough that he arrived in Moscow wearing a white fur hat, fully one foot in height, which would have looked better on Marlene Dietrich. (On the same pantomimic When-in-Rome level, he used to sport a cloth cap when visiting working-class constituencies at home.) But there was a discreet though discernible spluttering of rage when he was pictured wearing plus fours during a visit to a collective farm in the Ukraine. He looked 'as if he were at Chatsworth!', Malcolm Muggeridge later commented.[5] Worse still, perhaps, there was his habit of greeting all the Russians he met with the words, 'Double-gin! Double-gin!', the closest he could get to the Russian salutation *Dobrodjen* ('Good day').[6]

Still, he seemed to be winning. Despite jibes from Hugh Gaitskell and the Labour Opposition – 'Macblunder' – and the hostility of some sections of the Press, Macmillan and the Conservatives won the 1959 General Election with an overall majority of 107 seats, forty more than the Tories had enjoyed in 1955. Even Vicky's ironically-intended 'Supermac' cartoon (which had an aged, spindly-legged Macmillan flying through the air in a Superman cape and T-shirt) rebounded in his favour. Supermac he was, and for a couple of years at least, Supermac he remained. As another contemporary cartoon vividly illustrated, he had stolen Gaitskell's clothes ('Wot? ME trying to pinch YOUR clothes? Cor, it's obvious they're mine, ain't it?'). Labour was 'the people's party', but Macmillan had by-passed them and found an unexpected popularity with the people themselves. In part this was because everybody loves a winner, and over and above electoral considerations Macmillan always looked more like a winner than the rather prim Hugh Gaitskell. He certainly seemed to be bringing home the spoils of victory:

Let's be frank about it; most of our people have never had it so good. Go around the country, go to the industrial towns, go to the farms, and you will see a state of prosperity such as we have never had in my lifetime – nor indeed ever in the history of this country. What is beginning to worry some of us is 'Is it too good to be true?' or perhaps I should say 'Is it too good to last?'

Is it too good to be true? ... Is it too good to last? ... All his life Macmillan was prey to bouts of intense depression and a completely debilitating melancholia he called his 'Black Dog'. More than once he had to hand over power to R. A. Butler and go off alone to read Jane Austen for a couple of days. In private moments, particularly the early hours of the morning (which he reserved for private reading, writing up his diary and contemplation) it is tempting to imagine the publicly-unflappable PM turning those questions back on himself. Was it all too good to be true? Were these unexpected salad days too good to last? For a man so subtle, a man who when all was said and done was an *intellect* rather than a personality, a shaman rather than a showman, the reverberations must have been intense. And indeed his private letters and diary entries do provide glimpses of a man who knew his time was up.

Behind the music-hall bonhomie there was what can only be described as a less attractive side to the apparently affable old actor-manager. In his diary he noted that Gaitskell was 'a contemptible creature – a cold-blooded Wykehamist intellectual and *embusqué*'[7] while in letter after letter and aside after aside, he betrayed an aristocratic *hauteur* and arrogance far greater than even the form-book snobbishness of Lord Curzon at the beginning of the century:

> I am always hearing about the Middle Classes [he wrote to the head of the Conservative Research Department in October 1957]. What is it they really want? Can you put it down on a sheet of notepaper, and I will see whether we can give it to them.[8]

It is a matter of some speculation whether the devoted, middle-class electors of Bromley – who in 1959 returned Macmillan to Westminister with a majority of 15,452 – would have been so solicitous if they had known that their votes had been bought with a shopping-list jotted down on one side of a sheet of notepaper. (The electors of Orpington in Kent certainly weren't in March 1962. Then, at a by-election in the constituency which was embarrassingly both adjoining and very similar to the Prime Minister's own, the otherwise unremark-able Liberal candidate Eric Lubbock wiped out a massive Conservative majority of 15,000 and entered the Commons with his own very respectable majority of some 8,000.)

Beneath the faintly comic style there was something more serious going on, although that style was in itself part of it. (Not for nothing does Alistair Horne conclude his two-volume authorized biography of Macmillan with a chapter entitled '*Le Style, C'est L'homme*'.) The tweeds, the double-breasted Savile Row suits and baggy plus fours to which the Prime Minister remained so stubbornly attached years after younger parliamentary colleagues had transferred sartorial allegiance to the King's Road and Cecil Gee (or, come to that, Gannex) were only the outward manifestations of an inner, lower-case conservatism.

As the laughter died away and the Conservatives and the Prime Minister himself became more and more unpopular during the first few years of the 1960s, Macmillan came to resemble nothing so much as a gentleman at bay – 'old, incompetent, worn out', as he was himself later to put it.[9] On television every Saturday evening he was mercilessly lampooned (usually by David Frost or William Rushton) as a broken-down has-been in the BBC's satirical review *That Was The Week That Was*. On stage Peter Cook was also caricaturing him as a frayed and faded Edwardian grouse-moor grandee in the revue *Beyond the Fringe* which started at the Cambridge Footlights, toured the world and came home to roost in the West End for several years. Large sections of the Press too were turning on him with a vengeance and ferocity which – as on the occasion when Malcolm Muggeridge described him as 'a faded, attitudinizing, Turf Club bummaree'[10] – frequently outdid even the satirists.

When sorrows come, they come not single spies/But in battalions. In the years leading up to 1963, a year which easily outdid Dalton's 1947 when it came to *anni horrendi*, Macmillan must frequently have pondered those words and maybe even seen the wisdom of J. Alfred Prufrock's later line: 'No! I am not Prince Hamlet, nor was meant to be.' Like the Prince of Denmark he was hemmed in by sorrows many of which were, quite literally caused by spies and the alleged shortcomings of the security services.

We have already seen how, as Foreign Secretary, in November 1955 he had assured the Commons that 'Mr H. A. R. Philby' was not the so-called 'Third Man' in the Burgess and Maclean affair, and that he had not 'at any time betrayed the interests of this country'. Now, he (or, more accurately, the Lord Privy Seal, Edward Heath) had to admit that that was wrong. By the summer of 1963 Kim Philby too had gone, presumably to somewhere 'behind the Iron Curtain' (it was; on 30 July Tass, the Soviet news agency, reported that he had been given Soviet citizenship and a flat in Moscow) and all manner of other spies had been noticed crawling out of the woodwork in the corridors of power.

There wasn't quite a battalion, but there were more than enough to be going on with. The Burgess-Maclean-Philby trail had led inexorably to the doors of Buckingham Palace, and Anthony Blunt. 'Yes, we did suspect that Blunt was a wrong 'un,' Macmillan admitted in 1979.[11] In addition there were several other cases which received a greater degree of publicity. In October 1962 another homosexual, John Vassall, a civil servant working at the Admiralty, had been sentenced to eighteen years' imprisonment for passing information to the Russians. That was bad enough, but the Government was further damaged by the subsequent resignation of Thomas Galbraith, then the innocent Under-Secretary of State for Scotland but previously (and equally innocently) an Admiralty minister in whose office Vassall had once been employed.

Rather less seriously, the very next month Barbara Fell, who worked at the Central Office of Information, was given a two-year prison sentence for passing low-grade office secrets to her Yugoslav lover. Six months later there were still further scares. It was alleged that Sir Roger Hollis, Director-General of M.I.5 was a Russian agent and Graham Mitchell, his deputy, another Vassall. Mitchell, code-named 'Peters', had been spotted 'wandering around the loos in [St James's] park', Macmillan later recalled. [12] It did indeed seem a similar story – 'we thought it was boys' – but at least that time (and, *pace* Chapman Pincher, in the even weaker case of Hollis) there was no proof, no trial and no publicity.

Macmillan was frankly bewildered by it all. With the obvious exception of Miss Hall, all the spies were ostensibly 'gentlemen' – and yet they could behave like that! (Their apparent or alleged homosexuality was not in itself an issue with Macmillan. Although he often chided Butler for his progressive stance on such liberal measures as the legalization of homosexual acts and abortion – and he always remained against the abolition of capital punishment, another of Rab's liberal shibboleths – he does not seem to have been peculiarly 'anti-gay' or 'homophobic' – another phrase which he would have abhorred.) To him the issues were very simple. Ever the Edwardian – ever too the staunch Anglican – he believed that an individual's private life was his own affair, a matter for him and his conscience and not, emphatically *not*, for the daily papers. What he could not understand, though, was how anyone's conscience could allow them to spy or act immorally when his wouldn't allow him even to contemplate such things. There was a great gulf fixed between him and the Edwardian liberalism of E. M. Forster; ever the politician, however, he was also well aware how grievously one man's turpitude could damage the Government.

It was a combination of all this, of moral outrage and political nous, which produced an entirely characteristic outburst when Sir Roger Hollis told him: 'I've got this fellow [Vassall], I've got him!' Macmillan could not share the spy chief's glee, and expressed his feelings in words which bettered even Willie Rushton's parodies:

> I'm not at all pleased. When my gamekeeper shoots a fox, he doesn't go and hang it up outside the Master of Foxhounds' drawing-room; he buries it out of sight. But you can't just shoot a spy as you did in the war. You have to try him . . . better to discover him, and then control him, but never catch him.[13]

Cases such as Vassall's genuinely distressed him; as far as he was concerned they were minor sideshows which distracted him – and everyone else – from 'far more important problems'. But in March 1963 a scandal surfaced which could hardly have been more important, and grievously wounded both Macmillan and the Government. An Opposition question in the House of Commons alluded to certain rumours about a minister and invited a statement, thus forcing the Government's hand on an issue it already knew too much about.

A full six weeks earlier – while Macmillan was paying an official visit to Italy and, ironically, seeing Pope John XXIII at the Vatican – his Private Secretary and the Conservative Chief Whip had confronted the Secretary of State for War, John Profumo. Was there any substance, they asked, to allegations that a couple of years earlier the Minister had been consorting with Miss Christine Keeler, a 'model'? ('"Model" is the word which is nowadays used to describe a rather better class prostitute,' Macmillan noted in his diary a few days later.) No, there wasn't, Profumo replied – well, he had *met* her, but there had not been any 'impropriety'.

This was the line he took in a statement to the House of Commons on 22 March, the day after Colonel George Wigg had tabled his ingenuously-worded question. 'There was no impropriety whatsoever in my acquaintanceship with Miss Keeler,' Profumo declared, adding that in any case he had not met Keeler since December 1961. Downing Street and the security services were disposed to believe him. Macmillan in particular could not conceive of anyone lying to the House of Commons; not only was it 'not done', it just wasn't worth it. Echoing Trollope – who else? – he believed that 'the fact is if you "own up" in a genial sort of way the House will forgive anything.'[14]

He was probably right ('the House' has certainly forgiven many a properly contrite Member in more recent years); but Profumo had not only not 'owned up', he hadn't told anyone the half of an extraordinary story. Today, however, the principal facts are well known, and the story the subject of several books and at least one film.

On a weekend visit to Cliveden, Lord Astor's country house (much favoured by the Marlborough House Set half a century earlier) Profumo had encountered the nineteen-year-old Keeler swimming naked in the pool. This was in July 1961, and it had been an old-fashioned case of love at first sight. The minister and the model had been to bed together – but it was only later, Profumo maintained, that he learnt that Keeler was a 'model' rather than a model, and moreover one who moved in distinctly dicey circles. She stayed at the London flat of Dr Stephen Ward, a society osteopath who had once pummelled the Duke of Edinburgh but whom the police were even then suspecting of living on immoral earnings. Worse, she was also having some sort of affair with Yevgeny Ivanov, of all things a Naval Attaché at the Soviet Embassy in London.

If Keeler hadn't been involved with two gun-toting West Indians *as well* Profumo might have got away with his deception. As things turned out, however, in March 1963 one of them appeared in court having loosed off a few rounds at Ward's flat, and slowly things began to unravel in an embarrassingly public way. Ward began 'talking' in a vain attempt to save his neck (it didn't work; he was found guilty of living off immoral earnings and killed himself on 3 August); the *News of the World* and the *Sunday Pictorial* began taking a more-than-casual interest in Keeler's story; and the Minister was forced to admit that he had lied to the House of Commons. Shortly afterwards he resigned and disappeared into a dignified obscurity.

Which only left Macmillan. Alone at the centre of the stage and for once bereft of all the usual vaudeville props – and come to that a good script – the old actor faced the Commons on the afternoon of Monday, 17 June. 'Bowed and dispirited', he at least thought of Trollope and 'owned up'. His statement was a remarkably candid account of his own reactions to the case and, by extension, to the new dispensation in which such things were conceivable and even possible:

> On me, as Head of the Administration, *what has happened has inflicted a deep, bitter and lasting wound.* I do not remember in the whole of my life, or even in the political history of the past, a case of a Minister of the Crown who has told a deliberate lie to his wife, to his legal advisors and to his ministerial colleagues, not once but over and over again [. . .]
>
> *I find it difficult to tell the House what a blow it has been for me, for it seems to have undermined one of the very foundations upon which political life must be conducted.*[15]

It was a genuinely moving speech, with much more on the same line. Macmillan felt let down; he had 'been deceived, grossly deceived – and the House has been deceived', he said. But there was more to it even than that. It wasn't just one minister, one isolated incident. Suddenly Harold Macmillan seemed to be presiding over a country in which standards – normal, traditional British standards, *his* standards – had completely disappeared:

> In the late spring of 1963 men and women all over Britain were telling, and others were believing, embellishing and repeating, such stories as that nine High Court judges had been engaging in sexual orgies, that a member of the Cabinet had served dinner at a private party while naked except for a mask, a small lace apron and a card round his neck reading 'If my services don't please you, whip me', that another member of the Cabinet had been discovered by police beneath a bush in Richmond Park where he and a prostitute had been engaging in oral-genital activities and that the police had hushed the matter up, that the Prime Minister, Harold Macmillan, had known about some, or all, of these matters but had taken no action, and that a principal member of the royal family had been having sexual relations with one, if not two, prostitutes in circumstances that would have made exposure sooner or later inevitable.[16]

Macmillan's bewilderment gave way to a recurrence of the depression to which he was so prone. And this time the Black Dog would not go away. Butler later recalled his admitting that 'his heart was broken' by the whole business. Certainly, at the very end of his life, twenty years later, a residual bitterness was still apparent. Macmillan (by then the Earl of Stockton) told his biographer, Alistair Horne:

> In the old days you could be absolutely sure that you could go to a restaurant with your wife and not see a man that you knew having lunch with a tart. It was all kept separate but this does not seem to happen these days [. . .] Profumo was incapable of keeping the two sides of his life separate.[17]

Almost without the Prime Minister noticing, the world had changed. He was an old man – in the summer of 1963 he was already approaching seventy years of age – and already beginning to feel out of things. As part of what was to become an almost-obsessive hand-washing exercise, he wrote to the Queen that June: 'I had of course no idea of the strange underworld in which other people, alas, besides Mr Profumo have allowed themselves to become entrapped.' It was not his fault, he assured Her Majesty (and indeed it wasn't); but he then went on to speculate that there might even be 'something in the nature of a plot to destroy the established system'.[18]

That was a bit wide of the mark; one man's 'conspiracy' is seldom more than someone else's cock-up. And so it proved when, in September 1963, the report of Lord Denning's Judicial Enquiry into the whole sorry business was finally published. Fearing the worst – 'I shall have been destroyed by the vices of some of my colleagues' – Macmillan had himself agreed to appear before Denning, and gave evidence for more than half an hour. But he need not have worried. Despite its modish tone, complete with paragraph- and section-headings such as 'The Slashing and Shooting', 'Those Who Knew', 'The Man without a Head' and even 'The Man in the Mask' – no, not that 'member of the Cabinet'! – the judge's report came up with 'nothing sensational'. (Although that did not stop its becoming another of Her Majesty's Stationery Office's unexpected bestsellers.) For once M.I.5 was in the clear; national security had not been compromised. With the exception of the 'utterly immoral' Stephen Ward, it concluded, no one had done anything fundamentally *wrong*.

Politically, Macmillan was profoundly relieved by Denning's findings; he hadn't 'been destroyed' at all. Privately, however, it was a different matter. The report noted that 'there has been no lowering of standards'. Perhaps there hadn't – in general terms. But on an *absolute* level it all looked very different: *Profumo had lied* and everything seemed to be going to the wall.

Tired and ill, by the end of September 1963 the Prime Minister was thinking seriously about whether to resign and hand over to a younger man (the faithful Butler? Reginald Maudling? Lord Hailsham?) at some time in the near future. Political instinct, the support of the Cabinet and, above all, his own sense of fair play – his departure would, he knew, severely damage the Tories' chances in the forthcoming General Election – finally convinced him to stay, at least for the time being; but then his hand was forced. At the end of the first week of October, on the very eve of the opening of the Conservative party Conference at Blackpool, Macmillan was taken ill with what proved to be an acute inflammation of the prostate gland.

He was operated on almost immediately. And, while the Queen phoned every day to enquire about the condition of the man who, since the departure of Churchill, had become her elder statesman, while the Blackpool conference disintegrated into an unseemly scramble for the leadership, Macmillan himself quietly cashed in his chips. After the 'Night of the Long Knives' and a succession of stressful international incidents – Berlin, Cuba and most recently the Nassau summit – the Profumo affair had been the last straw. He was beginning 'to get very tired', he later explained to Alistair Horne, 'to lose grip . . . much more fatigue . . . Long time, seven years – at that rate'.[19]

Not least among the factors contributing to Harold Macmillan's depression in the aftermath of the Profumo affair was the disgraced ex-minister's background. Even in Macmillan's terms, Profumo was a gentleman, one more member of that public school élite which had governed the country with hardly a break for the past one hundred years. (Ironically, Hugh Gaitskell was another; and Macmillan's violent antipathy to him may well have been fuelled by residual notions of the 'class treachery' implicit in his 'defection' to the Labour party.)

An Old Harrovian, during the war Profumo had risen to the rank of Brigadier in the Household Cavalry before entering Parliament, only to lose his seat, like many another Conservative, in the General Election of 1945. Re-elected in 1950, he rose steadily until, in 1960, Macmillan appointed him Secretary of State for War. He was tipped for greatness; he was certainly 'Cabinet material'. He was apparently happily married and, although prematurely bald, still a good-looking man who was equally at home in the corridors of Westminster and at the showbiz parties of his wife's theatrical set. He had everything going for him; in 1963 at the age of just forty-eight he should have been among Macmillan's natural heirs.

It was perhaps this betrayal of promise which most hurt Macmillan (who, out of a sense of propriety, always forbore from giving his MP son Maurice – a mere six years younger than Profumo – any Government office). 'I do not live among young people much myself,' he had said during the Profumo debate. That was self-evidently true, and the satirists made much of the remark. But what was also true, and infinitely more painful for him, was the fact that the few young (or young-ish) people he *did* live among were failing to come up to the very demanding scratch which he and his generation had so effortlessly met half a century earlier.

In that, however, they were by no means alone. In the early summer of 1953, as Britain geared itself up for the Coronation, newspapers were confidently predicting the dawn of a 'New Elizabethan' age. *Woman* magazine extolled its readers to 'Knit Your Own Beefeater' (complete with 'the finest, fiercest whiskers') while the *Daily Express* had gone as far as to predict who would be the 'Modern Elizabethans'. They were a curious bunch; little – except a *pre*-Elizabethan celebrity – linked the prima ballerina Margot Fonteyn, the (American-born) poet T. S. Eliot and the inventor of the jet engine, Sir Frank Whittle, for instance. Nor, ten years on, were other, later postulants such as the speed ace Donald Campbell, the mountaineer Edmund Hillary and the verse-dramatist Christopher Fry to prove any more essential to the neo-Elizabethan *zeitgeist*.

Indeed, had they only had their wits about them – and known in 1953 what they could not have ignored in 1963 – the *Express* reporters could have come up with a far more representative list. (As David Bailey was to do in 1965 with his *Box of pin-ups*, a collection of thirty black-and-white photographs which included portraits of Michael Caine, Lord Snowdon, Jean Shrimpton, the East End gang-leaders and mini-celebrities Ronald and Reginald Kray, together with a clutch of pop singers including John Lennon, Paul McCartney, Mick Jagger and P. J. Proby.) However worthily glorious the likes of Eliot (b. 1888), Fry (1907) and even Whittle (1907) were, by 1963 they were hardly true representatives of the new postwar One Nation ideal. A list of 'Modern Elizabethans' drawn up that year would have been, like the year itself, far more modish and youth-orientated. It would surely have included the names of Ronnie Biggs, Charles Wilson, Bruce Reynolds and the other members of the gang which had held up a Royal Mail train in Buckinghamshire one night that August and made off with some £2,500,000. Like Bailey's, it would also certainly have featured the defiantly one-nation name of John Winston Lennon (born on 9 October 1940), together with those of his friends James Paul McCartney (18 June 1942), George Harrison (25 February 1943) and Richard Starkey (7 July 1940).

With a neatness not normally afforded to historians, the Beatles' first taste of the big time actually coincided with the Profumo crisis. 'Please Please Me', their first song to get to the coveted Number One spot in the *Melody Maker* chart, got there on 2 March 1963. Seven months later, on 13 October, as the nation sweated out the final few hours of the great succession contest – Alec Douglas-Home finally took over as Prime Minister on 18 October – the group made a live appearance on Independent Television's top-rated variety show *Sunday Night at the London Palladium* and London got its first real taste of what the papers were calling 'Beatlemania'. The smoulderingly dark-eyed Paul McCartney, it was noted, had only recently celebrated his twenty-first birthday; George's still lay four months ahead.

Macmillan was thus being more candid than we can now imagine when he admitted that he did 'not live among young people much'. The Beatles were less than half the 'young' Profumo's age and, physically at least, more than young enough to have been Macmillan's grandchildren. And they were far from being the only ones. Michael Philip Jagger (born on 26 July 1943) was also beginning to make his mark, while a whole new generation of young heroes was already in place.

John Osborne's Jimmy Porter had first raised his voice as long ago as May 1956 when *Look Back in Anger* opened at the Royal Court Theatre. John Braine's Joe Lampton first saw the light of day the following year when Eyre & Spottiswoode published *Room at the Top*. Neither was a public school or Oxbridge man. Neither had the time, the neck or the stomach for old school ties. Nor would either, in 1959, have conceivably voted Conservative. (Nor too, in all probability, would Jim Dixon, the university lecturer hero of Kingsley Amis's first novel *Lucky Jim* – but that had been published as early as 1954 when Dixon was already a lecturer and so hardly counted.)

It was difficult, however, to see any of them as a successor to Macmillan, or even Profumo. The mould had been broken, and although none could quite equal John Winston Lennon's credentials, they still represented the New Age. Somewhere along the line, the focus had changed – opinions differed as to whether it happened as a result of Churchill's speeches, the publication of the Beveridge Report, the passing of Butler's Education Bill in 1944 or even the accession of the new Queen Elizabeth. But everyone agreed that by 1963 as a nation we, like them, were no longer looking up to our 'betters'. Hence the satirists, and hence too a new self-absorbtion in which we, Us, the Mitchells and Gibbonses and above all the working classes emerged as the new heroes. The process was complete by the time *Room at the Top* appeared in 1957 (the same year as Richard Hoggart's seminal study of working-class culture, *The Uses of Literacy*), and for that reason alone its hero Joe Lampton can stand as the epitome of New Age man. Indeed, it would be difficult to construct a better one than the figure which emerges from just the book's opening chapters.

Joe has been brought up by an uncle and aunt (so his later success is not based on paternal influence) among 'the back-to-back houses, the outside privies, the smoke which caught the throat and dirtied linen in a couple of hours, [and] the sense of being always involved in a charade upon *Hard Times*' of a Northern town (so no money either). He has also served in the army – but as an NCO, not an officer like Macmillan or Profumo. Charm, he admits, is his only qualification: 'charm wasn't in itself a guarantee of success, but it seemed to follow ambition like a pilot fish'.

Over and above Joe's protean, Everyman nature, two further points about the novel also now seem to have contributed to its success in the late fifties. The first was that it opened in the past, 'ten years ago'. As early as 1947, then, someone was thinking the thoughts which were just occurring to us – 'it was as if all my life I'd been eating sawdust and thinking it was bread' – and not just thinking them but doing something about them! The second led directly on from there: John Braine had written the novel in the first person, so that it was, in effect, almost a vade mecum. Joe's aspirations were our aspirations. The parody good life which Ian Fleming had thought he was peddling to his 'A' class readership had, by 1957, already reached the streets of John Braine's Dufton and, by extension, our streets. And the irony was, it was exactly, word-for-word, brandname-for-brandname the same:

I wanted an Aston-Martin, I wanted a three-guinea linen shirt, I wanted a girl with a Riviera suntan – these were my rights, I felt, a signed and sealed legacy.[20]

Given that it too was written in the pre-Macmillan, pre-Never-had-it-so-good years of the late fifties, Michael Young's pithy 'Essay on Education and Equality' *The Rise of the Meritocracy, 1870–2033* (1958) could well have been an even more useful survival manual for Joe Lampton and a younger generation of (in a more modern phrase) upwardly-mobile *arrivistes*. Its central argument that, in the years following the passing of the 1870 Fisher Education Act, Britain had seen the emergence of a new élite which had come to prominence solely through 'intelligence-plus-effort' certainly seemed to chime well with the times. Albeit that he had done so a decade or more before Joe and the rest of us, Young himself even looked the meritocratic part (and all the more so when he was created a Life Peer in 1978). He had not got where he was because of family influence or money. He hadn't been to Eton, Harrow or even Winchester. Neither was he an Oxbridge man – as was made almost gleefully clear by a smart alec biographical note on the cover of the 1961 paperback edition of his book:

> Born in 1915 of an Irish mother and an Australian father, Michael Young states that he succeeded in learning very little at a number of schools in Australia and England before he was 14. His education began when he arrived at Dartington Hall, the experimental school in Devon started by Dorothy and Leonard Elmhirst. He has been connected with Dartington for thirty years, first as a boy and later as a Trustee trying to learn not only about education, but also about the arts, about industry, and about administration.
>
> Michael Young began to study sociology in 1954. He more or less simultaneously took a very late Ph.D at the London School of Economics and started his own research unit in Bethnal Green, called the Institute of Community Studies . . .

And yet *The Rise of the Meritocracy* was (and still remains) a deeply depressing book, a non-fiction shelf-mate for *1984*, George Orwell's typically bleak view of the future which had been published only eight years previously. Writing as if in the year 2033, Young describes two parallel movements, the 'Rise of the Elite' and the 'Decline of the Lower Classes'. Reread today, his book at first *seems* more relevant than ever; and the fact that in 1957 he could write 'history' so accurately, positively alarming:

The wrecking of Wren's store at Stevenage the Prime Minister regards as a local disturbance; its 2,000 shop assistants were undoubtedly incensed by the management's unexpected rejection of the four-day week. Destruction of the atomic station at South Shields might never have happened with a less provocative director. The walk-out of domestic servants was precipitated by the slowness of the Price Review, similar trouble in the other Provinces of Europe being evidence enough for that. Feeling against the Education Ministry was stimulated by the publication in April of the last report of the Standing Commission on the National Intelligence, and so on.[21]

Even now, still almost fifty years from Young's own *annus horrendus*, all that is old news. Urban riots, four (and even three!) day weeks, anti-nuclear protests – we've had them already. Ditto prices and incomes policies and plans for a United Europe. Parents and school governors have been 'against the Education Ministry' for the best part of a decade – but national intelligence testing is still a central part of the 1988 Education Reform Act . . .

Buzz, buzz . . . as Hamlet would have said. But, unerring though Young's social predictions were, they filled only the first page of a 190-page book, and even now, 120 years after the start of his merito-cratic era – and with only forty-three years left to go – it has to be said that for all their faults Britain's social and educational systems have not ventured down a Youngian path. 'Boarding grammar' schools have not been established to train the élite; quite the reverse. Compulsory intelligence testing and all the rest of what Oliver Stally-brass has called 'the grisly features or ultimately self-destroying charac-ter of Young's apocalyptic vision' has not come to pass.

Quite how far that vision is at variance with the facts, however, is most eloquently demonstrated by the book itself. Once again taking unfair advantage of hindsight, we might pause to glance at a com-parative chronology of the lives of a sample meritocrat, 'Walter Wiffen', and Ernest Bevin which it includes:[22]

	LORD WIFFEN (Born 9 August 1957, Bradford. Father, spinner)		MR ERNEST BEVIN (Born 9 March 1881, Winsford, Somerset. Father, farm labourer)
5–11	A Stream Primary School, I.Q. 120	5–11	Learnt to read and write at village school
11	11–plus exam, I.Q. 121	11	Left school to take job as farm boy

13	Bradford Grammar School I.Q. 119	13	Kitchen boy, Bristol
14	Ditto.	14	Grocer's errand boy
15	Ditto.	15	Van boy
16	Sixth form, I.Q. 118	16	Tram conductor, then van boy again
18	State scholarship, Cambridge University, I.Q. 120, Subsequently 2nd class B.Sc. (Sociology) and M. Sc. (Mental Testing)	18	Drayman
28	Lecturer on Human Relations in Industry, Acton Technical College, I.Q. 123	28	Secretary, Bristol Right to Work Committee
29	Commonwealth Fellow, Harvard University, I.Q. 115	29	Secretary, Bristol Carmen's Branch of the Dock, Wharf Riverside & General Labourers Union
32	Deputy Research Officer, United Textile Factory Technicians Union, I.Q. 115	32	Assistant National Organizer of Union
34	Ditto.	34	National Organizer of Union
41	Research Officer of Union, I.Q. 114	41	General Secretary, Transport and General Workers Union
59	K.C.T.U.C., Secretary of Union, Member of General Council, I.Q. 116	59	Minister of Labour
64	Raised to peerage, I.Q. 116	64	Foreign Secretary
72	Chairman, Education Committee T.U.C., I.Q. 112		
76	Assistant Lecturer, Acton Technical College (where he now is), I.Q. 104.		

Ehue fugaces indeed! How things have changed over the seventy-six years between the births of Bevin and 'Wiffen' - and even more profoundly over the mere twenty-three years which separate the original appearance of *The Rise of the Meritocracy* from today's strangely more conservative world in which less than a month separated the publication of two books whose very titles hinted at what had been going on in the interim.

David Cannadine's *The Decline and Fall of the British Aristocracy* chronicled 'one of the greatest, least recognized, and least understood changes in modern British history', highlighting many of the reasons – the destruction of literally thousands of the great estates, the effects of taxation and other economic factors – which have already been noted in these pages. Paralleling (if occasionally contradicting) Cannadine's 'serious and sustained' analysis, Jeremy Paxman's thesis in *Friends in High Places: Who Runs Britain?* will also be familiar. Things might be a bit rough for the nobs, he concedes, but the old Eton-England axis is (almost) as strong as ever. The book contains no less than forty-two references, some of them lengthy, to Eton and Old Etonians. Public schools in general account for another thirty-one.

Oxford and Cambridge universities (together with such adjuncts as the Oxford Union and the Oxford and Cambridge Club) are discussed on no less than seventy-six of its 340 pages of text. By contrast, there are just seven references to the Trades Union Congress and trade unions in general. The world of the polytechnics and technical colleges in which Young predicted that 'Walter Wiffen' would make his name is hardly so much as mentioned – while Young, 'Wiffen' and *The Rise of the Meritocracy* itself are ignored altogether.

Plus ça change, plus c'est la même chose ... 'Walter Wiffen' may still have his day; born in 1957, in Michael Young's projection he is still only a trade union back-room boy in his mid thirties. But it looks increasingly unlikely.

Even the 'working-class' credentials that were so important to him, Jimmy Porter, Joe Lampton, and Jim Dixon have now been officially removed. Data obtained by the Office of Population, Censuses and Surveys from the 1991 UK Census will for the first time be analysed by criteria from which connotations of class will be absent; rather, attention will be paid to 'job, education and lifestyle'. Government diktat will thus finally formalize the centrist, consensus, One Nationism which Churchill and Coward were propounding exactly half a century earlier. (No one as yet seems to have thought about which box real-life precursors of 'Walter Wiffen' such as Frank Chapple will tick, however. The former trade union leader, created a life peer in 1985, was asked to describe his 'lifestyle' in 1990. He admitted that he was 'still a keeper of racing pigeons', and insisted that he 'considers himself working-class'.[23]

Ironically, it seems far more likely that it will be Cannadine, Paxman and their likes rather than 'Walter Wiffen' who will be the true 'meritocrats' of the millennium. That, however, should hardly surprise us: in the introduction to his book, Paxman writes something of his background. Born in the very early 1950s (and thus only a few years older than 'Wiffen'), he was sent to prep school, then public school (Malvern) and Cambridge before entering the 'trade' of journalism. He concludes:

> It was something of a shock to discover that many of the eminent people I interviewed in research for this book believed that, because of the power of the mass media, one had become part of 'the Establishment' oneself. I hope not.[24]

He will thus have been − no, *was* − pleased by the obloquy he attracted at the 1990 Conservative party Conference for his often-quoted remark that when interviewing politicians he constantly asked himself, 'Why is this bastard lying to me?' On a deeper level, of course, he is right. He is not part of *The* Establishment. But with his 'posh' voice, dark suits, Paisley ties and high-profile on BBC Television, he is certainly part of *an* Establishment. Quintessentially, he is a New Elizabethan; a gentleman of the new dispensation.

Epilogue

The graves are overgrown and the crosses are marked with indelible pencil. Dead, yes; but not the Breed. The Breed never dies.
   — Sapper, *Mufti*, 1919

Throughout the seventy years since Sapper wrote those words their truth has remained self-evident. As we have seen, in the years between 1919 and 1990 – barely one man's allotted span – a Second World War, a period of enforced Austerity and a fair number of upstairs scandals all seemed to threaten the very life of the Breed, but somehow it managed to emerge virtually unscathed.

'Crippling' estate duties had somewhat cramped its traditional style, it was true. So too was the fact that, whether out of pure doctrine or just to appease diehard Clause Four socialists back in the local constituency parties, various Labour administrations had *attempted* to do away with Money, both new and old. One threatened to 'clip the wings' of the upper classes; another to squeeze the rich 'till the pips squeak'. But – maybe because the mere possession of money was never either the *sine qua non* of a gentleman nor something he would ever normally mention – all the strutting and fretting on political stages had remarkably little effect. For fifty, sixty, seventy years, while politicians (and political parties) came and went, the Breed continued to show an unexpected sturdiness and resilience.

Certainly, as Britain – no, let's keep the faith and still say England – entered the 1990s, very little *appeared* to have changed. More than a century after the Hon. Arthur Fitz-Gerald Kinnaird's Old Etonian XI's victory in the 1882 FA Cup, for instance, King Henry VI's 'College Rioiall' (which celebrated its 550th anniversary in the summer of 1990) was still a force in the land. One quarter of the members of the House of Lords – and *half* of all hereditary peers – had been educated there, according to a recent edition of *Dod's Parliamentary Companion*. In 1979 Old Etonians had filled no fewer than six of the nineteen seats in Margaret Thatcher's first Cabinet; not bad going for just one school, least of all in what was hailed as the dawn of a new, truly meritocratic era. In later administrations the proportion was to drop a bit, it was true. But at the time of writing roughly one in every ten Tory MPs is still an Old Etonian – by contrast, after the 1945 General Election the proportion was slightly more than one in four! – and more than a handful of the Old Etonians who continue to occupy seats in the House of Commons hold Cabinet, ministerial or shadow-ministerial portfolios. (Unsurprisingly however, the majority of the remainder continue to lurk on the Conservative back benches. There are just two Labour Old Etonians: the veteran campaigner Tam Dalyell and shadow Arts Minister Mark Fisher.)

If nothing else, then, at least the almost talismanic allure of Eton has survived the obloquy and vicissitudes of the last one hundred years. In his search for *Friends in High Places*, Jeremy Paxman seemed genuinely surprised that:

> The scale of Etonian involvement in the running of twentieth-century Britain is staggering. Between 1900 and 1985 there were just over 1,500 ministers of all parties. No less than 343, over one fifth, had been at school at Eton. (The next highest totals, Harrow with eighty-three ministers in the period and Winchester with fifty-four, came nowhere even remotely close.)[1]

As a gloss on that perhaps rather naïve discovery – and a further example of Eton's continuing ubiquity – we might add that at the end of 1990 not only was Her Brittanic Majesty's Principal Secretary of State for Foreign and Commonwealth Affairs (Douglas Hurd) an Old Etonian, so too were, among others, the editor of *Punch* (David Thomas), the actors Christopher Cazanove and Ian Ogilvy, an only recently retired Lord Chancellor (Lord Hailsham), Green campaigner Jonathon Porrit, the Archbishop of York (John Habgood) a clutch of business tycoons including Sir James Goldsmith and Charles Hambro, a senior television journalist (Ludovic Kennedy) and a radio quiz-show host (Humphrey Lyttelton).

In one sense, however, Eton's survival into the nineties is not quite as 'staggering' as it at first appears. It is hardly the still point in a moving world. *All* Britain's major public schools have jointly and severally seen off the attempts of previous (Labour) governments, well-meaning educationists and 'social engineers' to do them down. They are flourishing now as never before.

One hundred and nine years after the introduction of universal elementary education, with the exception of Mrs Thatcher herself and John Biffen, every member of the 1979 Cabinet had been to public school. And, as Paxman also notes, even now (1990) so too have 'seven out of nine of the army's top generals, two thirds of the external directors of the Bank of England, thirty-three of the thirty-nine top English judges, all the ambassadors in the fifteen most important overseas missions, seventy-eight of the Queen's eighty-four Lord Lieutenants and the majority of the bishops in the Church of England.'[2] (Coyly, Paxman neglects to include himself or any other member of the 'new Establishment' in the list. A random sample of these might include: his own *Newsnight* colleague, the black television journalist Wesley Kerr (Winchester); the former England cricket captain David Gower (King's School, Canterbury); the businessman Richard Branson (Stowe); the comedians John Cleese (Clifton) and Hugh Laurie (Eton) as well as *The Times* columnists Bernard Levin (Christ's Hospital) and Craig Brown (Eton).

Although only some seven per cent of the nation's children (principally its boys) are at present educated at public school – or in the current jargon, 'privately' or in the 'independent sector' – this is still a larger number than it was fifty years ago. Come to that, it is larger than it was as recently as ten years ago when Eton, Harrow and Winchester, decent 'second drawer' schools such as Rugby, Christ's Hospital, Radley and Dulwich and a couple of hundred lesser-known establishments educated just 5.8 per cent of our children.

Public schools are big business. Eton alone, with some 1,300 pupils, is as large as a big inner-city comprehensive; and fees at the most expensive schools are already approaching £10,000 a year. And yet few find it difficult to fill their 'Removes'. Waiting lists are not uncommon, and there is more than a little truth in stories of Wykehamists and Old Etonians putting their sons' names down for the old school on the day that they are born.

Evidently then, Eton and the 'independent' system is thriving, for all that many public schools now have girls in the sixth-form (or, like Christ's Hospital, have gone fully co-educational). Despite the fact that computers, careers officers and a National Curriculum have curbed their blithe unawareness of the outside world, parents obviously still believe that they continue to provide the *je-ne-sais-quoi* of gentility; that a public school education will give their sons 'a better start in life', a leg up the ladder – or at the very least a better chance of getting to 'Oxbridge'. No matter that child psychologists might now express reservations about the desirability of sending a boy of thirteen – or even seven, if he is bound for prep school – off to live with two, three or even thirteen hundred of his peers for weeks at a time, the practice still continues. And as a nation we still broadly condone it – tellingly, despite a lot of fine words, no government has yet got around to abolishing the public school system. Nor, it is fair to say, will any; not in the foreseeable future.

For, more than anything else, the survival of the public schools symbolizes the broad middle-class desire to 'better itself' and hence its implicit belief in the continuing existence of an upper class of gentlemen – albeit that today these very gentlemen not infrequently have to dirty their hands and engage in 'trade'. Despite all official exhortations to the contrary – everything from taxation changes to the Race Relations Act – the Churchillian notion of the 'One Nation' has thus never really existed, except on paper. Deep down, 'We' and 'They' continue to live on different continents; even though, just like the continents and cultures of Marshall McLuhan's 'global village', they are becoming ever closer. It is the gaps, however, which are significant. For, as we have seen, the uneasy symbiosis of Us and Them, the unholy alliance between a modern, non-materialist, values-based version of Disraeli's two nations has been one of the characteristics of twentieth-century Britain – and the principal reason for the Breed's unexpected survival. They have emerged as the heroes of the hour; the victors, at least on points. On a simplistic level we might say that, although their values and attitudes have generally come to be seen as anachronistic, patronizing and even downright philistine, no one has yet propounded anything better. Hence, simultaneously we continue to revere the Breed while insisting on reserving our right to belittle it.

An (anonymous) Old Etonian, identifiable as a member of the Breed by every syllable he uttered, was among the contributors to a BBC Radio series on class – itself tellingly entitled *The British Disease* – which was first broadcast in the summer of 1990. Recalling his school-days in the mid forties, he said:

> We lived in the most appalling conditions. And there were to be assisted places at Eton after the war. Busloads of people came down – I think it was from Leicester – to see whether they'd like their children to go [to Eton]. I've never forgotten them. They took one look at the conditions and said, 'Not for our little Johnny!' Well, it never did us any harm, really, honestly.[3]

Seldom can there have been a more graphic illustration of the co-existence of the two nations, before or after the inauguration of the Welfare State. There was the Breed, making the best of a frankly-Victorian status quo, and taking the privations of public school life like men. And there were the newly literate, aspirational middle- and working-classes, peering into a glass darkly, and not quite liking what they saw.

Forty years on, their – or at least their grammar-school-educated sons' – values had ostensibly become the values of the day. They were the centrally-heated, socially-serviced values of a generation brought up on an orange juice and cod-liver oil diet and groomed to inherit what would become the small-town legacy of Thatcherism. Forty years of the Welfare State had led them to expect something rather better – or at least more 'modern' and 'relevant' – than the ante-diluvian squalor of Eton: gleaming new multi-million-pound city technology colleges (CTCs) at the very least. And yet, and yet . . .

Behind the newly 'stone-clad' fronts ('façades' seems somehow ludi-crous) of a thousand newly sold-off council houses something akin to the old gentility persisted. An almost-unconscious behovenness to the country house values of the Breed was exemplified by the slip-on leather covers which gave a copy of the *TV Times* the look of a volume from the family library, and the 'antiqued' MFI shelves which groaned under the weight of the sets of glasses bearing 'your family's crest', obtained through a coupon in one of the Sunday colour sup-plements.

The votes of the 'skilled working classes' were in large measure re-sponsible for the Conservatives' election victories in 1979, 1983 and 1987, and it was not unnoticed that their conservative, self-interested attitudes also brought about a revival of 'Victorian values' and a rather bastardized version of Samuel Smiles's self-help doctrine. Less well understood was the fact that those very values underlay the spartan conditions and equally uncompromising regime upon which Eton, and by implication, all that it stood for had been founded.

The very term 'Victorian values' was used as the title of at least two books in the aftermath of the 1987 election.[4] And endlessly the much-derided 'chattering' (i.e. non 'wealth-creating') classes went on about them, sitting in their newly-gentrified homes (note the term) 'taking the piss' out of their new progenetrix as ineffectually as their parents and grandparents had tried to 'take the rise' out of that Ramsay Mac and, a little later, out of poor (*poor!*) uncharismatic Clement Attlee. So very little had changed; faced by the statistics which only a few years previously had shown that there were more than three million people claiming Unemployment Benefit (a larger number than during the 'Great Depression' which followed the Wall Street Crash of 1929) a few braying, middle- and upper-class voices were even heard on the streets, poignantly demanding that once again 'Something must be done!'

Nothing very much was, however. A flurry of Youth Opportunity Schemes, training packages, self-help incentive schemes and grants to the 'inner cities' (a term which actually meant 'outer inner cities': Brixton rather than Belgravia) got the unemployment figures down. A scatter of centrally-funded city technology colleges promised an updated 'grammar school' education – computer studies rather than classics – for the lucky few. But none of this really laid the foundations for a new Jerusalem. Nor could it have done when other, unofficial, uncollected or at least unpublished figures and a welter of newspaper stories were already telling the real story:

YOU RAN, SIR? ASKS
THE MODERN JEEVES[5]

GRAMMAR SCHOOLS TAKE OVER
BRITAIN'S BOARDROOMS[6]

It mattered little that Hugh Montgomery-Massingberd – an Old Harrovian, but, despite his name, never more than a Sancho Panza to a well-bred but dispossessed Don – was around to reassure readers of the *Daily Telegraph* that all things were well. No one saw it as other than straw-grabbing when in the autumn of 1990 he wrote that, although the number was 'steadily declining', there were still some 2,000 'traditional country estates' in Britain,[7] most of which were thriving as never before.

Similarly, Montgomery-Massingberd's lavish but tardy celebration of *Great British Families* (assembled with the assistance of Debrett's) – and indeed, his spirited but jejune rebuttal of the arguments advanced by David Cannadine in his book *The Decline and Fall of the British Aristocracy* – came too late. Nor could statistics and gobbets of Trivial Pursuit-like knowledge such as the fact that the Duke of Devonshire's Chatsworth estate still employed seven gamekeepers, three riverkeepers and, in its farms, farm-shops, shops and other enterprises, another 350 full- and part-time workers[8] quite persuade anyone – and least of all the still substantial number of *Telegraph*-reading members of the Breed – that all manner of things would continue to be well.

A further avalanche of Press cuttings chronicling the arrival of the 'new gentlemen' – the largely State-educated tribe whose totems or shamans were the likes of the Nottingham-based menswear designer Paul Smith, Jeremy Paxman, the unshaven rock star (Sir) Bob Geldof and many another member of the 'new Establishment' – squashed all that. In particular the feature pages (not least the 'Style' section of *The Sunday Times* and the more sober 'Real Life' columns of *The Independent on Sunday*) hailed the successive emergence of the Right-wing Young Fogey; the materialistic, too-busy-to-be-political, acronymic Yuppie (originally the Young, Upwardly-mobile Professional Person); his elder brother, the married Dinky (Double Income, No Kids Yet), the first-generation-Tory-voting, white socked Essex Man and the American-influenced, preppy UHB (Urban Haute Bourgeoisie). 'MOVE OVER YUPPIE: THE UHB HAS HIT TOWN'[9] was a recent but wholly typical headline. And as many another group, sub-group and society clique was identified by 'style gurus' struggling to cash in on the success of Peter York's discovery of the Sloane Ranger and (a little later) the Sloane Ranger Man in the pre-Thatcherite mid seventies,[10] it became clear that, one after another, these sleek, svelte, Porsche-driving Galahads were being tried for size against the most traditional image of a gentleman:

> Style File asks, is there a UHB in Britain? And it answers, most definitely yes. Although these bright young things 'are more likely

to give dances in Clapham or Wandsworth than Eaton Square or Mayfair' [. . .] their financial base has allowed them to outlive the now extinct yuppie, and the all-too-passé Sloane Ranger.

There may be a UHB living in your street; the signs are all too familiar: several trips to the dry-cleaner to have black ties or ballgowns cleaned; remarks such as: 'Mummy was *right* to say that they shouldn't have allowed divorced people into Ascot after the war – it would be far less crowded.'[11]

Among the new heroes Sloane Ranger Man was first in the field, and in many ways has remained their exemplar:

I am in the San Martino in Walton Street with a woman dress designer. Opposite us is a table of eight very big boys. They *all* wear pin-striped navy-blue suits, the trousers with turn-ups, narrow at the ankle but loose around the seat, and Bengal-stripe red or blue and white shirts. Two of the striped shirts have detachable white collars. The plumper, blander four wear black oxfords. These have specs and look like lawyers. The other four wear Gucci loafers – the plain kind, without the red and green ribbon. They *march* across the floor, snap to attention, slap each other, horse around. One says of another that he's the best mucker he ever had [. . .]

Then the boy nearest us falls over in his chair. The pine alpino chair overbalances, and he goes flat on his back, still in it. He isn't hurt, he's a big healthy chap, so he waggles his feet in the oxfords with the dark grey ribbed socks concertina'd round his ankles [. . .] Having discovered the trick, this boy repeats it regularly; they'll just be talking and – whump – over he goes, and the other Sloane Ranger men have these braying very ci-vi-lized conversations with the horizontal Jamie.[12]

The 1977 antics of Peter York's Jamie – so ironically reminiscent of Arthur Fitz-Gerald Kinnaird's football-ground gymnastics – were a taste of things to come. In the 1990 article already quoted, *The Sunday Times* paraded three sample UHBs. Half a generation younger than Jamie, there was the 'half-American' Bruce Merivale-Austin 'whose family divides its time between homes in Chelsea and Wales. The price of champagne and the decline in the class of person admitted to Annabel's [the exclusive London nightclub] are among his gripes'. More grotesquely, there were also Christopher Wickham and Bertie Lipworth, throwbacks to a distinctly pre-Raymond era:

Wickham is a 28-year-old stockbroker who once, during his university days, asked for the dates of his exams to be changed to enable him to attend Royal Ascot. 'The dates were set months ago,' protested his tutor – only to be told that the Royal Meeting dates had been established years ago.

Lipworth is understandably proud of his two central London addresses, one of which boasts a swimming pool. He once referred to the usefulness of the £415 minimum grant which all students received: 'Well, it pays my subscriptions to Annabel's and Tramp.'

Sloane Ranger Man, Essex Man, the Yuppie, the UHB; even the Dinky . . . each had money and – apart from the brief, post-'Black Monday' hiccup in the late 1980s – every intention of spending it. Newspapers were filled with stories of 'Hooray Henries' and 'Lager Louts' (originally another élite tribe, until it was discovered that the label better fitted a proletarian army of can-carrying football supporters.) City wine-bars and champagne importers reported record business; the proprietors of *Vogue* even launched a British edition of the preppily-American *GQ*, a glossy, male 'lifestyle' magazine that told its readers what to wear, who to meet, where to eat, which films to see, when to invest, and how best to get cheap holiday flights to Acapulco.

By the end of the eighties, however, there was at least the beginning of contextualization. In a BBC radio 'special' to mark the end of the decade, pop journalist and producer John Walters deployed a deadly irony when he came to sum up 'eighties man':

He's young, fit, with no thought for the morrow. He lives in a dock-side loading bay which has seen no loading for some years as it's now a split-level apartment which he bought as an investment. He knows about these things because his job is buying and selling money – which is just as well because he had to take out an extra mortgage when the Government sold him a number-plate with his name on.

He sips some expensive bottled water. He has shares in tap-water – there's no point in drinking the profits; and anyway, you don't know what's in it. A quick blow on the saxophone. He pulls on his amusing socks, trendy tie and it's off out to buy his favourite paper which headlines with the revelations of a lady who claims to have had a 'night of passion' with the late Elvis Presley. He exits, leaving his answering machine to take care of conversation.

Somehow, during the decade, this chap became a hero.[13]

But still no one seemed to notice that, far from finding their own style, with their 'telephone-number' salaries these young – not-infrequently teenaged – tyros and an almost invariably comprehensive school-educated pack of hangers-on had failed the test of originality and were merely aping the manners of those whom (publicly at least) it had become impossible or at any rate inadvisable to call their betters. Their profligate spending and conspicuously smug self-satisfaction, condoned or at least sanitized by references to 'market forces' and 'Thatcherism', only amounted to a parody of what had gone before. And the biggest irony of all lay in the fact that the full title of *GQ*, which became a highly-successful parish magazine-cum-vade mecum for the Yuppie and his successors, was *Gentleman's Quarterly*.

Beneath the champagne-popping, the double-breasted suits and the Bengal striped shirts, however, there were differences. In a world of high growth and low inflation, things did seem to be moving the Yuppies' way. The so-called 'Big Bang' had after all done for the City; deregulation on 27 October 1986 had put paid to its ineffably gentle-manly world in which a stockbroker's 'word was his bond' as effectively as it had to the stockbroker himself. Thenceforth he was a 'trader' – no more and no less honourable than the other traders who continued to make a living in Leather Lane or the meat, fish and vegetable markets which had for centuries impinged on the fringes of the City. The writing was on the wall the first day that a loud-voiced, long-tied pseudo-Yuppie turned up for work wearing a Next or Top Man equiva-lent of the chairman's double-breasted suit – and white socks above his 'loafers'. (Paxman quite properly devotes a chapter to a City now sartorially divided between 'Bowler Hats and White Socks'.) In the House of Commons the Conservative MP Sir John Stokes summed up the new dispensation when he lamented that 'the age of chivalry has gone – to be succeeded by one of economists and calculators'.[14]

Beyond the Palace of Westminster it was perhaps inevitable that it should have been on the *Daily Telegraph* letters page that an (equally inevitably) titled correspondent led the beleaguered Establishment's wailing and gnashing of teeth. Not only had there been a 'de-classing' of *The Times*'s court page, the *Daily Telegraph* itself had given up 'Mistering every man, and even youths' in the spring of 1990, Baron de Spon thundered. What was happening? Why, when he had started as a sub-editor on that same paper in the early 1950s, he and his colleagues knew everyone's place:

> ... there were strict rules about Mr. Broadly, this appellation was
> denied the working and lower middle classes unless the person was
> distinguished.
> We subs had great fun deciding who was worthy of the honour.
> Anomalies were bound to arise; for instance, trade union officials got a
> Mr, but unofficial strike leaders were very much barred.[15]

More subtly too, the changes which were affecting everything from
the suddenly high-profile 'trading floor' to the trade unions (etiolated
by 'Our' defeat of Arthur Scargill and the National Union of Mine-
workers, they were fatally weakened by Mrs Thatcher's talk of 'the
enemy within') were also becoming apparent in the boardroom. Over
as short a period as a decade, the majority of Britain's major companies
passed out of the control of public school-educated directors. Research
published by the London School of Economics at the end of 1990
demonstrated that, whereas in 1979 twenty-nine of the chairmen of
Britain's top fifty industrial companies had been to public school,
only ten years later just one of the chairmen surveyed (Guinness's Old
Etonian Anthony Tennant) had attended a major public school.[16] The
retailing mogul Sir Philip Harris (Streatham Grammar School) was
quoted as saying: 'I think the grammar school gives you more of
a basic education and is more linked to the needs of industry. Eton is
more for scholars.' Coming as it did less than three weeks before the
resignation of Mrs Thatcher (herself a past pupil of Kesteven and
Grantham Girls' Grammar School), that comment was an all-too-
accurate testament to the economic and social revolution over which
she had presided.

But by the end of the 1980s there was other evidence too of the
manner in which even the newly-thrusting, 'dynamic' companies which
were beginning to find themselves listed among the *Financial Times*'s
100 were taking their place in the new scheme of things. A good
number of them – and, indeed, of their new, state-educated executives
– were hiring that ultimate status symbol of the old ruling class: a
butler. Were he still alive, however, P. G. Wodehouse's Jeeves would
not have bothered to apply for the £20,000-a-year-plus-free-
accommodation post. Somehow, something else had changed.

Naturally sanguine, and more a 'domestic administrator' than a
mere 'gentleman's gentleman', Ivor Spencer, who runs the London-
based International School for Butler Administrators and House-
keepers watched it happen:

Today's modern butler is often a jogger and jogs before and after work, often with his bosses, who like the company; and because the butler is trained in karate and able to protect his employers from a mugger [. . .]

He is often a non-smoker and only occasionally drinks alcohol, is very fit and rarely overweight. Half of today's butlers are married and usually own their own homes.

Traditionally, butlers are called by their surnames, but 75 per cent are now called by their first names.[17]

Now that new money has taken over from old, [at the School] we have to be very careful who we are dealing with [. . .]

With a one-night booking we would expect you to fax us a confirmation of your order and send the money, or at least a money order, round by bike. There are certain situations in which a butler wouldn't be – *appropriate*.[18]

Il n'y a pas de héros pour son valet de chambre, noted Anne Bigot de Cornuel in 1728. Now more than ever, perhaps, we can appreciate the wisdom of her words. And in an age in which, ever since Lloyd George began selling peerages, mere status has been up for grabs, we can also see what, more than 100 years earlier, King James I was really saying when he told his old nurse: 'I'll mak' your son a *baronet* gin ye like, Luckie, but the de'il himsel couldna' mak' him a gentleman.'

The last few pages of this book were written while radio and television programmes were almost routinely being cancelled or interrupted by news broadcasts giving the latest details of the Conservative party's 'leadership crisis' in November 1990. Following the resignation of Margaret Thatcher on 22 November, three candidates stood for election to the post of leader of the party and, *de facto*, prime minister. Not much was made of it at the time, but the contest itself encapsulated the one-nation struggle which Britain had been engaged in for the past fifty years. Memories fade, however, and it might be as well to remind ourselves of the two candidates who challenged Mr John Major. Were he seeking to inherit Harold Macmillan's crown, the 'patrician' ex-diplomat Douglas Hurd (Eton and Oxford) would have been the natural successor. In vain, however, did he try to distance himself from his background. His father had only been a *tenant*-farmer of some 600 acres, he said. He had himself only gone to Eton because he had won a scholarship. (Even Hugh Montgomery-Massingberd was later to protest that this 'phoneyness' and 'silly inverted' snobbishness was hard to take: 'In fact, Hurd's dad was Conservative MP for Newbury and eventually a peer, agricultural correspondent for *The Times*, and he farmed near Marlborough, where he had been educated.')[19] But suddenly Eton and Hurd's ambivalent 'aloofness' – good for a Foreign Secretary who had to bestride the international stage, but a definite no-no for a Prime Minister and Conservative leader who had to bring unity to a party (and nation) dependent on the disparate allegiance of blue-haired women and Essex Men – counted against him.

For all his mace-waving, 'impulsiveness' and 'irresponsibility', in the early days the smart money lay on Michael Heseltine. Even after the inconclusive results of the first ballot the 'self-made' – but none the less public-school-and-Oxbridge-educated – 'Tarzan' was the man to watch. For all that he had precipitated the leadership contest itself, he was something of a paradigm of Thatcherism, a self-made middle-class businessman and entrepreneur. His impeccably-chosen ties and sharp, dark blue suits, his country house and London home in Chapel Street, Belgravia, only hinted at a personal fortune which was generally estimated to be in the region of £60 million. (Heseltine was rated at joint 148th in the 1990 edition of the *Sunday Times Book of the Rich*'s list of the nation's wealthiest people.) Even the student nickname 'Michael Philistine' began to work in his favour.

Nervous Conservative MPs 'took soundings' in their constituencies. Hurd was an anachronism, they were told; good where he was, a statesman, a 'grandee' – but not the man to be Prime Minister of Great Britain in the last few years of the twentieth century. Heseltine, on the other hand, had that ineffably twentieth-century quality – charisma. He was a maverick, a crusader, a swashbuckling Cavalier, an Earl of Essex for the new Elizabethan age; historical accuracy counted for nothing, his blond hair was everything.

And yet when the votes in the second ballot were counted in Committee Room 12 at the Palace of Westminster no clear winner emerged. Three hundred and seventy-two Conservative Members of Parliament could not agree who should lead their party into the next election and – in all likelihood – their country into the next millennium. Hurd's men forebore from wearing Old Etonian ties; the Heseltine contingent played down their man's 'iconoclasm'. All three candidates praised the gentlemanly spirit in which the election had been fought. And yet . . .

Hurd and Heseltine gallantly stood down within hours of the result being announced; in their different ways gentlemen to the end. And so it was, almost by default, that John Major, the forty-seven-year-old 'Yuppie' whose father had been a circus acrobat, who had been brought up in Brixton, gone to no university and even worked on a building site, emerged as Prime Minister and First Lord of the Treasury.

'Grey man', 'Essex Man', a mere 'number-cruncher', said the critics; a gentleman only in so far as he opened doors for women. The responsible Press – and the public – were more reticent, however. Tory MPs' 'soundings' had revealed a remarkable fact: after eleven years of high-profile Thatcherism, the prospect of a period of 'class-less', faceless 'Majorism' held considerable appeal to the nation. And Major himself played on his 'greyness' for all it was worth. 'PRIME MINISTER PREFERS "HONEST JOHN" APPROACH', proclaimed *The Independent* a couple of weeks after he assumed office:

> John Major confirmed yesterday that he is a grey man . . . with a grey man trying to get out [. . .]
> 'I shall be the same plug-ugly I always was,' the Prime Minister told listeners [to a local radio station] with remarkable candour.
> Margaret Thatcher softened her voice, changed her hairstyle, bought haute couture dresses and had her teeth crowned, but Mr Major said: 'I am what I am and people will have to take me as I am. The image-makers will not find me under their tutelage . . . They have neither approached me nor are they going to get at me.'[20]

Over in clubland the wags were remembering George Orwell and giving two cheers for democracy. This was what the people wanted! *Vivat Rex!* Few – a very few – remembered Churchill and the One Nation. Rather more were preoccupied with the new Prime Minister's notion of 'classlessness'. 'People should concentrate on what I do [. . .] Only a leader who comes to inspire widespread trust can bring the country round those awkward corners,' he was saying.[21]

But was he that leader? Was he man enough for the job? Could he inspire widespread trust? No one voiced such doubts about Mosley, or Churchill when they – and Margaret Thatcher too – 'emerged'. For all its glib, *post hoc* unanimity, the Conservative party and the Establishment it still represented was staking its all on Major. His classlessness, his very ordinariness would be his and our salvation. Or so the message went.

Behind the scenes, however, a lot of good old-fashioned harrumphing was going on in 'smoke-filled rooms' – especially when it became clear that Mr Major seemed set on taking Britain very much farther into the embrace of Europe than his predecessor would ever have countenanced. (Even before the end of his hundred-day 'honeymoon period' it was noticed that he was already calling the German Chancellor Helmut Kohl by his Christian name and receiving an affectionate *du* [rather than the more customary *sie*] in return.) 'Our Jack' was doing no more than acting in the national interest – as he saw it – but in the deeper recesses of clubland the idea of a Conservative prime minister even considering entering into closer – *any!* – relations with Germany and the European Community, not to say toying with the idea of eventual monetary union, seemed very rum indeed. Our national sovereignty – yes, our *Englishness* – was at stake. The very notion stirred tribal memories of the Gold Standard (even David had been in favour of that!) the farthing, the ha'penny, crisp white five pound notes and the good old pre-decimalized days when ten bob – *ten bob!* – would buy a gent's supper *and* pay the taxi fare home . . .

Only a couple of years after the Duke of Edinburgh had averred that the Japanese were 'slitty-eyed', there was a certain inevitability in the fact that it was Nicholas Ridley, then a member of the Cabinet, who gave fullest vent to these views. One of the grandest chams of the Conservative party, a rumpled, chain-smoking aristo – the younger son of a viscount and, inevitably, an Old Etonian – in an interview with the *Spectator* only weeks before Mr Major's emergence he had intemperately opined that the Germans were on the make, intent on world (or at least European) domination. And, he seemed to be saying, it wasn't just Jerry.

En bas les Boches! . . . That was the pure, un-reconstructed voice of the Breed. Sapper, it seemed, had been right all along. Despite spies and soft-pedallers, mashers, mavericks and Mr Major, the Breed had never died. Mr Ridley, it was true, had had to resign when the furore stirred up by his comments threatened to sour international relations. That was, after all, the decent, *gentlemanly* thing to do. But the point had been made – just as it had in 1878 when *HMS Pinafore* was first produced. Then, less controversially, W. S. Gilbert had exquisitely differentiated between the 'lower middle class' and the man we have come to call a gentleman. Inevitably, his final chorus hymns the latter:

He is an Englishman!
 For he himself has said it,
 And it's greatly to his credit,
That he is an Englishman!

For he might have been a Roosian,
A French, or Turk, or Proosian,
 Or perhaps Ital-ian!
But in spite of all temptations
To belong to other nations,
 He remains an Englishman!

Notes

INTRODUCTION
1. See in particular Philip Mason: *The English Gentleman: The Rise and Fall of an Ideal*.
2. Sapper: *Mufti*, p. 43.

CHAPTER ONE: The Old School Tie
1. Tony Pawson: *100 Years of the F.A. Cup*, p. 31.
2. The figures are taken from T. J. H. Bishop and Rupert Wilkinson: *Winchester and The Public School Elite*, p. 37.
3. See Brian Simon and Ian Bradley (eds): *The Victorian Public School*; and Jonathan Gathorne-Hardy: *The Public School Phenomenon*, p. 486.
4. The extent of this casual but nevertheless absolute control was brought out almost accidentally by the novelist and critic Andrew Sinclair (himself an Old Etonian) in an article in the *Daily Telegraph*, 19 September 1988:

> The old blue-on-black tie was a noose round the neck of English writing. 'One in five of the major novelists of the century', Anthony Powell once told me at Cambridge, 'was an Etonian'. The list was impressive. Osbert and Sacheverell Sitwell: Aldous Huxley and Anthony Powell himself: Henry Green and George Orwell: and Peter and Ian Fleming.
>   The literary editors and critics were just as impressive. Harold Acton and Peter Quennell and John Strachey: Alan Pryce-Jones of the *Times Literary Supplement* and the publisher Rupert Hart-Davis: and the dominant magazine editors of the Second World War, John Lehmann at *Penguin New Writing* and [Cyril] Connolly at *Horizon*. When the philosopher Freddie Ayer, the theatrical George 'Dadie' Rylands and the designer Oliver Messel were added to the list, Eton seemed a Pantheon, not a playing-field.

5. See Gathorne-Hardy, op. cit., ch. 3.
6. Ibid., p. 70.
7. Unpublished *Journal* of Minet, 1818–20; quoted, ibid., p. 66.
8. Thomas Hughes: *Tom Brown's Schooldays*, p. 118.
9. In what amounts almost to a memoir of his own time there, Hughes is

unusually reticent about the specific years of Tom Brown's schooling. We are told that he set out for his first half at Rugby 'in the early part of November, 183-' (Ibid., p. 63). But, apart from one final reference to Tom's being up at Oxford in 1842, that is all. For what it is worth, however, various pieces of internal evidence suggest that Hughes was writing about the late rather than the early 1830s. Chief among these is the fact that, while still in his second half, Tom is described as 'looking up from an early number of Pickwick, which was then just coming out' (Ibid., p. 135). The first, serial publication of Charles Dickens's *The Pickwick Papers* was announced in *The Athenaeum* on 26 March 1836.

10. Hughes, op. cit., p. 66.
11. Ibid., p. 201.

CHAPTER TWO: Anglo-Saxon Attitudes

1. Kenneth Rose: *Superior Person*, p. 61.
2. Hugh Montgomery-Massingberd: *Great British Families*, p. 99.
3. Duke of Windsor: *A King's Story*, p. 104.
4. Lady Cynthia Asquith: *Remember and Be Glad*; p. 64.
5. Patrick Hamilton: *Twenty Thousand Streets Under the Sky*, p. 26. (My italics.)
6. Duke of Windsor, op. cit., p. 47.
7. Ibid., pp. 86–7.
   The Duke concludes: 'My father had shot over 1,000 birds; I had even passed the 300 mark. He was proud of the way he had shot that day, but I think the scale of the bag troubled even his conscience; for, as we drove back to London, he remarked, "Perhaps we went a little too far today, David."'
8. The story is quoted in Rose, op. cit., p. 69.
9. Duke of Portland: *Men, Women & Things*, pp. 228–9.
10. Ford Madox Ford: *Some Do Not . . .* p. 11.
11. The nine so-called 'Clarendon Schools' were: Rugby, Shrewsbury, Winchester, Harrow, Charterhouse, Westminster, Eton and, for contrast the Merchant Taylors' and St Paul's day schools. Inevitably perhaps, in the years following 1864 they came to see themselves as a 'first division' among the 200 or so other schools then also represented on the Headmasters' Conference.
12. Report of the Clarendon Commission, Eyre and Spottiswoode, 1864, vol. I, p. 56.
13. Nicholas Mosley, interview with the author, 23 February 1989. In the early 1940s his father, the British fascist leader Sir Oswald Mosley was detained in Brixton Prison.
14. Tom Driberg: *Guy Burgess: A Portrait with Background*, p. 15.
15. I am indebted to Peter Robinson for drawing my attention to this, and

grateful to Edmund Hall who first suggested that Christ's Hospital was worth a mention.

16. Desmond Graham: *Keith Douglas*, p. 21.
17. Quoted in D. Jesson-Dibley: *A Pageant of Christ's Hospital*, p. 54.
18. Keith Douglas, undated letter to 'Kristin'. Quoted in Graham, op. cit., pp. 53–4.
19. Sir Philip Gibbs: 'The Deathless Story of the Titanic', *Lloyds Weekly News*, 1912. Quoted in Michael Davie: *The Titanic*, p. 22.
20. Quoted in Rose, op. cit., p. 246.
21. Ibid.
22. Ibid., p. 250.
23. Ibid., pp. 223–4.
24. Letter to Alfred Lyttelton, 29 August 1900. Quoted, ibid., p. 345.
25. Letter to H. H. Asquith, 1897. Quoted in John Jolliffe (ed.), *Raymond Asquith: Life and Letters*, pp. 27–8.
26. Letter to Margot Asquith, October 1897. Quoted, ibid., p. 33.
27. Quoted in Rose, op. cit., p. 21.
28. Duke of Windsor, op. cit., pp. 26–7. (My italics.)
29. Speech delivered by Lord Curzon at Derby, 28 July 1904. Quoted in Rose, op. cit., p. 197.
30. Ibid., p. 286.

CHAPTER THREE: Playing Hard
1. Bob Willis and Patrick Murphy: *Starting With Grace*, pp. 25–6.
2. Sir Arthur Conan Doyle: *Memories and Adventures*, quoted in E. W. Hornung: *The Collected Raffles*, p. xvi.
3. E. W. Hornung: *The Collected Raffles*, p. 176. Even here, however, Hornung makes little of the name:

   'Rich?' I echoed. 'Stephano?'
   'Si, Arturo mio.'
   Yes, I played the game on that vineyard, Bunny, even to going by my own first name.

4. Ibid., pp. 7–8 and 41.
5. Ibid., p. 37.
6. Ibid., p. 20.
7. Ibid., p. 166.
8. Ibid., p. 168.
9. Quoted in Alan Hyman: *The Rise and Fall of Horatio Bottomley*, p. 34.
10. Ibid., p. 51.
11. Ibid., p. 71.
12. Anne Edwards: *Matriarch: Queen Mary and the House of Windsor*, p. 135.

13. Undated letter from G. H. S. Walpole, quoted in Rupert Hart-Davis: *Hugh Walpole*, p. 34.

CHAPTER FOUR: 'Lovely Lads'
1. See Rose, op. cit., p. 287.
2. Quoted in Paul Delaney: *The Neo-Pagans*, pp. 55–6.
3. Verse by Frances Darwin, 1908.
4. A. E. Housman: *A Shropshire Lad*, XXXV.
5. Letter to Margot Asquith, October 1897. Quoted in John Jolliffe (ed.): *Raymond Asquith: Life and Letters*, p. 33.
6. John Buchan, *Memory Hold the Door*, pp. 53–4.
7. Letter to John Buchan. Quoted in Jolliffe, op. cit., p. 86.
8. Letter to Katharine Horner, 26 October 1905. Quoted, ibid., p. 138. John Jolliffe rightly notes that the reference to 'a half-witted old woman' is hardly a fair description of the pioneering garden designer Gertrude Jekyll, who was related by marriage to Katharine's mother's family.
9. Raymond Asquith in Lady Desborough's *Pages from a Family Journal, 1888–1915* (privately printed), 1916. Quoted in Nicholas Mosley: *Julian Grenfell*, pp. 124–5.
10. Heavily reliant on family papers, Mosley's account is completely convincing. Nevertheless, in *Julian Grenfell*, a pamphlet published by Burns & Oates in 1917, Viola Meynell attempts to paint a very different picture. Not only does she depict a Julian who 'had a serious conscious love of religion' (extrapolating from a single reference in a letter to his having read *The Imitation of Christ*, she extolls 'his love of Thomas à Kempis') she studiously avoids any mention of Ettie and her affaires, preferring instead to hold up Julian as 'a shining example of one of the great qualities the war has brought to light – that of filial love'.

    Never previously cited by any of Julian's biographers, though grossly unreliable the pamphlet is a perfect example of the sentimental hagiography to which members of the 'Lost Generation' were subjected in the years immediately following their deaths.
11. Anonymous comment, quoted in Mosley, op. cit., pp. 139–40.
12. A typescript copy of Julian's book was discovered by Nicholas Mosley during his research for *Julian Grenfell*. Its contents are fully described on pp. 149–56 of that book.
13. Letter to Diana Manners, August 1914. Quoted in Jolliffe, op. cit., pp. 191–2.
14. Horner's request probably warranted Raymond Asquith's scathing rebuke:

    Your letter asking for a gold pin for your servant does you great credit. May I send you out an emerald ring for his nostril? and some attar of roses for your charger, and a Dégas for your dugout, and a sheet or two of Delius for the gramophone – or would a little something by John Sebastian Bach be more seasonable in Holy Week? and 'some precious tender-hearted scroll of pure Simonides' for use in the latrines? It seems very horrible that you shouldn't have had these things long ago: but you know what our War Office is like . . .

(Quoted in Jolliffe, op. cit., p. 197.)

15. Lieutenant von Neubert, quoted in Lyn Macdonald: *1914*, p. 384. It spoils the story, but Macdonald goes on to note that Lord Charles Worsley's effects were never received by his family.
16. Second Lieutenant R. B. Talbot, Royal Field Artillery, quoted in Peter Parker, *The Old Lie*, p. 165.
17. Letter to Ettie Grenfell, 24 October 1914. Quoted in Mosley, op. cit., p. 239.
18. Letter to Diana Manners, 25 November 1915. Quoted in Jolliffe, op. cit., p. 220.
19. Viola Meynell: 'Julian Grenfell', article in *The Dublin Review*; reprinted as a pamphlet by Burns & Oates, p. 18.
20. Letter to Ettie Grenfell, 1906. Quoted in Mosley, op. cit., p. 94.

CHAPTER FIVE: The Hero and the Thug
1. Gunner B. O. Stokes, 13th Battery, New Zealand Field Artillery, quoted in Lyn Macdonald: *1914–1918: Voices and Images of the Great War*, p. 307.
2. Quoted in Quentin Bell: *Virginia Woolf*, p. 62.
3. Inevitably perhaps, it has never been possible to produce a truly accurate tally of the number of casualties. The first figures – covering both Britain and the Empire – were given in November 1918:

In the House of Commons Yesterday our total war casualties were announced as follows:

	Officers	Other Ranks
Killed	37,876	620,829
Wounded	92,644	1,939,478
Missing and Prisoners	12,094	347,051
Thus the grand total of casualties is		3,049,972.

(*Daily Mirror*, 20 November 1918.)

On several subsequent occasions these figures were to be adjusted upwards.

4. I have quoted only the final lines of Thomas's poem 'Old Men'.

5. Nicholas Mosley: *Rules of the Game: Sir Oswald and Lady Cynthia Mosley, 1896–1933*, p. 26.

6. Angela Hewins (ed.): *The Dillen: Memories of a Man of Stratford-upon-Avon*, pp. 160–1.

George Hewins ('the Dillen') was invalided home from France, where he was serving with the Royal Warwickshire Regiment, in 1916. Prior to returning to his native Stratford-upon-Avon he spent more than a year in hospital. Shrapnel 'had cut my thigh, made a wound eighteen inches long, three wounds in the back, ripped one leg open to the knee, and blown the top of my privates off'.

7. R. C. Sherriff: *Journey's End*, Act II, Scene 2.

8. Ibid., Act II, Scene 1.

9. Contemporary newspaper advertisements, quoted in Macdonald: *1914–1918*, pp. 331–2.

10. Trooper Sydney Chaplin, 1st Northamptonshire Yeomanry, quoted, ibid., p. 333.

11. Oswald Mosley: *My Life*, 1968, p. 70.

12. Diana Mosley, in a letter to the author, 22 April 1989.

13. Ibid.

14. Nicholas Mosley, op. cit., p. 4.

15. Oswald Mosley, op. cit., p. 35.

16. Diana Mosley, in a letter to the author, 12 March 1989.

17. Oswald Mosley, op. cit., p. 70.

18. George Nathaniel Curzon, in a letter to his wife, 23 March 1920.

19. Nicholas Mosley, op. cit., p. 70.

20. Robert Boothby, quoted, ibid., p. 83.

21. Oswald Mosley, op. cit., p. 150.

22. Ibid., p. 152.

23. Oswald Mosley's address to the electors of Harrow, October 1922. The italics are as in the original.

24. Richard Usborne: *Clubland Heroes*, p. 150.

25. 'Sapper': *Mufti*; quoted in Richard Usborne, op. cit., pp. 143–4.

26. 'Sapper': *Bulldog Drummond*, p. 17.

27. Ibid., pp. 21–2.

28. Ibid., p. 173.

29. Ibid., p. 16.

30. John Buchan: *The Thirty-Nine Steps*, pp. 20–1.

31. Leonard Woolf, quoted in Peter Ackroyd: *T. S. Eliot*, p. 304.

CHAPTER SIX: Every Other Inch a Gentleman

1. Clive Ellis: *C.B.: The Life of Charles Burgess Fry*, p. 120.

2. C. B. Fry: *Life Worth Living*, p. 46.

3. Ibid., pp. 79–80, *passim*.
4. Ibid., p. 90.
5. Quoted in Ellis, op. cit., p. 23.
6. Fry, op. cit., p. 152.
7. Ibid., p. 179.
8. Ibid., p. 187.
9. Ibid., p. 196.
10. Ibid., p. 193. (My italics.)
11. Ibid., p. 381.
12. Ibid., pp. 379–80.
13. Ibid., pp. 371–2 and 373.
14. Ibid., pp. 375–7, *passim*.
15. The story of how the crown of Albania was apparently touted around various delegates at the 1920 League of Nations Conference in Geneva is convoluted and fantastic-sounding. It is certain that it was offered to Herbert since he makes several references to it in his letters and diaries: 'The As (private) have invited me to be No. 1 big man'; 'Then [Lord Curzon] said I had better make it a fait accompli, go to Albania, get myself proclaimed. I said I did not want to have the Rupert of Hentzau business – it was too like D'Annunzio.' (See Margaret Fitzherbert: *The Man Who Was Greenmantle*, pp. 229–30.)

But Fitzherbert also quotes J. Squire, an authority on Albanian history: 'Certainly it was offered to no one else, except perhaps by propagandists wishing to discredit Albania or by journalists as a practical joke.' (Ibid., p. 231.)

On the other hand, in *Life Worth Living* Fry himself is convinced not only that he 'was well in the running for the billet' but that the offer was genuine: 'If a grandchild ever asks me what I did after the Great War (I mean the 1914 Great War) I shall tell him that I composed a speech which turned Mussolini out of Corfu and ran prominently in the race for the Kingship of Albania' (p. 305). In his biography of C.B., Ellis reviews all the evidence – though without acknowledging Herbert's rival candidature – and comes to the conclusion that although Fry's invitation came via Ranji it was in all probability genuine, neither black propaganda nor a practical joke. Only money stood in Fry's way: the Albanians had let it be known that they would like their new monarch to contribute £10,000 a year to the national coffers.

In 1928 the throne of Albania was assumed by Ahmet Zogu, the country's one-time Prime Minister, who ruled as King Zog until forced into exile by the Italian invasion of 1939. He died in 1961.

CHAPTER SEVEN: 'Something Must Be Done!'

1. Quoted in E. W. Swanton: *Gubby Allen – Man of Cricket*, p. 124.
2. Ian Botham, interviewed on BBC Radio 4, November 1989.
3. Quoted in Laurence Le Quesne: *The Bodyline Controversy*, p. 17.
4. Indeed, he had more than once done it before. Bill Bowes has recalled how, after he had repeatedly asked Jardine for an additional leg-side fieldsman during one of the pre-Test games, Jardine had suddenly said 'Have five!' and re-arranged his field accordingly. (See Le Quesne, op. cit., p. 61.)
5. Bill Bowes, interviewed in *The Bradman Tapes*, BBC Radio 3, 1989.
6. Quoted in Le Quesne, op. cit., p. 32.
7. Quoted, ibid., p. 52.
8. Ibid., p. 59.
9. E. W. Swanton, op. cit., p. 117.
10. Peter Vansittart: *Paths from a White Horse*, p. 7.
11. W. H. Auden: *Forewords and Afterwords*, p. 514.
12. He had been formally created Prince of Wales at Caernarvon (Caernarfon) in 1911, but in view of his subsequent changes of nomenclature – King Edward VIII, the Duke of Windsor – I shall continue to refer to him as David, the name by which Prince Edward Albert Christian George Andrew Patrick David was always known to his family and close friends.
13. Amid mounting uproar, Hardie had gone on with rather greater accuracy: 'In due course, following the precedent that has already been set [by the early life of the future King Edward VII] he will be sent on a tour around the world, and probably rumours of a morganatic marriage will follow, and in the end the country will be called upon to pay the bill.'

    David himself was later to describe the speech as 'uncannily clairvoyant'.
14. Duke of Windsor: *A King's Story*, p. 79.
15. Ibid., p. 76.
16. Ibid., p. 102.
17. Ibid., p. ix.
18. Ibid., p. 106.
19. Ibid., p. 130.
20. Ibid., pp. 25 and 187.
21. Ibid., p. 277.
22. Ibid., pp. 191–2.
23. Ibid., pp. 128–9. (My italics.)
24. Duke of Windsor, quoted in *Kenneth Harris Talking To ...* (Weidenfeld & Nicolson, 1971). See Frances Donaldson, *Edward VIII*, p. 134.
25. Duke of Windsor, op. cit., p. 214.

26. *The Times*, 18 May 1934.
27. Duke of Windsor, op. cit., p. 218.
28. Ibid., p. 219.

CHAPTER EIGHT: 'Cut Is the Branch . . .'
1. Unattributed; quoted in Valentine Cunningham: *British Writers of the Thirties*, p. 421.
2. Denis Healey: *The Time of My Life*, p. 35.
3. Quoted in Robert Skidelsky: *Oswald Mosley*, p. 129.
4. Ibid., p. 133.
5. Lady Mosley, in a letter to the author, 12 December 1989.
6. Oswald Mosley: *My Life*, p. 229. (Characteristically, Mosley went on: 'That capacity has not diminished but has grown with the years.')
7. *Daily Express*, 5 May 1927.
8. Oswald Mosley, op. cit., p. 247.
9. See Harold Nicolson: *Letters and Diaries, 1930–1939*, 2 July 1930.
10. Harold Nicolson's diaries, MS, 15 January 1930; quoted in Skidelsky, op. cit., pp. 196–7.
11. *Punch*, 17 December 1930.
12. Lady Mosley, interview with the author, 28 February 1989.
13. Christopher Isherwood: *Goodbye to Berlin*, pp. 203–4.
14. Brian Masters, *Great Hostesses*, p. 100ff.
15. Robert Rhodes James (ed.): *Chips: The Diaries of Sir Henry Channon*, entry for 16 June 1935, p. 49.
16. *Daily Worker*, 28 May 1934.
17. Muriel Spark: *The Prime of Miss Jean Brodie*, pp. 55–6.
18. Evelyn Waugh: 'For Schoolboys Only'; a review in *Night and Day*, 8 July 1937.
19. Oswald Mosley, op. cit., p. 286.
20. Quoted in Skidelsky, op. cit., p. 285.
21. Harold Nicolson: *Diaries*, MS, 6 January 1932; quoted, ibid., pp. 284–5.
22. Lady Mosley, interview with the author, 28 February 1989.
23. Lady Mosley, 28 February 1989.
24. Lady Mosley, 28 February 1989.
25. Lady Mosley, 28 February 1989. (My italics.)
26. Oswald Mosley, op. cit., p. 285.
27. Lady Mosley, 28 February 1989.
28. Lady Mosley, 28 February 1989.
29. Cullen's findings are summarized in a letter to the *Daily Telegraph*, 29 November 1989. (This letter was in itself another reaction to Lady Mosley's appearance on *Desert Island Discs* a few days earlier.)
30. Lady Mosley, 28 February 1989.

31. *Sunday Pictorial*, 4 August 1940.
32. Now, as then, references to *Doctor Faustus* or Goethe's *Faust* spring readily to mind. Not only was the latter one of Mosley's favourite works – I was able to examine his own leather-bound eighteenth-century edition while interviewing Lady Mosley at the Temple de la Gloire – but in his biography of Sir Oswald, Skidelsky entitles a chapter dealing with Mosley's post-lapsarian thought in the mid 1940s 'The Faustian Riddle' and even signs off 'with one of [Mosley's] own favourite passages from *Faust*: "Whoever strives/ Can be redeemed".'

CHAPTER NINE: The Yeomen of England
1. *Daily Telegraph*, 4 September 1939.
2. BBC Radio, 18 June 1940.
3. House of Commons, 13 May 1940.
4. Richard Buckle (ed.): *Self-Portrait with Friends: the Selected Diaries of Cecil Beaton*, p. 74.
5. Rhodes James (ed.), op. cit., p. 375.
6. Although of genuine concern at the time, the only modern investigation into the morale of the American bomber-crews seems to be the detailed research, undertaken in Britain, Europe and America by Granada Television for their 1989 documentary, *Whispers in the Air*. The following paragraphs draw heavily on material from that film.
7. Basil Wright: *The Long View: An International History of Cinema*, p. 177.
8. *Richard II*, II.i.31ff.
9. Cole Lesley, *The Life of Noël Coward*, p. 229
10. Quoted in Charles Castle, *Noël*, p. 177.
11. C. S. Lewis, in *Time and Tide*, September 1944.
12. See Peter Mellini: 'Colonel Blimp's England', *History Today*, October 1984, p. 35.
13. Quoted in Charles Castle, op. cit., p. 174.
14. Ibid.
15. Quoted in Ronald Howard: *In Search of My Father*, p. 18.
16. *Picture Post*, 30 November 1941.
17. Quoted in Howard, op. cit., p. 115.
18. Quoted, ibid., pp. 159–60.
19. In *In Search of My Father* Ronald Howard explicitly states: 'I still believe Leslie's death was an act of intent and not an accident' (p. 241). Ian Colvin's earlier study: *Flight 777* (Evans, 1957) reaches very much the same conclusion.
20. Quoted in Howard, op. cit., pp. 235–6.
21. Quoted, ibid., p. 102.

CHAPTER TEN: Straitened Circumstances

1. Anthony Howard, 'We Are the Masters Now', in Michael Sissons and Philip French (eds), *Age of Austerity*, p. 5ff. I am indebted to Howard's essay for many of the political anecdotes in this chapter. Similarly, I am indebted to Andrew Barrow's compendious *Gossip: A History of High Society from 1920 to 1970* for many of the lighter, 'social' stories. Trifling in themselves, when read in context they throw a fascinating light on the times.
2. Rhodes James (ed.), op. cit., p. 499.
3. Ibid., p. 473.
4. Ibid., p. 504.
5. Ibid., p. 474.
6. Ibid., p. 508.
7. George Orwell: *Nineteen Eighty-Four*, pp. 6–7.
8. *Daily Telegraph*, 7 August 1945.
9. Buckle (ed.), op. cit., pp. 170–1.
10. Rhodes James (ed.), op. cit., pp. 510–11.
11. Ibid., p. 511.
12. Sir Stanley Matthews, interviewed on ITV, 31 January 1990.
13. Ibid.
14. For a graphic account of the match, see Brian Glanville's essay: 'Britain Against the Rest', in Sissons and French (eds), op. cit., p. 139ff.

CHAPTER ELEVEN: The New Look

1. Glanville, ibid.
2. Quoted in Derek Stanford, *Inside the Fifties*, pp. 122–3.
3. Colin MacInnes: 'An Unrewarded Virtue: Britain 1945–51', *Queen*, 25 September 1963.
4. The former MP James Cross in an interview on BBC Radio 4, April 1990.
5. Alan Doig, from Liverpool University, speaking on the same programme.
6. Ibid.
7. James Cross, ibid.
8. Sir Stafford Cripps, speech to the Trades Union Congress, 1948.
9. David Marquand: 'Sir Stafford Cripps', in Sissons and French (eds), op. cit., p. 165ff.
10. Rhodes James (ed.), op. cit., p. 542.

CHAPTER TWELVE: 'Sex, Snobbery and Sadism'

1. Among the books, the revised (1980) edition of Andrew Boyle's *The Climate of Treason* is probably the most authoritative and covers the

whole field, from the early life of Philby, Burgess and Maclean to the unmasking of Anthony Blunt – in which, of course, the original 1979 edition of the book was itself instrumental.

2. Inevitably, perhaps, we do things differently now. Within an hour of the unmasking of Anthony Blunt as another member of the so-called 'Cambridge spy-ring' on 15 November 1979 it was announced from Buckingham Palace that 'the appointment of Professor Sir Anthony Frederick Blunt to be a Knight Commander of the Royal Victorian Order dated May 31st 1956 shall be cancelled and annulled and that his name shall be erased from the Register of the said Order'. (*London Gazette*, 16 November 1979.) A few days later there came a further ritual humiliation when Trinity College, Cambridge announced that Blunt had 'resigned' his honorary fellowship – and let it be known that the spy was the first man to lose such a position in the college's 433-year history.

3. Quoted in Humphrey Carpenter: *W. H. Auden*, p. 370.

4. Robert Cecil: *A Divided Life*, p. 135.

5. Lady Jackling, in conversation with the author, 7 July 1990.

6. Robert Birley, Burgess's history teacher at the time; subsequently Sir Robert and headmaster of the college. Quoted in Tom Driberg: *Guy Burgess*, p. 11.

7. This date (cited by Barrie Penrose and Simon Freeman in *Conspiracy of Silence*) seems right. On the other hand, given the date of Burgess's matriculation, in his history of the society, *The Cambridge Apostles*, Richard Deacon is clearly wrong when he lists Burgess as having been elected in '192-'.

8. It is an attractive theory and is developed in Julian Mitchell's 1981 stage play (and subsequent film) *Another Country* in which 'Guy Bennett', a thinly-disguised portrait of Burgess emerges from public school vowing eventual revenge on 'the prefects' who have humiliated him.

   Ultimately, though, the theory is too pat since it fails to explain the compulsive womanizing of Kim Philby and the normal heterosexual behaviour of John Cornford, Julian Bell and the majority of the other communist sympathizers at Cambridge in the early 1930s.

9. Unattributed story, quoted in Deacon, op. cit., p. 117. Davies was a rough contemporary of Burgess; Deacon notes that he was elected to the Apostles in '193-'.

10. Four years Burgess's senior and another Eton-and-Cambridge man, John Lehmann has given a graphic description of this in his strongly autobiographical novel *In the Purely Pagan Sense* (Blond & Briggs, 1976; G.M.P. 1985).

11. Nor did it pay very well. Burgess's BBC salary was rather less than £500 a year. Although this was supplemented by an allowance from his late

father's estate and Burgess himself always had an individual attitude to money, living beyond his means at Cambridge and ever after, the fact that his friends noted 'thick wads of banknotes' on a shelf at the Chester Square flat not unreasonably led Andrew Boyle to conclude that at this time Burgess was 'assuredly' receiving money from his Soviet controller. (Boyle, op. cit., p. 163.)

12. John Green, quoted in Penrose and Freeman, op. cit., pp. 209–10.
13. *Granta*, 8 November 1933, p. 90.
14. Cyril Connolly: *The Missing Diplomats*, p. 39.
15. Sir Frederick Everson, quoted in Cecil, op. cit., p. 139.
16. Lord Greenhill, quoted in Boyle, op. cit., p. 379.
17. Goronwy Rees: *A Chapter of Accidents*, pp. 188–9.
18. George Carey-Foster, in a letter to the author, 23 August 1989.
19. *Hansard*, 7 November 1955.
20. Ibid.
21. 'Control of the passes . . .' 11.1–4; W. H. Auden, *Selected Poems*, Faber & Faber, 1979, p. 3.
22. John Pearson: *The Life of Ian Fleming*, p. 254.
23. Ian Fleming: *You Only Live Twice*, pp. 178–80.
24. *007, James Bond in Focus*, Glidrose Productions Ltd and Marvyn Bruce Associates Ltd, 1964 (not paginated); quoted in Tony Bennett and Janet Woollacott: *Bond and Beyond*, p. 12.
25. Quoted in Pearson, *op. cit.*, p. 404.
26. Hugh Gaitskell, quoted in ibid., p. 410.

CHAPTER THIRTEEN: New Elizabethans
1. The *Daily Telegraph*, 29 May 1972.
2. See David N. Durant: *Living in the Past*, p. 12ff.
3. From July 1958 when the first fourteen (ten men and four women) were appointed, life peers have significantly altered the composition of the House of Lords. Today some 400 of them are grouped with hereditary barons and baronesses in the lowest order of the peerage. In the summer of 1988 the House of Lords comprised (in order of precedence): four peers of the blood royal, two archbishops, twenty-five dukes, twenty-eight marquesses, 156 earls and countesses, 103 viscounts, twenty-four bishops and 854 barons and baronesses.
4. Bernard Levin, *The Pendulum Years*, p. 431.
5. Quoted in Alistair Horne: *Macmillan: 1957–1986*, p. 122.
6. Lord Barber; quoted, ibid.
7. Diary entry, 4 May 1959, quoted in Horne, op. cit., p. 156.
8. Letter to Michael Fraser, 17 October 1957; quoted, ibid., p. 62.
9. Unpublished diary of Harold Macmillan, quoted, ibid., p. 479.

10. Malcolm Muggeridge, quoted in Levin, op. cit., p. 224.

11. Interview with Alistair Horne; quoted, Horne, op. cit., p. 466.

12. Ibid.

13. Ibid., p. 461.

14. Horne makes the point (ibid., p. 480) and identifies the quotation as coming from Trollope's novel *The Duke's Children* (1880) – inevitably, perhaps, part of the Palliser cycle.

15. *Hansard*, 17 June 1963. (My italics.)

16. Levin, op. cit., p. 49. In a footnote Levin adds: 'The author heard all of these stories at the time, most of them more than once, and all of them from people who believed, or professed to believe, that they were true.'

17. Quoted in Horne, op. cit., p. 495.

18. Letter to HM the Queen, 23 June 1963, quoted, ibid., pp. 485–6.

19. Interview with Alistair Horne; quoted, ibid., p. 529.

20. John Braine, *Room at the Top*, p. 31.

21. Michael Young, *The Rise of the Meritocracy*, p. 11.

22. Ibid., pp. 146–7.

23. *The Sunday Times*, 28 October 1990.

24. Jeremy Paxman: *Friends in High Places: Who Runs Britain?* p. xi.

EPILOGUE

1. Paxman, op. cit., p. 167.

2. Ibid., p. 156.

3. Unidentified Old Etonian in *The British Disease*, BBC Radio 4, August 1990.

4. James Walvin: *Victorian Values*, André Deutsch, 1987; Gordon Marsden (ed.): *Victorian Values: Personalities and Perspectives in Nineteenth Century Society*, Longman, 1990.

5. *Daily Telegraph*, headline, 16 April 1990.

6. *The Sunday Times*, headline, 4 November 1990.

7. *Daily Telegraph Magazine*, 22 September 1990.

8. Quoted, ibid.

9. *The Sunday Times*, 11 November 1990.

10. Peter York: 'The Sloane Rangers', *Harpers & Queen*, October 1975; 'Sloane Ranger Man', *Harpers & Queen*, March 1977. Both essays are reprinted in Peter York: *Style Wars*.

11. *The Sunday Times*, 11 November 1990.

12. Peter York, *Style Wars*, p. 61.

13. John Walters: *Kylie Culture*, BBC Radio 4, 30 December 1989.

14. *Hansard*, 22 November 1990.

15. Baron de Spon, letter to the *Daily Telegraph*, 25 May 1990. Rather too

gleefully, the Baron's argument was taken up on Francis Wheen's Diary page of *The Independent on Sunday*, 27 May 1990.
16. *The Sunday Times*, 4 November 1990.
17. *Daily Telegraph*, 16 April 1990.
18. Ivor Spencer, interview with the author; *Evening Standard*, 18 October 1988.
19. *Daily Telegraph*, 5 January 1991.
20. *The Independent*, 8 December 1990.
21. Ibid.

Bibliography

Publication details relate to first editions, except where these have been supplanted by more recent, generally available impressions. The place of publication is London unless otherwise stated.

Abdy, Jane and Gere, Charlotte: *The Souls*. Sidgwick & Jackson, 1984.

Ackroyd, Peter: *T. S. Eliot*. Abacus, 1985.

Arlen, Michael J.: *Exiles*. André Deutsch, 1971.

Asquith, Lady Cynthia: *Remember and Be Glad*. James Barrie, 1952.

Auden, W. H.: *Forewords and Afterwords*. Faber & Faber, 1973.

Barrow, Andrew: *Gossip: A History of High Society from 1920 to 1970*. Hamish Hamilton, 1978.

Bell, Quentin: *Virginia Woolf*, vol. 2, 1912–1941. Triad/Paladin, 1976.

Bennett, Tony and Woollacott, Janet: *Bond and Beyond: The Political Career of a Popular Hero*. Macmillan Education, 1987.

Bishop, T. J. H. and Wilkinson, Rupert: *Winchester and the Public School Elite*. Faber & Faber, 1967.

Blow, Simon: *Broken Blood: The Rise and Fall of the Tennant Family*. Faber & Faber, 1987.

Boyle, Andrew: *The Climate of Treason*. Revised edition, Coronet Books, 1980.

Braine, John: *Room at the Top*. Eyre & Spottiswoode, 1957.

Buchan, John: *Memory Hold the Door*. Hodder & Stoughton, 1940.

Buchan, John: *The Thirty-Nine Steps*. Hodder & Stoughton, 1915; second edition, 1924.

Buckle, Richard (ed.): *Self-Portrait with Friends: The Selected Diaries of Cecil Beaton*. Weidenfeld & Nicolson, 1979.

Campbell, Michael: *Lord Dismiss Us*. Heinemann, 1968.

Cannadine, David: *The Decline and Fall of the British Aristocracy*. Yale University Press, 1990.

Carpenter, Humphrey: *W. H. Auden: A Biography*. George Allen & Unwin, 1981.

Castle, Charles: *Noël*. W. H. Allen & Co., 1972.

Cecil, Robert: *A Divided Life: A Biography of Donald Maclean*. The Bodley Head, 1988.

Connolly, Cyril: *The Missing Diplomats*. Queen Anne Press, 1952.

Cunningham, Valentine: *British Writers of the Thirties*. Oxford University Press, 1988.

Davie, Michael: *The Titanic*. The Bodley Head, 1986.

Deacon, Richard: *The Cambridge Apostles*. Robert Royce Ltd, 1985.

Delany, Paul: *The Neo-Pagans*. Hamish Hamilton Paperbacks, 1988.

Donaldson, Frances: *Edward VIII*. Weidenfeld & Nicolson, 1974; Ballantine, New York, 1976.

Doyle, Arthur Conan: *Memories and Adventures*. Hodder & Stoughton, 1924.

Driberg, Tom: *Guy Burgess: A Portrait with Background*. Weidenfeld and Nicolson, 1956.

Durant, David, N.: *Living in the Past: An Insider's Social History of Historic Houses*. Aurum Press, 1988.

Edwards, Anne: *Matriarch: Queen Mary and the House of Windsor*. Hodder & Stoughton, 1984.

Ellis, Clive: *C. B.: The Life of Charles Burgess Fry*. J. M. Dent, 1984.

Fitzherbert, Margaret: *The Man Who Was Greenmantle: A Biography of Aubrey Herbert*. Oxford University Press, 1985.

Fleming, Ian: *You Only Live Twice*. Coronet, 1988.

Ford, Ford Madox: *Some Do Not . . .* Republished as Volume Three of *The Bodley Head Ford Madox Ford*. The Bodley Head, 1963.

Fry, C. B.: *Life Worth Living*. Eyre & Spottiswoode, 1939.

Gathorne-Hardy, Jonathan: *The Public School Phenomenon*. Penguin, 1979.

Graham, Desmond: *Keith Douglas*. Oxford University Press, 1978.

Hamilton, Patrick: *Twenty Thousand Streets Under the Sky*. The Hogarth Press, 1987.

Hart-Davis, Rupert: *Hugh Walpole*. Macmillan, 1952.

Healey, Denis: *The Time of My Life*. Michael Joseph, 1989.

Hewins, Angela (ed.): *The Dillen: Memories of a Man of Stratford-upon-Avon*. Oxford University Press, 1982.

Honey, J. R. de S.: *Tom Brown's Universe: the Development of the Public School in the Nineteenth Century*. Millington Books, 1977.

Horne, Alistair: *Macmillan: 1957–1986*. Macmillan, 1989.

Hornung, E. W.: *The Collected Raffles*. J. M. Dent, 1985.

Howard, Leslie Ruth: *A Quite Remarkable Father*. Longman, 1960.

Howard, Ronald: *In Search of My Father*. William Kimber, 1981.

Hughes, Thomas: *Tom Brown's Schooldays*. Puffin Classics, 1983.

Hyman, Alan: *The Rise and Fall of Horatio Bottomley*. Cassell, 1972.

Isherwood, Christopher: *Goodbye to Berlin*. Penguin, 1945.

Jesson-Dibley, D.: *A Pageant of Christ's Hospital*. (Privately printed), 1963.

Jolliffe, John (ed.): *Raymond Asquith: Life and Letters*. Century Hutchinson, 1987.

BIBLIOGRAPHY

◆

Lambert, Angela: *Unquiet Souls*. Macmillan, 1984.

Le Quesne, Laurence: *The Bodyline Controversy*. Secker & Warburg, 1983.

Lesley, Cole: *The Life of Noël Coward*. Jonathan Cape, 1976.

Levin, Bernard: *The Pendulum Years: Britain and the Sixties*. Pan, 1977.

Macdonald, Lyn: *1914*. Michael Joseph, 1987.

Macdonald, Lyn: *1914–1918: Voices and Images of the Great War*. Michael Joseph, 1988.

Mackenzie Jeanne: *The Children of the Souls*. Chatto & Windus, 1986.

Marsden, Gordon (ed.): *Victorian Values: Personalities and Perspectives in Nineteenth Century Society*. Longman, 1990.

Mason, Philip: *The English Gentleman: The Rise and Fall of an Ideal*. André Deutsch, 1982.

Masters, Brian: *Great Hostesses*. Constable, 1982.

Meynell, Viola: *Julian Grenfell*. Burns & Oates, 1917.

Midwinter, Eric: *The Lost Seasons: Cricket in Wartime, 1939–45*. Methuen, 1987.

Montgomery-Massingberd, Hugh: *Great British Families*. Webb & Bower/ Michael Joseph, 1988.

Mosley, Diana: *A Life of Contrasts*. Hamish Hamilton, 1977.

Mosley, Nicholas: *Julian Grenfell*. Weidenfeld and Nicolson, 1976.

Mosley, Nicholas: *Rules of the Game: Sir Oswald and Lady Cynthia Mosley, 1896–1933*. Secker & Warburg, 1982.

Mosley, Nicholas: *Beyond the Pale: Sir Oswald Mosley, 1933–1980*. Secker & Warburg, 1983.

Mosley, Sir Oswald: *My Life*. Nelson, 1968.

Nicolson, Harold: *Diaries and Letters, 1930–1939* (ed. Nigel Nicolson). Collins, 1966.

Orwell, George: *Nineteen Eighty-Four*. Penguin, 1954.

Parker, John: *King of Fools*. Macdonald, 1988.

Parker, Peter: *The Old Lie: The Great War and the Public-School Ethos*. Constable, 1987.

Pawson, Tony: *100 Years of the F.A. Cup*. Heinemann, 1972.

Paxman, Jeremy: *Friends in High Places: Who Runs Britain?* Michael Joseph, 1990.

Pearson, John: *The Life of Ian Fleming*. Jonathan Cape, 1966.

Penrose, Barrie and Freeman, Simon: *Conspiracy of Silence: The Secret Life of Anthony Blunt*. Revised edition, Grafton Books, 1986.

Portland, Duke of: *Men, Women & Things*. Faber & Faber, 1937.

Rees, Goronwy: *A Chapter of Accidents*. Chatto & Windus, 1972.

Richards, Jeffrey: *Happiest Days: The Public Schools in English Fiction*. Manchester University Press, 1988.

Rhodes James, Robert (ed.) : *Chips: The Diaries of Sir Henry Channon*. Weidenfeld & Nicolson, 1967.

Rose, Kenneth: *Superior Person.* Weidenfeld and Nicolson, 1969.

'Sapper': *Bulldog Drummond: His Four Rounds with Carl Peterson.* Hodder & Stoughton, (no date).

'Sapper': *Mufti.* Hodder & Stoughton, 1919.

Simon, Brian and Bradley, Ian (eds): *The Victorian Public School.* Gill & Macmillan, 1975.

Sissons, Michael and French, Philip (eds): *Age of Austerity.* Oxford University Press, 1986.

Skidelsky, Robert: *Oswald Mosley.* Macmillan, 1975.

Smith, Janet Adam: *John Buchan.* Oxford University Press, 1986.

Spark, Muriel: *The Prime of Miss Jean Brodie.* Macmillan, 1961.

Stanford, Derek: *Inside the Forties.* Sidgwick & Jackson, 1977.

Swanton, E. W.: *Gubby Allen: Man of Cricket.* Hutchinson/Stanley Paul, 1985.

Usborne, Richard: *Clubland Heroes.* Hutchinson Paperback, 1983.

Vansittart, Peter: *Paths from a White Horse.* Quartet, 1985.

Walvin, James: *Victorian Values.* André Deutsch, 1987.

Willis, Bob and Murphy, Patrick: *Starting with Grace.* Stanley Paul, 1986.

Windsor, HRH The Duke of, KG: *A King's Story.* Cassell & Co., 1951.

Wright, Basil: *The Long View: An International History of Cinema.* Secker & Warburg, 1974.

Wright, Peter: *Spycatcher.* William Heinemann (Australia), 1987.

York, Peter: *Style Wars.* Sidgwick & Jackson, 1980.

Young, Michael: *The Rise of the Meritocracy, 1870–2033.* Penguin, 1961.

INDEX